Frances Courtenay Baylor

**On Both Sides**

A Novel. Tenth Edition

Frances Courtenay Baylor

**On Both Sides**
*A Novel. Tenth Edition*

ISBN/EAN: 9783337000745

Printed in Europe, USA, Canada, Australia, Japan

Cover: Foto ©Andreas Hilbeck / pixelio.de

More available books at **www.hansebooks.com**

# A NOVEL.

## FRANCES COURTENAY BAYLOR.

*TENTH EDITION.*

PHILADELPHIA:
J. B. LIPPINCOTT COMPANY.
1892.

# PREFACE.

.

"On Both Sides" originally appeared in " Lippincott's Magazine" in two stories, or rather a story in two parts, called "The Perfect Treasure" and "On this Side," supposed to be illustrative of certain phases of social life in England and the United States. These are now bound together (as I earnestly trust that John Bull and his cousin Jonathan may be in the future, however divided in the past), and have been rechristened, to avoid a wealth of title which the author fears would only illustrate afresh the deceitfulness of riches, since no one story any more than one individual can reasonably be expected to carry out all that would be promised and vowed in three names.

F. C. B.

Elmwood, August 26, 1885.

# THE PERFECT TREASURE.

# THE PERFECT TREASURE.

## I.

LATE in the autumn of '73, Mr. and Mrs. Fletcher, wealthy and refined Americans of the best type, returned to England after an extended tour on the Continent, and decided to spend the winter in Cheltenham, one of the gayest and most agreeable of the English watering-places still, though not as fashionable as in the palmy days when poor George III. sipped the waters of the Royal Wells, and the fine gentlemen and court beauties danced, drank, gamed, raced, laughed, loved, lived in the idle profligacy and splendor of the period, and brought in their train such a crowd of tradesmen, parasites, henchmen, tire-women, lackeys, pleasure-seekers, and snobs as sent the place up from a village to a large town more rapidly than if a gold-mine had been discovered in the neighborhood.

It was agreed that Mrs. Fletcher should stay there while her husband "ran over to New York," as he phrased it, and put his affairs upon a footing that would admit of their devoting the following summer to Norway and Sweden and perhaps another winter to some unexplored country to be decided upon later. Both were inveterate travellers, and had the health, the

1*      5

spirits, and the intelligence which can alone make the social nomadism of our day either pleasant or profitable, to say nothing of a purse that gave to their journeys all the comfort of a royal progress without its *ennui.* They were not alone; for where is the American who has the courage or the heart to travel abroad with no other companion than the wife of his bosom? He may hate going about the world with a menagerie, and shrink from the prospect of rambling over strange countries in charge of several thread-paper females, being held accountable for the safety of sixteen Saratoga trunks, wrangling in unknown tongues, and paying enormous bills. He may feel that to regulate the largest business interests in the United States and manage any number of banks and factories and railroads is nothing to such an undertaking. He may even be the slave of the lamp, and have rubbed away half his physical and mental layers of strength and sensibility for twenty years that Mrs. Aladdin may live on Fifth Avenue and have a roc's-egg chandelier, and he may have always looked forward to a time when it would no longer be necessary to sacrifice himself to the American Moloch "business," and he could take that admirable modern substitute for the wings of a dove, a Cunarder, and with another "dearer self" seek the relaxation and amusement so sadly needed. But who ever carried out this delightful and impossible daydream? From the moment a trip to Europe is decided upon, the stars in their courses fight against such an arrangement. He tells his wife, who straightway communicates the interesting fact to their joint families, who think it (with certain modifications) "perfectly

splendid! It would be so nice for sister Lucy to go!"
or, "Margaret is out of health, and nothing else will
cure her;" or "Kate has a wonderful voice, which *must*
be cultivated;" or, "Mother has always wanted to go
abroad;" or, "Jack ought really to be sent to Heidel-
berg." And so that most unselfish and generous of all
male creatures (who ought always to be painted with a
nimbus around his head), the American husband, gives
in, after one or two feeble remonstrances, perhaps, and
sails on the "Scythia" or the "Russia" with a full comple-
ment of petticoated barnacles, and wears his necklace
of millstones ever after with the beautiful unconscious
grace of the hero and none of the airs of a martyr, and
hosts of foreigners hold up their hands and puzzle their
heads over the strange spectacle. At least they did,
until experience taught them it was a national peculiarity.

But this is straying from my theme, and is a very
roundabout way of saying that Mrs. Fletcher was not
left to languish alone in Cheltenham, but had the society
of a rather low-spirited mother-in-law, a cheerful sister,
and a charmingly pretty and accomplished cousin. A
furnished house on the Promenade was taken for these
ladies, and two hours after their effects were moved in
from the Plough Hotel one might have supposed that
the establishment had been organized for twenty years.

Not only was it in perfect order and provided with
every comfort and luxury, including a staff of well-
trained servants as noiseless as the white cats of the
fairy-tale, but some minor details had been attended to
that made their arrival seem almost like a home-coming.
The *jardinières* in the windows were a mass of color;

cut-flowers were placed about the reception-room; the London papers, aired and the leaves cut, had been laid on the drawing-room table; and two small red-plush tea-tables and sleepy-hollow chairs had been drawn near a glowing coal fire which was doing its best to take the chill off the November day. A comfortable-looking, round-bodied bronze tea-kettle hissed on the hob; a brisk, busy little clock ticked cheerfully on the mantel-shelf; and the ladies had hardly laid aside their wraps when Walton the butler appeared with a huge silver tray, which he bore in with as much dignity as if he had been offering them the keys of the city on a velvet cushion, or figuring in a Lord-Mayor's show.

On that tray was a set of dainty Worcester china, with a gorgeous tea-cosey extinguishing the too volatile butterflies on the teapot, and the thinnest possible slices of buttered bread, and a covered dish of the incomparable Cheltenham muffins, than which nothing can be lighter or browner or more *buttery* or more entirely satisfactory. And when Walton had asked in a husky whisper whether they "would be pleased to ring if there was anything more required," and vanished, there was an amount of tea-drinking done that would have shocked Dr. Johnson. "The trimmings," as Mr. Fletcher facetiously put it, were not neglected; and I doubt whether the accumulated noises of the solemn old house for the past century would have amounted to as much cheerful racket as was made by the merry family party.

"I am glad I am going home," said Mr. Fletcher, "instead of staying here in the trying *rôle* of master to that very superior domestic Walton. I couldn't do it: he would find me out in a week. I should never dare

to be helped thrice to anything, unless it was 'cold
boiled missionary,' of which he might approve, for he
looks like an archbishop. I felt that he was my master
the moment he took my overcoat down-stairs. I lost
confidence in my tailor on the spot. I felt as though I
had come home from school for the holidays, or done
something that I could only atone for by assuming an
apologetic attitude and entering upon a course of sys
tematic propitiation."

"Nonsense, Ned! how absurd you are!" commented
his wife. "Besides, he who propitiates under such circumstances is lost."

"Oh, you may be sure I didn't give way to the impulse. I frowned, and looked as though my temper
was bad, and got up-stairs as soon as possible. I
shouldn't in the least mind meeting the Prince of
Wales, or the Lord Chancellor; but there is something
inexpressibly awe-inspiring about the British flunkey.
Deny it as we may, very few Americans can honestly
say that they feel themselves a match for the majestic,
inscrutable creature."

"Dear me, Kate! you have never kept house in England; and, though you are a famous manager at home,
don't you rather dread the idea?" said the rather-
alarmed Lucy; but Mrs. Fletcher lowered her calm
eyelids and replied, "You'll see I'll be a match for them.
I shall make mistakes, of course, at first; but I shall
get one of the natives to enlighten me as to their system as soon as we present our letters, and show myself
*plus royaliste que le roi*, a rigid stickler for all my rights,
and a great respecter of theirs. It is the only way to
get along comfortably with servants anywhere."

"Katherine pants for the fray, as anybody can see," said Mr. Fletcher. "When I get back from New York I shall expect to find the magisterial Walton meekly engaged on the knives and boots, and the other servants mere door-mats. Even in the 'land of the free,' you know, there was something about her that made Bridget stammer when asking if she was the woman that wanted a 'gurl' and announcing that 'she was the lady that had come for the washing.'"

"We shall be fearfully cheated, and had much better have stayed at the hotel, as I suggested," said Mrs. Fletcher senior from behind the "Times," in a muffled voice of disapprobation.

The dressing-bell put an end to this discussion. Lucy and Jenny Meredith, who had been rambling about the room admiring the cabinets and old china, were promptly sent to their rooms, and the other ladies soon followed, encountering two rosy maids armed with hot-water cans in the hall outside.

A capital little dinner was served by the "archbishop," assisted by a very young and irresolute footman, who made wild dashes at the side-tables when anything was asked for, and was always headed off by his superior, who paralyzed him with a look, set down the dish he carried, substituted the proper vegetable or condiment with noiseless despatch, and retired into the background to await further orders. Indeed, he made a "function" of the meal, and the ladies exchanged glances when, on Mr. Fletcher's asking for a second supply of game, Walton glided forward and said respectfully, "Beg pardon, sir, it has all been served."

When the door finally closed on him after coffee had

been served, Jenny burst out with " What a relief! Really, Kate, that man makes a 'cold baked meats' affair of every meal; and, as for me, I feel like what I once heard called at a funeral 'the dear remains.' The oppressive stillness and overpowering gentility of this arrangement is quite stifling, and tells on my democratic nerves. Why not take one of those rosy pretty little creatures in stuff dresses and white caps as parlor-maid instead ? The way we all discussed the state of Ireland and the Tichborne case and the elections was something delightful to hear!"

" I've often thought," said Mr. Fletcher, " that, as we never can talk of anything that interests us before servants, it would only be fair to ask them what subjects would most interest them."

" And I think intelligent servants a fearful bore. You know in the South we are rather apt to think of them as ' it,'—an impersonal contrivance for giving us what we want, without any embarrassing or disagreeable features whatever," Jenny replied.

" Walton has a secret grief, or only one lung, or a great enthusiasm, or something that lifts him above his fellow-men, and the menial estate in which we find him only adds to his melancholy without obscuring his inherent dignity," said Mr. Fletcher. " Have you noticed, Kate, how like our print of Melancthon he is?"

" I notice that he is my *beau-idéal* of a servant ; and if I could only give him half my income and induce him to go home with us, I should feel it a bargain to be proud of. The conversation, though, is losing its intellectual tone, isn't it?" And Mrs. Kate led the way to the drawing-room.

In the course of the following week the Fletchers presented their letters of introduction to two influential families, and were received with the kindness which characterizes English hospitality when a guest is properly—*i.e.*, formally—commended, and which, although less promiscuous than our own often indiscriminate entertainment of man and *beast*, is equally genuine and hearty in its way. Mr. Fletcher was put up at the club as a visitor, though he protested that it was not worth while, under the circumstances. Tickets were sent for the approaching assembly, and invitations to luncheons, teas, drums, dinners, and parties of every kind poured in upon them. As a family they were received with great favor, and society was engaged in dealing, and Walton in shuffling, cards diligently for several weeks.

Mr. Fletcher was pronounced "an uncommonly gentlemanly, agreeable fellow." Mrs. Fletcher senior, who wore the blackest possible dresses and the whitest possible caps, was evidently of quite appalling respectability; and her manner, which had a curious rigidity that passed for *hauteur*, together with a way she had of trampling people down with the heel of assertion on all occasions, seemed to make a very favorable impression. Indeed, she was called "a most aristocratic old gentlewoman" by a certain *mondaine*, and took up the study of "Debrett's Peerage" and convinced herself that because her grandmother was a McSomething she was descended from Rob Roy.

People soon found that young and handsome as Mrs. Kate was, in the large, fair order of loveliness, she was not in the very least degree fast or flirtatious: so she received the high meed of praise embodied in "good form." As for the girls, they were both admired, though in very different degrees. Lucy, who had a pretty little figure, the national clothes-wearing faculty, and a pair of wonderfully fine eyes, with a yard or so of eyelashes veiling them, was thought "a nice girl," simply; but Jenny created a furor. She was a thorough-paced American beauty, of the flower-like and ethereal type, and had an air of distinction that was far more charming than any merely physical charm. She had been the belle of a second-rate Southern city, indulged beyond belief, and had really scarcely any education except such as a refined home and a love of reading had given her, and where she learned to dress, walk, dance, talk, and appear as she did, is a mystery which can only be solved by her versatile and clever countrywomen who achieve the same feat every day. Music was part of her family inheritance, and she played brilliantly. Always a delicate girl, she had not been kept closely at her books, yet gave every one the impression that she was very highly educated. Accustomed to the informal social atmosphere of a provincial town, she somehow never offended against the rigid *convenances* of English life, and in any capital of Europe would have been singled out for admiring notice.

None of the party had ever been long enough in England to know anything of its social aspects. Mrs. Kate's first care was to master the details of English housekeeping. She began by consulting a new friend, an old lady who had the reputation of being a domestic Wellington,—and together they went into the questions of beer-money, board-wages, charwoman's perquisites, tradesmen's books, coal-siftings, bread soakings, cheese parings, and the like marvels of good management. When Mrs. Kate got home that day, she said to the girls, "Well, I used to think that I knew something about housekeeping and economy, and all that, but it seems that I have been an ignorant and wasteful housewife after all. I find that I could have supported a couple of families on what I have always thrown away, and that in a well-ordered Northern household!"

. The very next day, as she was looking over the week's bills, with their confusing ha'pennies and farthings, the cook tapped at the door, entered, courtesied, and said, "If you please, mem, you have not yet mentioned what you want me to do with the drippings."

"Good gracious! what can the woman be talking about?" thought the mistress; but, like Mr. Toots at the commercial dinner when his neighbor suddenly demanded fiercely what *he* would do with the raw material, she replied, "Cook it," with diplomatic vagueness.

"Yes, mem, I quite understood about that; but what then?" urged cook.

"Why, set it aside to cool," replied Mrs. Kate calmly.

"And after that, mem?" said cook, driving her mistress unconsciously into a corner.

"I have not quite decided yet, but I will let you know to-morrow when I come down to give the orders. You can go now," responded the mistress with decision.

Go she did; and Mrs. Kate, putting on her bonnet, rushed around to her Mentor, and was told that "drippings," the fatty substance exuding from the various meats, formed an important perquisite in some households for cook, who sold it for eighteenpence a pound;

while in others an untold saving was effected by using
it to make cakes and fry fish.

The cook was in a state of subdued radiance when
she was informed that all the drippings were to be hers,
and great was the amusement of the Americans over the
episode. Mrs. Fletcher had demonstrated her capacity
for governing, and from that time everything went as
smoothly as possible. She found in Walton an invaluable aide-de-camp. A dozen times a day one or other
of the ladies, who had had the most afflicting experience
of the domestic service of America, would break out
into warm praise of that " perfect treasure,"—that swift,
noiseless, capable, respectful, honest creature. Walton
paid their bills and accounted scrupulously for every
penny; he picked up and returned careless Jenny's
purse over and over again; he ordered their bouquets,
bought gloves, matched ribbons with feminine discretion and success. He escorted them to and from all
sorts of places, was invaluable on picnics and excur-
sions, and several times went up to London on errands
for them. He was never tired, or pert, or saucy. He
never once forgot or neglected a duty, or seemed to see
or hear anything not intended for him. His talent for
admitting the right and excluding the wrong callers
was not the least remarkable of his gifts. In short, as
his mistress once exclaimed, with rapture, he was "the
most perfect product of European civilization, and there
isn't such a servant on the whole American continent."
Mrs. Fletcher senior was so impressed by the thoughtful
care for her comfort evinced by his sending the footman
with galoshes, wraps, and umbrella to church for her
whenever it rained, without waiting for orders, that she

confidentially told her greatest friend—the widow of a
general officer, much interested, like herself, in such
matters—that she was quite sure that Walton came
morganatically or surreptitiously of good blood, and
added that "the last of the Plantagenets died a butcher."

While he was developing all these excellencies in the
seclusion of the servants' hall, the young ladies of the
house were finding in the festivities of the season and
the novelty of their surroundings a fresh and piquant
interest. At the first dinner-party to which they went,
two or three things happened that gave unusual zest to
the prosaic occupation of eating. Lucy was taken in
by a stout gentleman, who, like Thackeray's aldermen,
seemed to have but one idea,—"gorging, guzzling, and
gormandizing,"—and did not address her until coffee
appeared, when he suddenly roused himself, and, mis-
taking her for her Southern cousin, asked whether it
was "her father or her grandfather who was a black."

Lucy had barely succeeded in setting forth her claim
to be regarded as a member of the Caucasian race, when
the conversation turned upon women's rights, and she
was obliged to disclaim the distinction of belonging to
that party, which no doubt reassured her companion as
to her feminine cast of character; for he presently
asked her if she was fond of sewing, and if she em-
broidered her flannel petticoats, as his sisters were in
the habit of doing.

Meanwhile, Jenny had fallen to the lot of a very High-
Church, pensive-looking young clergyman, and was con-
verting him, sentimentally, into pulp, while he was
trying to gain some insight into her favorite pursuits
by putting questions that puzzled her. "Do you col-

lect?" said he, with an earnest glance at his pretty neighbor.

"He means subscriptions, of course," thought Jenny; then, aloud, "No, never. I can't ask people for money— for anything. They either refuse altogether or patronize one for six months afterward on the strength of a fifty-cent subscription."

. "You have quite misunderstood me," put in the curate hastily, with a little blush. "I was talking of stamps, and autographs, and that kind of thing, you know."

Whereupon Jenny announced that she did not, and never would, "collect," and the conversation trickled feebly in another direction for a while.

Presently he said, with a profoundly interested air, "Do you splutter?"

"Splutter! splutter!" thought Jenny. "What *can* the man mean? Do I fall down in an epileptic fit occasionally and foam at the mouth?" Then, aloud, "No, not often. Do you?"

"I don't; but they all do at home. My six sisters are always at it."

"The whole family! It can't be fits!" thought Jenny, thoroughly mystified. "Dear me!". she. exclaimed. "Do tell me how they manage it."

The curate, enchanted by her dimpled vivacity, gave a very elaborate description of a process by which, with a comb, a tooth-brush, and a bottle of India ink, the exact impression of any fern can be transferred to paper, linen, or satin; and Jenny hypocritically promised to "try it some dull day when she had got herself on her hands."

That night the girls exchanged experiences as they

*b*　　　　2*

put on their dressing-gowns and took down their back-hair, and they agreed that the impossibility of knowing what would be said next gave an indescribable charm to the social situation in England; though Jenny, descended from a Virginian signer of the Declaration, and immensely proud, within well-bred limits, of her English ancestry, was rendered speechless on hearing that she had been supposed to be one or two removes from "a black."

Nor did their impression of the astounding lengths to which English frankness can go lose force as time went on: indeed, it seemed to them that all the things about which Americans are habitually most reticent were being dragged into the light. Family affairs, family scandals, money-matters, a thousand topics that at home were either never mentioned at all or discussed with closed doors in family councils, while furnishing food for the mild or malignant gossip of the world, they here found proclaimed from the house-tops by the people most concerned, and that with entire simplicity, as a mere statement of facts, with no apologies, no attempts at justification, and no faintest evidence of feeling personally implicated or compromised on the part of the narrator. It took the girls some time to adapt themselves to the change and wear just the right face when these surprising revelations were made. It was evident that no one else was at all astonished by them.

One afternoon some *amis de la maison* dropped in for five-o'clock tea, and in the course of conversation the subject of kleptomania came up. When everybody had contributed his or her share to the general stock of experience, anecdote, and comment, a charming young fellow, who was leaning against the mantel-shelf, lazily sipping his tea, smiled blandly, shifted his position so as to catch Jenny's eye, and said, " Queer thing, isn't it ? My aunt was had up for it in London."

The statement was made with perfect simplicity and an air of *bonhommie* which seemed to give it the aspect of any other agreeable *on dit :* it was received by the English people present as a matter of course, and excited neither amazement nor amusement.

Jenny and her cousin with difficulty smothered the desire to laugh outright, murmured some commonplace intended to be sympathetic, stole a glance at each other, though both knew it to be a lapse from good breeding, and were obliged to have recôurse to their handkerchiefs to conceal the smiles that would play around their mobile lips.

Later on, a discussion arose as to whether the Arabs were right in saying that no amount of age or experience avails a man in buying a horse or choosing a wife, when another young swell gave his emphatic assent to the truth of the proverb, and proceeded to illustrate his views as follows : " There's my grandfather. The old beggar had three wives, and, at the age of eighty, was about to marry his cook, when he died. Lucky thing, wasn't it ?"

These incidents provoked much lively comment when our Americans were again alone, and renewed laughter. Some of the party could not believe that they were not exceptional, and ought not to be set down to personal eccentricity rather than a national habit of mind. All thought that mortal frankness could no further go ; but ın this they were mistaken.

The next day a gentleman called, sat up very straight, holding his hat at the correct angle and wearing an air of mild expectancy, and, when the usual inquiries and greetings had been exchanged, turned to Mrs. Fletcher, and said, "I suppose you have heard about my brother Hugh?"  '

"Not I.  Is anything amiss?" she asked.

"Well, yes.  You see, Hugh always was a bad lot. He is the greatest rascal in England; regular blackleg. He has been going to the bad ever since he was weaned, and now he has run off with his wife's governess. Pretty little devil; been angling for him for months. Wife's a fool; crying her eyes out about him."

The visit over, the girls went off to get ready for a visit they had promised to make at a country-house fifty miles away.  Jenny was tying her bonnet-strings, when the postman's rap was heard, and presently the maid brought in a letter from the lady who had invited them.  Jenny tore it open, and read:

"THE LODGE, Tuesday, 10 A.M.

"MY DEAR MISS MEREDITH,—I write to say that my brother arrived quite unexpectedly last night from Bournemouth, with his keeper; and, as he is quite mad, and seems rather excitable just now,—though harmless enough in the main, poor dear!—it occurs to me that you and your cousin would prefer to come to us after he has left,—say Thursday of next week, and by the same train."

"I should rather think we would," commented Jenny, with *empressement.*  "Was there ever such a people for telling the truth, the whole truth, and nothing but the truth? ' *Tout se sçait*' in England, certainly. They all live morally in the Palace of Truth, with every door and window wide open. Only fancy the elaborate fibs that an American hostess similarly placed would have told, even if every creature of her acquaintance knew quite well that she had a brother in an insane asylum. I am not quite sure that I like English frankness. It often strikes me as indelicate, and always as astounding; but, after all, there is a good deal to be said in its favor. What is lost in refinement and finesse is gained in simplicity and sincerity. There is something very refreshing in the absence of the transparent social fictions to which we are accustomed. It is quite delightful to hear people say simply that they can't afford to do this or that, or to go here or there, instead of perjuring their snobbish little souls in fifty distinct directions in wild and wholly unsuccessful efforts to convince a sceptical public that black is white. There is Mrs. Harford, at home, for instance, whose daughter has been stretched on a couch for years with spinal disease, which the mother always speaks of as 'a little weakness of the muscles of the back.' And Mrs. Travers, who says that she has ' come out just to do some shopping in a simple foulard,' which anybody can see is a black alpaca of the rustiest description. Don't you remember how amused we were by that preposterous girl from New Jersey who wasn't going to Newport because her health was so shattered that nothing but a summer in a farm-house (with board at twenty dollars a month) could restore her? One is reminded of Scribe's diplomate, and the reputation for Machiavellian astuteness that he-achieved

as accidental envoy at a petty court by simply telling
the truth (which not a soul could be brought to believe)
about himself and his affairs.   I really think it would
be the only way for Americans to deceive each other
about such matters now, we have put so much talent
and ingenuity into our social white lies."

"Well, I hope it isn't immoral, but I prefer our system, decidedly," said Lucy.   "First, there is the intellectual gratification of a clever fiction, if it is clever, or
the satisfaction of thinking one could easily have invented a better, if stupid; with the comfortable *arrière-
pensée* that one is not being the least bit in the world
deceived by it in either event.   And I don't care to be
taken into people's closets and shown their skeletons.   I
like them dressed *à la mode* and properly presented in
the drawing-room.   When I first came over, Jenny, I
thought there was something about me that invited the
confidence of the British public, and that it would be
as unpardonable for me to repeat what was told me to
you or Kate as for a priest to publish confessions.   But
I know better now.   What is one to say when a man
announces, as Mr. Battersby did yesterday, that he
thinks, and has always thought, his wife the most thoroughly disagreeable woman in England?   It is really a
most uncomfortable position to be placed in."

The conversation was here cut short by a second
knock at the door.   This time it was Walton, who announced "a young person from Debenton & Freeman's,"
and, having received orders to show her up, disappeared
for a moment, and presently returned, followed by a
tall, handsome girl, carrying two large boxes of cloaks
and mantles, which she asked to be allowed to display

Permission was readily granted ; and it is needless to say that the remainder of the afternoon was devoted to the sacred mysteries of shopping, the trio twittering away like so many sparrows under the eaves, as the "young person," with many blushes and modest mien, tried on a succession of wraps, each of which looked a shade more stylish than the other on the slim, graceful figure.

That evening, as the girls were rolling up the Promenade, *en route* to a dinner-party, they caught a glimpse of the "young person," who had exchanged her black silk—the property of the shop—for a cheap print and a shabby shawl, and was hurrying home in the twilight to a cottage three miles away, where a widowed mother and five little sisters and brothers lived principally upon her munificent salary.

## II.

EARLY in the Cheltenham season the Fletchers were invited to come to "tiffin" at "The Bungalow," a charming little villa on the outskirts of the town, with French windows looking out on a model English lawn in front, and verandas covered with wisteria running around the other three sides. It was a delicious little nest, bursting with books, prints, souvenirs of travel, good bits of china and odds and ends that cried out to be examined, rugs with a bloom on them like a plum, snug corners that invited irresistibly the most insensible visitor and

rewarded him with unexpected glimpses of the grounds,
the conservatory, or the Malvern Hills, and everywhere
the last indescribable touch which showed that it was
a home, not a museum or a bric-à-brac shop, and that,
after all, its best furniture was the master and mistress
of the establishment.    Very clever, cultivated people
they were,—a retired officer (often described in the
community as "an old Indian," in allusion to his past
military service) and his accomplished wife.    They had
taken a fancy to the Fletchers on first meeting them,
and had shown them marked attention, producing so
favorable an impression that poor Mr. Fletcher's letters
from England were one hymn of praise of the Venables,
and he wrote back that he hoped he might, without
giving offence, say that he wished he either knew the
Venables and could therefore share the enthusiasm of
the family, or that they didn't and could not therefore
bore him further with accounts of their friends' astounding perfections.    A series of luncheons was one
feature of the intimacy, and the one in question was a
rather more formal affair than usual, given by Mrs.
Venable with the view of introducing her American
friends to some English cousins lately arrived in the
place,—Sir Robert Heathcote and his nephew and heir.

The baronet was a fresh-colored, well-preserved man
of sixty-five, with rather a brandy-and-watery eye,
genial manners, and that general *bouquet* of prosperity
which the possession of thirty thousand pounds a year
never fails to impart when it comes by inheritance.
His nephew was an extremely good-looking young fellow, of the conventional London stamp, not very bright,
but with plenty of conversational sixpences that passed

current everywhere and were often declared to be sovereigns by British matrons with marriageable daughters,
—a simple-hearted officer in one of the household regiments, and wonderfully unspoiled, considering that he
had been brought up in the purple—who knew perfectly
well the advantages as well as the disadvantages of
being a *bon parti*, and never meant to be taken alive by
any matron in the land, charm she never so wisely.
Besides these gentlemen, there were only two other
guests present,—a very shy, fair girl, who blushed
deeply whenever she was directly addressed,—Mabel
Vane by name,—and a quiet young London barrister,
who had the good fortune to be seated next to Jenny.

Sir Robert, with Mrs. Fletcher on one side of him
and Lucy on the other, naturally began (in a large,
hearty voice) to talk of America, and astonished them
quite as much by his breezy familiarity with the history,
climate, population, and peculiarities of Chicago, on
which he evidently greatly prided himself, as by his
utter ignorance of the rest of the country. He had
never crossed the Atlantic, he said, but fully meant to
do so, as he had a distant cousin out there who had a
town-house in *Oheeo* and a country-place in Saint Louis
(pronounced in the French fashion), to say nothing of
a friend, a Southern general, "quite the gentleman,"
who had done something very remarkable during the
war, he really couldn't say what; only of one thing he
was sure,—the general had been with Grant on the
Potomac. The ladies made polite responses to all this,
and, without meaning to do so, lapsed into the local
standard of pronunciation in naming the American
localities; but Sir Robert did not mind it. He clung

B     3

firmly to his preconceived idea of the way the names
ought to be pronounced, said "Just so" to all their ob-
jections, and insisted that, according to the Indian
standard, he was right. Nobody present having the
faintest idea what the aboriginal standard was, the discussion naturally fell to the ground, leaving Sir Robert
wearing the wreath and the smile of the victor.

His nephew was less fortunate. Attracted by the
delicate high-bred beauty of his neighbor, he had made
unusual efforts to monopolize her attention, only to find
that Jenny persistently appealed to her host or hostess,
to Mabel Vane, or to the quiet man with the keen,
clever face, on her right, for sympathy, or, if she turned
to him at all in talking, did so evidently from a well-
bred desire not to ignore him altogether. Her fresh
and original way of putting things interested them all,
and so piqued his languid interest that he did not lose
a word, and before the meal was over felt quite viciously
toward the unoffending barrister, whom he mentally
scored as " a poor devil with not more than five hundred
a year." The truth was that Mr. Heathcote, from a
long habit of looking down upon women as dangerous
or disagreeable creatures, all more or less bent upon
marrying the heir to " The Towers," securing the usual
settlements, and wearing the Heathcote diamonds, had
contracted a moral squint which showed itself in some
ugly little ways, well veneered as he was, and really
well intentioned in the main, and this Jenny, with the
*esprit de l'escalier* of the sex, had at once divined and
resented. Jenny having mentioned that she hoped to
have a season in London before going home, he said,
with animation, " Oh, yes; you really ought, you know.

You will have no end of a good time. Pretty girls always do. But I am afraid I shall not be allowed to do more than make my bow. English girls never look at me in their first season,—they all feel booked for a duke; but in the second they can see me across the Park; and in the third you have no idea how irresistible I am, and how the dear mamma dotes on me."

"Come, now, Arthur; you really ought not to make fun of the poor mothers," put in his hostess. "Only fancy what agonies of mind a woman with five daugh-. ters undergoes in England! We were only two, you know, but all the same when we both got engaged the same year I really thought mamma would have died of joy!"

The Americans thought this quite the most delightful speech they had heard for an age, and joined heartily enough in the general laugh that followed it, which had not yet died away, when the door opened and a tall elderly woman in deep mourning appeared. The hostess seemed a little disconcerted, but rose and greeted her cordially, saying, "Just in time for a nice *pâté*, Miss Frynne!" made a place for the new-comer beside her, and introduced her to the Fletchers. Miss Frynne had a perfectly stolid, expressionless face, a wandering eye, and a rather fidgety manner. She fingered her knife, fork, spoons, and napkins nervously until she was served, and then fell to and ate steadily and ravenously, with swift despatch but without grossness. Learning from some remark of Sir Robert that there were Americans present, something like a flash of intelligence passed. over her face, and she said with animation, to nobody in particular, "Do the birds sing there?" Now, the

girls had been asked so many absurd things about their
native country that they were rather sick of lecturing
on the subject, and, besides, misunderstood the temper
of this inquiry, and fancied it patronizing in tone: so
Jenny said quickly, "Oh, dear, no! they wouldn't dream
of taking such a liberty in a new country!" and Lucy,
"Why, of course! What an odd question!" almost at
the same moment; whereupon Miss Frynne hurriedly
begged pardon, and said,—

"No offence meant, I assure you, only they don't in
Australia," astonishing the girls in her turn. After this
she devoted herself to her pudding again, which she
pronounced "beautiful." But no words could paint
Jenny's amazement when, chancing to look at her a
few minutes later, she saw her put down her spoon,
clap both hands behind her ears, press some springs,
take off an auburn wig that covered a head as bare as a
billiard-ball, wave it about a few times, clap it on again,
settle the springs, pick up her spoon, and go on with
her pudding, quite unembarrassed by the performance.
It had been done so quickly and quietly that no one but
the cousins and their hostess had seen it. Mrs. Venable
gave the girls a meaning glance, and they said nothing;
but from that moment conversation was almost out of
the question for them, and they were always stealing
furtive glances at Miss Frynne to see what she was
about. Presently a general move was made, and, as
they filed into the drawing-room, Mrs. Venable dropped
behind, and said to the girls, in a perfectly tranquil,
matter-of-fact way,—

"She is a little touched, you see, but quite harmless,
poor dear, and not often as disagreeable as she was

to-day. She used to be a great friend of my dear mother's."

"But is she allowed to go about like this?" asked Lucy. And Jenny put in "All alone?"

"Not quite; I dare say we shall find her sister waiting for her."

In this Mrs. Venable was not mistaken, for on the first sofa they found Miss Anastasia Frynne, a cheerful, brisk little old lady, who took her sister and put her down in a corner with a book of photographs, saying authoritatively, "Sit there, dear, for a bit. We shall be going presently," and then came over to talk to the Fletchers, who, she said, were the very first Americans she had ever met. "You see, being in mourning, I go out very little" (the girls glanced at the bright scarlet cloak that enveloped her, at the magenta cravat tied in her throat, and the bow of cardinal ribbon that fastened her collar,—worn, it is true, with a black dress,—and thought that grief wore a cheerful face in England), "and so miss seeing people. Barbara is very confining, too. But I am sure I should find Americans most interesting,—really most interesting. I have read a great many books about America,—a very great many,—if I could only remember what they said,—the conversion of the natives, and all that. Is that work going on now, do you know? I should like to know more about it. Do the natives wear clothes? And what do they speak? Surely they aren't all as fair as you and your sister. Of course time and education, and all that, would make a difference, I can quite see."

Miss Anastasia was evidently laboring under an impression that the girls were reclaimed Indians, and they

were framing some sort of indignant explanation, when
she burst in again:

"Now, do tell me, what do people do in America to
amuse themselves?"

"Very much what people do elsewhere, I suppose,"
said Jenny. "They have dinners, and balls, and parties,
and go to the theatre and opera, and all that."

"Do they, now, *really?* Poor things!" exclaimed
Miss Anastasia, in the tone people employ when talking
of a Christmas dinner at an almshouse or Thanksgiving
Day at the penitentiary, adding, presently, "How very
interesting!" Then, getting up, she announced her intention of going, made her sister put on her things, and,
coming back to the girls, said,—

"You will let me come and see you, won't you? And
should you mind if I bring Barbara? Some people do;
but I don't see why they should, she is so very harmless; and she enjoys going about tremendously, though
you wouldn't think it, perhaps."

Lucy, though fully aware of the rudeness of the act,
could not stand this, and gave Jenny's elbow a warning
pinch. In vain: Jenny only smiled, and said she was
sure her cousin, Mrs. Fletcher, would be very happy to
see both sisters.

When they had gone, Mrs. Venable came up, and the
girls could not resist the temptation to repeat the choicer
portions of Miss Anastasia's conversation, spiced with
their own amusing comments, and afterward Mrs. Venable explained that the two sisters had lived all their
lives in that county, had only twice been up to London,
even, and might be pardoned a good deal on the score
of extreme provincialism.

"Oh, Katherine, what a delicious time we are having!" exclaimed Jenny as they drove home. "Talk of the discovery of America! what is it compared to the discovery of England? To find all these foreigners speaking my own tongue, to speak their tongue and feel myself a foreigner, and to be at home and abroad all day long, is just perfection. Don't dream of taking us on the Continent: it couldn't interest us half as much."

A discussion of the people they had just left followed, and the hope was expressed that they might see more of them except Miss Barbara.

"And Mr. Heathcote," Jenny put in.

In this they were not destined to be disappointed, for their new acquaintances all called early and often, and were, besides, met elsewhere at every turn (the maiden ladies excepted), and so became on more or less intimate terms with the Fletchers.

The Heathcotes, indeed, soon came to the house as regularly as the postman, and more regularly than the sun, and with a better knowledge of the pair came a cordial liking of the elder man, and a good-natured tolerance of the younger as a well-meaning but not particularly interesting and certainly very conceited person. Sir Robert delighted the ladies in many ways. He was so kind, simple, and sincere—so genuine, in short—that they really grew fond of him; and he was never happier or more entirely at ease than in their congenial and sympathetic society. He brought the girls books and music, sent Mrs. Fletcher's cablegrams, talked Spurgeon to Mrs. Fletcher senior (whose heart was much set on the destruction of the world, and who muddled herself continually with the prophecies and

their interpretation by various divines), and made himself, as he expressed it, "a house-cat,"—really a trusted
friend. At first they were much amused by what struck
them as oddities and eccentricities. He was an enthusiast about cricket, and constantly went to see the college matches, took part when he got a chance, and
talked rapturously of the play. Then, urged by the
girls, who had heard from his nephew that he was
musical, he would, after dinner, get up before a roomful
of people, and, without any consciousness, apologies, or
even accompaniment, roar out with capital spirit, if not
much voice, hunting-songs, Border songs, Irish songs,
in a simple, hearty fashion that was delightful. One
evening, when the talk happened to turn upon national
dances, what did Sir Robert do but get on the floor, and,
with Lucy for a partner, go through the sword-dance
and an Irish jig! The family being alone, and the girls
dull, this performance was rapturously applauded and
encored. Suddenly Sir Robert snapped his fingers and
wrung them violently as though he had been stung by
something, and started off with amazing celerity, his
coat-tails spread out like a fan, jigging and hopping
away for dear life in the Highland fling. When it was
finished, he dropped into the nearest arm-chair and
turned the reddest, jolliest, kindest face that ever beamed
upon a delighted audience toward the girls, crying out,
"See what you have beguiled me into, you rogues!"—
adding, as he mopped and composed himself, "I used to
be a famous hand at that kind of thing when I was a
youngster; but, God bless my soul! I haven't tried it
for an age."

Sir Robert had only been giving a rather unusual

proof that he was like the rest of his countrymen; for
even the cleverest Englishmen—men distinguished in
every walk of life,—men who have held the highest
positions of public trust,—men of the most liberal education, extensive travel, and widest experience—seem
to retain to the last a certain childlike quality of mind,
a relish for simple pleasures, a natural, homely, clean-
hearted way of looking at things that is beautiful,—
rare in our young people, and confounded with child-
'shness by many of our men.

"We should think Jay Gould or one of our Cabinet
officers quite mad if he had behaved like Sir Robert
to-night; but if I were a little boy I shouldn't at all
mind asking Mr. Gladstone to join me in a game of
marbles. I don't think he would trouble himself much
about the loss of personal dignity, and would put more
heart into it than into the reception of a Parliamentary
committee," said Jenny to Mrs. Fletcher, as they took
up their bedroom candles and filed up-stairs that night.

"True, Jane; but all the same I have no desire to see
the Stock Exchange and both Houses of Congress
doing the racket," that lady replied.

Next day, about eleven o'clock, the ladies were comfortably established around the drawing-room fire, and
Lucy was reading Froude aloud, when an interruption
came in the person of Walton, who tapped, entered,
stood near the door, and finally approached Mrs.
Fletcher, but still said nothing. Impatient to go on
with her book, Lucy at last said, by way of dismissal,
"We did not ring, Walton, and require nothing." But
that functionary lingered, and presently said, his eyes
on the carpet, his whole manner intensely respectful,—

c

"If you please, 'm, there is a party" (here he coughed discreetly behind his hand)—"a person describin' himself as a relation of the family—from America, which I was to say the name is Ketchum,—Mr. Job Ketchum. is what I was told."

Walton made little pauses between his clauses. He felt that he was impressive. Having finished, he cast one swift glance around the group, caressed thoughtfully his luxuriant side-whiskers, and dropped his eyes again, waiting for orders.

"Job Ketchum!" cried out Mrs. Fletcher senior, in a tone of horrified amazement.

"Cousin Job!" echoed her daughter-in-law feebly. "What on earth—" "can have brought him here?" she was about to say, but, catching Walton's deferential eye, she changed it into "can have prevented his telegraphing or writing to us to expect him?"

The look of gayety and cheerful comfort had quite died out of the little circle, and, feeling that they were betraying their consternation too plainly, Kate paid no attention to Jenny's plaintive "Who is Cousin Job?" but rose, saying,—

"Well, we must go down to see him." And with the older lady she walked out of the room and down the stairs. Walton, who had seated "the person" on one of the hall chairs until his claims should be investigated, had preceded them, and was hanging up a shabby overcoat and a new soft felt hat, hopelessly limp in the crown, on the rack, making a feint of brushing the latter carefully, that he might be present at the interview without seeming to wait for it.

Divested of his outer shell, Cousin Job appeared a

man of medium stature, carelessly arrayed in slop-shop
garments, having a pleasant, shrewd face, and a stamp
of immense vitality and energy about him. He hurried to meet his aunt, imprinted a sounding kiss on her
cheek, and said,—

"Well, this is nice,—to see relations in this strange
land! Been in London for a week, where I didn't know
a soul. I am delighted to see you all,"—with a heartiness and an air of feeling himself entirely welcome, now
that he had got among his kindred, that made both
ladies instantly ashamed of their secret sentiment, and
infused something more than politeness into Kate's
reception of him.

"Where is your luggage, Job?" she asked; "for of
course you are going to stay with us?"

"That's all the luggage I've brought" (pointing to a
shiny black portmanteau on the hall floor). "I didn't
want to bother with more, just for a flying trip. I knew
I could rig myself out over here if I needed anything;
but I guess I'll do as I am. When did you hear from
your husband?" said he, mounting the stairs as he
spoke. Then over his shoulder to Walton, "Here!
Bring that along up to my room, and get me some
water."

The ladies winced at this peremptory way of addressing "the archbishop," and were prepared for a revolt;
but Walton said, with his usual respectful air, "Yes,
sir. At once, sir," and, seizing the bag, disappeared
into the back premises.

"Hold on," said Cousin Job to the ladies; "I've got
something for you." And, running down the steps, he
undid a gigantic yellow-paper parcel he had brought

with him, and displayed a remarkably fine bunch of
bananas. "Those are for you, aunt. I remembered
you were fond of them when I saw them hanging in a
big fruit-store on Regent Street, and brought them
along. They ain't as good as you get over in New
York, but it was the best they had. Nice place that
was. There was the prettiest girl in there I've seen
since I landed. And, if you'll believe me, aunt, I saw
five little sweet potatoes, no bigger than an egg, hanging up in the window, labelled 'Madeira fruit.' I told
the man they'd kill themselves laughing at the idea out
in Tecumseh, Michigan, where I came from; and he
looked like an owl that's been hit over the head with a
shingle."

Displaying in his amusement a splendid set of white,
even teeth, and with an eye that twinkled with the
remembrance of his London adventure, Mr. Ketchum
rejoined his relatives on the landing, and together they
made their way to the drawing-room, to which the
girls, who had been hanging over the balusters meanwhile, had now prudently retreated. Here he was duly
introduced to Lucy, whom he had not seen since she
was a child, and to Jenny, whom he had never met,
and, remarking, as he walked about the room, that they
were "fixed up first-rate," and that their "parlor" was
unlike most English rooms, which he said were "hardly
big enough to swing a cat in," seated himself near the
fire and poured out a vivacious account of his trip across
the Atlantic, his detestation of and disappointment in
Liverpool, the English climate and hotels, and indeed
almost everything except the English beefsteak. Of
his private affairs, too, he talked with the utmost frank

ness. "I was pretty well cleaned out three years ago," said he, as he crossed his legs and contemplated a neat boot (which was the one evidence of dandyism about him, and flowed naturally from his having an uncommonly small foot), "but I kept a stiff upper lip, and I said to myself, 'Don't you let yourself get down in the mouth, Job Ketchum: you'll light on your feet yet.' And, sure enough, I made a change, and went into partnership with a friend of mine, and just prospered right along. And here lately I made a hundred thousand at a clip, on wheat. That'll do for a start, I guess. And I got tired seeing Sam Bates, the biggest man in Tecumseh he thinks himself, swelling around the place like the President of the United States, talking about Europe and what he did when he was 'abrard:' so I just put twenty thousand to my credit at Brown Brothers', and determined, if there was anything to see over here, I'd see it, as sure as my name was Job Ketchum. And here I am, ready for fightin' or fiddlin' or feastin', as the Irishman said."

The luncheon-bell interrupted the flow of his eloquence, and, looking at his watch, he exclaimed, "Why, what time do you have dinner at this ranch?"

"At six. But we will have something now," said Kate.

"That's right. I like to be fashionable when I can afford it. I used to take dinner—when I could get it—about twelve out in the mines in Colorado, and two is the hour in Tecumseh; but you are all high-flyers over here. Well, when I'm in good health I'm as good for dinner any time as five cents is for a ginger-cake. Don't put yourselves out for me," he replied, and, noticing

4

the girls' smiling faces, said to his aunt, "Nice lot of goods, these, aunt. All silk, and more than a yard wide, if I'm not mistaken."

At which the smiles developed into hearty laughter.

The afternoon proved a rainy one, and, for a wonder, no one called: so the ladies had Cousin Job all to themselves,—a state of affairs they were far from regretting. Learning that he proposed to spend a month (and, seeing their countenances fall, he reassuringly added, "And longer, if I like it") before "going the big circuit," they employed it in trying to give him some idea of the formalities and conventionalities of English society, insinuated a good deal of advice disguised as general information, which they hoped and prayed he would lay to heart, and with infinite tact contrived to set before him some of the most prominent reforms that would be expected of him.

"There is a capital tailor here, Cousin Job; and clothing is so cheap in England, you really ought not to go home without a complete outfit. Let me see: you will need a Park suit, and an evening suit, and a couple of morning suits, at once," said Kate.

"Nonsense!" said he. "Ain't this all right? And I've got another one in my bag that is better still. They ought to last me for three years,—made of the very best broadcloth. Why, I could get married in this out West: it's fine enough for anything." He looked down complacently at himself as he spoke, and Kate was obliged to yield the point for the moment.

She shifted her ground. "I dare say we shall have you 'the glass of fashion and the mould of form' in a little while,—a regular Bond Street swell," she said. " Of course you know that you will have to sacrifice your felt hat promptly, cousin. You wouldn't like to be conspicuous."

" Oh, no ; I'm sure he wouldn't," put in Lucy, sweetly.

" Everybody who is anybody wears a silk hat in England, except when they are in the country, and then a pork-pie is permissible," announced Mrs. Fletcher senior, with an aggravating air of being a supreme court and giving a final verdict.

This was unfortunate. With a thousand good qualities, Mr. Ketchum had some faults, and, for one thing, was as obstinate as a mule. He scented a feminine conspiracy, and planted all four feet firmly. He was not going to be led,—no, not he,—still less to be driven. So he made what he and a great many of his countrymen consider the proper response to any suggestion looking to the imprisonment of one of Columbia's freeborn sons in the strait-jacket of European conventionalities, and, though not generally profane, lost his temper, and said hotly, "Damn it! I am an American, and I shall do as I please."

After this, as may be supposed, an embarrassing half hour followed for all parties, which was broken by the girls saying that they must go and dress for dinner, as the Heathcotes were coming. Mrs. Kate followed them, and, leaving her dressing-room door open, wandered in and out of the girls' room while they were all engaged in this rite, reciting Mr. Ketchum's biography in fragments :

" You know, his mother ran away with a man the family detested, and went out to the West to live, and

this was the only son, and she indulged him to the top
of his bent and let him run perfectly wild. He came
on to New York when he was about twenty, and elec-
trified the family." (Disappearing for a while, and
then coming back.) "And—what was I saying? Oh !
Well, before he was twenty-five he had run through
everything he had, and the last we heard of him he was
washing bottles at a beer-saloon out in Colorado and
leading a very dissipated life. In fact, he was supposed
to have gone to the dogs altogether."

"It is no wonder, Kate, that you turned positively
green when you heard his name," said Jenny.

"Mamma asked him about it to-day, and he said it
was a pure invention; that he was really working in
the mines, and that the only thing he regrets about it
is that he sold a claim for fifty dollars to some man who
got thirty thousand out of it," said Lucy.

"It can't have been all true. At all events, he seems
all right now. But, I must say, I wish he hadn't turned
up here. Of course he is a gentleman at heart, and all
that, but he is dreadfully rough, and has absolutely no
*usages de monde;* and English people are so formal !
And I can't manage him a bit, as you see. What *will*
the Heathcotes think of him ? What on earth is he putting on for dinner, I wonder ! I pined to beg him not
to wear that awful green cotton necktie, but I didn't
dare. Oh, you may laugh, Jenny; but I don't find it
amusing at all," said Mrs. Kate, as she swept in for the
last time, fully arrayed.

The objectionable necktie was not visible when they
got down. Cousin Job had put on the other suit, which
looked to them an aggravated form of the first one,—

more hopelessly ill fitting as to the coat, baggier in the
trousers, shorter in the waistcoat, cut neither high nor
low, with linen bulging carelessly above it, and a very
narrow black cravat tied in a wild bow, with long ends,
and already showing a disposition to work around under
the left ear. He looked decidedly worse than before,
and all the more so by contrast with the Heathcote
men, who, in full canonicals and displaying about an
acre of spotless linen, had an easy unconsciousness of
being well dressed and the general *millefleurs cachet*
about them of their caste. Cousin Job looked at them,
and having long ago made up his mind that any man
who parted his hair in the middle must be a fool, made
no exception to this valuable rule in the case of the
uncle and nephew. They probably thought him—indeed, young Heathcote said as much, later—"an awfully
rum chap;" but both saw reason before dinner was over
to modify these impressions considerably. For, in spite
of the anxiety of Kate and the incongruous element
introduced at the eleventh hour, the meal went off very
pleasantly, even gayly. Sir Robert seemed delighted to
have an opportunity of learning something "from an
eye-witness" of Colorado and the Far West generally.
He asked some ten thousand questions about mining,
milling, the various ores, the climate, population, agricultural peculiarities, and geographical situation of the
border States, said "Just so" perpetually, as though he
had known it all before, and listened with avidity to all
Cousin Job said in reply.

Knowing the ground thoroughly, the American lost
sight of himself, talked not only fluently, but well, and
so appeared to advantage. Sir Robert grew more and

4*

more interested, and harked back to particular points
about which he said he was "not quite clear," begging
everybody's pardon if he was becoming a bore, and so
beguiled Cousin Job into further statements, and on to
reminiscences, and then to jokes, given in his native
vernacular, and of the flavor which is so relished by
English palates.

Mr. Ketchum had shown himself a man of sense and
wit, and knew it. His *amour-propre* soothed, he was no
longer on the defensive, and he grew every moment
more at ease. As for young Heathcote, he seemed exquisitely tickled either by the matter or the manner of
this recital, broke into what he considered frightfully
indecorous and unseemly guffaws, only to cork himself
up again with the utmost suddenness, and at last, when
Mr. Ketchum said something incidentally about "the
business end of a tin tack," gave way altogether, and
burst into the most uproarious and infectious fit of laughter. He went so far, indeed, as to slap his knee in his
ecstasy, referred to the tack with a fresh outburst of
hilarity several times during the evening, and repeated
the story the very first thing at his club next morning,
where, indeed, Sir Robert buttonholed old General
Bludger and poured out a mass of statistics about a
certain portion of America which he had been " credibly
informed was the greatest grazing-region of the world,"
advising his friend to send his sons out there.

But to return to the dinner. When Sir Robert took
up the conversational ball, he drifted into some of his
hunting experiences in various parts of Europe, Africa,
and India, and Cousin Job was obliged to concede mentally that the connection between the premises of his

favorite theory was not as perfect as he had supposed, and that he might be mistaken in his conclusion; in short, that "a creature bearing the outward semblance of a man, and not of a monkey," might have something in a head of which the hair was parted right down the middle that entitled him to the respect of his fellow-men. Having decided this, he ordered Walton to fill Sir Robert's glass, and insisted on giving as a toast, "The Anglo-Saxon race, first, last, and all the time." It was well received; and, the talk turning upon yachting, Mr. Ketchum said that he had met an English fellow out on the Plains two years before, who, he had heard, owned the fastest yacht afloat,—a splendid fellow, he said, named Bartow, and from Liverpool, he thought.

"I've met that fellow somewhere," put in young Heathcote. "Big, black man, isn't he, with a cast in one eye?"

"Well, he wasn't what we should call a black man, or even a 'colored pusson,' but he was dark, and there was a tendency to bolt the ticket in the right optic, I remember," assented Mr. Ketchum. "Who is he? What is he?"

"I don't know. I can't say, really. I've heard he was a kind of a—" (he hesitated, striving to pierce the aristocratic haze that veiled such occupations in his mind, and then went on)—"a sort of cotton fellow. Poor devil!"

This amused Mr. Ketchum in his turn, and, the *entente cordiale* being now complete, he ordered more champagne, and it was not long before Kate fancied that he had already taken rather too much, and heard with dreadful anxiety his demands to have his glass refilled.

Walton, whom nothing escaped, caught her eye as it travelled toward her cousin for the twentieth time, and understood the whole situation. His conduct from that moment was worthy of Talleyrand. The way he contrived to be deaf and blind, and out of the way, and coming presently but never got there, and only half filled the glass once after that, was masterly; but he reserved his great *coup* for the moment when Kate had given the signal for the ladies to retire (with outward calm, but a sinking heart) and Mr. Ketchum had ordered him to "bring up a half-dozen bottles of that champagne." Then, inscrutable as the Sphinx, he stepped up, with his usual quietly respectful air, to his mistress, and said, "I beg pardon, 'm, but it is all out. The order was not left in time, and Brown & Wentworth's young man has just been round to say it will be sent in first thing in the morning, and hoped you would excuse it."

Kate, being a woman, understood like a flash, and with graceful apologies insisted that the gentlemen should forsake the dining-room as soon as they had enjoyed a cigar, unless they preferred the Continental fashion of accompanying the ladies. Cousin Job would, she knew, with his American ideas of gallantry.

Thus appealed to, Cousin Job rose, young Heathcote opened the door, and they all trooped back to the drawing-room, where the remainder of the evening passed delightfully.

Before leaving, Sir Robert confided to Kate that her cousin was "a most shrewd, clever fellow,—a delightful fellow," and had offered to put him up for the club, in spite of a meaning cough from his nephew.

When they had gone, Job very much surprised the

ladies by saying, " Well, Kate, you were right, after all.
I guess my clothes ain't quite the cheese. I'll go and
get myself fixed up to-morrow at that place you were
talking of to-day. What's the name ?" and allowed
that lady to tell him that his cravat had slipped quite
round behind, and that he *must* remember to put a pin
in when he dressed himself, without showing the least
annoyance.

---

### III.

COUSIN JOB was as good as his word. Before the
girls were down next morning he went out for a walk
on the Promenade, and came home to find his aunt
enjoying the fashionable intelligence in the " Looker-
On," in which, among the arrivals, figured the name of
" Mr. *Joseph* Ketchum, United States." " Call that a
newspaper !" said he indignantly when his attention
was called to the interesting fact. He took it in his
hand, flipped it scornfully with his thumb and middle
finger, and, after careful examination, protested that it
was not to be compared for one moment to the " Te
cumseh Clarion." He was still talking about it when
Kate came in and changed the current of his thoughts.
" Well, you are all a lazy set here !" said he in greeting.
" I have been up for two hours, and been pretty much
all over the place, and I stopped at that store you told
me about, and told the man to make me the finest suit
he knew how to turn out, and to be quick about it
There was a chap there that smiled me in and smiled

me out, and wanted me to buy everything on the shelves *bad.* He soft-sawdered me for half an hour, and offered to make me an overcoat like the one they had just sent the Prince of Wales, at 'living rates.' But I laid my fingers on my nose and told them I sabed all that, and that if he thought we weren't up to snuff in America he was mistaken, only it was General Grant's coat over there, and that I was used to making up my own mind; if I wanted anything I would get it, and if I didn't he would have to get up very early in the morning to sell it to me. And he begged my pardon when he saw he had waked up the wrong passenger, and said that he hadn't meant to try any tricks of trade; theirs was a most respectable house; only if I had any 'borders' they would be glad to execute them."

"What did you say to that, Job?" asked Kate.

"I told him if he would stick to that programme he might make something out of me yet; but that as the prince and I weren't running in the same fire-brigade, it didn't matter about our being dressed *exactly* alike."

Great was the amusement of the ladies as they thought of the interview, and they exchanged eloquent glances across the table, while Mr. Ketchum devoted himself alternately to his breakfast and a map of the town which was spread out beside him.

"Cards to the Benedicts' ball on the 21st, girls, and a very kind note from Sir Robert, to say that he means to get a ticket for Cousin Job," said Kate. "Isn't it nice of him? It is *the* ball of the season, you know, and if there were pasteboard admittance to heaven it could hardly be more coveted than cards to the Benedicts'."

"I am delighted!" cried Jenny and Lucy in a breath, both girls having known for some time of the coming event, and having dresses from Paris ordered for the occasion and worthy of it.

"But, Kate, I do so wish we could get a ticket for Mabel Vane and take her with us. Only think of it! she is eighteen, and as pretty as a pink, and has never been to a ball in her life! Such a frightful case of destitution in the upper classes has never come under my notice," said Jenny. "This is the way I came to know it. She was here yesterday, and was saying that she supposed we were very gay, and I asked if she was going to this ball, and she said, 'Oh, no! I can't afford it, even if there was a chance of my getting a ticket, which there isn't. Papa, you know, was a poor clergyman, and since his death mamma and I have always lived in lodgings, and we have no great friends, and can't entertain, and so we are quite out of the current. I often wonder how it would seem to be like other girls. Mamma says that there are five hundred girls here, and only one hundred men, and that if I could go out it wouldn't be the least use,—that it would only be a great expense for nothing, I should never get an offer, and I am better as I am. But I don't care for that, and I do so long to go to *one* dance, even if I had to sit against the wall all the evening.' Poor child! her eyes were full of tears, and I felt so sorry for her, and yet her English way of putting it was so comical that I could hardly keep my countenance."

"It is a shame! It's perfectly abominable!" put in Lucy. "Why, if I have been to one party I've been to five hundred of various kinds; and Mabel says that she

thinks herself awfully lucky to be asked in after dinner
at a few houses, or occasionally to luncheon. And she
is such a sweet little thing, and such a thorough lady."

"I wonder at it," said Mrs. Fletcher senior pensively.
"I have heard that her father was a third-cousin of the
Earl of Carsford,—or is it the Marquis of Wolhampton?"

But this nice genealogical point was never settled;
for Cousin Job, who had been breaking three eggs into
a tumbler and stirring them with the most unnecessary
display of energy, while Walton, unable to bear the
sight, had retired precipitately to the butler's pantry to
avoid losing any portion of his specific gravity, now
looked up and said, "I can't understand how girls can
get so far below par in England. Buyers seem to be
backward in bidding, and holders anxious to realize.
The old lady in Threadneedle Street is carrying more
petticoats than her trade will warrant. Now, about
that young friend of yours, Kate. If money will do it,
just get her a ticket, and we will take her along with
us and see that she has a splendid time! Why, out
West she'd have eight or ten fellows haunting the house
every night, and sending her bouquets, and serenading
her, and ready to jump over the moon to please her."

"Money can't do it, but influence can, Cousin Job,
and we will see what can be done," replied Kate. "She
shall go if we can possibly manage it."

By what arts and machinations it was managed will
never be known, but, although a member of the Benedicts' Club had offered twenty pounds for a ticket that
very morning, and failed to get it, Jenny, on the next
afternoon, received from her friend the barrister, with
Mr. Lindsay's compliments, a large square envelope

containing an enclosure requesting the pleasure of Miss
Vane's company on Wednesday the 21st at the Assembly
Rooms. Putting on her bonnet, she rushed round to 38
Portarlington Gardens and demanded Miss Vane so imperiously that the small "slavey" who opened the door
asked "what ever was hup," lingering on the landing
after ushering Jenny up-stairs to catch if possible some
hint of the news she scented. The whole house was
"hup" when her errand became known. Mabel could
hardly believe her senses, and was radiant with delight,
Mrs. Vane equally fluttered and profuse in thanks.
The question of raiment for this lily of the field coming
up, Mrs. Botts, the landlady, who had once been maid
to a countess, was called in, and gave her opinion at
great length: the dress must be white tarlatan, she
should say, over a silk slip, with a "top" cut low in the
neck, a white satin sash and slippers to match, which
was what her ladyship had worn on an even greater
occasion, and it would set off Miss Mabel "wonderful."

Miss Marsh, an old lady on the second floor, who
walked nine times round the square every day at the
same hour, starting out for this cheerful tramp, was
attracted by the sound of voices and looked in, heard
what was going on, and, trotting back to her room,
brought down a box of Roman pearls, which she said
had belonged to a dead sister, and would Mabel do her
the favor to wear them? Mabel would not, but thanked
her as prettily as possible, and, it being generally agreed
that the "stuff for the gown" must be bought at once,
the two girls started off in high glee, and shopped so
briskly and sensibly that in half an hour the foundation-
stone of Mabel's palace of delights was safely laid: the

c      ~                  5

dress, the gloves, the slippers, the satin, were being
borne home in parcels that bulged delightfully and fore-
told to one pair of blue eyes at least a world of bliss!

The intervening days dragged their slow length along
for the girls, and were improved by Cousin Job in sight-
seeing, which he went about in a perfectly fanatical
way, determined that nothing should escape him, and
being guided solely by what his "hand-book" said, and
not in the least by what he himself wished to see. Sir
Robert put him up at the Club, where he amused himself by initiating certain gentlemen into the mysteries
of draw-poker, and teaching them, as he put it, "to
brew egg-nog on scientific, old-Virginia-forever principles." The first was decorously christened "American
whist" by Sir Robert, who explained to General Bludger
that the latter was "one of the American drinks,—
something like the 'eye-opener' and the 'raise-the-
dead,'"—two beverages that he firmly believed to be
national in reputation.

At a flower-show in the Montpelier Gardens, which he
facetiously dubbed a "shower-flow," because everybody
was driven into the tents and summer-houses three
times during the afternoon, Mr. Ketchum met Mabel
Vane, and, taking a tremendous fancy to her, showed it
by staying gallantly by her side and shielding her from
the rain with his enormous umbrella. Finding that she
had on thin shoes, he disappeared for a moment, and
greatly surprised her a little later by turning up with
her overshoes and mackintosh, which he had sent one of
the Park guards for. Poor Mabel, whose only experience of the sex so far had been one of scant civility or
utter indifference, was quite overpowered by such a proof

of thoughtfulness, and blushed herself into a state of damask-rosiness in acknowledgment of it that gave gratitude a new and very beautiful complexion to Mr. Ketchum, who was accustomed to rendering such little services on all occasions, and rather used to their being taken, more or less, as a matter of course.

The day of the ball arrived. Mr. Ketchum, when the arrangements for the evening were being discussed, insisted on getting a carriage and taking Mabel to the ball, and Kate had great difficulty in making him understand that it would positively shake Cheltenham to its centre and be flying in the face of all English conventionalities, that Mabel wouldn't go, and that it was not to be thought of. She had settled all that. Walton, who was perfectly trustworthy, should go for her in Mrs. Fletcher's carriage and bring her down to them; and, once under the wing of a chaperon, she would, with the other girls, be taken "properly" to the Assembly Rooms.

"And do you mean to tell me, Kate Fletcher, that they trust a girl over here with a footman sooner than with a gentleman?" he demanded hotly.

"Yes, I do. I can't help it, and I am sorry you are vexed, Job, but indeed it wouldn't do," said she, which set him off in one of his eager, emphatic orations, calling upon heaven and earth to witness the absurdity of such a social regulation, and winding up with,—

"Well, I shall send her a bouquet, anyway. I suppose that isn't a scandalous proceeding?"

"Oh, no! quite proper. It isn't often done, unless people are engaged; but still—"

"Oh, go along, Kate! You must have lost your

senses!" ho interrupted, and, clapping on his hat, left
the house.

Ho had boon gone some hours. The girls were in
the drawing-room, entertaining the Heathcotes and Venables; and Kate, a little apart from the others in the
bow-window, which commanded a view of the street
and front steps, heard a ring. She bent forward to see
who it was, and caught a glimpse of a man in a towering white beaver hat, and, even at that distance, with
something queer about him. Another look,—a stranger
*in full evening dress, at one o'clock in the day!* Another,
—the stranger turns, and—oh, horror! oh, "agony,
rage, and despair!"—it is Cousin Job!

It may be an ignominious pang that rends her bosom,
but Kate is a woman of the world; she feels it to be
quite equal for the moment to battle, murder, or sudden
death. In five minutes he will be in that room, and
there is that odious young snob of a Heathcote, who is
always sneering covertly at Cousin Job as it is, and
doesn't understand him at all, sitting opposite, immacu-
lately arrayed, his hat held in his hand at an eminently
correct angle, his offensive eye-glass screwed firmly in
his eye! It is a perfectly unbearable situation, she
thinks. There is nothing that can be done, and, with
a crimson face, she sits still, waiting to hear the fatal
step on the stair. It doesn't come, and she glides out
of the room and down as far as the first landing, where,
looking down, she sees Walton and Cousin Job parleying
near the front door.

"Who is up-stairs?" asks Mr. Ketchum.

"The Miss Frynnes, sir, I believe; but cook answered
the door."

Walton knows that Mr. Ketchum detests these esti-
mable women for some reason, and takes his chance.
Fixing his shrewd, gray eyes on him, he adds, after a
pause, "The tailor sent home some things for you, sir,
and would be greatly obliged by your trying them on
at once. His man will be back in 'arf an 'our to know
if they suit."

Mr. Ketchum still hesitated, holding his hat in his
hand and rubbing the nap energetically with his silk
handkerchief. "Tell him to come back to-morrow," said
he, and moved toward the stair.

"Oh! And, if you please, sir, I took a note up to
your room, brought a moment since, which the maid
from Portarlington Gardens said was to be give you as
soon as you came in."

Mr. Ketchum stopped: for the life of him he couldn't
help blushing, and, to hide it, he turned brusquely away
and walked off to his room.

Walton had gained the day, and, unconscious that he
was being observed, leaned against the wall, and, throw-
ing back his head, laughed the laugh of the successful
diplomat whose skilful evasion of some obstacle has
enabled him to carry his point.

It was the first time Kate had ever seen the real
Walton, and it gave her rather a startled and unpleasant sensation,—a feeling that he was too clever by half,
thankful as she was to have the social calamity averted
that she had so much dreaded. But the sensation was
only momentary. "He is doubtless attached to the
family, and knew we should be mortified. It was very
nice of him. Really, Walton is a nonpareil among servants," she thought.

5*

As she was making her way back, the drawing-room door opened ; farewells were being exchanged, and in a few moments the guests were safely out of the house, and she was relating the agonizing experience of the last half-hour to the girls.

Jenny laughed until the tears ran down her cheeks: "Oh! to think of his putting it on at the shop and wearing it home! And with a white hat!" she cried.

"And that awful green cravat! My dear, it is my belief that he means to be *buried* in that cravat," said Kate. "It was a fearfully narrow escape!"

"Why didn't you let him come up? It would have been such a crucial test of the breeding of those people. Sir Robert and the Venables would have been a shade nicer than ever; but can't you fancy the galvanic shock it would have been to young Heathcote? But no, Kate. Seriously speaking, I wouldn't for the world have had Mr. Ketchum put in such a disagreeable position before that horrid man. He is a kind, generous, splendid fellow, and worth a dozen of such people ; but all the same he would have looked exquisitely ludicrous, and we should have been obliged to go about à *l'Anglaise* and tell people that he was a little mad, and we hoped they didn't mind. It is the drollest thing I ever heard of. You are such a worldling, Kate, that I wonder there is a particle of coloring-matter left in a single tube of your hairs."

"I shall tell him that he may break all the Commandments, and blow up the House of Parliament, and set fire to Windsor Castle, and trample on the union jack, and throw vitriol in the face of the Princess of Wales, if he likes, but that he is *never*, NEVER to put on a dress-suit before nightfall in England, on pain of *death*," said Kate. "I know he has grown up out of the world, on the frontier; but, still, how could he do such a thing?"

No spectator was present at the interview that en sued, of which Kate only reported that she said very little, and that Cousin Job took it in good part.

When nine o'clock came, Mabel appeared, looking too quaint and pretty for anything. Her dress was cut in the fashion of a very remote period, with what was known then as a "baby-waist," and queer half-long sleeves. She was sitting bolt upright on the edge of the sofa when Kate came down, evidently afraid of crushing her dress and soiling her gloves. Her eyes shone with pleasure, and a more charming picture of youth and innocence it would be impossible to find. She was as fair and simple as an English daisy, Kate thought, as she came forward with an air of modest self-possession and her usual charming little blush: "Do you like me. Mamma says that I do very well, but that no one will notice me among so many splendid people in Worth gowns and all that, and that I had better give over thinking of myself at all and make up my mind to enjoy looking on."

Kate noticed that she had on a white carnelian neck lace, shamed into looking almost blue by the white, lovely neck, and said, "Come here, dear, and let me see," gave a disapproving frown to the English over-skirt, which she found fearfully and wonderfully looped, sent for some pins, and rearranged it tastefully in a twinkling, pinned a charming bunch of natural flowers in her dress, insisted on giving her a little silver châte-

laine, turned her about, giving any number of those
mysterious touches which produce such an effect when
given by a woman with a genius for dress, and at last
pronounced her " an ideal *ingénue*," and assured her that
if she lacked anything it was rouge, pinching the girl's
rosy cheek.   She then went off to tie Mr. Ketchum's
cravat, and that gentleman presently returned with her,
looking extremely well, and protesting that she had tried
to get him to wax his moustache and part his hair in
the middle, but that this was against the constitution
and by-laws of the State of Michigan, and that he was
"quite enough of a Tussaud wax figger" as it was.

Jenny and Lucy, coming in resplendent in Paris
dresses, walked up and down to give the family a private view of these artistic constructions; much oscula-
tion followed between the girls, everybody suddenly discovered that it was very late, and, after much muffling
and shawling, they all rolled away at last to the ball.

The ball had the three great requisites for such an
entertainment,—good music, a capital floor, and a supper calculated to compensate all the heavy dowagers
and sleepy papas for their sufferings as chaperons.
The spacious rooms were beautifully decorated, the
orchestra from London was fiddling away in the gallery, the dancers were spinning and whirling at a tremendous rate in the circles chalked off on the floor, the
master of ceremonies, who was nearly as imposing as
Walton (and no earthly dignitary could be more so),
stood near the door.   Our party advanced.   Sir Robert
stepped out from a mob of gentlemen and offered his arm
to Mrs. Fletcher senior, and Jenny had already taken
that of a certain young barrister (in preference to Mr

Heathcote, who consoled himself with Lucy), and a
stout clergyman, who had just finished waltzing what
he called the "*troy temps*," offered to escort Kate.
Mabel slipped a timid hand under Mr. Ketchum's awk-
wardly-proffered elbow, and they all made for the
benches on the upper side of the room, where they cast
anchor. Jenny looked about her, and felt as an actress
does when she gets a whiff from the footlights; Mabel
was terrified by the glare and the crush and the crowd,
and felt herself morally a grain of mustard-seed and
the least of all these birds of Paradise; Kate began to
scan the toilets, Mrs. Fletcher to look up the great ones
of the company; Mr. Ketchum remarked that it was
the biggest fandango he had seen, and that the Assembly Rooms compared favorably with any hall that he
knew "on the other side of the pond." Kate offered .
to introduce him to some of the girls, but he declined
for the present, and stood behind Mabel, looking down
admiringly upon the fair head bent every now and then
over his huge bouquet, which had already created a
sensation at Portarlington Gardens.

Jenny, as a belle and beauty of recognized position,
was soon surrounded by men, and, generously intent
upon "Mabel's having a good time," brought them all
up and presented them in turn, having previously interested them in her *protégée*. The consequence was
that Mabel's programme was soon half filled up. Out
of the twenty-three dances she was engaged for twelve,
and Mr. Ketchum, who was already down for four of
them, was begging for a fifth, when her first partner
arrived, and she tripped off joyously with him and
joined the dancers. Job saw her making vain efforts to

catch his step (with small success), her pretty face wearing its most anxious expression. He seemed to combine
in his own person the worst traits of all three classes
of bad dancers,—the teetotums, the wobblers, and the
go-aheads. When he ought to have gone ahead, he
spun around for five minutes, as if his operations were
confined to a hearth-rug; when he ought to have tem-
porized for lack of space, he dashed madly ahead; and
whenever called upon to guide his partner decisively in
any direction, he wobbled infuriatingly first to the right
and then to the left in an embarrassing series of false
starts, very trying to a novice. Job was secretly delighted. Like most Americans, he could use his feet
with the same dexterity as a French actress does her
hands, and he waited impatiently for his turn to come,
which it did very soon.

Mabel came back to her chaperon looking flushed and
harassed, made a meek little speech expressive of her
regret at not being able "to quite catch his step" (skips
would have been nearer the mark for a performance
which was a mixture of waltz, polka, mazourka, Highland fling, and Irish jig), and, with a "Now-then!" expression of triumphant satisfaction, Mr. Ketchum had
taken his place. At what "fandangos" he had graduated in the graceful art is not known, but he danced
beautifully, and Mabel, who had taken lessons and had
moreover been practising the "American reverse" for a
week before a dingy old pier-glass at her lodgings, felt
herself borne along in an inspired whirl, forgot that she
was dancing at all, in the technical sense, and did not
stop until the last strains of the "Morgenblätter" had
died away. In all her experience, confined hitherto to

a lonely Welsh curacy and Portarlington Gardens, there had been nothing like it, and she was radiant.

Meanwhile, Jenny had taken several turns, and was resting for a while in a little bower of ferns and foliage-plants that opened into the ball-room. She was with her friend the barrister, who was commenting upon the scene before him. "Who is that girl there in yellow?" he asked.

"Where? Oh, in the corner. Smythe is her name, I believe. Pretty, isn't she?"

"No. Not according to my ideas. She looks as though she didn't tub. Dash of the tar-brush there, I should say."

"Oh, no! Impossible! You should not say such things, really. Besides, she isn't so dark at all."

"It isn't her skin only: her hair has got that awful kink. I hate it. One of my aunts went out to New Zealand in the early days and got carried off by a Maori chief; and I often wonder what I should do if a lot of blackamoor cousins turned up in the Park on some sunny day in the height of the season and laid claim to me. Awful lark it would be, wouldn't it?"

Jenny burst out laughing, and agreed that it would certainly not be pleasant: "I have never heard you mention any of your relatives before. Have you a mother and sisters?"

"I've got the usual supply of mother, and shoals of sisters. My mother came down from town to-day with one of them,—Edith, the eldest."

"Did she?" replied Jenny, with animation. "Why didn't you bring her with you to-night? But I suppose it was too late to get a card."

"Oh, she never goes to balls. She is on the shady side of forty, and never goes in for anything in the shape of amusement, except penny readings for the deserving poor and those awful parish tea and harvest-home things. She got me to one of them *once*, but I don't think she will ever do it a second time. She is a district visitor, and has a soup-kitchen and all that: she really is an excellent creature, but she'll never get a husband in the world."

"What are the others like?" asked Jenny, delighted with this brief biographical sketch.

"The next one is named Gertrude, and she is quite *passée*, too, and rather like Edith: curates, and croquet, and that kind of thing, you know. She is awfully plain, poor thing! and makes herself no end of a frump by the way she dresses. The third one is very pretty, and is married to a fellow in the Carbineers; and the fourth was thought the best-looking girl that was presented the season she came out. She is down in the country now, though she hates it most awfully. It is a confounded shame to keep her there; but the governor says she has had two seasons, and played her cards very badly,—going and getting engaged to a missionary,— and can't have any more. I dare say he will take her up, though, when he comes round. I wrote her to-day to give the old chap his head and not oppose him, and it would all come right."

"And is that all?" asked Jenny, hoping that it was a large family. "How very sad for your sister! People can't always control such things, and I suppose she had forgotten that Cupid has sovereigns for wings nowadays and always perches near the Bank of England."

"I am sorry for her, too. She is my favorite sister, and she was awfully cut up about it. But what was the use? There is another, Caroline, just out of the school-room, and disgustingly slangy and horsey and doggy. I'd like to shake it all out of her, but she is the governor's favorite, and does exactly as she pleases. The three others are still in the nursery, thank heaven!"

"What a lot of you!" exclaimed Jenny.

"Do you think so? We don't consider ourselves a large family at all. The mater was one of sixteen."

A pause followed this statement, and then Jenny began again.

"Is yours a pretty part of England? Not that I need ask, for it is all lovely, so far as I can see."

"Pretty well. Good hunting country, but rather flat. I don't like it. I prefer London fifteen months out of the year. I have just got myself a tiny little bandbox of a house in May Fair, and shall get myself a cat or a dog and settle down as a selfish old bachelor. I can't marry: I've nothing but a beggarly allowance and a confiding tailor while the governor lives, which will be forever. I went to see his medical man not long ago, and he told me he was good for fifty years yet. I went off then and signed the lease for my house. There will be a capital town-house, and all that, when I come into the property; but I am tired of the life I have been leading, and want a den of my own, where I can be as much of a bear as I choose."

"How long is your lease?"

"Seventy years."

"Why, what possessed you to lease a house for seventy years?" asked Jenny, in utter surprise.

"Oh, I thought I might get used to it and want to stay; and I wasn't going to be bundled into the streets any day."

Jenny could not conceal the amusement afforded her by this idea: "An American would as soon think of flying. I never heard anything so absurd. Why, you are thirty years old now! May I ask if you expect to live to be a hundred?"

"I don't know. One of my great-aunts got to ninety-nine, and her physician said he could have made it an even century if she hadn't eaten a Welsh-rarebit for supper one night. He was awfully savage about it. You see, she lived at Bath, and it would have given him a tremendous boost with all the other old women there, if he could have managed it."

Just then a couple whisked past the door, and Jenny remarked,—

"That Miss Porter is lovely, and dances better than any girl here, I think."

"If I tell you something, will you be vexed?"

"No; certainly not."

"I am afraid you will."

"Not unless you are very rude; and I am sure you won't be that."

"Are you sure you won't mind a bit of criticism?"

"Of course not," she replied, much puzzled.

"Well, then, you dance beautifully, but you don't kick out your legs enough at the back."

At this perfectly unlooked-for and astounding remark Jenny turned into a peony. Quite misunderstanding her furious blush, he said,—

"There, now! You are angry! I said you would be

vexed! I'm always putting my foot into it. What I meant was that I admired Lady Florence Foster's way of dancing. Look at her. Here she comes, now."

Jenny looked, and saw a huge blonde girl with a pronounced attack of "Grecian bend" (which was *à la mode* then), who certainly was making lively play with her heels, her body bent forward at a most extraordinary angle. When she could utter anything in answer to his penitent apologies for having "vexed" her, she said that she was "not angry, exactly, but—"

"What! You don't like her dancing?" he asked.

"No; I think it frightful!" she declared, and was spared further argument, for at that moment a tall, fair, languid man, who had been introduced that evening, approached her. When immediately in front of her, he stopped, glanced at his programme and then at her, and said pensively,—

"I think I'll give you No. 10."

"I beg your pardon, but I don't think you will," she replied, angry indeed now. (Jenny, who had had an embarrassment of riches in the matter of partners ever since she went to dancing-school, a belle in white frocks and a blue sash!—Jenny, who had been in the habit at home of dividing her dances between two or three eager aspirants, and had always been made to feel that she conferred an honor on the object of even this temporary preference!) Outwardly civil, there was something in the ring of her voice that made him glance with interest at the fierce little thing looking up at him with such a flash of scorn in her brilliant eyes.

"No. 11, then?" he said.

"I am engaged," she replied curtly, without referring to her programme.

"No. 12, say, or 13, then," he perseveringly suggested.

"My card is quite full," she answered, with no conventional regrets.

"A supper-dance, then," he stupidly insisted.

"I must definitely decline the honor." And, rising, she bestowed upon him the faintest inclination that ever did duty for a bow, and, taking Mr. Lindsay's arm, moved away. "It takes my breath away, quite," she said to him. "Did you ever hear of such a piece of impertinence? I rage when I think of it! He'll give me No. 10, forsooth! Good heavens! Do you mean to say that English girls put up with that sort of thing?"

"No; of course not. At least, nice girls don't. Some girls might. It is they who make themselves cheap, and they ought not to complain. But the fellow's a cad: anybody can see that. Don't mind him. He is an awful ass."

He seemed much annoyed by the episode, and, seeing this, she dropped the subject. Some time afterward she heard that the mirror of chivalry, whom she had so roundly snubbed, felt very sore on the subject, and had spoken of her to the Venables as "a spiteful little Yankee."

That night was a memorable one for Jenny in many ways. For one thing, Mr. Heathcote, who, as an eligible *parti*, had undergone agonies of mind first, misled by her gay and gracious manner, lest she should marry him, and next, when he better understood her, lest she should not, having come to the conclusion that she was essential to his happiness, plucked up his courage, proposed, and was "definitely" refused as a partner for life.

Meanwhile, Mr. Ketchum had been making a brilliant record for himself. The good-natured fellow took out at least a dozen of the young ladies who sat round the room in long and melancholy rows, fair, fresh, stout-looking girls most of them, in pink and blue and green and white,—a partnerless generation, rather heavy all round, it must be confessed, with, in. consequence, only a few names here and there on their programme, and awful gaps (and gapes, indeed) between. It was a dismal business for many of them; and why they went at all to such a harrowing form of entertainment was a mystery to our Americans. They were quite grateful for Mr. Ketchum's politeness, and it may be safely averred that he lost nothing by it with the mammas, to whom he was likewise most attentive, taking relays of them up to supper, and rendering them a thousand good offices, with his usual amiability and unselfishness. He even forgot his dislike to Miss Frynne when he saw her sitting neglected and forlorn in a corner, carried her off to the supper-room, got her a liberal supply of oysters and *pâté de foie gras*, ordered a bottle of champagne,-- to which she did full justice, he thought, accustomed as he was to the abstemiousness of his countrywomen,— and, on her stating that she wished to go home, took her to the cloak-room and put her into her modest cab.

When Mrs. Fletcher senior was quite worn out, and the feat of collecting the girls for the third time had been accomplished, after Lucy had begged for the inevitable "one more," which Mr. Ketchum had taken for

*e* 6*

granted, and was spinning out with Mabel, the party followed Miss Frynne's example.

While waiting for their carriage in the passage, Mabel met an old lady whom she knew. "Hasn't it been a delicious ball?" she cried. "Only to think of it! I have danced every dance. I haven't sat out one. Mamma will never believe it."

"Yes, yes, my dear. I saw you. It was all very fine. I only hope it will last," said the matron severely, shaking her head dubiously by way of farewell.

When they got home, Walton had a blazing fire for them and a nice little supper, over which they lingered for some time, Mabel having been dropped at Port-arlington Gardens *en route*.

"Six dances with Mabel, Mr. Ketchum! Take care, or you will have to put on your explanation-coat. The affections of the British virgin are not to be trifled with in this reckless way. You are not in America now, where men devote themselves to every pretty face they fancy and girls pride themselves on being engaged six deep," said Kate, as she rose from the table and shook a finger warningly at her husband's cousin.

> "She hath two eyes, so soft and *blue:*
> Take care! Beware!"

sang Jenny. And, relapsing into prose, "And remember that I will not have the daisy trampled upon. No flirtations permitted on the premises."

"I am not flirting," protested Mr. Ketchum.

"Oh, then you are in earnest?" she replied, putting him promptly on the other horn of the dilemma. "Flirtation is attention without intention, you remember. Good-night." And Jenny laughingly disappeared.

"She's a pretty one to lecture me about flirting! She has been mopping up the pavement with Heathcote for a month, and will have him asking to pay her board-bill for the rest of her life in another week. Anybody can see which way that cat is going to jump. Oh, the women! the women! Do you think Miss Jenny likes that London barrister, Kate? I hope not. He tells me he can't put up the necessary securities, to say nothing of margin; and a poor man engaged to a poor girl is like a pig under a gate,—he can neither get in nor out." And with this characteristic aphorism Mr. Ketchum betook himself to bed.

## IV.

THE playful warnings Mr. Ketchum had received had no effect upon his relations with Miss Vane, unless, indeed, they served to accelerate the pace of his wooing, —for such it now was. But for this attraction, he would long since have exhausted the sights of a provincial town and bolted the historic scenes of the neighborhood at a gulp, as it were, and then rushed off to do the same thing elsewhere with the same fretful haste and joyless expenditure of energy. And, in spite of his infatuation, Mr. Ketchum felt that he was wasting precious time, of which he should not be able to give any satisfactory account to his recording enemy Sam Bates, who was always standing in the background of his mind, asking

him what he had seen "abrard." His ideal had been to
"do" England, Ireland, Scotland, Wales, France, Bel-
gium, Germany, Switzerland, Spain, Italy, and the Holy
Land "inside of three months." This was the time he
had allowed himself for that hurried race over many
thousand miles of foreign territory—with its insane
jumble of hotels, railway-carriages, cathedrals, picture-
galleries, scenery, peoples, and tongues—which once in
a lifetime the American "business-man" allows himself,
usually when already threatened with softening of the
brain and most in need of repose.

Whether moved by this consideration or not, Mr.
Ketchum certainly conducted his sentimental campaign
with vigor and discretion. He tipped the little slavey
so magnificently that when she saw him coming she
flew to the door as though she had been shot out of a
mortar, and on opening it gave him a series of courtesies and quite flattened herself against the wall. She
thought him, as she confided to Mabel, "the 'andsomest
and most liberal gentleman as ever was," and took a
burning interest in the progress of the affair, as indeed
all the women in the house did. She would knock at
the Vanes' door and say, "The American gentleman is
down below again, mem: is he to be allowed up?" Or,
"The gentleman said as 'ow you wasn't to be disturbed
on no account, and this package was to be give particular into Miss Vane's h'own 'ands, w'ich I 'ope you'll
overlook the thumbmark, seein' I was a-doin' the grates."
She wore a chronic air of repressed excitement all the
while, and quite neglected the penny-dreadful romances
on which she was wont to feed her youthful imagination,
for a more fascinating reality.

Mr. Ketchum came to know Mrs. Butts by sight, and always had a pleasant word and smile for her. One day he met the old lady on the first floor, and, hearing that she had lost her favorite cat, sent her a beautiful Maltese mouser, almost all tail, to fill the aching void. He astounded Mrs. Vane by the number, the variety, and the generosity of his benefactions in all directions, and poured a Pactolian stream of flowers, books, and music, the only things he could offer, upon Mabel's head. Hearing of a crippled lad in whom they were interested, he sent him ten pounds, and, being asked by a clergyman to subscribe to a "Home for Disabled Seamen," of which he was chairman, amazed that gentleman by giving him a check for a hundred. His reputation for liberality grew apace. Cabmen fought for him, beggars followed him, florists sent him specimen bouquets, tradesmen inundated him with cards, and begging-letter-writers exhausted all their arts upon him, without, however, making a penny out of this shrewd creature, who knew better than most men how to make, save, and spend money. But, if he had an eye for and hatred of shams, he had a heart easily moved by real distress, and, unhappily, there is only too much of that in England, so that he was always giving, if not to the daughters of the horse-leech, to consumptive widows and reduced gentlefolks, orphan children and old women. It was no part of a scheme for conquering Miss Vane's heart, of course; but if it had been he could not have better succeeded in winning her confidence. To these two lonely women, accustomed to the rigid economies and colorless vistas of a tiny fixed income in which there was room for neither hope nor despair, which curbed every gen-

erous impulse and tamed every wild desire, Mr. Ketchum
was a constant source of wonder. He brought with him
a breath of his native prairies, and his large ideas, hopes,
views of life and its possibilities, the breadth of his
horizon, the force of his energy, impressed them more
and more. He seemed the splendid flower of conditions
undreamt of in their world,—a world in which every
ounce of tea was carefully weighed and the caddy
watched with a vigilance that was never to sleep from
the cradle to the grave, in which a gnawing anxiety as
to how much was being cut off the leg of mutton down-
stairs was one of the gravest interests of an immortal
soul, the cleaning of soiled gloves and remodelling of
old dresses religious rites.

It amused him beyond measure, when admitted on
a sufficiently intimate footing to know of such things,
to find that he had been agonizing Mrs. Vane by his
reckless way of picking up the poker and vigorously
uprooting the fire. She had feebly remonstrated in
a playful way once, telling him that "one could not
punch a friend's fire until one had known him seven
years," and he had said, "Well, I suppose two can
do it if one can't, and Miss Mabel can help me if she
likes." He never realized the enormity of his offence,
until he discovered that, though ostensibly a Christian
Englishwoman, Mrs. Vane was really at heart a fire-
worshipper. She had a grate half full of clay balls that
retained the heat and effected an untold saving in her
"coals." The sacred fire was built up and renewed at
stated hours by the slavey in lieu of a vestal, and then
became to all intents and purposes an altar which no
one was ever allowed to desecrate by a touch. "Why

don't you have a fire?" he would ask, in entire good
faith, on coming in on bitterly cold days and finding the
ladies in a chilly room, decorously engaged on some bit
of needle-work before a handful of coals built into a
pyramid in the centre of the grate.

"We have got one! There was a beautiful blaze not
five minutes ago. Mabel, dear, you might lift that lump
*a little* on the right, and stir it *very* gently, if Mr.
Ketchum feels cold."

Such as it was, Mr. Ketchum sat by it a good deal,
warmed, let us hope, by a more sacred flame. He got
two severe colds, it is true, that resulted in quinsy and
a swelled face, by sitting in that cheerless lodging-
house; but they did not cool the ardor of his suit,
which a refrigerator would have been powerless to
affect, and Mabel was not sorry when he was well
enough to resume his visits.

Curious affairs they must have been, those interminable talks between people who differed in a thousand
things and agreed perhaps in a dozen. It was a duet,
chiefly, between Job and Mrs. Vane, punctuated by
Mabel's bright smiles and blushes and neat platitudes,
for she was a gentle, good little girl, obedient to a fault,
accustomed to see life over her mother's shoulders, and
it would have seemed to her quite shockingly bold to
have taken a leading part in any conversation. It
seemed the most unlikely thing in the world that these
two should ever have cared for each other, yet somehow
the great Leveller smoothed the way to a perfect understanding and affection between them, she seeing and
valuing the fine qualities, the real refinement and goodness, that lay hidden under what had struck her as

roughness and eccentricity, and he recognizing under the conventional crust of a formal manner a sweetness and unselfishness and womanliness that seemed to him little short of adorable.

Matters were at this interesting and satisfactory stage when Mrs. Vane became suspicious and put a sudden stop to their further progress. Hearing that Mr. Ketchum visited and sent bouquets to other young ladies of his acquaintance, as indeed he did, being of a gallant and amiable turn of mind, she took it into her foolish old head to think of him, and, what is more, speak of him, as "a desperate flirt." Mabel was impressively warned not to believe a word that he said. She was kept up-stairs when he called. She was made to return, with polite, frigid little notes, as loans, the books he had given her. If they met on the Promenade, Mrs. Vane was always there too, and gave Mabel's arm a warning squeeze, which said that she was to bow and cross the street. The poor child was not even allowed to walk in the square opposite Portarlington Gardens, for fear of meeting the ogre who was crunching all the young women's bones in the place.

Mr. Ketchum was completely mystified by this fine display of feminine tactics, and confided his woe to Kate at great length. Not only was life valueless and existence unendurable, but, among other things, a picnic that he had long planned was completely spoiled, since Mabel would not come to it.

"Are you sure she won't?" said Kate the comforter. "I don't know about that. Let me ask her."

To this he joyfully assented, and, for some reason, she was not only cordially received, though she went as his ambassadress, but Mrs. Vane accepted the invitation for herself and her daughter.

Hearing this, Mr. Ketchum threw himself with more than his usual energy into the preparations for the occasion. He ordered the luncheon from London, and, when the caterer murmured something about its being an expensive proceeding, exclaimed,—

"Oh, blow the expenses! That isn't your lookout This is my funeral. I want an A 1 lunch, I tell you, and the whole thing done as well as you know how to do it. No rag and bobtail odds and ends, now, and wine that will bore a hole through our sides! I want the best that is to be had, and am willing to pay the piper. And look here: I don't want a teaspoonful of ice-cream in a butter-plate, either! And send plenty of those fellows of yours in swallow-tails, to run the thing as smooth as greased lightning. Do you understand?" Just such instructions had never been left at that shop; but there was no misunderstanding the general tenor of them, and in spirit they could not have been better carried out, as was shown when the day came.

"These people have been polite to you, Kate, and I don't want you to be under any obligations to them. Ask them all," he had said. She replied that, in her husband's absence, she had not entertained to any great extent, but that she had given a number of small affairs and did not feel herself weighed down by her social obligations.

"Well, never mind! ask them anyway. We'll take the town and paint it red!" said he, as he went off whistling "Captain Jinks of the Horse Marines."

A large party assembled on the day chosen,—a fine,
mild day, full of suggestions of spring, and as well
adapted for the expedition as though it had been
ordered on purpose. A long string of carriages went
rattling out of the town into the lovely country beyond, past Cranham Wood to Witcomb, where it had
been agreed that the remains of a Roman villa should
be visited. Arrived at the spot, the party came to a
halt, and, after endless chatter and delay, dismounted
and formed into a straggling procession, which struck
into a foot-path that led through a farm-yard full of
comfortable-looking animals, hay-ricks, and poultry into
a succession of fields, and brought up at two small stone
thatched huts near the border of the wood. Entering
the largest of these in detachments, all the ladies fell
into the regulation fit of rapture over what remained
of the remains, and gazed with enthusiasm at certain
spots in the tessellated mosaic pavement which, with
the aid of a vivid imagination and the eye of faith,
could be made out to have been intended for fishes.
Most of the guests felt but a languid interest in this
piscatorial display; but Mr. Ketchum got out a foot-
rule and went to poking and peeping and measuring
with much zeal and intelligence. He discovered that
the lintels of the door-way leading into the next room
were of massive stone and more than six feet high;
that the floor of the room rested on pillars three feet
high, and each about one foot square, set sufficiently far
apart to permit combustibles to be thrust in between
them and the whole room heated. He tipped the guide
and got two bits of the tesseræ and dug up a bit of the
cement. "Hang it! I must find out how those old

scalawags did this! They beat the world at it!" said
he, as he tied the relics up in a corner of his handkerchief. He stared for ten minutes at the hypocaust
under the flooring, calculated the amount of wood and
coal it would take to "run" it, and declined to leave,
though Kate assured him the others were getting restless, until he had satisfied himself as to what became of
the ashes, and wondered what people in Tecumseh
would say if he bought it and transported it bodily
there. The interest he exhibited in this antiquarian
research surprised his relatives, who could not understand the attraction it had for his practical mind.

At last he consented to move, and, taking carriages,
they drove rapidly to Birdlip and up to the door of
"The Black Horse" Inn, where everything wore an extremely festive air and a small army of servants was
drawn up to meet them. Entered from the street, the
house was in no way remarkable, but it must have been
artfully contrived to heighten the effect produced on the
mind when, walking straight through a long, narrow,
dark passage, they came out suddenly upon a lovely
garden laid out on the very verge of a cliff which sloped
almost perpendicularly several hundred feet to the valley of the Severn and commanded one of the most extended, varied, and beautiful views in all England. The
Americans were especially enraptured by it, and, long
after the other ladies had gone in to lay aside their
wraps, Jenny and Kate and Lucy and Mrs. Fletcher.
stood in a group on the terrace, picking out and admiring in detail the white Roman road stretching straight
across the valley, the Severn winding through it, the
towns of Gloucester and Worcester with their spires

and cathedrals dotting it, the abbey tower of Tewkes-
bury rising out of the woods in its centre, the beautiful
Malvern and Shropshire hills that encircled it, and a
thousand features besides of this most charming land
scape.

By this time the party had assembled in a closed pavilion, which, thanks to the upholsterer and the florist,
had been completely transformed. The dull gray light
of an English winter's day had been shut out; it was
brilliantly lit, and the long, bare, dismal room was gay
with bunting and mirrors and flowers, and at the upper
end an orchestra was playing delightfully. Mr. Ketchum
had kept his preparations a secret even from his relatives, and, like his other guests, they found this feature
of the entertainment a most agreeable surprise. On
their complimenting him upon it, he said that he was
"determined it shouldn't be a one-horse, Jim Crow
blow-out, if he had anything to do with it." Mrs. Vane
stood transfixed when she arrived at the door, near
which her host was standing. "Look here! Why
don't you leave your gums outside?" said he, glancing
down at her feet.

"What? What did you say?" she exclaimed.

"Your gums. You have forgotten to take them off."

"Take off my *gums!* What on earth do you mean?
How can I? or why should I, if I could? I beg pardon,
but I really can't have understood you," said she, putting on her glasses and peering at him in her near-
sighted way, completely mystified.

"Why, your shoes I am talking about. Don't you
see?" said he, pointing at them as he spoke.

"Oh!" she exclaimed,—a full, long-drawn English

"Oh!" with volumes in it,—"you mean my *galoches.*"
And then she sat down and laughed more heartily than
she had done most likely for twenty years over what
was to her mind an exquisitely absurd mistake, and,
seizing Miss Frynne, who was passing, began, "What
*do* you suppose they call galoches in America, my dear?
*Gums!*" and she related what had passed, and both
ladies found in it a whole comic almanac. They are
relating it to this day, no doubt, amidst cries of "Really,
now!" and "How very remarkable!" "What very
curious people the Americans must be!" from their astonished friends, who, truth to tell, are easily surprised,
and find the least variation from English customs amazing in a people who, though they went to housekeeping
three thousand miles away a good while ago, and have
naturally got to calling some things by different names,
are in the main more easily understood than the worthy
inhabitants of Scotland, Ireland, Wales, or even England, outside the large towns and below a certain rank.

When the dancing had gone on with immense spirit
for a couple of hours, luncheon was announced. It was
called that, but was really an elaborate banquet, in which
every delicacy that Covent Garden Market could furnish and a French *chef* convert into delicious *plats* was
served to perfection. At each lady's plate there was a
lovely bouquet and a charming little souvenir of some
kind, ordered from Paris by Mr. Ketchum, each one an
elegant and tasteful trifle, and as nearly as possible of
equal value. To each was fastened a card, with "Mr.
Job Ketchum, Tecumseh, Michigan," engraved on it in
large letters, and, though there have been prettier names
and better-known places, I doubt whether any gentle-

7*

man's card ever gave more entire satisfaction. There
was the prettiest possible little flutter around the table
as each package was opened and its contents admired
and compared, and beaming glances and cordial thanks
were poured out on the smiling host, who I am afraid
lost a good deal of both in his effort to catch Mabel's
timid, pleased glance as she unrolled the tissue-papers
folded around her dainty tortoise-shell fan.

"If you please, 'm, one lady has been overlooked,"
whispered Walton (who was presiding over the affair
with a dignity and omnipresence remarkable even in
him) to young Mrs. Fletcher. "What would you wish
done about it? Would one of the family, beggin' your
pardon for making so bold, be willing to give up—"

"Certainly. You see everything, Walton.' Take
mine," she said. And a moment later Miss Frynne,
who was quite at the other end of the table, received,
with a neat apology from Walton, her share of the
goods the gods had provided. Partaken of under unusual circumstances and in such pleasant company, the
little feast seemed a piquant improvement upon ordinary
entertainments, and put every one into a state of brilliant good humor.

All the conditions for thawing English reserve were
in force, and although the entire party did not make as
much noise as ten average Americans would have made
under the same circumstances, there was plenty of ani
mation in the subdued current of sound, and it was
evident that pleasure was at the helm as well as Walton,
who, to pursue the simile, had taken command of all
Higginson and Chuffey's young men early in the day,
and felt as bold as an admiral on his own quarter-deck.

When they rose from the table, Mr. Ketchum walked round to where Mabel Vane was sitting, took a lovely rose from one of the *épergnes* and offered it to her. With a shy look at him and an anxious one in the direction of her mother, she accepted it and held it in her hand.

"Put it in your dress," he commanded rather than suggested, and Mabel, flushing painfully; and mindful of her mother's instructions, began to say, in her low voice,—

" I—I would rather not. At least—" here she caught Mrs. Vane's eye, and saw with surprise that she was smiling and nodding amicably in Mr. Ketchum's direction. Mrs. Vane had been hearing from Miss Frynne that Mr. Ketchum had "pots of money, and was no end of a catch." She had been deeply impressed by the present display, and had suddenly concluded that she would reverse her policy of the past two weeks. Glad of the permission implied by her mother's glance, Mabel said, by way of reparation, " I am afraid it will fade. However—" She did not finish the sentence, but put the rose in her belt. Mrs. Vane joined them, and was overpoweringly civil to Mr. Ketchum. She was too sorry to have missed him so often lately, but she had been selfishly absorbed in some private matters, and Mabel had been obliged to keep her room a good deal. Dear child! her throat was so delicate! But he must come very soon again and spend a nice long morning and tell them some more about his exciting adventures in—what was the name of the place?—Colorado.

Mr. Ketchum did not understand the situation at all, but, nothing loath, promised readily enough, and promptly asked Mabel for a dance, which she cheerfully

accorded. Everybody had drifted back to the pavilion
by this time, and dancing was going on with more zest
than ever. In the course of the afternoon Mr. Ketchum
danced five times with Miss Vane, and not much with
any one else.

"Depend upon it, he is in earnest, dear Mrs. Vane!
I am sure your Mabel is about to make a most brilliant
match," whispered Miss Frynne. "Only do be sure
about the money. It is so very difficult to find out
anything about foreign fortunes."

And, though she parried her friend's congratulations
discreetly and affected to pooh-pooh the idea, Mrs. Vane
revolved in her own mind a dozen schemes for landing
the big fish that had strayed into her net, and marked
out her own line of conduct definitely.

It was almost nightfall, and Mr. Ketchum was disposing of his guests in the various carriages, when he
heard a hubbub in the inn, and turned back to see what
was the matter. It was briefly this: Lucy had gone
back to the edge of the cliff to get a last view of the
valley, which came very near being her last view of
anything, for her foot slipped in some way, and she slid
down ten feet, stopping on a ledge that, fortunately,
jutted out just there. How it happened that Walton
heard her shriek, and, seizing one of Chuffey's men and
a couple of table-cloths, managed in a few minutes to get
her back on terra firma, and bear her, half fainting, to
the house, she never knew; but it was one of that invaluable servant's most striking peculiarities that he
was never out of the way and never in it. Here was a
sensation that afforded ample food for comment as the
party drove home in the twilight.

"Where did you get that fellow?" Sir Robert asked Mrs. Fletcher senior. "He is one of the best servants I ever saw. If you are not thinking of taking him to America with you, I should like to take him into my service. He is a quick-witted chap, and a plucky one, too, by Jove! That was a neat thing of his, getting your daughter up from that place like that. Most servants would have left her to tumble off into the valley while they ran all over the place collecting a mob of people and pointing out the wrong spot."

"And hasn't he a *good* face, Sir Robert? Such an honest, open countenance! I am sure we never, never can repay him," she replied.

The lights of Cheltenham were twinkling in the distance, and Mr. Ketchum, who had saved a seat for himself next to Mabel, was wishing the town a good deal farther off, when Mrs. Vane bent forward and addressed him: "If you have no engagement, could I see you to-morrow?"

"Why, of course you can," he replied, heartily. "I am always at the service of the ladies. About what time?"

"In the morning, some time. About eleven, I think, if convenient."

Not long afterward, they were all exchanging farewells and telling Mr. Ketchum what a "charming affair" and "immense success" the expedition had been.

"I hope you have had a happy day," Mr. Ketchum said to Mabel, "and that I shall see you to-morrow. I have said 'Damn it!' pretty often lately when I have found that door shut on me, though I generally draw things mild. Shall you be at home?"

*f*

Before Mabel could answer, Mrs. Vane interfered:
"No: Mabel, unfortunately, is obliged to go to the dentist's to-morrow. You must put up with an ugly old
woman for once," she said, with what she meant for a
meaning glance, Mabel standing by and hearing of this
arrangement for the first time.

At the appointed hour next day Mr. Ketchum made
his appearance in Portarlington Gardens, and was
almost instantly admitted and taken up to Mrs. Vane's
shabby-genteel little drawing-room, where she was
waiting to receive him. As far as he had thought of
the interview at all, he had quite made up his mind
that he was to be consulted on some business matter.
"Women are always getting into a muddle in money
matters and sending—generally when it is too late—for
some man to pull them out," he said to himself. He
was confirmed in his impression by Mrs. Vane's thanking him effusively for his kindness in coming and apologizing for the inroad she was making upon his time.
He saw that she was ill at ease and somewhat nervous
in manner, and, with a view to helping her, said kindly,
"Well, now, what is it? Here I am, ready to do
anything in the world that I can for you and Miss
Mabel."

"You are very kind; really, most kind. Thank you
very much for it," she murmured, putting down the
cushion on which she was making macramé lace and
looking at him.

"Oh, no, I ain't. What are men for?" he rejoined.

"I am about to approach you upon a very delicate
matter,—a very delicate matter indeed,—and it is highly
embarrassing. But I have a sacred duty to perform,

and I must do it, no matter what impression I may make upon you," she went on.

"Now, don't you bother your *cabeza* about that, my dear madam. I have told you already that you can count on yours truly to command," said he, leaning back in his chair and thinking, "In a mess with her stocks and bonds: I'd bet my bottom dollar on that." Then, aloud, "You are in some sort of fix now, ain't you?"

"If you mean trouble and anxiety, you are right, dear Mr. Ketchum. Never was a woman more sorely perplexed; and, reluctant as I am to say anything to you that—"

"Oh, that's all right. Go ahead. Never mind," he interrupted.

"Then, if you will pardon the natural solicitude of a parent, the only surviving parent of a most lovely and interesting young girl, placed in a position of most terrible responsibility" (here she took out a black-bordered handkerchief and put it up to her eyes, while Job shuffled uneasily in his seat, thinking, "Great Scott! I hope she isn't going to let on her water-works!"), "I beg of you not to be offended, dear Mr. Ketchum, if I ask you what your intentions are in regard to my dearest child."

"What's that?" exclaimed Mr. Ketchum, sitting bolt upright in his chair and staring at her with a fierce frown, his whole body galvanized into immediate interest. "What's that you are saying?" he repeated curtly.

Mrs. Vane trembled inwardly at the change in his manner, but went boldly on: "I am asking what your

intentions are with respect to my daughter, Miss Vane,"
she said, putting the case more formally. "You cannot
be blind to the fact that from the very first you have
gone out of your way in every place and company
where you have met us to shower upon her the most
pronounced and compromising attentions. You have
singled her out repeatedly; you know that you have,
perfectly well. It is useless to deny it. And I have a
right to ask whether, after coming here day after day
for weeks, and sending my child books and flowers and
music and boxes upon boxes of sweets, and dancing
with her in public *five times in succession*, you mean to
go away from here without making her a proposition
of marriage?"

Her temper had risen; gone were her mellifluous
accents, and her voice was as sharp and rasping as a
fish-wife's as she turned and glared at poor Mr. Ketchum,
who, instead of attempting to answer any of the charges
on which he was arraigned at the maternal bar, only
sank back in his chair, and exclaimed, "Well! If this
don't beat the Jews!" He was so completely taken
aback that he was positively speechless for several minutes, and returned Mrs. Vane's stare with interest.
Then, to that lady's intense astonishment, he suddenly
burst into a roar of laughter, and, getting up from his
seat, walked rapidly up and down the room, shaking his
head from side to side, waving his long arms about, and
exclaiming, "This beats everything! This gets me, and
no mistake!"

When the paroxysm of laughter had spent itself, he
resumed his seat without apology and turned a quizzical
face and a pair of twinkling eyes upon Mrs. Vane, who

had spent the interval in bouncing about on the sofa in a state of fury.

"Is it, has it been your intention all along to compromise my daughter by engaging in a meaningless and contemptible flirtation?" she jerked out.

"Not if the court knows itself," he replied coolly. "But, if it comes to that, I should say that *you* are doing a great deal more to compromise her than I have done. What *have* I done, by the by? I should say that, on a rough estimate, I had paid five hundred girls as much attention in my time, and nobody ever thought anything of it."

This was a direct realization of Mrs. Vane's worst fears and suspicions, and she broke out upon him: "That sort of thing may be customary in *America*, Mr. Ketchum, where I have heard that the relations between the sexes are of a most extraordinary character; but let me tell you that it will not do in respectable *English* families. You have done my daughter a great wrong. You have blighted her future and kept off other men."

A fresh twinkle lit up Mr. Ketchum's eye at the idea of his being supposed to have frightened off a hundred or two of Miss Vane's suitors, when that guileless child had already told him that he was the only man who, as she put it, "had ever been at all—well, you know, nice to me," or whom she had known intimately.

"I don't want to crowd the mourners," said he. "If she wants any fellow to take my place, I'm ready to take a back seat. I'll ask her about that."

"You shall do nothing of the sort," snapped mamma.

"I have a good deal to say to her about that and several other little matters," rejoined he calmly.

8

And she, seeing that the battle was going against her, had recourse to the last refuge and safety-valve of the sex, and burst into tears. She loved Mabel, and was really distressed and upset by the result of her interference. She dared not let the child know what she had done, feeling instinctively that it would be regarded as unpardonable. "Don't tell her," she whimpered "She would never forgive me. And I thought I was acting for the best."

This speech not only changed the whole current of his feelings toward her, for he saw in it a genuine expression of maternal affection and solicitude, but it brought the delightful assurance that Mabel knew nothing about her mother's little plan for bringing him to book. "Now, look here! You stop crying," he said in his usual friendly tones. "I love your daughter, and I mean to ask her to be my wife. I'm a rough fellow, and I ain't fit for such a dainty, pretty piece of goods as that; but I made up my mind to it the first time I ever set eyes on her sweet face. But you oughtn't to have tried to hurry up the corpse as you have done. It may be the custom over here, but it ain't a pretty one, to my thinkin'. A man ought to be ready to go down on his knees before a woman like that, and it hurts him to think of her being speculated with. If I thought Miss Mabel had a hand in this, I'd take the next steamer. But I know she hasn't. It would never come into her innocent mind. She'd never do anything she oughtn't to. She's the sweetest woman that ever trod shoe-leather." He spoke very gently, and made little pauses after each sentence, while Mrs. Vane cried copiously in her corner. "You haven't got anything to

fear from me. I want to do what's right and square,"
he went on presently. "I'll ask her this very day, if
you say so. Lord! I wish I'd been a better man!"

At this Mrs. Vane took her hands down suddenly
from her face, and, with a real burst of womanly feeling, grasped his hand and shook it warmly, half crying
all the while. "You are a good man, Mr. Ketchum!
You have made me ashamed of myself. If Mabel will
marry you, I shall be glad and proud to have such a
son!" she cried.

Five minutes later, this stormy interview had ended
and Mr. Ketchum was walking down the long beautiful
avenue of elms that leads from the Queen's Hotel to the
Promenade, when whom should he see, "timid, and
stepping fast," but Mabel, looking a thousand times
lovelier than ever in the light of his new resolution.
"You are a cheerful-looking young lady to be coming
from the dentist's," he cried out gayly as he advanced
to meet her. "You can't have suffered any to hurt."

"No, I haven't. It was all a mistake. When I got
there, the man told me that his appointment was with
mamma for next week! I can't think how she could
have supposed it was I. She has a book for engagements, and is so very accurate about her entries, as a
rule. It is very odd. But I was not sorry to escape.
I went off to Heath's at once, and—only fancy!—I
found quite a new azalea, the Princess Maude, a lovely
thing! I ordered a pot of it to be sent home, and mean
to surprise mamma with it at breakfast."

Mr. Ketchum had joined her, and was walking back
with her to Portarlington Gardens, which was five
squares off, and at which they arrived three hours

later, after a long walk in the country beyond Lans-
downe Crescent and the outlying villas, down several
lanes that led they had no idea where, and over daisy-
starred fields that to them formed a tolerable substitute for the garden of Eden ; returning in a shower
under one umbrella, a blissful, bedraggled, engaged
couple !

"Well, Kate," said Mr. Ketchum to his cousin that
evening, "I have gone and done it at last! I have
played my last card, and, if I know anything about it,
it's the biggest trump in the pack. I'm engaged to
Mabel Vane."

Enthusiastic exclamations of "Goodness gracious !
You don't mean it! How perfectly delightful! I am
*so* glad !" and a hearty embrace followed.

"Yes," he resumed thoughtfully, poking the fire for
once in a tranquil way, "it seems too good to be true.
A plain, rough fellow like me. It's wonderful! But
one thing is certain : she might have taken a handsomer
man, and a more palavering man, and she could have
found a better one easy, but none of them could treat
her any better than I mean to. She shall have everything on top of this green earth that I can give her!
And you were right, Kate. That mother of hers got
out her lariat to-day and tried to rope me in! I never
was so surprised in all my life. I was completely euchred
for a while. The bottom fell right out of my tub."

"Oh, dear ! How delicious! Do tell me all about it.
Begin at the beginning," cried Kate in her most eager,
excited voice.

He related what had passed, and they were still talking when Walton slipped in with his usual cat-like tread

to announce dinner. The last thing Mr. Ketchum said was, "I cut loose from all my rough associates long ago; I got tired of that life. And one thing more, Kate, I've shaken hands with *whiskey*. I don't mean to so much as look at an empty beer-bottle without having blue goggles on. I've said it; and when I say a thing I mean it."

A week later the personal surroundings of the Fletchers had considerably changed. Mr. Ketchum had gone off at last to the Lakes, the Heathcotes to Surrey, and the Venables to the Isle of Wight. A fortnight later Mr. Fletcher arrived, having come over partly on business and partly to take his family home, and causing a sensation by his announcement that he meant to catch the next Cunarder.

Ladies, unlike stones, collect a larger amount of moss the more rolling they do, and it took vast quantities of packing-cases to hold all the things that Mrs. Fletcher had bought because they were "so cheap, and would cost five times as much in New York."

It would have been a tremendous undertaking to get ready in so short a time, but for Walton, who contrived that everything in the house should go on as usual, while he ordered, selected, packed, with incomparable judgment and despatch, the Fletchers' personal effects, verified the inventory of the house and replaced what was missing, took notes, left cards, and did a thousand last things as no one else could have done them. Mr. Fletcher was so charmed that he offered him a large advance on his wages if he would go to America with them; but he respectfully refused, with many expressions of gratitude for the esteem in which he, was held.

"What do you think of doing, Walton?" asked Mrs. Fletcher.

"I'm going abroad, 'm; I have heard of something there that will suit," he replied, and they reluctantly forbore to press him further about remaining in their service.

When they finally tore themselves away from the charming town in which they had grown to feel at home, and where they had received great kindness and hospitality, Walton accompanied them as far as Liverpool, was useful—indeed, invaluable—up to the last moment, and went down the Mersey with them in the tug, in charge of their smaller pieces of luggage, and especially of one dressing-bag of Mrs. Fletcher's containing several thousand dollars' worth of diamonds and a quantity of other valuables. Each member of the party tipped him handsomely and parted from him with effusion,—almost tearfully, indeed, knowing that they should ne'er look upon his like again until they returned to Europe. As he was stepping on the tug, Mr. Fletcher said to him,—

"What did you do with that bag,—*the* bag, Walton?"

"If you please, sir, I gave it to Mrs. Fletcher."

"Oh, all right. Good-by, again!"

Ten minutes before, Mrs. Fletcher had made the same inquiry, and he had made the same response, except that—in the confusion of the moment, doubtless—he had substituted "Mr." for Mrs. Fletcher. When they were well out to sea, Kate asked her husband what he had done with her bag, and, after a long discussion, ending in a quarrel, they concluded that there had been some dreadful mistake, which Walton would be sure to rectify, and that they must telegraph as soon as they reached New York.

We must go back to mention that Mr. Heathcote and Mr. Lindsay came down to see them off, bearing Sir Robert's "regrets at not being able to have the same miserable satisfaction." The poor man at a cricket-match a few days before had received a ball almost full in the face and been terribly hurt. His nephew was disgusted. "They wired for me, they thought it so serious, and when I got there I went up to his room on tip-toe. And when the old chap heard my step he sat up suddenly in bed, all bandaged and bloody,—a perfect spectacle,—and called out—what *do* you suppose?—'Who won?' Did you ever hear of such an infatuated old idiot in all your life?" he remarked to Jenny, to whom he renewed a former proposal, only to get the same answer. "Is there any one else?" he asked, coming back again after he had said good-by all round, and Jenny, with one of her rare, deep blushes, said simply, "Yes: he is waiting for me in New York now." And Mr. Heathcote rushed off without another word, or so much as a last look.

Mr. Ketchum made a portion of the grand tour he had planned, and returned to America with the understanding that he was to claim Mabel in a year.

Mrs. Vane said something to him about "settlements," very meekly, before he left.

"What's that for? Mabel will have all I've got," said he, much annoyed.

"But suppose you lost your money. It would be so dreadful for my dear Mabel, away off there among strangers."

Mr. Ketchum was not convinced, but yielded. "Very well, then. I will settle fifty thousand on her; and don't you mother-in-law me any more." '

Mrs. Vane was too enraptured to mind his vexation in the least, and he, repenting of his little speech, sent her twenty pounds of English breakfast-tea before sailing, "to keep that caddy of hers full without her sitting up with it day and night."

When he got home he forwarded some credentials for which she had asked. They consisted of four letters, one from his uncle, one from a member of Congress, one from a Methodist minister, and one from a firm of bankers. They reached Mrs. Vane at breakfast one morning under cover from her prospective son-in-law, and Mabel sat opposite and assisted at the tremendous ceremony of opening and mastering their contents. The first one that Mrs. Vane picked up was written on immaculate paper in a rather illegible but gentleman-like hand, and sealed with a crest, at which she peered curiously for five minutes. It ran as follows: '

"WABASH AVENUE, CHICAGO, April 3.

"MY DEAR MADAM,—My nephew, Mr. Ketchum, writes me that he has had the good fortune to win the affection of your only daughter, and begs me, with all the ardor of a lover, to do what I can to promote his suit. I don't think that I could do more than justice to his many fine qualities, and will only say that while he has grown up under peculiar conditions, and has lacked some of the advantages to which he is entitled by birth, he is, as you have doubtless discovered, a man of sterling worth and innate refinement, kindly in temper and generous to a fault. He has the ability to surround your daughter, if she should marry him, with every comfort, and I know will, as far as possible, guard her from every breath of hardship or misfortune. He has been a devoted son and brother, and in a man I believe these are generally regarded as good guarantees that he will not be found wanting in a nearer relation. My wife writes by this mail to Miss Vane, and, with cordial regards to her, I am, my dear madam,

" Faithfully yours,

" ALEXANDER FORBES."

"How very charming! How entirely satisfactory this is!" Mrs. Vane exclaimed as she handed the letter across the table to her daughter and took up the second. She raised her brows; the envelope was yellow; on being opened it disclosed a sheet of ruled paper, and in what she thought a queer hand she read,—

" WARSAW, INDIANA, April 5.

' This is to certify that I have known Job Ketchum, man and boy, now for more than twenty years, and believe him to be an honest, correct, and respectable young man. Any mother could, in my opinion, trust a daughter in his hands. The only fault I find with him is that he is not a professing Christian; but I hope there will yet be an abundant outpouring of grace upon him, and that he will then connect himself with the church of which his father was a member in good standing up to the day of his death. In the bonds of Christian fellowship,

" EBENEZER D. ROOT."

"Mabel, dear, this is really too puzzling for anything. It seems to be from some sort of Dissenting minister. Can Job's family have been *chapel*-people? And it sounds like a character for a gardener or footman. You mustn't mind my saying so, but it really does. And that 'Warsaw.' There must be a settlement of Poles out there. But I never heard of any Polish dissenters. Did you? I can't make it out."

While Mabel was trying to read the riddle, Mrs. Vane opened the third letter, at the head of which were the name and address of a firm of bankers and brokers in Lansing, Michigan. It was addressed to Mr. Ketchum:

"JOB KETCHUM, ESQ.: DEAR SIR,—Your favor of the 13th inst. received. Contents noted. We take pleasure in stating that we have had extensive business dealings with you for five years past, and can bear witness that we have always found you a reliable gentleman of the highest integrity. Your credit and standing among business-men is first-rate, and we endorse you without the least hesitation.

"Very respectfully,
"Yr. obdt. servants,
"PRATT, HAYNES & Co.,
"*Per J. B. Hodges.*"

Mrs. Vane knew nothing whatever of business-men, but was impressed by the practical tone of this letter, and gave it to Mabel, with a smile, saying, "From dear Job's bankers. If he has to be in trade, it is as well that his credit should be so good."

The smile deepened into a little laugh of satisfaction

as she picked up the fourth letter and saw the heading, "House of Representatives, Washington, D. C., March 29."

"From a member of the American Parliament!" she exclaimed. "How very nice!"

And Mabel, who, with her usual reserve, had said nothing all along, jumped up, and, running round to the back of her mother's chair, read the letter over her shoulder:

"DEAR MADAM,—This will be sent you, I understand, by my talented young friend Colonel Ketchum, one of the most elegant gentlemen it has ever been my happiness to meet, a leading citizen of my State, and one of the stanchest champions of the people in their present godlike struggle with the bloated monopolists now prey ing on their vitals and sucking away their very life-blood. As a man and as a patriot, General Ketchum needs no endorsement from me, the humblest of the people's servants.

"Hoping to welcome him and his lovely lady before long to our broad prairies and hospitable hearths, I remain, madam,

"Yours truly,
"ANDREW JACKSON SINGER."

When they had got at the end, mother and daughter looked at each other.

"Dear! dear! I had no idea politics were running so high in America. Things seem in a very bad way," ejaculated Mrs. Vane. "And what *does* the man mean by his 'lovely lady?' Why can't he say wife, pray?

It really is most unpleasantly ambiguous. And how odd it is that they should all lay such stress upon his being a gentleman! What else should he be? Well, dear, let us hope it is all right; though it is most awfully queer."

On some points, what she considered the important ones, Mrs. Vane's mind was quite at rest, and she made no difficulties,—indeed, took Job to her heart at once, and wrote him so many letters that she nearly drove him wild, polite correspondence, conducted with unfailing regularity, not being much in his line.

"I am not engaged to your mother that I know of," he wrote to Mabel; "but it seems to me that I hear from her by every mail, and she expects an answer to every one of her letters. Do explain to her that I only write to my own mother once a week."

At the appointed time he went to Cheltenham, and he and Mabel were duly married—with a wealth of carriages, postilions, and wedding-favors that made him wretched—from the house of Mabel's third cousin, who, as she was making a good match, "took her up" for the first time and gave her a gorgeous wedding-breakfast.

From England they went to Paris, where Mr. Ketchum spent a small fortune on his gentle, dazzled little wife; and from there he took her all over the Continent and the East, and brought her back triumphantly to America, where he installed her in a lovely home of her own.

The English mother-in-law thinks herself lucky if she is allowed to spend a month every year with a married daughter; but Kate was not surprised when Mabel wrote, "Mamma is to come to me and make her home with us and be at no expense whatever. Was there ever anything so noble and generous as my dear husband?"

Is it necessary to say the Fletchers never got back that bag, and, after much telegraphing and writing and the employment of the best detective talent, only traced Walton as far as Spain, and found out that the dignified, able, incomparable "perfect treasure" was—a ticket-of-leave man?

He had, before entering the Fletchers' service, been for two years in the service of an English officer, who thought as highly of him as they had done.

"I shall never get over it, never!" exclaimed Jenny. "The foundations of society are completely broken up for me. I wouldn't trust Cardinal Newman now, or Mr. Gladstone, or Charles Francis Adams!"

"Well, Jenny, Walton was an excellent servant, none better, but there was always *something* about his expression that I didn't like," commented Mrs. Fletcher senior, who, like the Pope, had set up as infallible, and could not afford to be surprised by an earthquake.

# ON THIS SIDE

# ON THIS SIDE.

## I.

ONE day in the spring of 1878, Mr. Job Ketchum, of the firm of Ketchum & Richardson, brokers, Kalsing, Michigan, came down to his office an hour earlier than was his custom, in order, as he told his wife, that he might "buckle down to his work and get things ship-shape again," which was his way of saying that he meant to attack the business and correspondence that had accumulated in an absence of six weeks from home. Arrived there, he seated himself before a large desk abounding in pigeon-holes and strewn with papers, en-ergetically unlocked three drawers in turn, glanced into and relocked them, and then looked about him, uncer-tain where to begin when there was so much to be done at once. His clerk, a sharp-faced young fellow, who had greeted him familiarly on his entrance in high-pitched, nasal tones, now approached, picked up a letter from a heap on the desk, perched himself on a table close by, swung his feet idly, and with a rasping laugh called attention to certain peculiarities in the envelope and address of the document in his hand.

"Here's a communication from one of your fine Brit-ish friends," he said, "postmarked Leemington, Wah-

wickshire." (Pronounced in a broadly American fashion,
that would have puzzled an inhabitant of the town in
question not a little.) "Big seal, with some tomfoolery
or other on it, and addressed, as sure as my name is Tom
Price, to 'J. Ketchum, Esq., Kalsing, Colorado, Michigan'! There's an idiot for you, full-blown."

"I don't believe it. Give it here!" exclaimed his employer, holding out his hand for the letter; then, recognizing the handwriting, he could but smile a little to
find the accusation true and have fresh evidence that
English haziness about America is pretty much now
what it was when Mr. Joseph Ball, barrister, of London,
used to send voluminous epistles across the Atlantic to
his beloved nephew "Major George Washington, at the
Falls of the Rappahannock, or elsewhere in Virginia."

"Queer," commented Mr. Ketchum, "they—" Here
he looked up, caught the look of impudent triumph on
his clerk's face, and broke off to say, "Not that it's any
business of yours, Tom Price, that I can see. I don't
take much interest in your wash-list to speak of, and
I'll thank you to leave my letters alone in future. Perhaps you may have heard of the man who made a large
fortune by attending strictly to his own affairs. You
are as sharp as a steel-trap about most things, but
you've got no more notion of being a gentleman than a
pig has of being a gazelle."

"Oh, pshaw! I guess I'm as much of a gentleman
as most," replied Mr. Price, not at all offended, his amiability being as invincible as his vulgarity. "And I don't
care if I ain't," he added frankly. "I don't see that it
would put anything in my pocket. What are you so
mad about, anyway? Correspondin' with high and

mighty Britishers don't agree with you. Pity you
can't teach 'em a little geography; but I suppose they're
above learnin' it."

"I suppose you are good at it, now, ain't you?" asked
the artful Mr. Ketchum, in a voice full of flattering
suggestion.

"I believe you," was the prompt response; and Mr.
Price got down and swaggered around the office with
his hands in his pockets. "Before I was six years old
I knew the capital of every State in the country, and
most of the rivers and big towns. I knew Colorado
wasn't in Michigan before I cut my first tooth. I never
heard of such disgraceful ignorance in all my born days,
—never!"

"Well, if you know so much about geography, suppose you just tell me where Yorkshire is," said Mr.
Ketchum, coming to the point.

"Yorkshire?" stammered Mr. Price, blushing furiously and taken suddenly quite out of his depth.
"Yorkshire? Yorkshire? Why, it is in Scot—no,
England, to be sure," he said boldly, his shrewd eyes
fixed on his employer's face.

"That was pure guess-work," commented Mr. Ketchum, mercilessly. "Well, what part of England?"

"Why, it's in the south—" (here Mr. Ketchum nodded
affirmatively) "western,—that is to say, eastern part,
ain't it?" hazarded Mr. Price slowly.

"No, it ain't!" exclaimed Mr. Ketchum. "You get
you a map of England, young man, and don't you talk
any more about ignorance until you have studied it a
little and are better posted. You had better sing small
about geography for a while. Because you've lit your

little tallow candle and got twenty feet or so into the tunnel, don't you go supposing that you know all about the bowels of the earth. Put that in your pipe and smoke it. Lay it down as a fixed fact, Tommy, that what you don't know is a good deal more remarkable than what you do, and that running up three columns at a time is pretty smart, but it isn't squaring the circle."

Mr. Price muttered something to the effect that nobody knew or cared to know anything about such an out-of-the-way place; but he was as nearly abashed as it was possible for him to be, and it was some time before the flush died out of his thin face, as he bent over a ponderous ledger. Not to be "posted" was acutely humiliating to him, for he prided himself upon being habitually in that mysterious state of knowingness which is not culture, but a substitute for it with men of his calibre; and his discontent finally took shape in a determination to change his subscription from the local newspaper to a New York daily of repute. As for Mr. Ketchum, he leaned back in his chair, not ill pleased with his share in the late discussion, one of many such into which he was continually being drawn, and in which he felt obliged to sustain the *rôle* of champion of all England, partly because he was a better judge of international questions than most of his countrymen and liked to see fair play, and partly from love and loyalty to his wife, a shy, timid little Englishwoman, who never took up the cudgels for her native land, no matter how preposterous the statements made about it, but only rolled her eyes beseechingly at her husband, as much as to say, "Dear Job, do you hear them? Do tell them it isn't true at all "

Thus inspired, it is no wonder that Mr. Ketchum grew quite eloquent in defence of English institutions sometimes, and rather against his convictions was silent at others. But, at the same time, he did not develop the faintest symptom of Anglomania, as a weaker man would have done. There was no change in his dress, speech, or habits, and when he went to England he became at once the champion of all America, showed the most ardent patriotism, and in all places and companies was a national standard-bearer, defending republican institutions with immense spirit, if somewhat whimsically, and gaining the respect even of those who differed from him most widely and radically.

Mr. Ketchum had no sooner made himself acquainted with the contents of his letter than he sprang out of his chair, seized the morning paper, looked at the shipping-news, made a rapid mental calculation, and put himself at the telephone, which was hardly invented before he had adopted it (connecting his house and office, for one thing) and subscribed for all the shares he could get. In a little while he succeeded in establishing communication with his wife, thanks to his masterly use of an instrument which requires a full half-hour of "Hello!" and "What's that?" treatment before it can be induced to repeat the simplest message for most people.

It was:

"Is that you, Daisy? Are you there?"

"Yes, love. It is I."

"Good news for you, Mrs. K. I have just had a letter from Sir Robert Heathcote, saying that he is on his way to this country with his nephew, another fellow, coming out here to settle, and some women-folks,—your cousin among them."

Mrs. K., evidently aghast: "Dear me! Is *she* coming? Only fancy!"

"Not fancy at all, my dear, but a melancholy fact. She—they will all get in to-morrow."

"You don't mean it! Are they coming out West?" (plaintively.)

"Yes, of course."

"Then you might ask them to stop over from the Saturday until the Monday, if they come this way."

Mr. K., energetically: "From Saturday until Monday? Why, Daisy Ketchum, I wonder you ain't ashamed to say such a thing! As if I'd do such a thing, especially to people who have come three thousand miles and very likely been sea-sick the whole way! I wonder at you! I thought I had cured you of all that 'Saturday-until-Monday' business. We might ask them to stop and take a glass of water with us as they cross the continent, if you are bent on being hospitable."

Mrs. K., answering the accusation made against her by implication: "It isn't that; but you know what a piece of business it is to entertain my cousin. She will give more trouble than the Emperor of Germany could and all his suite, and she will not care for America a bit; and how on earth shall we amuse her? I don't like her, and I don't want her, and that is the truth, dear."

"With the bark on. No more do I; but she is in the country, and it won't do not to ask her, especially as she is with friends of ours."

Mrs. K., with resignation: "Perhaps you are right.

dear. She'll have to come. Awful nuisance! Ask them, then, for a week."

" A month, you mean."

Mrs. K., desperately: " Job, if you ask her for a month I shall be quite wretched."

" I can't make it less. A month at least, Mabel."

Mrs. K., submissively : " Very well, dear. You know best. As you please."

" I please to make it three weeks, then, good child."

" Thank you. Three weeks of my cousin is equal to a cycle of anybody else. How she will hate America!" ·

Mr. Ketchum whistles a few bars of Yankee Doodle defiantly, and then says, " Hear that ?"

" Yes."

" There are several lines of steamers plying between this country and Europe, I believe.

" I wish she was going home in one of them, instead of coming out."

" Now, Mabel, don't worry. I'll take the whole thing off your shoulders, and get a housekeeper and order everything from New York in first-rate style."

" Is Mr. Price there ?"

" No, he has just gone out." (Frightful fib on Mr. Ketchum's part, and the two men exchange glances.)

" Then here's a kiss for the dearest husband in the world! Do come up to breakfast soon,—stewed kidneys and buttered toast !"

" All right. I'll be up directly,—as soon as I have answered Sir Robert's letter. And Mr. Price hasn't been out at all, Daisy."

A faint, indignant " Oh, Job! How could you ?" and the telephone closed.

Mr. Ketchum was late for breakfast, after all, but explained his detention satisfactorily: "I sent Sir Robert
a batch of letters of introduction,—one to the Browns,
—and promised and vowed in your name that you
would write to your cousin by the first mail to say that
you were pining for a sight of some English relative in
your miserable American home."

"You are not in earnest? Surely you didn't say
that?" Mrs. Ketchum queried, rather anxiously, for she
was a very literal person, and was never quite certain
whether her husband spoke in jest or earnest.

"Well, you will find it safer not to take *all* my remarks at their face value," was his reply. "You ought
to have heard Tom Price trying to pump me this morning about the party. He's got curiosity enough to set
up a dozen villages and two dozen convents. He'll not
close an eye now until he finds out every single blessed
mortal thing about every one of them. He asked
Richardson what he gave for his new carriage, and got
no satisfaction; that was six months ago; and, if you
believe me, he no sooner saw him come in to-day than
he stepped up to him and said, 'You needn't have been
so close about that carriage of yours. I've found out
all about it. It isn't new at all. It's second-hand, and
you gave four hundred and thirty dollars for it, and
forty more to have it done over.' You ought to have
seen Richardson's face. He could have bit a ten-penny
nail in two; not that he cared so much about that, but
it's everything. If he steps into a restaurant to take a
dozen oysters, there is Tom. If he goes into a bar-
room, Tom mentions it at the dinner-table,—Tom is his
wife's brother, you know, and lives with them. If he

buys a new suit, Tom finds out what he gave for it; likewise cigars, buggy-drives, and treats of all kinds. If he owes any money, Tom knows about that. In fact, there's nothing he don't know. Not that he has camped on Richardson's trail, but just because he is a born detective and would cross-question a corpse if he got the chance. He is a calamity on casters. Richardson isn't an ornament of the Young Men's Christian Association exactly, or superintendent of a Sunday-school, and hates being dogged around like poison; but he might as well try to escape death as Thomas J."

"His sister Lucy is not at all a nice person, I think," commented Mrs. Ketchum.

"Oh, I can't stand her at all. She is nine distinct varieties of born fool, and would talk the ears off a brass monkey. He has sense, at least, and is a good-hearted chap, as easy to get on with as an old shoe. I don't mind telling him when I had the measles, and what I paid the doctor, and how old my grandmother was that nursed me, and what her maiden name was, and her husband's name, and the names and sex of all her children, and how well off she was left, and a few dozen other things, unless I happen to be busy, and then I give him a file to gnaw, pretty quick."

Mrs. Ketchum was accustomed to her husband's way of putting things, but was now listening to him with the ears of her English cousin.

"Dear Job," she said, "how you do talk! What curious expressions you use!"

"What do you mean? I talk like other men, don't I?" he said quickly. "I haven't taken out a patent for it, at any rate. I know what you mean. You mean

10

that I don't talk like an Englishman. Don't you?" he demanded, with some asperity.

Mrs. Ketchum colored violently, and then said gently but honestly, "Yes, dear. Don't be vexed at my thinking that. I don't really wish you to be different in anything from what you are."

"Well, it is lucky that you don't," he replied, his face relaxing, but his tones still emphatic, "at least as far as making an imitation Englishman of myself is concerned. I was born an American, and I expect, with the blessing of heaven and the permission of the court, to live and die one. Not that I don't like the English,·and respect them, too. Any sensible man with a level head is bound to do the last, whether he does the first or not, and it's all nonsense Americans being down on them. It is true that they made the mistake for a while of giving us two fingers when we were holding out both hands with our hearts in them; but they know better now, and it is stupid to harp any longer on that old string. They are fine, brave fellows, and tell the truth thirteen times in the dozen, and if they are not our relations I don't know where we are to look for any, for my part. I don't want any Frenchmen or Italians in mine, thank you. It is my belief that the Lord has divided the footstool between us and asked us to stand sponsors for the human race. But all the same, when I see some of those fellows in the East, with their plaid suits that it would take two men to show the pattern, and their side-whiskers, and their umbrellas, and bath-towels pinned around their hats, hawhawing and swelling around, hoping to be mistaken for Englishmen or anything but Americans, I swear I'd give my Susquehanna preferreds if I could put every mother's son of them to rounding up cattle out on my Colorado ranch for ten years, until they came to their senses. There's Sam Bates, now,— Sam's last is to call the whole of this continent outside the city of New York 'the provinces'! I asked him when the king his father was going to make him governor-general of them, but the gump only simpered and looked as if I had paid him a compliment."

" Is he a New-Yorker?"

"*No—o!* Not any more than I am a South-Sea Islander. He was born and raised right here in Tecumseh. His father had no frills. He was as good an old grocer as ever sanded sugar, took to shaving notes, made a pile which Sam got and spends in 'Noo York,' as he calls it, and was gathered about ten years ago. Pity old Bates can't see how it's going: he'd regret over having made a dime. A fortune is like a razor, and, unfortunately, parents never can tell whether a son will shave with it or cut his throat. I hope that youngster of ours, Daisy, will turn out a man, and not a monkey or any other sort of brute."

Mrs. Ketchum, as proud possessor of the dearest and downiest little baby in the world, was quite shocked by this speech, and said decisively, "Of course he will. How can you doubt it, dear? You ought not to speak so harshly of Mr. Bates. Perhaps he is just naturally a foolish sort of creature."

" Well, I do try to remember that the Lord made him, but he is certainly one of heaven's light-weights. I'll try not to square at him any more than I can help, though."

With this concession the meal closed; indeed, for Mr

Ketchum it had practically come to an end some time
before, for the most elaborate dinner never occupied his
attention for more than twenty minutes, the simpler
meals an incredibly short time; and after having taken
what he wanted it was usually his custom to walk about
the room while his wife calmly and leisurely attended to
all her little duties,—slowly poured out her tea, chipped
away at her egg more slowly still, and ate slowest
of all, wholly uninfluenced by his restlessness.  He
would stop for a moment, sometimes, to watch, with a
bantering twinkle in his eye, the calm movements of
her pretty, white, beringed fingers and tell her that
"threescore years and ten was all she could count
upon, though there was Thomas Parr, to be sure." And ·
she would smile, and say that "one must breakfast
comfortably," and assure him that it was "quite unnecessary to fidget about so, time saved not always being
time gained."  But neither ever succeeded in either ac-
celerating or retarding the natural pendulum that ticked
so busily and incessantly in his case, with such long,
reposeful swing in hers.

Being in a talkative mood on this particular morning,
Mr. Ketchum grew reminiscent over his cigar, and had
a great deal to say about Cheltenham, the beautiful
English town in which he had met and married his wife,
the people he had known there, and so on by natural
transition to their expected guests, for whom, in American fashion, he was willing to put himself out to any
extent, anxious only that they should see and enjoy as
much as possible, and generously ready to meet any and
every demand that might be made upon his time or
purse.  As for trouble, he was quite willing to take that.

too, but all unconsciously, the word being either left out of the American host's Worcester Unabridged or translated as pleasure.

It was not often that the husband and wife got such a long, quiet talk, for reasons that will presently be explained.

When he finally discovered how late it was, he exclaimed, "This ain't business much, but I have enjoyed it. We are not exactly wretched without our old ladies, are we, now? I wonder if they wouldn't like a trip to California or Cuba some time? Good-by, Daisy. See that Frawlein gets her beef-tea at twelve."

This is clearly the place to make the reader acquainted with all the persons just mentioned, and to explain their connection with the Ketchums. When Mr. Ketchum transplanted his English daisy from the meadows of Gloucestershire to his native prairies, he felt in duty bound to offer the same advantage to the parent-root, which he thought must otherwise pine and droop, forlorn and miserable, away from its fair little flower. To drop metaphor, he thought himself the natural guardian and protector of his wife's widowed mother, and as a simple matter of course asked her to make her home with him. From the moment she came under his roof he treated her with the indulgence which alone was possible to him in any intimate relation with women, and for a whole year that lady revelled in a luxurious suite of apartments set apart for her exclusive use, her own carriage and servants, and the belief that she would sooner or later get entire control of her daughter's establishment. At the end of that time Mr. Ketchum brought his own mother home, for reasons as

*h*          10*

obvious and natural, and installed her on the same floor, across the hall, with exactly the same privileges, indulgences, and comforts.

He congratulated himself upon this arrangement very much, if a little prematurely.

"Your ma has had a hard life of it, and so has mine," he said to his wife; "and they are both getting old, and I am determined that they shall have everything they want. I've got plenty to do it with, and we'll just all live along together here as snug as sardines. I ain't a-going to make any difference between them, down to a paper of pins, and I know you ain't the woman to do it either."

In accordance with these views, Mr. Ketchum gave both ladies exactly the same allowance of pin-money, christened them facetiously "Mother and T'other," put one on his right hand and one on his left at table, and behaved with the most absolute fairness and the most admirable kindness in everything, from the greatest to the smallest question that came up. Mabel, who loved and admired her husband's generosity, imitated it as well, and never was there less room given for jealousy or heart-burning in any household that was ever organized. Mr. Ketchum himself saw to their comforts,— their bedroom fires, port, steaks, tonics, and what not, —and Mrs. Ketchum was an affectionate, respectful daughter to both alike, anxious to consult their tastes, anticipate their wishes, and obey their very distracting and somewhat imperious commands, for their advice and counsels were apt to take the latter shape. A more complete and ideal paradise for two weary old women, who had been battling with poverty and misfortune respectively for sixty and sixty-five years, it would be impossible to conceive; yet, such is the perversity of human nature, neither of them was satisfied, happy, or particularly grateful. One would have supposed that there was no room for the serpent to wriggle in, try as he might; yet he was there, in envy and jealousy, malice and all uncharitableness, pride and love of dominion. All Mr. Ketchum's thoughtfulness, generosity, and benefactions were poisoned to each by the thought that the other shared them. Did he bring home a box of particularly fine grapes for Mrs. Vane, that lady was certain that its counterpart was reserved for her rival. Did he surprise his mother by sending her up a handsome silk dress of the most superior quality, she knew quite well that another dress had been cut from the same piece for Mrs. Vane. And so the honest fellow got but tepid thanks, and went delicately, like King Agag, fearing to tread on one or other of the sensitive plants, whose "feelings" would hardly bear being breathed upon, though they had small care for the feelings of others; and Mabel was ever gentle and good and patient, and the two foolish old bodies squabbled over everything that came up, and made themselves very ridiculous and very miserable. The usual attitude of the belligerents was one of ill-repressed sniffs and sneers: the warfare was illogical and deathless, though rarely did it find vent in open outbreaks. These, when they came, occurred always when Mr. Ketchum's restraining influence was removed, for, with all his indulgence, he was emphatically master of his own house, and could, as he expressed it, "put his foot down," indeed, plant both feet firmly and squarely and stamp on other feet that

got in his way. Once at table, when Mrs. Ketchum
senior had openly taunted Mrs. Vane with being a de-
pendant on *her* son's bounty, and Mrs. Vane had taken
the ground that the third-cousin of an English earl conferred an honor in accepting anything at the hands of
social inferiors who were only too glad to purchase good
blood at any price, Mr. Ketchum had got into one of
his rare rages, and had frightened them so thoroughly
and rebuked them so sternly that for a month afterward
all was as beautifully calm and bright as moonlight in
the tropics.

As a rule, he would good-naturedly laugh and joke
away the little clouds that arose on the domestic horizon, or whisper to his wife, "The ladies! God bless
'em!" and she would say, "Dear mamma is really most
trying at times." Husband and wife were in perfect
accord and sympathy, and quite resolved to do their
duty, no matter how disagreeable.

But, as if this situation were not enough to try the
temper and exercise the tact and forbearance of any
couple, a third element of discord had been added some
time before the period of which this treats. It happened in this way. Mr. and Mrs. Ketchum had spent
the previous summer in England, and while there the
latter was much shocked to receive one day a letter
from a former governess, written actually from the
union, into which the worthy woman had drifted, owing
to a complication of misfortunes,—the failure of a bank
containing her little savings, ill health, and old age.
She begged to see her "*theure allerliebste Schülerin*," and
of course Mabel went to her at once, and had her gentle
heart much touched by the friendless and forlorn state

in which she found her old friend. And what should Job do but go and see the poor creature himself, carrying more life and sunshine into a dingy institution and a despairing soul than either had ever known before!

Fräulein Faustina Schmidt was certainly not the loveliest of her sex at her best, much less in the faded print bed-gown that served her for every-day wear and the black hood that framed her broad, roughly-hewn German face (restless Mr. Ketchum had insisted on seeing her at once, and would hardly have waited had it been the queen instead, desirous of appearing before him in her coronation-robes); but had she been young and lovely, and an heiress besides, she could not have met with more kind and considerate treatment from our American.

How she ever gathered the gist of her visitor's eccentrically-worded conversation and quavered out her assent, surprise, and gratitude, no one knows, but in a very brief time the royal-hearted fellow had settled all her future, hired a nurse for her, ordered her clothes packed on the morrow, and herself to be transported bodily to Brighton to convalesce. After this he went all over the establishment, made various shrewd and searching comments on what he saw, resisted several direct and indirect attempts to lighten him of a shilling, and finally left behind him enough money to give the inmates what he called "a good, square meal, reckoning eight to a turkey and trimmings," and to provide enough tobacco for the luckless old men and tea for the peevish old women to last three full months.

As he was about to drive off, a fancy struck him, and he hailed the functionary with whom he had just parted.

"What would it cost to stuff 'em with oysters?" he said.

"Beg pardon, sir?"

"The turkeys, I'm talking about. I'd like those poor old dead-beats to know an oyster when they meet it in the next world."

The official stared, confounded by the proposition and the terms in which it was made.

"For us, sir, you mean, I suppose. Thank you, sir. It would be a matter of—"

"I mean for the whole lay-out."

"For them *paupers*, sir? You never can be meanin' to do such a wicked thing, beggin' pardon for makin' so bold."

"Oh, that's your opinion, is it? Well, it ain't mine. I guess I'll be forgiven for it. They don't have such a lively time, that you should grudge 'em this little blow-out. Poor things! it would be money in their pockets if they never had been born. Well, speak up: what's the damage?"

Thus rebuked and solicited, the official named twice the sum necessary for the purpose, and was told that oysters must be considerably dearer in the country than in London, and got something more than half; and away rattled Mr. Ketchum, having first announced that he was "coming down to see the thing out." This he actually did, ten days later, and a chapter might be written about his visit and his interviews with the clergyman of the parish, the doctor, and various local magnates.

He gave his wife a lively enough account of the affair afterward: "They were all out in all their war-paint and feathers,—regular paper-mill display ; had been getting ready, evidently, for a week," he said. " Poor things! I took down a lot of gooseberry champagne, and when the corks began to pop every eye was glued to the nearest bottle and glittered like the Ancient Mariner's. Nobody said a word. When it was poured out, some gulped down the glassful and seemed to have a palate a mile long, and others seemed to dole it out almost a drop at a time. You could see it was kingdom-come to 'em. I haven't had as much fun for a coon's age. And you ought to have seen them when the first oyster struck 'em full and fair all round and went straight to the spot! I would have given anything for their photographs taken in the act. Mean, coppery little things I thought 'em, no more like our Blue Points than chalk's like cheese ; but they didn't know the difference. We drank the queen's health, and the President's, and the army, and the navy, and the church, if you please, and they tried to get in a lot of the ' gen-erous benefactor' business, but I put a stop to that mighty quick. There was one old champion gorman dizer, about ten thousand years old, that ought to be dead to-day if he isn't. And—Lord, Lord!—the songs! It was worth every cent of the money, and more too." Then, after a long pause, " There is nothing for the old lady but blood-letting, and we—that is, the United States —have got to hold the basin, Daisy," he concluded.

Mrs. Ketchum had not bargained for such complete success as resulted from her attempt to awaken her husband's interest in her ex-governess, and, when he announced that he meant to take Fräulein Schmidt home with them, she could not believe her ears. A

small—a very small—pension was as much as she had
dreamed of, and to her mind would have been a munificent return for such services.

"To *live* with us ! You surely can't mean it, love?
What an extraordinary idea !" she said, in quite a loud
voice for her. "What put it into your head ?"

"Why, you see, she hasn't got a friend on the face
of the green earth except us," he replied simply, as
if that covered the whole ground. He turned a frank,
pleasant face toward his wife for a moment as he said
this, quite unshadowed by doubts or misgivings, and
then went on brushing the short-cut, bristling hairs on
his head, as if his object was to brush them off, for this
conversation took place early in the morning, when
Mr. Ketchum was effecting a toilet by means of his
usual energetic methods.

"But to *live* with us ?" murmured his wife.

"Yes. Why not? All she wants is a seat in a
chimney-corner for a few years with kind people. She
has taught school for fifty years, and has got nothing
but rheumatism to show for it and death to look forward to. I guess, now, we can take her in out of the
cold, can't we, Daisy ?"

Mrs. Ketchum had all the acquiescent meekness of
the English wife, and would have submissively consented to almost any proposition of her husband's, but
she had something more, and it was this quality that
led to a rather unusual and impulsive demonstration on
her part. She ran swiftly across the room, put both
arms gently around her husband's neck (it was impossible for her to be other than gentle), gave him several
kisses, and then stood off and admired him unaffectedly.

"Why, hello, Daisy! What's up? Want fifty pounds?" said he.

"No. It's only that you are *such* a dear!" she explained, in her ordinary tranquil tones. "There never was any one like you, my dear husband, and I do love you for it." Woman-like, she did not state what "it" was, but she did better,—she understood and sympathized with it.

"But what will the mothers say?" she presently asked. "They will never submit to it, not even for a twelvemonth,—never! I really think they would leave the house first."

"Oh, no, they wouldn't," said Mr. Ketchum coolly. "They are a great deal too sharp for that. They are not going to saw themselves off a limb for a bird's nest."

The astute Mr. Ketchum was not mistaken, and Fräulein Schmidt was soon successfully grafted on the family tree, rested thankfully in its wide-spreading shade, and ate gratefully of its generous fruit without frightening away other birds of gayer plumage with a better claim to lodge in its branches. Mr. Ketchum, to be sure, displayed some tact and generalship in the affair. That is, he gave the enemy no notice of the intended movement beforehand, offered no apology at any time, and left his wife to make all the explanations. In his jolly, off-hand manner there was a tinge of authority that the mothers correctly interpreted, as he introduced Fräulein Schmidt to them and then installed her himself in a comfortable room and told her that she was "just to make herself at home."

"If you don't see what you want, ask for it, as the stores say. I guess you'll do now, won't you?" he said to his *protégée*, who shed copious tears, called upon "loved heaven" and "the dear God" a dozen times in a vain attempt to express her gratitude, and could scarcely believe her good fortune, which seemed made of the stuff that dreams are, until she had spent a week in unpacking a certain hair-trunk (blistered and labelled and brass-nailed to a wonderful extent) and had arranged and rearranged its contents in the ward-robe-bureau, closet, and chest of drawers with which she was lavishly supplied.

The rival mothers were completely taken aback. They thought it best to temporize for a day or two, and then open fire. Mrs. Ketchum senior accordingly came into the room where her son was on the third morning after his arrival, prepared for conflict. She was a delicate, refined-looking woman, with very large, light-blue eyes, emphasized by arched brows, which she sent up in an aggrieved way almost to the roots of her white hair as she took a rocking-chair, apparently that she might make a virtue of sitting bolt upright in it, and demanded imperiously an answer to certain questions. "Is it possible, Job, that you mean that horrid German creature, that eats with her knife and is perfectly odious in every way, to stay here perma-nently?" she said, after some talk between them.

"That's it, ma'am. You've hit the nail *right on the head.* She'll stay here until the undertaker asks to see her on a little matter of business; and I shall expect everybody in this house to treat her with politeness and respect," he replied.

"I'll have nothing to do with her,—nothing whatever," she snapped. "How many more foreigners are you going to take upon yourself to support, pray?"

"I can't say, really. I ain't an emigration-agent, exactly,—no fellow can be who wouldn't rather tell a lie on credit than the truth for cash,—but I rather like founding a house for indignant females as far as I've got. It keeps things moving along lively. Look here, mother: don't let's have any more of this. You've got all you want, haven't you? If you haven't, you know very well you can have it quick enough. What do you want to go pounding the saw-dust out of that old Dutch doll for? Live and let live."

"You mean that you are going to keep her?"

"Yes. She is here, and here she is going to stay. And, mind, she's got to be treated right; and that's all about it."

"Well, my son, far be it from *me* to dictate, or ever *advise*, any course of conduct to any one in this house. Only, I'll not stay here any longer. I'll go to my brother John's, where, if I am to be overrun at all, it will not be by foreigners and paupers. And mark my words: you'll fail in business yet fooling your money away as you do, and buying—"

"You mean my uncle John's?"

"Yes, of course."

"Well, I didn't know. You seemed to lay so much stress on his being your brother, I thought perhaps there was some mistake. Now, here is the way that is: You know I am more than glad to have you stay with me as long as you find it agreeable, mother; but if you would rather be with your brother John of course I

won't interfere. My object is to make you as happy
and as comfortable as I can. When would you like to
go?"

Here was a dilemma out of which there was but one
way, and that a way Mrs. Ketchum was not disposed
to take just then; so she said, "To-morrow," very
haughtily and huffily, and left the room. Whereupon
her son wore his shrewdest smile, being privately convinced that she would either not go at all, or, going,
would remain a very short time indeed.

At the same time, in another part of the house,
Mrs. Vane was taking her daughter very roundly to
task about the same thing. She was a large, florid
woman, who, in order to give effect to the position she
took up as martyr, on such occasions was wont to put
on her dressing-gown, tie a handkerchief around her
forehead, and, vinaigrette in hand, approach the griev-
ance of the moment, whatever it might be, warding off
every return-blow in the discussion by pathetic allusions to her "poor head" (which never ached so badly
as to prevent the fullest expression of her own views
and sentiments), and retiring when utterly worsted
behind a huge miniature-brooch of her husband, than
which no warrior ever had a more effective shield.

"What is this most extraordinary news," she began,
"that I hear from the servants—the servants, mark
you—about that foolish, half-witted old body, Frawlein
Schmidt?"

"What do you mean, mamma?"

"That she is regularly unpacked, and calls this her
'so beautiful home.' Weak as you are, you never can
have asked her to stay here for any length of time.

And what duplicity to keep from me the fact that she was coming!"

Mrs. Ketchum explained her husband's wishes and views, and Mrs. Vane burst out afresh:

"I never heard such a mad idea in my life! You should really see a doctor about your husband without his knowledge. Keep her for life! A creature that has no more claim upon him than any other beggar in the street! And do you mean to say that you have given in to the arrangement?"

"Would you have me oppose my husband, mamma. and anger him without just cause?"

"You have cause enough, I should think. The maddest idea! Pray, are there no hospitals or asylums in America, that gentlemen's houses are to be turned into such? Assert yourself, Mabel,—assert yourself, and send the woman away this very day when Mr. Ketchum is gone to his shop, or office, or whatever he calls it."

"I cannot, mamma; and I would not do anything so wrong, if I could. How can you wish me to displease or deceive my husband?"

"No *gentleman* would ask such a thing of his wife."

"Mamma! How dare you! I will not allow—will not tolerate—"

"Mabel! This to your widowed mother! What would your dear papa say if he could hear you?" (pointing impressively to her brooch.)

"I beg your pardon, mamma. I did not mean to speak rudely or forget the respect due you; but you must not, you must not, mamma, say such cruel things of my dear husband. He is the best of men, the kindest, the most indulgent, the most delicate in all his dealings with me, and—forgive me for saying so—with you, and with everybody. I brought husband nothing, as you know, mamma. I have no right to object to his asking anybody that he sees fit to his house for as long a time as he deems best. Everything here is his, to do as he pleases with. Not that he would have Fräulein here if I objected. But I don't object. I wish whatever he wishes. I am quite willing to be guided by him in everything. And it certainly is not a proper thing for *you* to object,—you, to whom he has been more generous and considerate than any English son we have ever known, you, whose every wish has been consulted, for whom every luxury has been provided, whose allowance is larger than that of any duke's daughter at home, and who owe everything to the man-who you say is not a gentleman. Not a gentleman, indeed! Oh, oh, oh, oh, mamma! oh, oh!"

Mabel had probably never spoken with anything like the same energy and boldness in her whole life; but the fire of indignant eloquence was soon quenched in tears.

"My poor head!" murmured Mrs. Vane, and applied her vinaigrette first to one nostril and then to the other; but her daughter was wounded to the heart and was wholly unmoved by her terrific sufferings. Indeed, she sobbed so violently as quite to alarm the mother, who had always seen her quiet and self-controlled. "My dearest child! My own love! You must not excite yourself so about nothing. You must really be calm," she said. "I have said nothing to put you about so. I don't deny that Mr. Ketchum is a most worthy man, an excellent man—"

"Go away, mamma, I beg, and leave me to myself."

"That's right, love; lie down for a while until you are more composed. You are getting as nervous as the American women, really. Dawkins shall bring you a cup of tea."

"I wish nothing, except to be left alone," Mrs. Ketchum maintained, in a choked voice.

"What! Am I to consider myself *ordered* from the room?" called out Mrs. Vane tragically. "Very well. So be it. I leave not only this room, but this house. I am going *home*. But remember, ungrateful, wicked daughter that you are, *you have a child!*"

With these mysterious and threatening words Mrs. Vane stalked out of the room, all offended majesty, unopposed and unrecalled.

Is it necessary to say that, in spite of these stormy passages between certain members of the Ketchum household and the distinct declarations of war and choice of exile made by both mothers, Mrs. Ketchum senior's "brother John" had no demand made upon him for hospitality or protection, and Mrs. Vane's passage to England was not secured in any steamer whatever?

That very night Mabel found a deeply-affectionate, remonstrant, apologetic note from her mother pinned to her dressing-table. It was a fad of that lady's to address numbers of such to her about anything and everything, although they were under the same roof, and she was doubtless glad to have such a topic to discuss at length with the fatal fluency, the profusion of adjectives, the scarcity of ideas, and the utter absence of punctuation that characterized her style. Mabel read the production with a serious face, as of one performing a disagreeable duty, and it took so long that her husband asked who her correspondent was.

On being told he laughed gleefully, and, as he kicked off a boot, said, " What the mischief is she always writing to you for, when she sees you all day long and can say anything she wants to? Lord, how she must love it! It's my belief that she makes pot-hooks and hangers on the slate, now, and sends them to the young one in his cradle; and how she is ever going to reconcile her mind to dying and going out of this world, knowing that she can't write back and tell all her relations and friends and acquaintances what it's like in the other one, I can't imagine. I hope it won't rile you for me to say so, but your mother's letters always remind me of old Peck's sermons, Daisy. I took you to hear him once, in Tecumseh, you remember. You never know where you are, and there is no stop in 'em. It's ' firstly,' and 'secondly,' and ' thirdly, my brethren,' and ' whereas,' and ' moreover,' and ' in this connection,' and ' again,' and ' nevertheless,' and ' now,' and ' lastly,' and ' again,' and ' to sum up,' and ' again,' and ' in conclusion;' and you ain't done then for twenty minutes or safe until you hear the Doxology. What's all that about, anyway?"

Mabel gave him a moderate and medicated account of the interview she had had with her mother, and he listened with much interest.

" Why, *my* mother took off her collar and let herself loose to-day on the same subject," he said ; " but she saw it was no use, and knocked under this afternoon, finding that I was bent and determined on having Frawlein's plank in the platform, no matter who bolted. Women are mortal queer, savin' your ladyship's presence, anyway. When I was sowing enough wild oats for ten, ma was as good and kind to me as if I had been all the twelve apostles instead of only one, and that the wrong one. She never blamed me nor reproached me; she didn't even sit up for me and weep over me, but just loved me right along through the whole thing and waited for me to come to my senses. But now that I am a good little boy, comparatively, with a pocket full of Sunday-school tickets from my teacher, she finds fault with pretty nearly everything I do, it seems to me. Well, now that the fire is out and the engines have gone home, I hope we'll have peace; but it isn't going to be peace on any terms, I can tell you."

When Mabel awoke next morning she detected Dawkins, her mother's maid, in the very act of fastening another note to her pin-cushion,—an unconditional surrender this time.

But all the same Mr. Ketchum had only won one of the victories which are worse than a defeat. The character alone of the warfare was changed, and from having been deadly enemies the mothers became allies welded together by a common prejudice, intent upon defeating a common enemy. The new system was so subtle, so ingenious, and, above all, so thoroughly feminine that it worked to a charm for some time, under Mr. Ketchum's very eye and superintendence, as it were. Poor old Schmidt was sent to Coventry, was snubbed, was beaten with many rods, all small ones, was cuffed and collared morally twenty times a day, if such violent terms can apply to buffetings and assaults to which she offered no more resistance than if she had been the softest of feather pillows. She dearly loved

i

to go to her room and read her Jean Paul or Klopstock or Goethe until some time after midnight, but, being forbidden to do so, meekly extinguished the gas in her room at nine o'clock and made no complaint. She tried to train some ivy that she had brought with her inside the sill of her window, near which she was wont to sit with her sewing; but when the allies declared that it would inevitably attract spiders and earwigs, and swept it all away, she submitted without a word. At table the allies never offered her anything, took her seat whenever it suited their convenience, without apology, and took great pains to show her that they considered her conversationally a non-combatant and socially an inferior. Of some of these petty persecutions Mabel was ignorant; to others she closed her eyes as the least of two evils. At last, one day, Mrs. Vane, emboldened by what she thought her son-in-law's obtuseness, pushed rudely past poor Fräulein as they entered the dining-room and seated herself in that lady's chair at the breakfast-table, waving her hand to Fräulein, and saying, "You can go down there somewhere—anywhere."

Fräulein obeyed: she would have sat under the table, had she been ordered to do so, quite without remonstrance.

Mr. Ketchum's eye followed her. "Isn't that Frawlein's seat that you have taken by mistake?" he asked of Mrs. Vane.

"Yes; but that don't matter," she replied. "She'll do where she is."

"I disagree with you. I must ask you to take your own, and to keep it in future," he said, with more dignity than she had ever seen in him.

"Don' move, I beg, I bray," pleaded Fräulein, much alarmed by the domestic situation.

"Do you mean to say that you give a *governess* precedence over *me?*" Mrs. Vane indignantly demanded of her son-in-law.

"Who's talking of precedence, madam? I mean you to be polite in my house to my guests. That's what I mean," said Mr. Ketchum, in a low, distinct voice, and said no more.

Mrs. Vane did not rage, did not weep, did not quit the table. She, to the amazement of her ally, the consternation of Fräulein Schmidt, and the surprise of her own daughter, said, "I beg your pardon. I have been rude. I am in the wrong," and went to her own place, a conquered woman.

"Precedence, indeed! I'll see whether Frawlein Schmidt is ever again insulted in my house, as I know she has been in more ways than one," said Mr. Ketchum to his wife.

Next day when the dinner-bell rang, what should he do but march up to poor old Schmidt, offer her his arm, take her in to dinner, put her on his right hand, and help her first to all that was furnished forth on his mahogany! Nor was this a mere caprice. He made it an invariable rule henceforth, no matter who came to the house, and was neither to be reasoned, coaxed, nor ridiculed out of it, to the end of the chapter. It was his idea of precedence; and, although it was not that of Debrett or the "Almanach de Gotha," we get more than a hint of it in a much older work,—the Book of Books.

Fräulein Schmidt after this enjcyed all her privileges,

rights, and immunities. She had a student-lamp, for one thing, and flowers in all her windows, and a cat, and a canary, and the pleasure of darning and mending her benefactor's clothes,—the last being a luxury that she insisted on. Terrified at first to find herself so conspicuously distinguished by Mr. Ketchum, she soon grew accustomed to it, and dwelt securely and happily in that best of all asylums, a good man's home. As for the mothers, if they were away when this story opened it was entirely due to their wish to see Niagara,—a satisfaction that Mr. Ketchum was willing to give them, if only to mark his approbation of the angelic behavior that followed and flowed from the stand he had taken about a certain guest.

## II.

Mr. Ketchum was somewhat mistaken in the calculations he had made as to the probable time the "Britannia" would take to reach New York. That steamer, with his friends and friends' friends on board, to say nothing of other passengers in whom he felt no interest, was off Bedloe's Island a good ten hours earlier than he had supposed possible, to the distraction of a certain florist who had been ordered by telegraph to send off "the finest basket of roses to be had in New York" by the pilot-boat, to greet the strangers before they had so much as set foot on American soil. Interpreting his instructions liberally, this artist had taken great pains to prepare one of the *chefs-d'œuvre* on which he prided himself,—an enormous wire structure full of hot-house beauties, with a parasol of maiden-hair and rose-buds suspended above it, the whole requiring the best efforts of two able-bodied seamen to deposit it in the cabin of the "Britannia." There it was much admired by the passengers while the steward hurried away in search of a certain gentleman, who presently came back with him, —a somewhat elderly, squarely-built, stout man, with iron-gray side-whiskers, dressed in a pepper-and-salt travelling-suit, having a field-glass slung across his ample chest, wearing a cork helmet that he removed as he descended the gangway smoking a brier-root pipe, which disappeared about the same time in one of his pockets, and diffusing a genial air of good feeling and high living, breeding, and fashion,—in short, Sir Robert Heathcote.

If this gentleman had in an eminent degree the indefinable everything that announces to the looker-on, not only of Vienna, but from Dan to Beersheba, an Englishman, and to a practised eye can no more be counterfeited than the flavor of oyster or olive to the cultivated palate, the two young men accompanying him may be said to have fairly recked of Bond Street, St. James, Kensington Gardens, Pall Mall, the Guards' Club, Tattersall's, Lord's,—any and all resorts where English men-about-town are wont to congregate. Both were tall, both handsome, but the good looks of Mr. Heathcote (Sir Robert's nephew) were of the dark, worn, and dissipated order, while his friend Mr. Hugh Ramsay was a young Adonis of five-and-twenty, such as is frequently to be seen in London parks, of average brains and

barely respectable attainments,—a model of manly
beauty, simple and honorable in character, modestly
self-reliant in manner, rosy as any girl, with a girl's
trick of blushing, and a voice which it is no exaggera-
tion to call delicious,—the sort of man that always
looks and seems about to be charming, yet really says
little and does less to justify the fervid liking he is apt
to inspire in the breasts of most women, and a good
many men, almost at sight.

He approached the table now and fell into one of his
usual graceful attitudes as easily as a kitten or a child
might have done, and, though it would not seem difficult of accomplishment to sit on the arm of an easy-
chair, holding a Scotch cap in the right hand, while the
left arm describes a curve that enables a shapely hand
(well cared for and adorned by a handsome cat's-eye
ring) to rest lightly on the left hip, another man would
have found it an impossible feat after a month of pos-
turing and posing, at least so far as achieving the same
result is concerned. Mr. Ramsay had a great and happily unconscious gift for attitudes, and did the simplest
things in an especial and incomparable manner of his
own. He did not even take a seat like other men;
while his manner of rolling his umbrella or drawing on
his gloves had all the effect of a new idea, and seemed
an exhibition as original as it was attractive, not in the
least a matter of course.

The florist had disappeared by this time, but a card
dangled from the handle of the pretty parasol which
said all that was necessary, and, having examined it,
Sir Robert looked with some interest at the flowers, and
said, " Very friendly of Ketchum, upon my word ! Very

friendly indeed! He is the man I was telling you of this morning, Ramsay, that lived out here,—in the Western part. A very good fellow; an original: one doesn't meet his like every day. In trade, of course, but not in the least like our Brummagem fellows. Just so! We must have the ladies out to see these."

"The beggar must have pots of money, to throw it away like this," said Mr. Ramsay, half enviously.

Looking around for a servant to take a message, Sir Robert saw the unctuous steward bearing down upon him with another large bouquet, less elaborate than Mr. Ketchum's, but also beautiful.

"If you please, sir, this has just been left by a person," said the man, with a fatuous air of personal gratification.

Sir Robert, without a word, looked at the card attached, which was glazed and had written on it, in fashionable-boarding-school characters, "For the ladies of Sir Robert Heathcote Baronet's party," and underneath, "From Miss Bijou Brown."

"This is from a Miss Brown, some friend of Ketchum's, I dare say," he said, with an amused but genial smile. "Very kind, I am sure. Let the ladies know that I wish to see them here" (turning to the steward).

"The plot thickens!" exclaimed young Ramsay. "There will be a third presently, for that chap and myself" (nodding toward Mr. Heathcote, who was leaning languidly against the wall, an impassive witness of what was going on). "A lyre, most likely. Do they do this sort of thing often over here?"

"Can't say, really," replied Mr. Heathcote. "Never been here before. I should like to land at least before setting myself up as an authority on American customs, though I know a chap that wrote a book about it without ever leaving his rectory in Dorset,—not half a bad book, either, giving the Americans what they would call 'particular all-fired fits.'"

Mr. Heathcote said this with the air of a man who is being witty and knows it. He considered himself an authority on American slang, though he had just disclaimed any knowledge of American customs, and was in the habit of using it a good deal (with a certain elephantine clumsiness and dislocation of terms) at his club, where it met with hearty uncritical appreciation, as well as in many drawing-rooms, where mothers with marriageable daughters were apt to be convulsed as by a second Talleyrand, called him "a clever, satirical, malicious creature," and told him that he ought to be ashamed to make those poor Americans so ridiculous. Mr. Ramsay laughed now, having always had an infatuated admiration for what he called "Heathcote's Far-Western expressions," and, having exhausted this sensation, consulted his watch, saying, "How goes the enemy? I must toddle. I've got some things to put up.—Oh, I beg pardon!"

This last was addressed to a young girl against whom he had jostled in turning round,—one of the ladies of his party, who was closely followed by the other two.

"What lovely nosegays! Where did they come from, Ethel dear?" asked the eldest of the trio, the Honorable Augusta Noel, an elderly gentlewoman of charming appearance and dignified bearing.

"Dear! dear! I had no idea there were such roses in America!" exclaimed her friend Mrs. Arundel Sykes,

in a deep chest-voice, that reverberated as if it had
come from a female bassoon, but was harsh in tone,
exaggeratedly English in its inflections, and distinctly
patronizing. "How very kiawrious! And what au
extravagant profusion! Whose are they?"

"Yours, partly," said Sir Robert, and explained the
situation.

"Most civil and kind of them," commented the Honorable Augusta. "It is so very pleasant to be welcomed
like this to a foreign country."

"Yours were sent by Mabel Vane's husband, you
say? They must have been grown under glass. What
does the man want of you? Depend upon it, he is
trying to make something out of you," said Mrs. Sykes.

"Not at all. You quite mistake him," replied Sir
Robert quickly.

Mrs. Sykes took up Miss Brown's card and inspected
it: "'Miss Bijou Brown.' What an extraordinary com-
bination! And glazed! And with that 'Baronet,' too.
Very queer indeed! And who is Miss Bijou Brown
when she is at home? And why should she be sending
us flowers? I don't understand," she said.

"It is simple enough. She is a friend of the Ketchums, no doubt, and, being here in New York, has sent
these out of politeness and regard for them. There is
nothing remarkable about it that I can see," said Sir
Robert, "except that it is remarkably civil."

"Oh, yes, to be sure. That is all very well. Only, I
suppose we shall have to *know* her; and that may be
awkward. I don't wish to know her, I'm sure," said
Mrs. Sykes, speaking with conviction, and thinking of
the card. (Mrs. Sykes would not have cared to know

Joan of Arc or St. Paul had either used glazed pasteboard, at least until they had received the hall-mark of
society in spite of the awful fact.) "Well, well, we are
in America now, and I suppose it doesn't matter. We
must expect everything in the way of indiscriminate
association in a country where there are no class
distinctions."

"None? Surely you exaggerate, do you not?" asked
Miss Noel.

"Oh, not in the least, I assure you," affirmed Mrs.
Sykes, with warmth. "I've read Miss Alcott's books,
and a lot of other American works, and they all tell the
same story. Not only do the gentry, or what we are
used to regard as such, visit the tradespeople, but if the
cook should develop a talent for music, or painting, or
anything of the kind, the family rejoice like the Biblical
female over the lost piece of money, send her abroad to
cultivate it at their expense, and seem quite charmed to
have her come home and marry the son of the house."

"Dear me! How *very* dreadful! I can't fancy it for
a moment! So very destructive of personal dignity,
and subversive of social order," said Miss Noel. "I
almost regret having brought Ethel."

"Pooh! stuff! Ethel is all right," said Sir Robert.
"You don't suppose I am going to have Tom, Dick, and
Harry introduced to my niece! I shall be the judge of
all that. To be sure, it is rather difficult to place them.
I have known numbers of them, and the only thing I
have learned is that, as a general rule, it is safest to
avoid officials. They must hold titles in republican
contempt, to judge from some of the people they bestow
them upon. The most vulgar fellow I ever knew in all

my life was their minister to Karlsbaten, and one of the most delightful was a man I met out in Egypt, a most accomplished, clever, gentlemanly fellow,—a dentist. Just so! But all the same, depend upon it, they have their share of social distinctions: their society could not hold together otherwise, and caste is one of the funda mental natural laws of all society, whether it rests on an aristocratic, plutocratic, bureaucratic, or simply inherent foundation. However, my rule is to take people as I find them, and among fifty millions of people I should think it would be quite possible for us to find some who are our equals, perhaps a few who are even our superiors."

"Oh, really!" said Mrs. Sykes, in scornful dissent, and had no time to say more, for there now came up to her certain fellow-passengers—a Mrs. Washington Hitch-cock and her two daughters—intent upon making their adieux and final compliments. This was accomplished on their part with grace and warmth, and met with a civil response from the Honorable Augusta, a neutral one from Ethel Heathcote, who, in the face of recent disclosures, dared not give expression to the wish she had formed to know more of the new acquaintances, and a distinctly haughty and repressive one from Mrs. Sykes, who thought it one thing to know people at sea and quite another thing to know them on land.

Friendliness with her was a fluid condition of mind and manner, adapted to ocean and watering-place life, but apt to form into a thick deposit of ice across which she skated to *terra firma* at the close of a voyage or season, leaving rueful or indignant acquaintances to think what they pleased. She now made it so clear

that she considered her relations with the Hitchcocks
to have been of this temporary character that those
ladies bowed themselves stiffly off the scene.   Ethel
hastened after the girls and shook hands again, murmured something about the pleasure she had had
with them, and "the awfully jolly voyage," and also
expressed a hope that they might meet "somewhere"
again, blushing a good deal while she made this atone-
ment, and feeling extremely uncomfortable.

Her aunt took Mrs. Sykes to task as follows: "Surely,
Georgina, it was not necessary for you to be so—well,
positive.   I fear you have given offence.   And you
know Mrs. Hitchcock kindly gave up her cabin to you
when she found it was making you so ill to be near the
screw, besides showing us other civilities.   Really, I
feel concerned that you should have repulsed her as you
did."

"Oh, never fear.   That kind of people who dress up
to the nines and wear their diamonds when they travel,
are in the habit of putting out small attentions at
interest and quite used to the cold shoulder in return.
They are accustomed to being sat upon.   They like it,
expect it, thrive upon it, I assure you.   It is the only
way to deal with them," replied Mrs. Sykes coolly.   "I
met two families at Scarborough last year that I did
not care to keep up with afterward, though they
amused me at the time, so I cut them all dead in the
Park a month ago.   But they didn't mind it in the least,
with the exception of one daughter, a red-haired dowdy
of a girl with whom I had been rather intimate in a
way.   She was perfectly furious" (Mrs. Sykes called it
"fiawrious'); "but the others, on the contrary, bowed

most graciously to me after that at the opera, and told a friend of mine that I was the most delightful woman they had ever met. I should never have taken them up but that I got the use of a drawing-room facing the sea out of them without its costing me a penny, and I knew I could drop them whenever I liked. A vulgar lot, of whom I am well rid."

"You—surprise me," said her companion, though "disgust" would have better expressed her meaning. "But the Hitchcocks are not at all vulgar,—a little over-dressed perhaps, but not more so than a good many people in the highest society at home. I can't think why they wear their diamonds in the daytime. It is such an extraordinary thing to do."

Sir Robert, who had walked away at the beginning of the conversation, now came back again to ask if they were quite ready to land, and the two ladies, remembering a number of last things that required their attention, retired to their cabins again, where Mrs. Sykes's deep voice might have been heard giving explicit directions about her "darling Bobo,"—a Dandie Dinmont about which she gave herself endless concern, and for which she felt apparently all the fondness that the most doting parent could lavish on a favorite child. Mrs. Sykes had once been a mother, but always a devotee to dogs, and, when people complimented her upon the appearance of her little daughter during the brief stay it made in a world of woe, she was wont to reply, "My baby is all very well, of course" (tepidly); "but" (with enthusiasm) "you should see my dog! He has got no nose at all!"

Perhaps it may be well to take this opportunity of

saying that Mrs. Sykes was a middle-aged widow of
ample fortune and aristocratic connections, who belonged to the genus lately and accurately defined as
" globe-trotter;" an aggressively clever, well-informed
woman, an insatiably curious woman, who yet travelled
all over the world that she might enjoy the *éclat* of
having seen and done everything and been everywhere
rather than for any pleasure it gave her, unless indeed
it was a pleasure to assure herself (and everybody else)
that there was " no place like England ;" a woman
coarse of nature, destitute of tact, and profoundly selfish, who could make herself very agreeable or perfectly
insufferable, just as she saw fit.   Returning from Siam
three months before Sir Robert planned his tour in
America, and hearing that he meant to take with him
his niece and nephew and their maternal aunt, the
Honorable Augusta Noel, she skilfully fastened herself
on the party, knowing from experience that it was certainly less expensive and might prove more agreeable
to travel in that way than alone, and stating frankly
that she had to do America,—everybody was doing
America,—and she had best get it over and done
with.

Another addition was made to the party later, in the
person of Mr. Hugh Malcom Farquharson Milman
Ramsay, the younger son of a younger son, who, growing tired of supporting this wealth of title and its
possessor on the salary of a Foreign-Office clerk, had
conceived the idea of making a future for himself in
America, where, although he knew nothing whatever
of business and had the habits and tastes of a man with
thirty thousand a year rather than eighty, he had

mapped out for himself an abnormally successful and brilliant career.

"I give myself five years in which to make a million and come back to England," he said to young Heathcote.

"How are you going to do it?" his friend inquired.

"Oh, in mines and things," explained the sanguine innocent. "You watch your chance and put in a little capital out there, and before you know where you are you find yourself rolling in money. I have been reading a lot about it lately. You strike a vein, don't you see, or a railroad comes along, and there you are. Not that I mean to live in America, I can tell you. When high tide comes, I'll sell out and put every shillin' of it in the Bank of England, and come home and turn country gentleman, and marry, and all that."

In this easy and agreeable fashion did Mr. Ramsay lay up much wealth for himself in imagination and prepare to eat, drink, and be merry, not knowing what would be required of him in the way of knowledge, capacity, and energy in order to earn so much as one trade dollar making up in piety the weight it lacks in silver. Acting on this belief, he drew out of the funds his entire fortune, consisting of a thousand pounds left him by a maiden aunt, and with immense eagerness and delight set himself to take the plunge he had determined upon,—ordered fourteen suits of clothes of Poole, bought the newest and best gun, the most ingeniously jointed and reeled fishing-rod, the most gorgeous dressing-case to be found in London, not to mention equipments for twelve horses, a great bundle of canes and umbrellas, a case of pistols, a travelling-clock, despatch-boxes, Cockle's pills, Pears' soap, Lubin's "White Rose," eau

de Cologne, and a thousand other things suggested in
" Bell's Life" by army-men who had been stationed in
Canada, by friends who had "done the States," and by
the general public, with something less than fifty pairs
of shoes, boots, gaiters, slippers, tennis- and racquet-
Oxfords, and the trees to keep them in shape; all of
which he regarded as essentials for the intending colo-
nist which it was unlikely he could procure in America
"anything like so good, if at all."

To purchase all these things and have them packed
under his own eye, to pick up his rifle and, shutting one
eye, aim at an imaginary buffalo in full gallop, and drop
it again with a click of the tongue and a radiant expression betokening sated ambition and intoxicating
victory, to set up his rod and give it a dexterous whirl
worthy of Izaak Walton, that sent his fly into the far-
thest corner of the hall adjoining his bedroom at his
London lodgings, and draw in an enormous mountain-
trout from California, to examine every buckle and strap
of his saddle and fancy himself careering across the
prairies on a wild mustang in pursuit of some sort of
game, was the keenest pleasure this enthusiastic sportsman had ever known or was likely to know.  He told
all his acquaintances, with an awkward shamefacedness
that betrayed his satisfaction, how tired he had grown
of England, which was always the same old two-and-
six, and how he meant to "cut it" and go out to the
backwoods of America.  He also continued to buy this
or that up to the last moment and to give the tradesmen
very particular instructions about furnishing articles
adapted to his great purpose.  Altogether he contrived
to get a great amount of satisfaction out of the journey

before it began at all, and when he got on board the
" Britannia" was able to boast with good reason that,
from his tent and his portable shower-bath to his English
breakfast-tea and a sovereign's worth of gold-beaters'
skin, nothing had been forgotten. While the others had
not given individually such scope to their desires or
taken such comprehensive views of the situation, all of
them had brought about five times more stuff than there
was any necessity for, unless, indeed, they had been
going into the heart of Africa for an indefinite period ;
and the collective total was so various and extensive
that Sir Robert felt called upon to make some sort of
apology for it to the custom-house authorities in New
York. Those officials were still peering dubiously at
the Ward case for plants of Mrs. Sykes and the complete photographic apparatus of Mr. Heathcote, when
a gentleman came up to Sir Robert and introduced himself as Mr. Brown, explained that he had been asked
by his friend Mr. Ketchum to make their acquaintance,
shook hands formally with the three men, bowed gravely
to the ladies, and made some polite inquiries about their
trip. This gave them time to observe that Mr. Brown
had an air of spotless-cambric respectability and a
family-prayers voice, was very well and very quietly
dressed, and had a dignified cordiality of manner that
was admirable.

" My carriage is waiting to take you to your hotel,"
he said, when the last chalk-mark had been scrawled on
the last trunk. " There it is" (waving his hand toward
where a handsome carriage was standing, drawn by a
beautiful pair of Kentuckian thoroughbreds).

Sir Robert looked inquiringly at the ladies, and Mrs.

G   k          13

Sykes, ever eager to save a sixpence, came forward graciously, saying, "We shall be very pleased to avail ourselves of your kindness, I am shore.—Miss Noel? Ethel?"

Those ladies were close behind her, and with Parsons, a prim elderly maid of indescribable stoniness, boniness, and efficiency, now followed Mrs. Sykes's lead, and were assisted into the landau. Mr. Brown, when they had rolled away, told Sir Robert that he would call very soon, pleaded a business-engagement, and called a cab. Before getting into it he put his carriage at Sir Robert's disposal and that of his party during their stay in New York, without either ostentation or Orientalism, in all simplicity and sincerity, and so was driven rapidly off on his own errands. The three Englishmen followed him in another cab, and as they peered out curiously at the unfamiliar streets through which they were passing, Sir Robert said, "Mr. Brown is a man of ability, I should judge. Fine head. Remarkable frontal development. I observed him with interest. I wonder if his is the national type. There must be a national type, you know. Stimson had a paper in the 'Fortnightly' lately in support of his theory that the Americans are rapidly reverting to, or rather assuming, the aboriginal type,— high cheek-bones, coarse hair, and so on; but all the same I shall trust only to the results of personal observation and maintain an independent judgment meanwhile. Very curious and interesting speculation, is it not, how far a race can be affected by climatic conditions, diet, and all that? Attractive man Brown, very. And extremely civil of him, I must say, to offer his trap for our use."

" A fellow with horses like those at home would hardly do as much for his own brother," replied Mr. Heathcote.

Arrived at the hotel,—chosen because it was the hotel of the country and *not* kept on the European plan, —Sir Robert faced that great American fountain of absolute authority and irresponsible power, the clerk, with the unconscious courage that animates a boy in his first battle. He did not know the danger, and so knew no fear, and had no idea of what he was doing, when, after stating particularly that he wished a room with a southern exposure and being assigned one with a northern one,—a fact ascertained by taking his bearings with a pocket compass as soon as he was installed, —he marched down-stairs and boldly rebuked the gorgeous young man with the solitaire pin who had betrayed his confidence, and who, paralyzed perhaps by such audacity, forgot to either threaten or command, but called a servant and bade him " take that there lord's things up to 36 from 24, and be quick about it, too."

Sir Robert had not been long in his new quarters when a telegram was brought to him from Mr. Ketchum, which read as follows:

" Delighted to know that you are on the right side of the pond at last. Would have run on to meet you if it had been possible. String of the latch on the outside, remember, now and always."

The next day's post brought letters also from Mr. and Mrs. Ketchum urging the whole party to come "right out to the West and make Kalsing their head-quarters during their stay in the country." At least, this was what Mr. Ketchum wrote. His wife said that she would be very pleased to receive them whenever they might appoint a time, and suggested their taking a "sleeper" from New York, besides giving them the exact distance and a good deal of information about the trains.

Established at the hotel, the various members of the party proceeded to occupy or amuse themselves as best suited their respective tastes and characters for a fortnight. Miss Noel went promptly to Trinity the first afternoon, to return thanks for a safe voyage, after which she came back and rested quietly in her room. Mrs. Sykes, who was made of equal parts of steel and whalebone and did not know the meaning of fatigue, bought a guide-book (shop-worn, at a reduction), and, accompanied by Parsons, tramped up and down Broadway until tired of the full pulse of trade, when she took the elevated road up town, honored with a rapid and supercilious survey the Metropolitan Museum, asked there what three churches were considered best worth seeing in the city, tramped to each of them in succession only to give a brief stare of detraction, and returned to the hotel satisfied,—at least with herself.

"A narrow, dirty street," she reported of Broadway; "but the shops well supplied, at ruinous prices. I met the Hitchcocks. Wasn't it odd? And who do you suppose was walking with them, and actually stopping at the house? The Duke of Marlshire. I've seen him often at home, and am not mistaken. I stopped and told her we were here, but she was as haughty as Mrs. Siddons, if you please. After that I went up to a museum with a lot of stuff in it of one sort or other;

there wasn't time to see much, but I got quite enough of it; and then I did a few churches, very tame and uninteresting. How did you like Trinity, which I believe is the crack church? I was told to go there, but didn't."

Miss Noel had liked Trinity, had thought "the service respectably conducted and the hymn-tunes pretty," and had not found the changes in the ritual as numerous or startling as she had expected.

"Oh, my dear," Mrs. Sykes went on, "what *do* you think that bouquet cost that Mabel's husband sent Sir Robert? I passed the shop on Broadway and recognized the name, which was peculiar, and thought I would just ask. Fifty dollars! Ten pounds! Was there ever such a senseless piece of ostentation! And, talking of flowers, I noticed a most curious Yankee fashion to-day. In the windows of a great many houses that I passed there were huge bouquets flattened against the panes, so as to be seen from the street and impress the passers-by, I suppose. I had never seen such a thing, so I stood stock-still at one place and gazed rural-fashion, and pointed it out to Parsons with my umbrella. And just then a lady came out of the house, and I said, 'What's that for? Can you tell me? Why do you make a vulgar show of the flowers you get, instead of keeping them about your rooms for your private enjoyment?' And, would you believe it? the rude creature walked off without a word. American manners, I suppose."

In the hotel Mrs. Sykes certainly found ample food for her peculiar order of intelligence, and made almost hourly "returns," in election parlance, of all that was

happening around her to Miss Noel, who, being differently constituted, did not enjoy the same advantages
for observing the singular people among whom she
found herself. "So very odd," Mrs. Sykes would say
in her throaty, strident tones, and laughing her guttural
laugh. "There are five women in one of the 'parlors,'
seated in five rocking-chairs, and they have been plung-
ing backwards and forwards without intermission for
the last two hours like mad women, trying to find some
vent for their nervousness, and not one of them usefully
employed. I saw it myself. The door was ajar, and I
caught a sight of three of them, and I pushed it open
a little to get a better view, and found two more doing
the same thing. The woman I noticed at dinner, the
one in yellow satin and point-lace and diamonds, *of
course* (as far as I can see, every other woman in New
York wears a black silk and solitaire ear-rings; even in
the tramway, but this creature's dress was a satin *mer-
veilleux* of the best quality),—well, my dear, that woman,
arrayed as a duchess might be for a garden-party at Marl-
borough House, is the wife of a draper's clerk, and gets
herself up like that every day for a four-o'clock dinner
at the *table-d'hôte.* I expected to hear that she was
some great personage,—the wife of a cabinet officer, or
something of the sort. A draper's clerk! Fancy the
wife of the floor-walker at Whiteley's or Marshal &
Snelgrove's going on like that."

"Most likely a silly woman who puts everything on
her back and doesn't know how lacking in good taste
and good sense she is not to dress as becomes her station and lay by for a rainy day," was Miss Noel's placid
reply.

But, if these and other things gave occasion for disapproving or sarcastic comment on Mrs. Sykes's part, there was at least one other that struck her in a more favorable light. And this was the bill of fare. She scanned it closely the first day, and ordered but a moderate share of the good things set forth, under the impression that she was paying a certain sum for each dish. But when the steward, sharply interrogated as to the cost of each viand, explained the system on which the hotel was managed and the great fact dawned upon her that she could have anything and everything on the *menu* without its costing her a penny more than if she were to dine on pulse and water, a marked change was observed in the lady.

"That is quite another thing," she very truly said; and now it took two experienced waiters to minister to the widest range of gastronomic experiment that can be imagined. Always blessed with an enormous appetite, and feeling the opportunity a golden one, there was scarcely a dish that she did not order at least once, and certain expensive luxuries she was never without, while in the matter of ices it must be confessed that letters three can alone describe her conduct. She studied the bill of fare, if possible, more earnestly than ever, though with a different object in view, and has got a pile of them now among her papers somewhere, mournful souvenirs of a bright and beautiful past that will never come again.

Sir Robert was likewise struck by this feature of American hotel-life.

"I don't care for all the glare and glitter of this place, and I can't see why they should fetch me a jug of iced

water every time I ring my bell, but I certainly like the
American plan of paying a fixed sum for inn accommo-
dation and no extras.   The way I have been regularly
fleeced on the Continent with *bougies* alone is really a
scandal," he said.

All the party did the regulation sight-seeing, but Mrs.
Sykes went at it with tireless, deathless energy, and
kept Mr. Brown's carriage dashing over the city morning, noon, and night.   It had been devoted to the ladies'
service, and Mrs. Sykes, who was the sort of woman
whom the French describe as *maîtresse femme*, took it
upon herself to give all the orders in connection with it,
and used it so unsparingly that at last Miss Noel, after
many remonstrances to which no heed was paid, spoke
to Sir Robert about it.   He gave Mrs. Sykes "the English of the thing," which was that she had behaved
shamefully, and that he would not permit Mr. Brown's
kindness to be so grossly abused, so that the carriage
was dismissed at the end of five days, with a handsome
tip to the coachman and a note of apology and thanks
to his master.

Mr. Ramsay and Mr. Heathcote had a small adventure
that was amusing at the time and became a standing
joke with them in after-years.   Going out to see the
town on the day of their arrival, they got over a great
deal of ground, made various sage reflections on what
they saw, and found themselves about noon a long way
from their hotel and decidedly hungry.   Not long after
making this discovery, they came upon an inviting-
looking French restaurant and agreed to have luncheon
there.   Both were extravagantly fond of oysters, and,
after some consultation, called the Alsatian attendant

and ordered in good *quatre-ving-sang* French "*sans weeters*," being, as they expressed it, "peckish, uncommonly sharp-set," and feeling quite equal to the order. They also asked persistently for *l'ale pâle de Bass*, thinking thus to describe accurately their national beverage, but, in spite of this handsome concession to his nationality, succeeded only in puzzling Alphonse thoroughly. Finally that genius had an inspiration. "*Ah! c'est de la bière!*" he exclaimed, and forthwith produced several stubby bottles with the right trade-mark. They asked for "biscuits," but for answer had a French loaf and accompanying pats of butter furnished them, after which Alphonse disappeared for so long that they were about to make violent demonstrations of some sort, when he returned, gravely bearing a huge tray containing dishes full of enormous oysters, and followed by other waiters bearing other trays loaded in the same manner. The tiny room was quite blocked with them finally, and the two young men first stared with all their eyes, and, seeing at last the difference in size between the English and American oyster, burst into a perfect roar of laughter, in which they were joined by Alphonse and his crew, who had simply thought the order another evidence of English eccentricity.

I am afraid it cannot be denied that both of these young men were bored by the Astor Library, which they visited next day; but perhaps it was only that they reserved their admiration for purely American institutions. It is certain that they went into a bar-room of the best class, and watched with keenest interest the accomplished gentleman who brewed two different beverages at the same time, poured the contents of one glass into another at impossible distances, and described a sherry-cobbler rainbow behind his back without spilling so much as a drop in the effort. Moreover, they each bet a half-sovereign that they could imitate his feats successfully, tried to do so, and failed. Being asked to name what they would take, they chose two concoctions called "Moses's Milk" and "Settler's Friend," which they assured him were well-known American drinks, but of which he had never heard. They drowned their defeat in a delicious preparation for which that bar-room was noted, and then went back to the hotel, where they spent the next hour drenching themselves with water in a futile attempt to reproduce the rainbow that had so fascinated their imagination.

They had just given up, in despair and joined the ladies in the drawing-room, when Miss Bijou Brown's card was brought in, and that young lady followed closely upon it.

A tall, graceful girl, with what in more poetical days used to be called "a kiss-worthy face," fresh, bright, and sweet, eyes like two patches of brown velvet, but with spikes in the iris, a quick, bird-like turn of the head, a wave of the gold-brown hair wholly unconnected with pins, irons, or papillotes, small feet, small hands, and a rather thin voice as full of light and shade as the face in its varying inflections,—such was the lady who, with an *aplomb* that made elderly Miss Noel feel positively shy and awkward, came forward, made herself known to each member of the party, and, dropping into a chair, straightway seized the helm of conversation, and kept it during her entire visit. With a great flow of language and pleasant glances to the right and left, Miss

Brown acquitted herself of her social *devoir* with a frank naturalness that was not the case or simplicity of the highest breeding, but was very attractive, and with an entire absence of embarrassment and constraint which girls in other countries are not apt to achieve at eighteen. Ethel made round eyes at her, as if still in the nursery, Mrs. Sykes listened to her with an amused smile of superiority and Miss Noel with one of kindly interest, as she fluently explained that the Ketchums were her next-door neighbors in Kalsing, where she spent her summers and until recently had passed the winters as well, that she was intimate with them and thought Mabel "perfectly lovely," and was very happy to make acquaintance with her friends, and so on.

"She was not thought a beauty at home," put in Mrs. Sykes. "Nice-looking, rather, but certainly not lovely. Still, over here I suppose she would be above the average. I am forgetting that the Americans consider themselves to have the prettiest women in the world, though I must say that I have not seen even a moderately good-looking one since I landed."

At this speech Ethel colored with annoyance, and Mr. Ramsay shuffled his feet uneasily; but Miss Brown only laughed, and said, "Haven't you? I didn't mean that Mrs. Ketchum was a beauty. She is such a fine woman, though, we all think, and is liked by everybody."

"A fine woman you call her?" exclaimed Mrs. Sykes, with animation. "Then she must have grown at least a foot and expanded to match. She used to be rather undersized than otherwise : there was never very much of her."

Miss Brown felt puzzled, but, it being evident to her that they were talking at cross-purposes, she changed the subject by saying that her especial object in coming that morning had been to ask them all to a theatre-party she was giving the same night.

"What! Do you hire a theatre and give all your friends an invite?" demanded Mrs. Sykes, prepared for anything in the way of American extravagance. "What is it like? What do you do? Is it one of your favorite amusements here? I never heard of one before, but can guess a little what it is like."

"There wouldn't be many of them if we had to go to all that expense," replied Miss Brown, answering one of these questions. "Oh, no! we all go to the theatre together and have a little supper at Delmonico's afterward, that is all; but we think it a pleasant way of entertaining our friends."

"And how are we expected to get there?" asked Mrs. Sykes, ruthlessly rubbing the bloom off an intended courtesy. It was not only that she was utterly destitute of tact, but that, possessing it, she would have thought it much too expensive a luxury to indulge in, when there was a question of her being, as she afterward said to Miss Noel, "let in for the hire of a cab both ways."

"Don't bother about that. Popper will send for you; and you had better have an early dinner, perhaps, for it is Salvini, and he's perfectly splendid!" replied Miss Brown, rising to go. "There will be another Englishman in the party," she added, and looked brightly around; but, if her new acquaintances felt this to be a gratifying piece of intelligence, they all concealed it

under aspects of varying stolidity and unexpressed disapproval, and she got no reply but " Oh, really!" from
Mrs. Sykes, which expressed a good deal, if she had
only understood it.

" I asked him on purpose, thinking it would be so
pleasant for you to meet, and that it would be nice for
Miss Ethel to have somebody from her own country to
talk to and flirt with," she went on. " He's a lovely
little man. The girls here are all wild about him."

" You are very kind, my dear, and we shall be pleased
to go with you," said Miss Noel, "but you mustn't be
putting ideas into my Ethel's head."

" Goodness gracious alive! Has she had to come all
the way to America to get that idea, at *her* age?" inquired Miss Brown, with her merriest laugh.

" What is my age?" asked Ethel, smiling, and addressing the visitor for the first time.

" I can't tell a bit. You are as fresh as though you
were fifteen, and as grave as though you were fifty, at
least when your aunt is around," was Miss Brown's
audacious reply, at which the two girls looked at each
other and laughed, and, with the Free-Masonry of their
age and sex, decided on the spot to be friends. So much
good nature and friendliness had not been thrown away
upon Ethel, though she had only rewarded it with
monosyllables. Miss Noel now thanked Bijou for the
flowers sent on shipboard, and, after more ladies' last
words, the pretty visitor was gallantly escorted down-
stairs and put into her carriage by Mr. Ramsay.

She had hardly driven off when an old friend of Sir
Robert's and flame of his nephew's—Mrs. De Witt, *née*
Jenny Meredith—came to call. Sir Robert, who had

been writing letters previously in strict seclusion, was addressing a note to "The Lord Bishop of Maryland" when this interruption came. Down dropped the pen instantly, and he was soon shaking Mrs. De Witt's hands with an enthusiasm and heartiness he did not often exhibit. Mr. Heathcote slipped in a few phrases somewhere among his uncle's fluent greetings, and then retired to the fireplace, from which he blushingly and pensively regarded his lost love during the remainder of her stay, paying small attention to Sir Robert's "God bless my souls," his assurances of his delight at meeting her again, his inquiries for mutual friends and protestations that she was handsomer than ever, but hearing clearly every word of her clever and gracious replies, and acknowledging to himself that she was, if anything, more charming than in the old Cheltenham days.

"Ass that I was ever to have thought that I could confer any distinction on that woman by asking her to be my wife," he thought. "She would grace a throne; and but for my confounded conceit she might have married me. That disgusted her utterly, and no wonder!" It will be seen from this that time and disappointment had had a wholesome effect upon Mr. Heathcote's character and given him a much more modest opinion of himself than he had once entertained; but he was mistaken in his conclusion, for Jenny Meredith had been attached to Colonel De Witt for two years before she went to England, and had engaged herself to him the day she sailed. Sir Robert had thought that Mrs. De Witt was in California, and it appeared that she had only very recently come to

New York, and had, through his banker, accidentally learned of his arrival and that of his relatives.

"We have the tiniest little house that ever was, near Babylon, Long Island;" she said, "and, like Mrs. Skewton, I always sleep with my head in the parlor and my feet in the kitchen. But it is a great saving in house-maids, and I am by no means the most miserable of my sex. You must come out and see the 'nut-shell,' as we call it. Name a day when you can come and take a high tea with me. With paupers like us *on mange, mais on ne dîne pas.*"

"*Babylon* did you say? Did I understand you to say that you lived at a place called *Babylon?*" quoth Mrs. Sykes. "How very extraordinary!"

"Yes; but, you see, I am a woman of nerve, and my husband a soldier by profession. And there are worse places. We have tried Versailles, Kentucky, and Whis-key City in the West, and it is a distinct improvement on both places, I assure you," said Mrs. De Witt, laugh-ing, and so took her leave, having made herself so agreeable that even the "globe-trotter" had something amiable to say of her.

"Really, quite a charming person, and not bad-look-ing. But she can't be so frightfully poor as all that. Her lace was lovely, and real, I know, for I came up behind her while she was bidding Ethel good-by and *felt it,*" was her characteristic comment. "I am glad we are asked to drink tea with her. She said her hus-band had some photographs of those curious cliff-cities of the Mexican Americans in Anazona, or whatever it is, and I mean to get a couple out of him for my diary if I can."

Mrs. Sykes and Sir Robert both kept diaries, hers being an illustrated one, and forming part of a series which she had kept in all the countries where she had travelled,—very entertaining reading, and made more attractive by her really admirable sketches, supplemented by photographs.

In spite of Miss Brown's suggestion about an early dinner, it was rather late when the party from the hotel presented themselves in her father's box, where she was seated awaiting them, looking her prettiest and as if clad in white samite, an immense bouquet on the railing in front of her, and a crimson *sortie de bal* thrown over the back of her chair.

She received them quietly, assigned them their seats, and introduced them to the two other guests present,— Mrs. Conway, a gorgeous matron in blue velvet, stout and stupid, and the Englishman of whom she had spoken. Bows were exchanged between the opposite sexes. Sir Robert and Mr. Heathcote met their countryman with the affectionate effusiveness for which Britons are· noted; that is, they gave him a haughty stare and then shook hands with him limply and ignored him utterly. In the confusion attendant upon getting seated, no one noticed a little scene that took place in the back of the box between Mr. Ramsay and Mr. Drummond of London, as the stranger was called by Miss Brown when she presented him to the others.

" What the deuce are *you* doing over here?" demanded Mr. Ramsay, by way of greeting.

" I don't see that it is any business of yours," replied Mr. Drummond coolly, returning with interest the scowl he had received.

"Oh! all right!" said Mr. Ramsay, and took a seat as far from him as possible and proceeded to look as disdainful and as thoroughly out of humor as a man very well could for some time,—indeed, until Miss Brown diverted his thoughts into more agreeable channels. Even this *adoucissement* did not last long, for when that young lady in her capacity of hostess turned round and addressed various pleasant remarks to Mr. Drummond, Mr. Ramsay straightway relapsed into his former mood, and, not being an adept at concealing his feelings, was either offensively silent or disagreeably curt of speech the whole evening.

While Mr. Ramsay, like a grown-up school-boy, was giving vent to his disgust with the incurable honesty and constitutional incapacity for sophistication which causes Englishmen of his type to be liked and trusted or disliked and ridiculed according to the mental habits and moral bias of the people with whom they are thrown, another member of the party was in a state of mind that precluded the possibility of enjoying Salvini's performance, though her discontent arose from a much more trivial cause. This was Ethel Heathcote, who had been placed in a front seat, under the full glare of a chandelier as well as in full view of the audience, and, owing to having been hurried off by an imperative uncle, had forgotten to bring her gloves. Now, Ethel, like many English girls, was afflicted with hands that had an awful trick of turning red,—yea, like unto the lobster,—and had given much time and the most anxious thoughts to curing this defect, but so far with no result but that of aggravating the unfortunate peculiarity. Not only did the hands appear to grow uglier

every day under cosmetic treatment, but the objectionable rose-flush mounted slowly but surely to her very
elbows, and made her wretched. She was sitting tugging
furtively at her uncompromisingly short elbow-sleeves,
with tears of vexation in her pretty blue eyes, when
Bijou noticed the movement and asked what was
wrong.

"Oh, dear, it is so tiresome! Do let me hide myself
somewhere. I came off without my gloves, and only
see these awful hands of mine! Scarlet! Positively
scarlet!" murmured Ethel, in a distressed whisper.
"Dear, dear! what shall I do with them?" she added,
pulling a fold of her overskirt over the objectionable
members.

"Wait a minute. They are not so bad at all. You
only think so because they are yours. Hold on, and
I'll look in my coat-pocket and see. I think I've got a
pair there that will fit you," whispered Bijou back
again, consolingly. Accordingly, Miss Brown looked,
found no gloves, put her head out of the door, spoke to
an usher whom she found there, and returned to her
seat. Five minutes later there was a knock at the door,
which Ethel did not hear, owing to her interest in
Desdemona. An envelope was handed to Bijou, which,
when unobserved, she quietly tore off, and, going back
to Ethel, slipped into her hand a pair of eight-buttoned
*gants de Suède.* The relief of Sebastopol was nothing
compared to Ethel's as she breathed out a fervent
"Thank you very much indeed; but a fresh pair?" and
hastily drew them on. It may not be out of place to
mention that Bijou got another pair next day, with an
eminently lady-like note stating, in Ethel's bold hand

but rather weak style; "that some girls would have been rathei glad to see another placed at a disadvantage, and other girls would not at all have cared how other girls appeared;" also that "one would not so much have minded how one was dressed in one's own country, but that one did not like to make one's self ridiculous in the eyes of foreigners," as well as that the writer was hers affectionately, "Ethel Maude Heathcote," from which it will be seen that if Miss Brown did a little kindness she was certainly paid for 't in the right kind of coin. Rich as Mrs. Sykes was, perhaps she was bankrupt in this particular, for, having occasion to borrow Bijou's exquisite fan during the evening, she kept and used it during her whole stay in New York, and finally sent it home, a good deal the worse for wear, wrapped up in a fragment of newspaper, without a line of acknowledgment, by Parsons, who for very shame invented a civil message on her own responsibility. But for these episodes, the evening passed very much like others of its kind. Mrs. Sykes talked a little in a patronizing way to Mrs. Conway, put the usual number of questions, swept the audience from side to side again and again with her *lorgnon*, and gave such attention to the great artist who was playing as she had to spare. Sir Robert and Mr. Brown talked incessantly between the acts, and intermittently during the performance. The girls were vaguely moved by it, and Mr. Ramsay at certain points very much so; as, for instance, when Othello springs like a tiger upon the crouching Iago. "If I had that chap I'd break every bone in his rascally skin! What does he let him off for like that?" he asked, with sparkling eyes.

When they had all helped to murder a most lovely and unfortunate lady, and the curtain had fallen and Salvini had committed the unpardonable sin of appearing before it, they went off to Delmonico's and had a delightful little supper, at which Mr. Ramsay continued pointedly to ignore the existence of Mr. Drummond, and Miss Brown was always casting herself *à la* Quintus Curtius into the gulf that separated them; and so the affair ended.

When Miss Brown got home that night she felt an unaccountable sense of disappointment in thinking over the events of the evening. "He's the handsomest and the 'swellest' fellow, as they say here, that I ever saw, but I am afraid he has got an awful temper," was one conclusion that she jumped to.

Driving back to the hotel in their cab, Mr. Ramsay said to Mr. Heathcote suddenly, "Who do you think that chap was that they had there? That was my cousin, Arthur Plummer."

There seemed to be a voluminous biography in the bare statement.

"The deuce it was!" exclaimed Mr. Heathcote. "I thought there was something familiar about his face, but I haven't seen him since we were at Eton together. I thought he had been transported or hanged long since."

"And so he would have been, if he had got his deserts," rejoined Mr. Ramsay. "They haven't heard of him at home for years. I was never so astonished in all my life as when he showed up on this side. I wonder where he got the money to come? If it hadn't been for the women and all that, I'd have kicked him out of that, pretty quick. He isn't fit to sit in the same theatre with them. If he thinks I am not going to tell of him, he is vastly mistaken, that's all. I shall go to Mr. Brown the first thing in the morning and expose him. Hang it all! To think of his turning up over here now!"

Mr. Brown was out of town when Mr. Ramsay called next day at his house, but was expected back in a few days, the servant said, so that, after spending several minutes in trying to decide whether he would ask for the daughter and pour into her ear the particularly plain and entirely unvarnished tale he had come to tell, his shyness got the better of him, and he left cards instead. These being promptly taken up to Miss Brown, that young lady exclaimed, "Too bad!" and darted to the window to get a glimpse of the retreating visitor, after which she inspected the cards again with an interest hardly justified by the narrow strips of pasteboard on which was inscribed, in plain text, "Mr. Ramsay, of Ferneyhaugh," and, in pencil, "Ninth Avenue Hotel."

---

## III.

"Lay out my red satin gown, Parsons," said Mrs. Sykes to Miss Noel's maid, when the time came to dress for the De Witts' entertainment. "It is nearly gone now, to be sure, after three seasons' wear; but it will do nicely for America."

"And what shall I do about the spots all down the

front, mem?" inquired Parsons. "And the bottom
flounce do look 'opeless; there's nothink to be done
with it, as I can see."

Parsons's services had been "occasionally" proffered
to Mrs. Sykes by her mistress, and she was already
tired of the endless demands made upon her.

"Oh, all that will not be noticed. It really doesn't
matter over here. It will answer quite well as it is, I
am sure, for this kind of thing," said Mrs. Sykes,
serenely convinced that any dress of hers was good
enough to grace an American entertainment given by
people who confessed themselves poor and who lived
near Babylon, Long Island.

Parsons did what she could to furbish up the dis-
gracefully-shabby robe in question (with an eye to
future perquisites, it must be confessed), but it remained
a piece of tawdry finery, and a very unbecoming one
besides, for the day was warm, and it imparted an additional flush to a face already as highly colored as a
chromo,—vivid blue as to the eyes, almost magenta as
to the cheeks, auburn-haired, and boasting an array of
very white, large teeth.

But if nature had added to these tints prominent
features and a chin which, as the one retiring thing
about Mrs. Sykes, surely needs no apology, she had
given her one of those beautiful figures which she
seems to reserve especially for her ugliest daughters,
and fortune had added other figures which are thought
by some persons to be much more satisfactory in the
long run. Mrs. Sykes was tall, perfectly proportioned,
graceful, and occasionally dressed as well as any French
woman.

"Americans have a silly idea that all Englishwomen are frumps, and I'll take one box of my French things to show them that they are not the only women in the world who know how to dress; but that will be for great occasions, should there be such by any chance. I don't mean to waste my best things on them, as a rule. I'll go in for 'republican simplicity,'" she had said on leaving London.

It will be seen, then, that if she wore her oldest gown to the De Witts' it was from insolence, and not in the least from indigence; and she saw her mistake when she got there, and repented in satin instead of sack-cloth.

Nor was she better satisfied with the toilets of her companions. Miss Noel came down in a rick silk, cut in a wonderful way, the skirt much longer in front than at the back, most eccentrically looped in a series of little pleats set very far apart on the sides, long and plain in the bodice, and enlivened about the neck with a wide fall of cotton lace, and no less than five neck laces, graduated from a velvet band and brooch about the throat to a long string of lapis-lazuli beads that fell almost to the waist. But all the same she looked the handsome and refined old gentlewoman that she was, and kept the Chesterfieldian "*ton de la parfaitement bonne compagnie*" in a costume that would have vulgarized many women of great pretensions to gentility. As for Ethel, she was got up as only an English girl of the provincial type ever could be.

"The two of you are bad advertisements for Parsons," observed Mrs. Sykes, with her usual unbridled frankness, when she saw them. "Not that it matters very much. Miss Noel must be past caring for such things, and you are a good little thing, Ethel, but you are one of the girls that no man would ever look at twice. But, really, to put you in a short black slip and a trained overdress of tarlatan and a beaded cashmere jacket is too bad of Parsons. I·had not thought it of her. To be sure, she is country-bred, and has only had the annual hunt ball to provide for, but still she must see that you are a couple of guys."

"You are extremely uncivil, and I don't agree with you at all," said Miss Noel. "This is a good, serviceable gown, that I expect to last me for years, and all done over quite recently; it can't have been three years since it was turned upside down and inside out and all this lace put on. What is the matter with it? As to dear Ethel, she looks as nice as possible, I think. She wore that very frock to an archery meeting at the castle before we left, and the countess asked to be allowed to take off the pattern of her josie, saying that she had not seen anything like it before."

"That I can well believe," replied Mrs. Sykes coolly. "She never will, out of the provinces. I always think when I go down there that it is easy to see what became of the three thousand dresses that Queen Elizabeth left behind her. They drifted into the remote counties, where the women have been making them over once in fifty years ever since. No, no. If Ethel is to make anything of a figure in the world, or hook so much as a fifty-pound curate, she will have to get a London maid,—a French one she can't afford. A girl with no beauty and no money *must* have clothes. Thank heaven! I shall never have any daughters to marry off. When I think of my four sisters out season after season husband-hunting, and the youngest a good thirty-three, I feel that I can't be too thankful that I married when I did. Excuse my speaking so plainly about your dress, but I never could see the good of mincing matters; and you'd better act on it as soon as you get home, and not wait until Ethel begins to go off, when it may be too late."

Poor Ethel, who had come down-stairs with an agreeable consciousness of being well dressed, was much disturbed by these comments. Nor was she reassured by her brother, who presently came in.

"What is the matter with you, Ethel?" he said. "There is something wrong with you, but I can't tell what it is. You seem to wear the same things that these American women do, but you don't look as they do. You can't know how to put them on. It can't be the thing to see a yard of carpet between your gingham petticoat—"

"It is a silk slip, and was five-and-six a yard, I'm sure," Ethel put in ruefully.

"Well, silk, then—and that frazzled Darwin that goes over it of muslin."

"Tarlatan, dear."

"Well, tarlatan, if that's the name of the stuff. Hang it! all I know is that you are a regular scarecrow in it—"

"Oh, Arthur!"

"And a pretty laughing-stock you'll be to these Americans," he concluded.

"You know I have only thirty pounds for my allowance, and that my maid's wages come out of that," she remonstrated. " You don't know what it costs to dress like an American. Bijou Brown told me only yesterday that she gets a hundred and all her worst bills paid, and no question of a maid, and lots of presents."

" Why don't you send Parsons packing, and do your own hair and all that, like the American girls ?"

" Do my own hair ? I never could. I haven't the least idea how to go about it."

" Then you are a great stupid, that's all," remarked Mr. Heathcote, with all a brother's talent for making himself agreeable.

" Perhaps, if it is so bad, I had best stay at home," Ethel said to her aunt. " I can see that Arthur is ashamed of me and considers me a fright."

" Nonsense, my dear. Don't mind him ; and" (lowering her voice) " don't mind Mrs. Sykes either. An English lady does not *wish* to look as though she had just stepped out of a fashion-plate. I consider that Mrs. Sykes has lived too long on the Continent to be a judge of such matters. It is all very well for tradespeople and parvenues to lay such stress upon apparel, but you can afford to dress as you please, within certain limits. I have always thought myself that French costumes look best on French actresses. It is no ambition of mine to see my niece enter such lists. Really, my love, you look unusually well this afternoon; and though Mrs. Sykes evidently thinks me dreadfully old-fashioned, my own idea is very different. It seemed to me that this top looked a little *fast* looped up like this. I should have preferred to have it plainer; only Parsons was so set about it that I yielded."

The " nut-shell" proved to be a charming little villa

set in well-kept grounds, gay with flowers and striped awnings, and having more than its share of veranda, wide, steep-roofed, and invitingly cool. There was the usual *entourage* of such places,—a windmill, a tennis-court, hammocks, benches on which lay books not over-wise, and a merry, unpretentious little fountain that plashed pleasantly all the summer long on a remarkably small capital in the way of water, thanks to the engineering skill of a certain officer who had diverted himself and a small stream at the same time, devised pumps, laid down pipes, and spent a good deal of time and money proving that "anybody can have a fountain at a trifling outlay."

Across the front lawn, sloping graciously toward a westering sun, came Mrs. De Witt when she heard the carriages stop at the gate, looking almost as nice as she was in the coolest, freshest of white dresses, and having the warmest welcome for her guests, whom she received in her own gay and gracious fashion. She was merely eager to meet them as promptly and cordially as possible; but Mrs. Sykes at once set the little attention down as a recognition of her superior rank, and was hardly out of the phaeton before she fell to patronizing the place and its mistress as affably as possible, in a way that set Miss Noel's teeth on edge.

"Quite a pretty place you have got here,—quite a pretty place, though dreadfully out of the way. And a nice lawn,—the best bit of turf I have seen since I landed. Yes, really; I am sincere. I think it would be thought a nice lawn at home. *Quite* English."

"Oh, we shouldn't dream of having English turf over here," said Mrs. De Witt, in her very clear treble. "We

know our place better. We can only offer you a little
sparse and defective American verdure here and there
that dies away in a green and yellow melancholy later
in the season."

"And what shrubs have you got there? I never saw
them before. When they are grown they may prove
quite ornamental, though I don't think them well
grouped, I must say. You want to open out the view,
not shut it in; and there should be more variety of
tint in the plantations over there. What are those
rather thinnish bushes with long, glossy leaves?"

"Mere native shrubs. I forget the name. Not worthy
of your notice, I assure you. As common as possible,"
replied Jenny. "Dear Miss Noel, I am so pleased that
you should take all this trouble to come to us. Ah!
here comes my husband, Sir Robert,—Colonel De Witt,
—the only colonel in America, as you will soon find."

She then presented him to each of them more particularly, for, though he had called upon them, they had
not met, and as they sauntered back to the house even
Mr. Heathcote admitted to himself that his successful
rival was a remarkably handsome man, of polished
manners. He had been accustomed to think of him as
"a Yankee chap," and he was prejudiced against Yankees. He had met a good many florid specimens of the
race on the Continent, whom he chose to consider typi-
cal Americans, and of whom he was disposed to say,
with Jaques, "God be with you! Let's meet as seldom
as we can."

As they approached the veranda they got clearer and
clearer views of a party of five ladies and six gentlemen
assembled there. On their arrival, more introductions

followed, after which Mrs. De Witt carried the English ladies off up-stairs to lay aside their wraps. Even in her hasty transit through the house Mrs. Sykes had time to observe through open doors certain effects of portières, family portraits, bric-à-brac, and what not, that were reassuring, and to see that the villa was a gem of a place, small but perfect, having about it not only an air of great refinement, but a stamp of originality. It was irregular, to be sure, to be shown up-stairs by her hostess; but "*autre pays autre mœurs.*" She was less sure of her ground, somehow, and mitigated her condescensions considerably. She prepared to make herself agreeable according to her best lights, and, on their return to the veranda, took the easiest of the easy-chairs and voluntarily renewed her acquaintance with Mrs. Hitchcock, who was of the party. That lady, however, almost immediately made some excuse, and slipped away to another seat.

"That woman has a perfect detestation to me," thought Mrs. Sykes. "I suppose that insignificant little man of the same name is her husband, and that it is they who have brought the duke. These De Witts must be people of more consideration than I had thought. The men seem *du monde*, and the women too, which is a better criterion. And a bishop of something, too,—not that colonial bishops amount to much. Still—" Here her reflections were cut short by the prelate in question, a divine of much port and presence, in whose creed turtle-soup and moselle counted for two of the Thirty-Nine Articles, and whose broad person savored far more of New York or London than of the New Jerusalem. The bishop took the seat vacated by Mrs.

Hitchcock, put his finger-tips together easily in semi-clerical fashion, and diffused bland remarks in a fat voice that issued from the back of a thick throat made up of three tiers of chins. He spoke of England as "the nursing-mother, under Providence, of the Church," and described his visits to his "brothers of London and York." He really liked England, went there as often as he could, had no objection whatever to being called "my lord," and always got into his apron and knicker-bockers the day he landed in Liverpool. He was quite lionized there, and felt that he presented a pleasing contrast to other American bishops of inferior social gifts. Indeed, he once explained the difference between himself and a gaunt, careworn territorial missionary, whose lawn sleeves were utterly destitute of worldly starch, and who cut a sorry figure at a certain general council, by whispering impressively to the nearest English prelate, "Converted from the Methodists!" "Ah! I see," said his lordship.

As for Mrs. Sykes, she talked away in her most animated strain on a great variety of topics, and, being a clever, a widely-travelled, and a well-read woman, made a very pleasant impression for some time,—indeed, until she began to show the cloven foot which it was simply impossible for her long to conceal.

"You consider yourselves to have some sort of connection with the Establishment, do you not?" she said.

"Friendly relations, but no entangling alliance. You recognize the quotation, of course. It is our religious no less than our political policy," the bishop replied.

A sharp course of cross-questioning ensued as to the organization, position, and influence of the Episcopal

Church in America. Mrs. Sykes was surprised to find that the Church did not boast a single archbishop. The bishop as good as promised her one before another decade, and signified that New York would be the see to furnish him.

"You'd like to be chosen, wouldn't you? You would be a very good man for it," said she.

The bishop blushed with gratification at finding such appreciation, though it was disconcerting to hear a private conviction publicly expressed. Mrs. Sykes was a delightful woman. He disclaimed the honor, of course. "New York is not my diocese, you know," he said.

"Never mind. Perhaps you'll get it all the same by some fluke," said Mrs. Sykes encouragingly, and then pursued her inquiries. Having grasped the idea that the Church had no subsidies from the government, no tithes, nothing, she went into practical considerations, and wound up by asking the bishop point-blank what his salary was, and how he managed to "screw" it out of the faithful.

The bishop was annoyed. He mentioned the sum collected, but was silent as to the manner of collection.

"Why, that's less than the cook at the 'Reform' gets!" cried Mrs. Sykes, on hearing it. The bishop was disgusted. Mrs. Sykes was odiously gross now. Happily, a musical bell tinkled in the hall at this juncture, and he was spared the necessity for a reply, for this meant that tea was about to be served, and a gentleman from Boston, who had been talking to Sir Robert, came forward and offered Mrs. Sykes his arm, Mr. Porter by name,—a cool, severe-looking man, a kind of abstract of the exact sciences, with weak eyes and a trick of

looking beyond the person with whom he conversed, at
some fixed point, real or imaginary. There were women
—rather foolish ones, be it said—who would sooner
have been shot from a cannon, like the Barnum prodigy,
than to have endured a prolonged *téte-à-téte* with him,
and men of some intellectual pretensions and even
achievements who would have shrunk from it as an
ordeal, for Mr. Porter was a kind of reagent, which,
applied to vanity, affectation, pretentious ignorance, or
charlatanism, exposed them mercilessly. But he and
Sir Robert got on common ground at once and had a
delightful talk. They began with the bird-fauna of the
United States, and the occasional additions made to it
from Mexico, Central America, and the West Indies,
and from this went on to ornithology in general, geology, botany, the Mauvaises Terres, the Dismal Swamp,
the Great Cañons and Salt Lake, the Mississippi River,
valley, and delta, the Yosemite regions, the oil-wells of
Pennsylvania, and so on. Then followed a discussion
of the Quakers, the Shakers, the various communistic
societies established from time to time in the country,
the Mormons, the Penitents of New Mexico. Finally,
they had an argument as to whether the religion of the
American Indians was or was not a pure theism, bringing out a few legends and other specimens from Mr.
Porter's mine of information about the aboriginal tribes
which especially charmed Sir Robert, who asked permission to make a note of what had been said, and
began with an important entry to the effect that "pol-
lywog was the Indian name for tadpole." He also put
down "a curious and most poetical belief that the rainbow is the heaven of the flowers," and "a remarkable

prejudice of the Cherokee women against hair on the face of their warriors, which it is their practice to pluck out as fast as it appears, in order, as George Eliot said, to keep it 'distinctly human.' Extremes meet here, certainly." There was another note, for which Mr. Porter was not responsible. It was this: "The houses of the early settlers in America were built of rude logs, to which long, thin boards were nailed, which, doubtless from the haste in which such buildings were constructed, came to be called *clap-boards*, being clapped on without loss of time by the natives, impatient to secure shelter as soon as possible."

It had not escaped Sir Robert all this time that Mr. Porter had high cheek-bones, a tall, lithe figure, and a delicate, aquiline nose. Could this be a national type? Was it the beginning of a reversion to the aboriginal model? He put some questions. Mr. Porter acknowledged that he often felt himself disagreeably cramped by the artificial restraints of a high state of civilization, and irresistibly impelled to throw them off; he confessed to a fondness for bright colors; he was never happier than when shooting or fishing in the Adirondacks. There seemed to be something of a case for Stimson, and Sir Robert's eye brightened. But here Mr. Porter's savage impulses ended, and further inquiry elicited the fact that his mother was Scotch, and that he only represented the second generation born in this country, his grandfather having been an Englishman, so that it was too soon for him to have "reverted" to any extent to the Choctaw or Tonkaway type as a result of climatic conditions. Nor did the physique of the other men present shed any light on these interesting problems.

*m*

Colonel De Witt looked more like an Italian than any-thing else, though he came of an old family, as American families go. The bishop might have been English, Danish, Swedish, German,—anything that was fair, ruddy, ample. As for Mr. Hitchcock, he was as nearly featureless as possible, a sort of pasty nonentity phys-ically, though a magnate financially. But Sir Robert reflected that it was too soon to generalize and reach conclusions. Great patience in collecting data, and elasticity in applying them so that a given result (determined beforehand?) may be reached, are the two indispensable essentials of scientific investigation. He would be patient.

The two young Englishmen had all this time been amusing themselves admirably, sitting metaphorically at the feet of Beauty in the persons of three attractive girls,—Edith Bascome, of Baltimore, the youngest and prettiest member of a family that had been producing belles and beauties for quite a century, and two sisters, the Parker girls, from Philadelphia, as unlike as possible, one being tall and as fair as Faust's Marguerite before the footlights, the other a midget of a woman, of a dark, striking, handkerchief-box type of loveliness, dressed in a sheeny stuff of old gold, with a great bunch of Jacque-minots at her round little waist. Mrs. De Witt glanced at them more than once, pleased by their good looks, smiles, and vivacious nothings, more especially by the familiar air of the two men, handsome and high-bred, whose every word and look, attitudes and platitudes, brought back a long train of associations,—the amuse-ments, impressions, and dormant recollections generally of her own life in England.

" What an air of *education* English legs have, to be
sure !" she mused. " Walking or dancing, standing or
sitting, they seem always to be playing a part rather
than executing a natural and involuntary function.
There is something studied about every one of Mr. Ramsay's incomparable attitudes, graceful and easy as they
are, yet he can hardly have acquired them of some
Turveydrop,—the lazy grace with which he has just
wiped his face and tucked his handkerchief in the front
of his waistcoat, for instance. What is that he is saying about his brother Bill ? I didn't catch it, but
nothing flattering, I am sure, from the queer expression
of the girls. Something about his 'nasty temper' and
its being impossible for his wife to live with him.
Certainly the English have less reason to dread the
awful day when the secrets of all hearts shall be revealed than any other people, for everybody will have
heard theirs, with the fullest particulars, beforehand.
I wonder if Mr. Heathcote admires Edith ?"

Edith was Mrs. De Witt's cousin, and it was a dis-
puted point in the family whether Edith or Jenny had
given the more perfect expression to the well-knowr
Bascome features, complexion, and hair.

" I was told before I left home that I had better ' ab
squatulate' Baltimore if I wanted to preserve my peace
of mind, as it had two American institutions in perfec·
tion,—pretty women and canvas-back ducks,—and it was
' a tarnation deal' easier to go there than to get away
again," Mr. Heathcote was saying to Miss Bascome
" But, no matter if I am 'flabbergasted,' as you say
over here, I am going all the same. I met a fellow in
Paris last winter who was from there and made me

promise I'd come. He's a kind of 'top-boss' there, I fancy, and promised to do me the honors."

"Couldn't we skedaddle over there together some time or other?" asked Mr. Ramsay, anxious to show that he also had a certain command of American idioms. "Bill was there when he came over here, and said it wasn't half bad fun."

"Do come," said Miss Bascome. "I really think you will amuse yourselves for a little while famously. Why not go there at once from here?"

Mr. Heathcote instinctively grew cautious. "I can't do that. In fact, it is altogether uncertain whether I go at all," he said.

"I shall not be there; but mamma and papa and the boys are at home, and they will be delighted to receive you and put you up at the club, and all that. And everybody will be as nice as can be to you. Englishmen, when they are nice, are very well received there," she hospitably urged.

"Thank you for the implied compliment. I didn't know before that I was nice. I would rather go there when—when you are at home, Miss Bascome," said Mr. Heathcote, rather *sotto voce* and feeling that he was committing himself quite seriously. He had been much struck by a certain resemblance, and had been comparing the cousins privately all the afternoon to see how far it went. Something of the same freshness and spontaneity of manner there was, but he was not yet ready to admit that anybody could be as charming as Jenny Meredith, as he always called Mrs. De Witt in his own mind. Edith had not Mrs. De Witt's brilliancy and quick sympathies and rare fibre of soul; but

she had a charm of her own. She was a thoroughly
refined girl, a sufficiently intelligent one, more conscientious and practical than most of her ugly contempo-
raries in all that appertained to her *métier de femme,* and
distractingly pretty. Now, Mr. Heathcote was accustomed to girls who looked more or less agitated when
he approached or accosted them, much more paid them
compliments, but no faintest trace of consciousness or
gratification was visible in Edith's face. She neither
blushed and looked down nor smiled and looked up over
this compromising declaration, or any other of the
speeches that Mr. Heathcote hazarded during the evening. She apparently regarded him as indifferently as
though he had been his own grandfather, and said carelessly, "Very well. I shall not be back for a month;
but if you chance to come then I'll take you about and
present you to all the prettiest girls in the place and
do what I can to make it a pleasant visit."

She was not intending to monopolize him, then, as
some girls had tried to do before now, and she was willing to introduce him to any number of possible rivals,
—unlike a certain young woman who had told him
only a fortnight before, at a Brighton ball, that "she
never introduced eligible men to other girls, not even
her dearest friend,—as she was not going to lose a lot
of dances, and perhaps a chance of settling herself for
life, when it could easily be avoided by a little management and judicious fibbing." He knew that a nice
English girl would never have said such a thing, and
had been disgusted; but he also knew that, grossly or
adroitly, he had been flattered, followed, and angled for
ever since he attained his majority, and remembered

with a feeling of relief that the relations between the sexes were said to be entirely different in America. He did not know what they were, but it would be pleasant to find out, to lay aside the social strait-waistcoat that had bored him so of late and forget that the matrimonial net was spread for his feet. "I shall certainly come,— in about a month," he said, and then, from force of habit, added, "But it will not suit my book at all to stay long."

"You will bring your sister, of course," said Edith.

"Oh, no; not at all. Why should I?" said he.

"Why shouldn't you, pray? Wouldn't she like it?"

"I dare say. She's always as pleased as Punch to be taken about by me; but it is a bother having women around."

"A bother, indeed! You should feel it an honor to have a sister to protect and care for and make happy in every way possible," concluded Edith, in a tone of decided disapproval.

This was a new gospel, and Mr. Heathcote received it in silence. He had eight sisters,—quite enough to protect him, he thought. He was by no means madly devoted to any of them, but was least indifferent to Ethel. As to making them happy, such an idea had never been so much as suggested to him before. On the contrary, it had been the mission of the girls to make him happy; at least they had been trained to give up to him and submit to him in everything. "I have dozens of them,—a whole covey. If I did that, I should never do anything else," he said, after a moment.

"Very well. What of that? You couldn't be better employed. It would be as good for you as for them," said Edith severely. "And that's what men are for. They were not put in the world to amuse and gratify and pamper themselves from morning till night."

"I expect—that is, a fellow expects to deny himself lots of things and give in and philander around his *wife*, Miss Bascome,—that is, if he ever marries," replied Mr. Heathcote, making the remark as much of an impersonal and abstract aphorism as possible. "But a sister, now, is a different thing."

"Do you think so? I don't agree with you at all. And I am sorry for the wife. Bad brothers are not apt to develop in a few weeks into good husbands. For my part, I wouldn't marry any man, not if I loved him with all my heart, that was unkind to his mother and sisters. I wouldn't be such a fool as to suppose that I could transform him into a devoted husband."

Mr. Heathcote stared. Her decision of tone and manner amused him, as did the didactic tone of her remarks. The plump way in which she brought out the "not if I loved him with all my heart," and that round, unvarnished "fool," was very novel. An English girl of her class would have blushingly said something about "liking" the man in question, and avoided the last expression altogether as unladylike. He was interested.

"Then you expect to get a devoted husband?" he said.

"I hope to," said Edith honestly, "when—if—" And now at last came her blush,—the dearest little blush that ever rose to a girl's cheek and vanished again.

Mr. Ramsay all this time had been rattling away in the most cheerful manner to the Parkers, who put in an animated "Is *that* so?" or "How perfectly lovely!"

or " What an awful shame !" as the circumstances do
manded.   For the last five minutes he had been talking
to them of London slang.

Edith had caught a " Tell us some more, do," from
the youngest Miss Parker, who now broke in with,
" It's just too funny for anything, Edith.   A ' tizzy' is a
sixpence, and a ' bobby' is a shilling,—twenty-five cents
of our money,—and a ' pony' is a hundred dollars."

The two gentlemen laughed.

" No, no ; a ' bob.'   A 'bobby'. is a policeman," explained Mr. Ramsay.   And all the party being at the
age when it is possible to laugh at everything or
nothing, availed themselves merrily of the privilege.

This was the only information imparted ; and the
conversations were not at all like the one Sir Robert
was having with Mr. Porter, a few feet off; neither
were there any *bon mots, jeux d'esprit,* or witticisms of
any kind ; yet every member of the quintette had
found it extremely pleasant and amusing.

Ethel had fallen to the lot of a certain young lawyer
of the self-confident, aggressive type spoken of by
many persons as " a smart man," and reputed to have
" a great flow of language."   Fluent he was, in a showy,
superficial sort of way ; but his talk was all machine-
made, and only " flowed" on the coffee-mill principle,
as he ground out the same thing over and over again
at successive entertainments, without often finding so
good a listener as Miss Heathcote.   An interest he had
for her that he little suspected.   He fancied that he
was captivating her by the play of his mind.   The real
truth was that he sported a " goatee," the first that she
had ever seen, and she found a sort of fascination for a

while in watching the singular tuft as it rose and fell
with each phrase or smile: indeed, so absorbed was she
in the contemplation of this unique hirsute adornment
that once or twice she quite forgot to make a proper
response to what he was saying. His manner struck
her as familiar, audacious, "shoppy :" it was smart, and
had none of the deference that need not be spoken but
should always be felt. He asked Ethel how she liked
America, and, on her saying, "It is all different to
England, but has been very diverting so far," exclaimed,
"'Different'! I should rather hope it was," and then
went on to express an intense dislike for her native
country and all its institutions, founded upon a brief
tour in it taken the year before. The hotels, people,
manners, and customs had all alike failed to please him.
The royal family were imbecile all the way through ;
the prince would never come to the throne; the aristocracy was doomed; London society was the most
corrupt in the world. All this knowledge, and much
more, he had gained in a two weeks' residence at the
"Langham." He had never been able to get a glass of
iced water outside of that institution. The climate
was the worst on earth. The House of Lords dropped
its *h*'s habitually, and the Earl of—he couldn't remember the title—had said that "It wasn't the 'unting that
'urt the 'orses, but the 'ammer, 'ammer, 'ammer on the
'ard 'ighroad."

Ethel listened indignantly to all this intelligent criticism, and even when his uproarious laughter died away
she could find no words in which to confute it. The
largeness of the statements and the invincibility of the
ignorance confounded her. She was still trying to give

some adequate expression to her excited feelings, when he, noticing and rather enjoying her chagrin, had the fine tact to add, "You are very wise to come over here. Perhaps one of our Yankee boys will take a fancy to you, and then you'll be all right. America is the only country that is fit to live in."

"An English gentleman dropping his *h*'s! You don't know anything about England; and I wouldn't marry a Yankee, not if—" she began warmly.

But at that moment Colonel De Witt came up, and laughingly said, "Don't be rash, Miss Heathcote. Here is the most charming young fellow, a 'Yankee' officer, waiting to take you inside, and perhaps ultimately to the altar."

The lawyer rose. "Take this chair near Miss Ethel: I am going," he said to the gentleman who now joined Colonel De Witt.

"Odious creature! The idea of his daring to call me 'Miss Ethel,' when I never saw him before!" thought Ethel, more angry than ever.

"I've made her furious," the offender said to Colonel De Witt, as they walked off. "They can't bear to be told about their *h*'s. But she needn't talk. She says 'at tome' and ''otel' herself."

Colonel De Witt felt annoyed. By an unlucky chance the lawyer had dropped in on them that afternoon: he had not been invited. "They give to 'hotel,' as to the word 'trait,' its original French pronunciation," he said.

"Oh, pshaw! They don't know how to speak their own language," the lawyer replied, with conviction. "In some parts they didn't understand me at all at first."

Miss Noel had been placed between the bishop's wife and another dignitary, a major-general in the regular army, of commanding presence and much social prestige. This officer sat bolt upright in an uncompromisingly straight-backed chair, and talked in short, staccato sentences in a huffy, bluffy, chuffy way which suited him, somehow, as a *vieux moustache.* His body had always the air of being on drill, while his legs seemed always on furlough. He turned his whole body when he wanted to look to the right or left, but his legs he continually twisted and untwisted about the rounds of his chair like clumsy creepers, or shot them out suddenly in front of him, to withdraw them as suddenly.

Miss Noel recognized the *tenue militaire,* although he was not in uniform, and asked the general if he had seen much foreign service "in Mexico and South America and about there;" deplored "the sad struggle between the Northern and Southern Americans, whose wounds she feared were hardly yet healed;" and rejoiced that slavery was done away with forever.

"It is more than I am," said the general, whose turn of mind was pessimistic. "I'd put every one of them back to-morrow if I could. It is the only system for them. My son has an orange-plantation in Florida that ought to have yielded him seven thousand this year, and he didn't get seven hundred. And why? Stolen! Stolen by those miserable darkies down there. Don't talk to me of the future of that race. They've got no future,—unless you call the almshouse and the penitentiary one."

"Dear me! How very dreadful! Can't the govern-

ment restrain such lawlessness in some way? Has
their moral sense been appealed to?"

"Moral sense? Moral fiddlesticks!" said the general.
"Excuse my warmth. You might as well appeal to a
leopard and ask him to change his spots. I'd like to
tie every one of them up by the thumbs for a week.
The country is topsy-turvy, and has been ever since
the Fourteenth Amendment passed. There isn't a
servant in it, not even in the army now. We are in
the hands of the Irish; and you know what that is,— .
anarchy at home, disgrace abroad."

"You surprise me," said Miss Noel. "What a state
of affairs!"

"It is all true. Politics are in a pretty state when
you can't pick up a paper without seeing that the Irish
vote must be conciliated and the German vote gained:
it will be the Swedish vote soon, and the Chinese vote,
and the French vote, and the Italian vote,—not the
American vote at all. The only sensible party this
country has ever produced was the Know-Nothing
party. Who ought to rule this country? The people
who were here before all these foreigners poured in,—
the American people, of course, madam. And who
does rule it? The riff-raff of Europe."

Miss Noel listened most attentively, and ejaculated
"Only fancy!" when he had finished.

"And where are the Indians now?" she asked, with
unconscious irony. "I hope they are not giving trouble,
too?"

"Breaking out all the time, on the contrary,—mur-
dering the whites right and left whenever they get a
chance." said the general.

"Is it possible? In what part is that? I had supposed that they were being rapidly civilized."

"Out West," said the general.

"Really! Sir Robert can't know that, surely! That
is where we are going,—the Western part,—the State
of Michigan," said Miss Noel anxiously, visions of being
scalped and tortured and made prisoner running through
her mind.

"Oh, there is no danger there,—none whatever," said
the general reassuringly.

"What do you think would be the best policy to
adopt in dealing with them?" asked Miss Noel.

"Shoot 'em," said the general decisively. "Kill the
last one of 'em, and then we shall have peace, and so
will they, and not until then."

Miss Noel wrote nine letters next morning before
breakfast, and gave in several of them a comical enough
*résumé* of the condition of affairs in America as gleaned
from "an official of wide experience and high rank,"
showing that the country was a prey to factions of
the most ignorant and turbulent kind, that the experiments of freeing the slaves and civilizing the aborigines
had proved utter failures, and prophesying the worst
things.

"They carry the seeds of disunion in their own
bosom," she wrote, "and the late war was only the first
of a long series of struggles more gigantic and terrible
than any the world has yet known, I fear." Congratulations on the British constitution followed, and the
wisdom of being born in the right place, and then the
remark, "The fourteen new amendments to the Constitution seem to be working very badly, and it is to be

hoped may soon be repealed. And the worst of it is
that there seems to be no remedy for all this; for when
I asked the official with whom I was talking (whose
name I reserve, having met him at a private house)
why the government did not take such and such measures, he said bitterly, 'Congress? Is it possible you
expect anything from Congress? Ah, you are a foreigner.' And when I asked if there were not other
tribunals, he said, 'Yes; there was a Supreme Court,
that had falsified election returns and put into office a
President never elected by the people.' Of course with
a corrupt judiciary all is lost."

There was a good deal more talk between Miss Noel
and the bishop's wife, and even the general, with which
we are not immediately concerned, it being high time
to say something about a high tea which has already
been kept waiting too long.

A model meal it was,—not ostentatious, yet elegant,
well cooked, faultlessly served, and bounded at the head
and foot by a host and hostess who could almost have
made pulse and water ambrosial, so perfectly did they
understand the art of entertaining. A seat had been
added for the very superfluous lawyer, Mr. Crosby, who
had not had the breeding to take himself off, and he
was just beginning to grind, when his neighbor, Miss
Noel, looked across the table and saw Mrs. Sykes with
her eye-glass up staring fixedly at the handsome silver
*épergne* before her.

"Dear me!" said that lady alertly. "Can that be a
*crest* that I see?"

"On the *épergne?*" asked Mrs. De Witt. "Yes. My
husband's. An old family piece, that has quite recently

come into our possession through the kindness of a friend, who, strange to say, found it at a jeweller's in Charleston, and rescued it just in time to prevent its being melted down and converted into teaspoons."

"An *old* piece, you say? How very extraordinary! I thought Americans had no grandfathers," said Mrs. Sykes, restoring her glass to its place, her brows still keeping the arch of surprise.

Mrs. De Witt flushed, and was about to retaliate, but, remembering that she was in her own house, stopped. She caught Miss Noel's uneasy look, and felt repaid for her self-control.

"Unlike the Smiths," she said, "who, according to their delightful representative, 'invariably sealed their letters with their thumbs,' we have arms; but I know better than to sport a crest, as if I were a peeress in my own right, or a reigning princess, and my husband, as far as I can see, uses his nose, but he is so painfully near-sighted that I am never sure what he is about."

"We don't want any crests and idiotic stuff of that kind in this country. We have done with all that nonsense," said Mr. Crosby, sweeping away paltry distinctions with his right hand. "We don't care a cent what a man is; we aim to be free and equal. We have got no aristocracy over here, thank heaven, and never will have."

"Ah!" said the duke. "Do I understand you correctly? Your position is that of absolute political and social equality? You visit your butcher and baker, then, and sit at table with your servants? Logical, but scarcely agreeable, I should fancy."

"Nothing of the sort," snapped Mr. Crosby angrily.

" I never sat down to a meal with a servant in my life,
any more than you have."

" I beg your pardon.  I did not mean to be discour-
teous, but the fact is that, to be consistent, that is what
you ought to do.   You hold yourself aloof on the
ground of his being the inferior and you the superior.
There you have a distinction at once.   You republicans
all want to level up, but not to level down.   It has
often struck me forcibly that the one thing Americans
do want is distinctions, if they would be honest enough
to confess it.   They are determined to do and be everything; they are out-and-out the most ambitious people
I have ever known.   It is laudable ambition for the
most part, but has lately found less honorable expression in the genealogical and heraldic craze, with its
attendant search for distinguished ancestors, family
portraits, spindle-legged furniture, and heirlooms generally.   I am a good deal in America, as you know, and
have amused myself by observing its growth.   When
I first used to visit here, I could count on the fingers
of one hand the carriages having any heraldic device;
and now every other trap one sees has a regular soup-
plate of an affair on the panel that would do for the
Guelphs and Habsburghs, only that they very likely
would prefer a quiet brougham with perhaps not so
much as a monogram on it.   I take it that those of you
who are really entitled to bear arms—and the number
is greater than you think—have either let them fall
into disuse or used them under protest intermittently,
and taken up an apologetic attitude toward the American people for having unwittingly been born gentlemen.
And now a whole lot of cads, that have no more right

to a coat of arms than I have to the mitre of my friend the bishop here or the gown of the chief justice, have coolly manufactured out of whole cloth the most ridiculous insignia that were ever seen, aided and abetted by certain bogus 'heralds' colleges' that do a thriving business, I am told."

"I know of two such," said Colonel De Witt. "And I have heard that the manager of one of them was once an undertaker in San Francisco. It is to be hoped that he lets the dead past of his patrons bury its dead."

There was a laugh, and the duke went on: "I give you my word that I passed by a handsome house in a certain city, not long ago, that had a stone escutcheon carved over the door on which there was nothing but a bar sinister! I could not help it—I roared with laughter! Honest man! he had no more idea that he was proclaiming to the world that he was a bastard than another man would have that he was a bore. And another day I saw a carriage standing in front of a shop, very well set-up, so much so that it attracted my attention, and, if you please, it had on it the Percy arms, with the motto of the Aglonbys,—a north-country family that I know."

"Ah, poor human nature!" sighed the bishop. "Vanity and vexation of spirit."

"Yes, that is it," said the duke. "Human nature will have distinctions of some sort, and titles too. The Quakers, in their effort to get rid of forms, have become rigid formalists, and, in trying not to dress like the world's people, stickle for a particular color or shade and give themselves twice the trouble that their neigh-

I     n          17

bors take. I have no idea that Mr. Crosby there would be mortally offended if he saw his name in the morning papers (as I did another fellow's) as 'Grand Potentate of the Ancient Arabic Order of the Mystic Shrine,' whatever that is. Let me see. I noticed another. Ah, yes! A lady at a ball given by our minister in Wash ington,—'Mrs. Assistant-Fish-Commissioner Robin-son.'"

"The only title that I ever thought entirely satisfactory was that of the Emperor of China,—'Brother of the Sun and Moon, and Grandfather of the Fixed Stars,'" said Mr. Porter.

"That is final: there is no going behind that record, not even in a Presidential canvass; it will bear any amount of scrutiny," said Colonel De Witt.

"Well, as I said before," remarked Mrs. Sykes, "I never knew that there were any grandfathers in America."

The duke turned upon her a look that certainly did not express admiration, and said, "You are out there entirely." Then, addressing himself to Mrs. De Witt, he said, "You have, and have always had, a gentry in this country, men of more or less good birth, antecedents, achievements, refinement. I could mention a number of names at the North and the South that are as well known in this country and as highly thought of as the O'Connor Don in Ireland, the Master of Napier in Scotland, the Howards and Stanleys of England. The only difference I see between England and America is that with us the fact is officially recognized and regulated. It does seem to me that the whirligig of time is revenging the South, which has been so tremendously laughed at for its aristocratic pretensions and 'first families of Virginia' by the North. You must excuse these comments, Mrs. De Witt, as well as my rudeness in monopolizing so much of the conversation. In interests and in heart I am quite half American, and I have made them in that capacity, not at all as a foreigner."

"A foreigner! God bless my soul! I never thought of it before, but I must be one, too, over here," exclaimed Sir Robert. At which there was another laugh, and many kind assurances from his hostess that he was nothing of the sort, as well as a choky speech from the general to the effect that he was a brevet American. Mr. Crosby's batteries were silenced, but he swelled and raged inwardly, and was so curt to Ethel that she turned from him to the general on the other side, and was rewarded by hearing that officer's views on certain ecclesiastical points.

"I hate bigotry; that is what I hate. That is why I can't stand the Roman Catholics and the Episcopalians. I'd like to put a barrel of gunpowder under those two churches and blow them both up," said that apostle of charity. Such moderation was rather alarming to Ethel, who wondered that a man of his rank should be "a Dissenter,"—and a Dissenter the general was, though not in her sense.

The talk ceased to be general, but was very briskly kept up, especially by Mrs. Sykes, who "pumped" Mr. Porter about the De Witts, the bishop, and others searchingly, and was getting very dry answers, when the move was made to return to the drawing-room,—or parlor, as Mrs. De Witt persistently called it, on the ground that "a withdrawing-room" did not match a cottage, and a "parloir" exactly expressed the use to which she put the pretty little apartment in question.

"Some *musique de digestion* is what we want now," said Mrs. De Witt to Mr. Ramsay. "I am told you sing. Do give us something."

He seemed reluctant to comply with the request, and declared that he was "an awful duffer at that kind of thing, and would be sure to make a mess of it," but yielded finally. Mrs. De Witt played the accompaniment to "O Fair Dove! O Fond Dove!" admirably, and Mr. Ramsay, in one of his best attitudes, looked ineffably handsome, and "mourned, and mourned, and mourned," without expressing any grief whatever, or so much as a shade of expression, in a mellow voice of agreeable tone and no cultivation, to the enslavement of all the ladies present, especially the youngest Miss Parker.

Mrs. Sykes was then asked to sing; and, after the usual conventional excuses, and making as much of her condescension in consenting as Patti could have done, she swept over to the piano, took her seat, arranged her skirts elaborately and her music still more elaborately, and favored the company with "Non e ver" in the style of an actor in a certain London burlesque, who repeats three verses of a song and then says, "Ladies and gentlemen, these are the words; you will find the air outside." Lessons a many Mrs. Sykes had had, from Campana, and Trebelli, and heaven knows who. One saw that she had received good training. She took her notes properly, and paid attention to all the "fortes" and "pianos," and died away utterly at "*con sentimento*," but voice she had none, past or present.

Wild applause followed, except from Ethel, who said to
her aunt, "What does she mean by singing *my* song ?"
with that extraordinary proprietorship in a printed
composition which Englishwomen alone claim, and
Mrs. De Witt, out of courtesy, asked for another. This
done, Mrs. De Witt and her cousin played Schubert's
" Les Inséparables" charmingly, and a waltz of Wald-
teufel. Then Ethel's turn came, and, refusing to sing,
she played a sonata of Beethoven very conscientiously;
and then Miss Parker played the zither as if for Titania's
court; and last of all her sister was asked to sing,
having been kept, like good wine, for a farewell bumper.
She might have sung " Au bon Père," for she gave " O
Rest in the Lord !" like an artist or an angel, whichever
you prefer, being a passionately-musical creature, with
a noble voice and the advantage of five years' hard
study abroad. Everybody was charmed, or nearly
everybody.

"Professional, of course," said Mrs. Sykes. "No?
Then going to be. People don't sing in that theatrical,
pronounced style in private life. You will see, she will
go on the stage."

There is no knowing how long the party would have
gone on urging Miss Parker to give them " one more,"
or "just this," but Mrs. Sykes rose and began making
her adieux while it was still early, and would not hear
of staying. So carriages were ordered, and they were
soon rolling away in the darkness, leaving the De Witts
to talk the affair over,—the extraordinary good looks
of Mr. Ramsay, the ducal behavior and that of Mr.
Crosby, Miss Parker's voice, Mrs. Sykes, and even Miss
Noel's overskirt, which Jenny pronounced " delightful,

—as English as Windsor Castle." Its owner she thought
"a high-bred, charming old gentlewoman." Her opinion of Mrs. Sykes was not so favorable.

"She belongs, I can see, to what I call the Crom-
wellian class in England, because they cause the English
name to be dreaded in the remotest parts of the globe,"
she said.

Many other entertainments were given to the party
during the fortnight of their stay in New York, all of
them far more brilliant than the modest one described,
and set down in Mrs. Sykes's letters to her sister as
"fully up to the mark of May Fair." The French
costumes appeared at them, and Mrs. Sykes herself
was as gracious as she knew how to be, and secretly
much impressed. Mrs. Hitchcock and her daughters
showed Ethel and Miss Noel every attention. They
did not call at all upon Mrs. Sykes, finding out that she
was not a relative or even intimate friend, and explaining that she had been rude to them. But that lady did
not stand upon ceremony, and, from motives of purest
curiosity, went to see them one day with Ethel, and
inspected and criticised their handsome house, furniture,
and pictures with all her own *sang froid*.

Of one of the latter she remarked, "That may be
thought good here, but at home we should call it third-
rate,"—and when she left she said to Ethel, "The idea
of an English duke staying in a house with a door-plate
to it, like a veterinary surgeon's or a dressmaker's! If
it had been a foreign title, one could have understood it.
I can't make it out at all."

Several ladies at the hotel called as soon as the party
registered without having any knowledge of them or

pretence for doing so, and with no object in view, as far as they could discover, unless it was to find out "which one the lord was," and what their plans were, and why they had come over. As might have been expected, these did not prove very desirable acquaintances; but one of them, who was very rich, and whose heart was better than her grammar, asked Mrs. Sykes to join a party that she had invited to go some distance up the Hudson. Mrs. Sykes was dubious about it until she found that she would be at no expense, and then was "delighted." She announced to Miss Noel that she was going, and that lady was surprised, but only said,—

"Ah, well! I shall be a good deal absorbed by some friends of my own,—Americans. I met them in Switzerland three years ago, and only think of their coming a distance of two hundred miles to see me! Is it not the friendliest thing possible? And they seem to think nothing of it, I assure you."

Mrs. Sykes took all her prejudices with her, and looked at nothing from a stand-point of good will. She found no resemblance whatever to the Rhine in the Hudson,—which is not an unpardonable sin. She complained of the boat, ridiculed the passengers, patronized her benefactress, and destroyed all that worthy woman's pleasure in the outing by holding her personally responsible for everything that displeased her, or that failed to come up to her standards, or that she thought unsightly,—the hardness of the pillows, the flies, the advertisements posted up, the roads, the dust, the very weather! She made the whole party change their plans to suit her whims, and, when they returned, politely informed her hostess that she was "precious glad

to bo back again, and had had quito enough of rural
America." Sho also atoned for tho loss of dignity sho
had sustained in putting herself under an obligation to
a person whom sho thought her social inferior by taking
no further notice of hor, beyond bowing distantly when
they chanced to meet. Miss Noel told hor that the
Browns had left town for Kalsing, and that her friends
had como and gone as well.

"They were too dear and kind for anything; and,
only fancy, they asked mo and Ethel to spend six
months with them! Did you ever hear of such a
thing?"

All the members of the party had amused themselves
so well in New York that they left it with regret; but
their plans were made, and they never thought of
altering them.

On the day fixed, Sir Robert sent off a packet to his
solicitor, telling him where to address him and asking
him to number his letters, paid the hotel bills, counted
his change methodically, entered the amount expended
in his note-book, and was ready to move. Mr. Ramsay,
who was supposed to have applied himself to and to
have mastered the American system of checking bag-
gage, bought the tickets, and showed Ethel what he
called "the brasses," saying he hoped he wouldn't lose
them, as it would be "confoundedly awkward" if he
did, and there would be "no end of a piece of business
to recover the luggage." Parsons became again a peripatetic mass of parcels. Mrs. Sykes sold her red-satin
gown to the housekeeper for more than sho had given
for it originally, and gave the chambermaid who had
attended her ten cents. Final courtesies— flowers,

books, notes—poured in upon them, and they left for Washington and the West "much pleased with what they had seen of the Northern Americans."

Lest any one should accuse Mrs. Sykes of ingratitude, it should be said that when the duke (who had been barely civil to her, though very nice to the others) called on the morning of departure and wrote down an address for which she had asked him, she was deeply appreciative of the trifling service, and brown-sugared · her voice to any extent in making her acknowledgments.

"Thank you so *very* much," she said. "It will be of the *greatest* use to me ; and I do hope to have the *honor* and *pleasure* of meeting your grace again some day."

To which his grace made no reply whatever.

## IV.

THE most brilliant and attractive of American cities was looking its best when "the allied forces," as the English party laughingly called themselves, invested it. Congress was still in session, pleasure very much at the helm. The numerous parks were lovely with the first vivid flush of green, and already boasted their fairest flowers, the little children just escaped from their winter hot-houses. The streets were gay with throngs of people, even at other hours than those when the Departments give up their employees. Smart carriages rolled smoothly down the wide asphalt avenues by day, containing maids or matrons, richly dressed, poring intently over their social ledgers and day-books in the shape of visiting-lists, making an occasional entry under protest, or scoring off thankfully, almost devoutly, entries already made, as they stopped at first one house and then another and either left the customary heaps of pasteboard or stopped to make a call. And at night the same carriages took half the dear five hundred to meet the other half at innumerable entertainments, and everybody agreed that flesh and blood could not stand the wear and tear of such a life much longer, but continued to go everywhere all the same. The wives of certain officials felt that they at least had stood it as long as mortal woman could, and envied Miss Kilmansegg one of her golden possessions, while counting their "days," that they might apply their hearts unto other matters, if not to wisdom. The soul of the eligible young man sickened at the sight of fresh invitations or the thought of chicken-salad. The heart of the susceptible young lady had been broken over and over again by naval officers, army officers, foreign attachés, and agreeable strangers at large. But, like that thrilling story in which the hero swallows the contents of a vial of arsenic, shoots himself through the head, and then leaps from London Bridge into the river, exclaiming, "The end is not yet!" the season held its own, in spite of all its tragedies, comedies, romances, and sensations of every kind. And, to look on that social surface on whose brow "Time writes no wrinkles," one would have supposed that Moore's millennium had come, and that "not tear nor aching heart could in this world be found."

Mrs. Sykes had opposed stopping in Washington, on the ground that it was "quite unnecessary," as the Capitol, which was "the great card of the place," could be distinctly seen from the train as it moved in. Left to herself, she would certainly have bought the little book of views of the city offered for sale *en route*, transferred them to her diary with a *réchauffé* of the descriptions attached, and gone her way more than content. But she was overruled; and even she found a little that she could admire here and there, in the public buildings, the handsome avenues, and the charmingly individualized houses, that have so entirely the air of having been built for homes, instead of being run up by the block to contractors' orders and then converted into homes.

They put up at the hotel recommended by the De Witts; and next morning Sir Robert, being desirous of making certain inquiries, was told that "Mr. Maffy, at the office," would "post him" about everything. The official to whom he was thus referred proved to be a very pale young gentleman, with a general air of having sat up all night, a rapid utterance, and a perfect willingness to impart all the information desired as to the situation of the post-office and the nearest bank, the hours when the foreign mails closed, and so on. He was so obliging, too, as to add certain supplementary suggestions—"wrinkles," he called them, and certainly "extras," though not charged as such—as to what Sir Robert should do, see, and avoid, not only there, but throughout America. There was no difficulty, either, about finding out where the residence of his minister was, latitude being reckoned from there, instead of from

Greenwich, in Washington,—real-estate agents making their "ad" (*captandum vulgus*) of a house as "in the *immediate* neighborhood of," "twelve blocks north of," or "on a line of cars leading *directly to*, the British Minister's." Affecting spectacle of American respectability sheltering itself under the ægis of St. George!

Having got all this information, Sir Robert posted certain letters and notes, and then said to Mr. Maffy, "Should you think it likely to remain fine? Have you usually good weather at this season?"

"First-rate," replied Mr. Maffy confidently. "Yesterday was a sample of what we get about now. How are your ladies this morning? All right, I hope; but if they are tired, and would like to stay in their rooms, I'll see that their meals are fixed up to suit them and sent up. And if they would like anything to read, I'll send them up something. I've got all Messrs. Bulwer and Dickens's works, and I subscribe for several magazines."

Deathless, unquenchable gallantry was the key-note of Mr. Maffy's character; but Sir Robert did not understand the situation at all, and stared in an evidently perplexed way at the speaker.

"What should they stay shut up in their bedrooms for on a beautiful day like this?" he asked. "If they want anything to read, they can send out and get it in."

With this he took himself off, leaving Mr. Maffy with an impression that he was "not a polite gentleman at all,—probably *jealous*," and carrying away a confused idea that Mr. Maffy was "an impudent fellow," who had meant—he could not say what; whereas the truth was that Mr. Maffy prided himself on being "a polite gentleman," and was not conscious of any social gulf between himself and the people stopping at the hotel that could not be bridged by these small attentions, which he was very much in the habit of showing.

The ladies were much amused when told of the incident, said he must be "a most droll, curious creature," and thought Mr. Maffy was "trying to take them in, perhaps, in some way."

"What do you say to a good, brisk spin?" suggested Sir Robert. "I have not stretched my legs, except to potter about a bit in New York, since I landed, and I am longing to get out in the country again."

It seemed that they all felt the need of a constitutional, and off they tramped accordingly to Georgetown, and far beyond, enjoying their walk as people do with whom walking is not merely the getting over so much ground in a given time at a certain pace, but a fine art. Nothing escaped them. The earth, air, and sky, the rocks, trees, plants, the note of every bird, came in for a share of notice. They botanized a little, and Sir Robert whipped out a trowel that he had brought, and Miss Noel had her pocket-microscope with which to inspect each treasure-trove as he enthusiastically transferred it either to his pockets or, when those began to overflow, to her basket; and both were quite charmed by "the plants of the country." They found a fern just beginning to uncurl its fronds which neither of them had ever seen before, and which awakened an intoxicating hope that they might be "the first to introduce it into England;" a lily something like their own Thames water-lily, and "quite worthy of an English garden;" an anemone which Sir Robert remembered to have seen in Palestine and considered to be the one that eclipsed Solomon in all his glory; "delicious" bits of moss, "fascinating fungi," and delight without end. While Sir Robert was cutting off buds, twigs, leaves, and bits of bark to be inspected and dissected at his leisure, Mrs. Sykes, quite fresh from Murchison and Hugh Miller, was interesting herself in various stones and pebbles which she had observed or picked up. Even Ethel and the two young men, having been trained to use their eyes, found a great deal to enjoy. The scenery was by no means unappreciated, and the ladies did a little sketching,—Miss Noel making two water-color blurs representing nothing whatever to the ordinary eye, and Mrs. Sykes dashing off a very clever and spirited outline of a view that pleased her, to be worked up later. The "spin" was an affair of twelve miles, and they came back to a late luncheon as fresh, to all appearance, as when they started, ravenous, and delighted to have gathered more than thirty plants quite new to them.

They intended to repeat the experience very often. but it proved the only quiet, tranquil episode in their stay, for their letters of introduction, having been presented, met with an immediate and generous response, and they were sucked at once into the social whirlpool, from which it would have required a strong effort of will to release themselves. Invitations of every kind fairly rained upon them, and visitors poured in without end. They dined at the White House,—at least some of them did,—at their own minister's and other ministers', went to parties and receptions at the houses of the Cabinet officers, teas, luncheons, *déjeûners-à-la-four-*

*chette,* Germans, entertainments innumerable, to say
nothing of concerts and lectures and operas. They made
acquaintance with hosts of people, who vied with each
other, it seemed to them, in showing them every kindness and a most lavish hospitality,—people from Maine
and California and Illinois and Cuba and the countries
lying between,—very charming people most of them, and
a few as odd as possible, Washington being a net that
catches every kind of fish, from a whale to a minnow,
and some varieties rarely seen elsewhere. They differed so radically from each other in appearance, manner, voice, and speech, and opened such an extensive
field for observation and comparison, that Sir Robert's
search for a national type became a very serious business indeed, especially as so many other things claimed
his time and attention. A busier baronet was never
seen. He attended the Congressional debates and took
a lively interest in the questions discussed, pronounced
the Senate the most dignified legislative body that he
had ever seen, and the House "an alert, business-like,
practical set of fellows, though not particularly states-
man-like in appearance and behavior." He thought
"the speaking surprisingly good," and compared the
speakers with this and that orator in the French Cham-
ber of Deputies or the Reichstag. He made "thumb-
nail sketches," as he called them, of the more prominent
members, often hitting off a likeness admirably in a
few lines, and a *précis* of the most eloquent speeches,
for the diary, together with an account of the lines
upon which the two great parties were laid down, and
of their leaders. He looked up Indian legends at the
public libraries, and transferred such as pleased him to

the diary. He went all over the Treasury, and informed himself as far as possible about the c rrency,
especially its more interesting features, the c ins now
rare and no longer in use, such as the Continen al paper
money, the pine-tree shillings, the Granby and Carolina
elephant coppers, the golden eagle of 1796.   The national banks and the financial condition of the country
had to be looked into, and the result was recorded in
the diary in facts and figures that would have satisfied
Mr. Gradgrind,—formidable statements that fairly bris-
tled with statistics, tabulated expositions of the im orts,
exports, cotton-, tobacco-, and corn-crops of the United
States for about fifty years, with more than incidental
mention of the war debt, and an argument in favor of
a national floating debt.   He went to the Patent-Office,
and came back with his head one nightmare of screws,
rods, boilers, engines, pistons, patents, to express in the
diary a profound respect for "the amazing inventive
talent of the Americans."   He revelled in the Smithso-
nian, and made an acquaintance that developed into
intimacy with a savant there, "who laid him under a
considerable obligation" (*vide* the diary) by presenting
him, "on the first occasion of meeting," with a fish
from Lake Champlain of a period when it was *à la
mode* for fishes to wear their bones externally, as Aus-
tralian cherries still do their stones.   He made a pilgrimage to Mount Vernon, and the diary glowed with honest
admiration of and veneration for "the great and good
Washington, who had the genius of Napoleon without
his selfish ambition and cruelty."   He went to Arling-
ton also, and proved conclusively in the diary that
"Washington and Lee were really Englishmen once

removed." He carefully measured what Mr. Ramsay called "the chimney they are puttin' up down by the river to *John* Washington," and contrasted it in the diary with other public monuments in various parts of the world. He got histories, maps, geographies, biographies, and went about his American studies with an energy and thoroughness which never relaxed during his stay in the country, and which made him eventually better informed about it than ninety-nine men out of a hundred born in it. Englishmen are apt to be either grossly ignorant of it or to know it in this way. And with all this he returned scrupulously every call made upon him, neglected none of the social duties, and enjoyed its pleasures, dining nightly with judges, professors, admirals, generals, Senators, and personages generally. It is not surprising that he thought Washington "an uncommonly pleasant place," and declared with truth that he "met every day a great number of very interesting and agreeable people."

As for the young people, they amused themselves with equal success, if in quite different ways. Mr. Ramsay achieved his usual immediate popularity. The leader of the German paled before him. If he could have taken himself apart in sections, like a telescope, he could not have accepted half his invitations; and at parties, although he danced badly in spite of the most painstaking attention to his steps, it would have required a wheelbarrow, almost, to carry away the favors he received. Although so remarkably handsome, he was not conceited or spoiled, but so perfectly simple, natural, and human, indeed, that as an ugly man he would have been agreeable, and it was he attracted and

*o* 18*

pleased everybody. Mr. Heathcote was also liked. Instead of keeping up his London habits and sharing the immortality of the famous Hussar regiment, whose officers give beautiful balls and attend them, but only with the distinct understanding that "the Tenth don't dance," let girls sit partnerless and hostesses plead as they will, he suddenly abandoned the Turkish position entirely. He waltzed, and gallopaded, and quadrilled, and would have polked if he could have got a partner. He tried to learn several new dances, and might have been seen twirling away like a West Point cadet until all hours in the morning, when there could be no philanthropic motive whatever for such exertions. Partners were plentiful, and it seemed to him that he was simply being numbered with the fogies by holding aloof; and then the girls were so pretty, and danced so well, and the floor and music were so good!

As for Ethel, whom should she meet at her very first ball but the young officer whom Colonel De Witt had presented to her in New York, Captain Kendall! A fortunate encounter; for, accustomed to the beautiful toilets, bright vivacity, and gracious manners of American girls, the men present were rather disposed to think Ethel "heavy," and to avoid her in consequence. She was certainly very solid in tissue, somewhat stolid and lymphatic in temperament, unbecomingly dressed, and lacking in grace; yet any one looking below the surface could not but have felt the charm of her sincerity and simplicity, would have noted the clear truthfulness of her eyes, the perfection of her complexion, the general refinement of her face, with its regular features, and hair drawn with uncompromising plainness straight back from the temples to be coiled in a low knot. The captain had certainly done so. Her shy and stiff manner had not repelled him, her sensible and thoughtful replies pleased him, he had remembered her with uncommon distinctness, and was more than satisfied to find her in Washington. He devoted himself to her almost exclusively that evening, he called upon her promptly next day, and caused a small commotion by asking thoughtlessly for her alone, though he had the pleasure of seeing Miss Noel as well. He would have taken her to the theatre, also alone, had not Miss Noel, startled by these unusual demonstrations, insisted on her declining; Ethel having rejected the only compromise offered,—namely, that she should "take Parsons along." He sent her very lovely bouquets, and might have made the most decided impression upon a very true heart, had not that always unmanageable, universally troublesome organ chosen to attach itself to Mr. Ramsay, whom she had known from childhood, who called her by her Christian name and was very fond of her in a way, though not at all in the same way, and who was entirely unconscious of the state of her feelings.

Stimulated by Sir Robert's industry, as well as by meeting so many incarnations of American geography in the persons of ladies from the North and South, East and West, Miss Noel got a huge map, which she tacked up on the wall; also a paper of pins. Every time any one called, she would, on finding out where they were from, stick a pin at once in her map, and so gradually got quite an idea of the overwhelming whole. "You can't think what a capital plan it is for one who is dull and hasn't a good memory," she said. "The names of the places are so very odd, and the distances so great, that I should never be able to master the subject abstractly. But this plan answers nicely, and impresses localities on my mind quite wonderfully. When some one says, 'I am a Californian,' I think, 'Oh, that is a place I know. That nice, attractive Mrs. Hudson lives there that told me about the vineyards, and the Chinese servants, and the marvellous climate, and fruits, and flowers.' And if another visitor proves to be a Maine —what do you say? not Maniac, I hope,—I immediately say to myself, 'That very superior woman Miss Marlowe was from Maine; and how delightfully she talked of the forests, and the loggers, and the life there!' I shall really get very well up on it in a little while, and in such a pleasant way! I get things a little mixed sometimes, but one must expect that;—yesterday, for instance, when I asked Mrs. Blair if the cotton-fields of Massachusetts were not very beautiful when the bolls were maturing, and she had to tell me that I was talking arrant nonsense; not in those words, though: she was far too polite for that. I am sure I saw the cotton-fields of Massachusetts represented in a panorama once at Bath, called 'America in Sixty Views,' to which I went as a girl with dear mamma. There was a dreadful slave-driver, I remember, carrying a wand with an iron tip heated red-hot, and the blacks all wore orange and red turbans, poor things! But perhaps there has been some great change of climate, owing to the forests having been cut down, and it can no longer be grown there. And you heard Miss Marlowe laughing at me for saying, 'Kansaw,' following the pronunciation of Arkansaw. But still I am learning a great deal every day,— learning how very ignorant I am, for one thing."

" If you consider yourself ignorant, what do you. think of the gross ignorance of the American women?" said Mrs. Sykes. "They know nothing of the natural productions of their own country whatever. Their knowledge of the vegetable world is confined to edibles, and I doubt if they would know those if they saw them growing in the garden. As for the rest, I don't believe they know gorse from heather, or fungus from moss. You know that you have not been able to get any in- formation about the plants you got the other day, ex- cept from Miss Marlowe. Geology they have barely heard of. I haven't met one who knew so much as the order in which the strata succeeded each other from the primitive rocks up to the cretaceous, tertiary, and alluvial formations, or the principal fossils found in them. I doubt if they know granite from chalk. It is really lamentable! They are merely painted, affected, arti- ficial dolls!—that is what they are,—extravagant and idle beyond belief, as far as I can see. I can't make out how they ever got the name of being charming."

Miss Noel conceded that the fair sex in America had " not been trained to love and observe nature," but she stoutly defended them from the other charges, without, however, succeeding in silencing Mrs. Sykes, who had mounted her favorite *cheval de bataille.* According to her, American women were "most disappointing" in every respect. They were all "too pale," "too thin," "too dark," too something, they had no "figgers," they were "forward," and "boisterous," and "vulgar," and "dreadfully overrated." But, such as they were, she "would say *one* thing for them," they were "vastly superior to the men,"—whom she was always asking to account for the fact. She was much vexed with Miss Noel sometimes for not agreeing with her. The truth was that, while Miss Noel regarded everything and everybody in her own kindly fashion, pleased and pleasing, liking and being liked, praising where she could honestly do so, and excusing the faults and defects that she saw for the sake of the virtues and merits that so greatly outweighed them, Mrs. Sykes looked at the new world in which she found herself through what the Duke of Argyll calls "the glass of custom and traditional opinion," a short-sighted, unfortunate substitute for that large vision which sees the traits, peculiarities, habits, customs, manners—in short, the social and political condition—of other nations than one's own through a sympathetic and therefore true medium, and finds, consequently, much that is deserving of admiration and imitation as well as condemnation. Too many English people take these glasses wherever they go, and like them none the less because they can see nothing but England through them, no matter what part of Europe, Asia, or Africa they may·be in. Mrs. Sykes had a pair of uncommon magnifying power. If a thing was "English," it was superlatively excellent. If it was not "English," it was ridiculous and odious. All the inevitable differences between England and America (neither numerous nor striking when certain facts are remembered) she set down as so many instances of hopeless degeneration and perversity. The' Virginians of to-day, who are much more like the English people of two hundred years ago than the present inhabitants of the great little island, might with equal justice reproach the latter with having changed (as they think) for the worse and lost that fine old flavor of rigid conservatism and invincible prejudice which true Britons and Churchmen should always preserve at any cost.

The one thing that Mrs. Sykes did understand and respect in America was its riches. Attentions and courtesies were worse than wasted upon her. So utterly did she misinterpret the meaning of her reception, with all its delicate thoughtfulness and generous hospitality, that she only grew ruder, more patronizing, more insufferable, with every fresh proof of what she chose to regard as her importance, until Miss Noel was thoroughly ashamed of her, and Sir Robert protested that if he had known what sort of woman she was, nothing could have induced him to allow her to join his party. She was not sensitively alive to their disapproval, however, and only felt herself to be making a kind of royal progress through her loyal provinces, receiving the homage that was her due, and dispensing such scant approbation, haughty recognition, or severe blame as became her position and as the circumstances called for. Still, her subjects were sometimes perverse and rebellious, as subjects have been known to be. A good many people came between the wind and her nobility, and nothing was ordered quite to suit her. It is just possible, too, that in spite of her satisfaction with herself, her French dresses, and her Mayfair manners, she was vaguely conscious that she was by no means as popular as the other members of the party. She would have been less popular still if the people who were showing

her, in her capacity of stranger, various attentions could
have heard her saying again and again, "How tremendously we are being run after, to be sure! I was never
so made up to in all my life."

Other outlets for her energies soon presented themselves besides social ones. Miss Noel had one day
wheeled a little table before her, and, with her herbarium outspread on it, was·intently classifying and ar-
ranging a new acquaintance—half pansy, half violet—
which she was loath to crush between two stiff boards,
when the door opened, and Mrs. Sykes burst in upor.
her, looking extremely animated, not to say excited.
"What do you think? Who do you suppose is staying
in this house?" she said. "The most wonderful luck!
You'll never guess, so I may as well tell you at once.
A Mormon elder from Utah! Isn't it delightful? I am
quite wild about it! Such a chance! I shall send him
my card, get up some story about wishing to buy property out there, or something, and ask to see him. I
dare say there will be no trouble about it; and I have
dozens of things to ask him."

"You would not do such a thing, really?" remonstrated
Miss Noel. "You can't mean to have anything to say
to the creature. What would your friends at home say
if they knew it?"

"Oh, they wouldn't mind, at all. Most of them would
quite envy me the opportunity. Besides, it' doesn't
matter much what one does over here: it can't affect
one's position there," Mrs. Sykes replied.

"You will not seek the man, surely?" said Miss Noel,
horrified.

"Oh, won't I, just!" said Mrs. Sykes. "I'll see him

before another twelve hours goes over my head. I may go out there, you know, and he would be very useful to me: so I mean to butter him up one side and down the other beautifully, and play my cards so as to get asked to stay at his house, if possible, and then put down everything I see. I should adore visiting a Mormon family: shouldn't you?"

"I should expect the roof to fall in upon me. Not for any consideration, short of absolute necessity or the clearest demand of duty, would I cross such a threshold," said Miss Noel. "I don't at all like his being here. How did you hear of it?"

Mrs. Sykes made no reply. She would not have minded giving her authority, but she was already absorbed in her prospective interview, and was maturing her method of cross-examination so as to leave nothing unasked that she could wish to know, or that would add to the interest of her diary; not that she adhered fanatically to facts in that voluminous record, but because truth in this case might be far more dramatic than any of her fictions.

Mrs. Sykes had no British reserve, or, indeed, reserve of any kind, and always interrogated everybody promiscuously that she met when she reached a place. She had just learned this interesting piece of information from a housemaid whom she saw gossiping and sniggering in the hall as she pointed out to a sister maid a tall, dark, severe-looking man of the most rigid aspect who was going down-stairs. All that day she thought of scarcely anything else, and she felt that Fortune favored her when, the following morning, as she was leaving the hotel-restaurant, she espied through an open

door the object of her deepest interest, reading the
papers in a small parlor opening into the passage she
was traversing. Without a moment's indecision, she
walked into the room. "Excuse me intruding like this,"
she said briskly. "Here is my card. I am travelling
in America, and I wish to talk with you particularly,
if you are not too much engaged."

The gentleman whom she addressed looked at the
card, and bowed stiffly as he said, in a sepulchral sort
of voice, "Be seated, madam : I am at your service."

"I have heard of you," Mrs. Sykes began, "and I
have been curious to meet you."

The stranger bowed solemnly again and unbent somewhat. He wondered whether his arduous service ir
and devotion to a certain cause were getting abroad.

"I never was more curious than I have been to see
some of your people," Mrs. Sykes went on,—"not even
the Singhalese, who reverse the thing, you know. I
am very much interested in them, I assure you. They
must be quite out of the common,—the life, and all
that."

"If you are making any stay in this country, madam,
you will have every opportunity of making their acquaintance ; and I trust that you will carry back with
you agreeable impressions of the American people,"
replied the stranger, with the national desire to propi-
tiate the foreign critic. "In the course of my missionary labors I have travelled all over this country pretty
much, and I don't think there can be a more beautiful
or prosperous one in the wide world. How do you like
what you have seen ?"

"Oh, it's all very well, I dare say,—very rough and

new, of course, and there has not been time enough to ornament it yet, I suppose. But you were saying your missionary labors took you about a great deal. Have you had much success? Is that what you are doing here? I should think that you would do better in the poorer parts, among more ignorant people; at least I have been informed so," said Mrs. Sykes.

"I have done very well in Washington,—far better than I had thought at all likely. I have secured in a month's stay over two hundred names. It is true that the wealthy do not respond to the call as the earnest of more moderate means, often the poor, do; but still I have no reason to feel discouraged, and I would like to say to you—"

The stranger was interrupted by what he felt to be a rude and frivolous demonstration on the English lady's part. Mrs. Sykes had thrown herself back on the sofa, and she laughed unrestrainedly as he spoke.

"It is no sort of use appealing to *me;* none whatever," she said, and laughed afresh. "What fun it will be to tell them of it at home!" she thought.

"Very well. I never intrude myself upon persons who are prejudiced against the cause. It is useless, and does more harm than good," said the stranger, with dignity.

"Quite so," agreed Mrs. Sykes. "And, now that there is no question of making a ''vert,' I should like to ask you a few questions immensely. I suppose yours is very flourishing society, and gaining in numbers and influence every day?"

"It is, I am glad to say."

"And you don't think it a shame and a scandal to be

running about the country on such an errand ? You feel that you are doing religion a service, eh ?".

"Certainly ; most certainly. How could I think anything else ? How could anybody ?"

"Well, that is a matter of opinion, you know," said Mrs. Sykes. "A good many people disagree with you. You are married, of course ?"

"I am a widower, madam," replied the lugubrious one, much surprised.

"Not much of one, I suppose," said Mrs. Sykes vivaciously. "You will be taking another in that one's place shortly, shall you not? How many have you had ?"

"I lost my all a few months ago. I shall not marry again," affirmed the stranger, with decision, wondering whether the lady before him "could *possibly*—well, exactly—" He did not frame the thought more clearly.

"You don't—you can't mean to say that you have only had *one* wife ?" exclaimed Mrs. Sykes, feeling it impossible that she should be so grossly defrauded.

"Two, madam. Both dead now," sighed the unfortunate husband. "Amiable, excellent women, both of them,—helpmates in the truest sense of the word, but gone now, gone to the better country."

"Only *two ?* Why, I thought you would have had at least a dozen!" expostulated Mrs. Sykes in a most aggrieved voice, deprived of an expected sensation.

"A dozen, madam! May I ask what you mean by such an extraordinary speech ?" demanded the stranger.

"Extraordinary? Not extraordinary at all. Aren't you a Mormon elder,—Elder Stebbins, from Salt Lake, —pray ?" replied Mrs. Sykes, with spirit.

"No, madam. Permit me to inform you that I am nothing of the sort; nothing of the sort, madam. I am the agent of the American Tract Society, madam, and a Presbyterian minister," said the stranger, with heat.

"How very tiresome! How disappointing! Why didn't you say so at once?" exclaimed Mrs. Sykes, indignant as at a deception attempted instead of an impertinence achieved; and, without a word of explanation or apology, she swept out of the room, leaving a highly respectable member of society almost paralyzed by the interview.

Mrs. Sykes's sense of humor was not strong; but when her vexation had worn off at the untoward result of investigations conducted in a perfectly business-like spirit, she related amusingly enough to her companions her late adventure. "To think of my having got hold of a 'meenister' of the Kirk, a dreadful old tombstone of a man, and bored myself like that, and wasted all that time! It is really too provoking, and yet, in a way, laughable," she said.

"I hope you mean to write him a note of apology. He must have been scandalized; and no wonder," suggested Miss Noel. "You owe it to him, really. Pray do it at once."

"Oh, dear, no; I shan't bother about him any more. But how can I get to see the other one? I had rather it seemed accidental, if it can be managed," replied Mrs. Sykes reflectively.

So well did she apply herself to this problem that, aided by Mr. Maffy, she conceived and carried out that very day a plan for seating herself at the same table

19*

with the elder, fell most casually into conversation with
him, and displayed some ingenuity as well as exercised
unusual self-restraint in making her inquiries. But,
alas! she was not the first person who had tried this
little game. The saint, a very commonplace-looking
person, answered politely enough the initial questions
about the climate, scenery, and industries of Utah ; but
when, warming with her subject, Mrs. Sykes fired a
whole group of interrogation-points at him, all bearing
directly upon his most private and personal affairs and
peculiar religious views, the elder quietly informed her
that he made it a point never to gratify gentile curiosity
about his domestic arrangements, and, without further
ceremony, left the room, to her great disgust.

"It doesn't signify in the least," she reported. "I
am going out there, and trust me for finding out all
there is to know. But fancy his impertinence! And
—do you know? it is a curious thing—he spoke with
a Devonshire accent. I meant to ask him about it, only
he took himself off so suddenly."

It was a sensation for the entire party when, later in
the day, the elder sought out Sir Robert and announced
that he had been born on his estate, and had lived there
until he was a lad of twelve, when he ran away to
London and from there had eventually come to America.
Sir Robert with some difficulty recalled him as "old
Widow Pratt's grandchild;" and the elder asked effusively after "the old place" and such people as he remembered. He answered in his turn all the questions
put by the baronet, and offered to do the honors of
Utah should he come there. He also asked who Mrs.
Sykes was, and remarked that she was "a rare one for

pokin' and pryin' into other folks' business; but he was not going 'te-u' give her any satisfaction."

Before leaving, he also expressed a whole political essay in his imperfect fashion. He had given much cogitation to the pros and cons of expatriation, first and last; and, although no longer a British subject, he had enough loyalty left to be offended and perplexed by a rumor that had reached him.

"They tell me, sir, that her majesty has written a book that can be had for fifteen cents," he said, and then, after a moment's reflection, added, "*It was time to leave.*"

On the strength of the tie between them, Sir Robert went so far as to remonstrate with his late tenant on his faith and practice, but quite without effect.

"God bless my soul! I can't get over it. I remember him a curly-headed, rosy-cheeked little beggar, hanging over the fence with his hands full of buttercups. And to think of him now! He is a precious rascal, of course, but I was rather glad to see the fellow, I must confess," said the baronet to Miss Noel.

Mrs. Sykes met the elder in the hall after hearing all this.

"Ah, Stebbins! Is that you?" she said, stopping him promptly and putting up her glass, as if uncertain about so insignificant an identity. "Sir Robert has been telling me of you. Quite a romance, to be sure. Very likely I shall be out in Utah before long, and you may be of service to me in some little ways."

Stebbins shuffled his feet awkwardly and blushed, and then habit, the habit that is second nature, asserted itself. He was no longer a Mormon elder, no longer an

American citizen; ho was just "Stebbins," Widow
Pratt's grandson, "ono of the lower classes," and Mrs.
Sykes was Sir Robert's acquaintanco and equal.

"Very well, mem. Lot me know when you come,"
he muttered, and so shuffled away, uneasy, but subju-
gated by one blow from the lion's paw. Mrs. Sykes's
change of attitude had forced from him the natural,
involuntary tribute that an ex-privato pays to a general
officer when his hand flies to his cap in a military salute
before he has timo to reflect that he is out of the
service.

"The *idea* of my wasting civilities on Stebbins!" said
the victorious Mrs. Sykes, giving an account of the
way she had "sat upon" the elder, "and of his being
so uppish to-day. He'll not presume again, I warrant;
and I'll make use of him."

"Ah, that was before the Mormon conquest," Sir
Robert replied laughingly. "Stebbins may be founding
an aristocracy, or helping to, out in Utah, for all we
know. You should be careful how you offend him.
Curious problem that, the Mormon one, and growing
more serious every day, I hear. Perhaps history will
be talking of the Mormon conquest in earnest some
day. Given unlimited fanaticism and unlimited prosperity, and why not? The government does not seem
able to cope with it at present, from all I can gather.
It strikes me, looking on the surface, that it is a weak
administration; or perhaps the fault lies deeper,—I
think it does myself,—in the republican principles un-
derlying it. I keep my eyes open, I observe for myself,
and several things have struck me. The people seem
to have no respect for the authorities; and that is a

bad sign. Only yesterday I heard his Excellency the President grossly ridiculed by a cabman; and having occasion to get into the tram,—not that I take it if I have three 'blocks,' as they say here, to go, like the Americans, but I was some miles off and late for dinner, —well, in it were two young fellows who were chaffing each other all the way. And one of them said, 'Billy, why don't you get yourself up in style, and wear a diamond pin and a stove-pipe hat and sport a gold-headed cane?' And his friend said, 'What do you take me for? Do you take me for a member of Congress? I wouldn't be found dead in that rig. I am sorry my style doesn't suit you; but I get fifty dollars a month, and I am poor, but honest, instead of coming of rich but respectable parents.' *I understood. Official corruption, you see.* This morning, too, when that negress brought home my washing, she surprised me by asking if I had any influence. 'Influence, my good woman!' I said; 'what do *you* want with influence? Whose influence do you want?' 'I wants infloonce, sah. I wants to get de Patent-Office washin'; dat's what I wants infloonce fur,' she said.

"A remarkable state of affairs, is it not, my dear Augusta? I was talking of it with a member of the Upper House last night at dinner, and he admitted that everything was got by political influence. He seemed a good deal amused, I thought, but still there was the fact. And he granted that the civil service of America was not in an ideal condition. Merit, length of service, and fitness for it count for very little, 1 judge; and the fact that the thousands of government employés in this place alone live with the sword of Damocles suspended above their heads, good, bad, and indifferent, the public servant of three months and thirty years alike, speaks for itself. It is not only that they have no assured future in the shape of pensions and regular promotion, but that they have no present. They can make no plans, they dare not establish themselves in homes that may have to be broken up any day; and they are quite as liable to be dismissed for no fault as for the gravest offence. How such a service manages to get or keep intelligent, conscientious, and faithful servants is a mystery to me. I have learned all this from a good many sources, and, wishing to verify it, asked my host last night, a member of Congress with whom I dined at Waelcker's, whether my information was correct. He admitted reluctantly that it was. A very well informed man, an able man I should say, who would give trouble on the opposition bench, but he did a most extraordinary thing! I was never so taken aback in my life. It was after dinner, and I was waiting for the servant to bring me a light for my cigar, when he positively drew a match across the sole of his boot and offered it to me, saying, 'Here you are. Go ahead.' A thing I should have discharged a footman for, and very embarrassing in a host. He meant nothing by it, I saw, any more than by another thing later, when I asked for a glass of water, and, the butler not hearing, he nodded toward me, and said to the man, ' Give him some water,' in the most cavalier fashion, and went on with his conversation. Just so. As to matches, I see that an American will draw a match anywhere. I do not think his mother's grave would be safe from it."

The dinner-party to which Sir Robert alluded was anything but a tame affair, and, although he did not know it, he himself had somewhat grated upon the sensibilities of his host.

One of the guests, also a member (with a rabid dislike to England), was not long in directing the conversation into international channels, and inevitably odious comparisons were soon drawn,—mildly by the baronet, as if it were not worth while to insist too ardently upon the value, stability, and perfection of English institutions, any more than upon the value of the sun to the earth, strongly by the member, who defended everything American promiscuously, because it was American, with immense spirit,—with so much energy, indeed, that the glasses rattled as if in a San Franciscan earthquake as he brought his fist down on the table with more and more emphasis. A looker-on could not but have been amused to see the two men,— the member burly and pugnacious, his elbows on the table, one sleeve pulled up nervously a little, a clinched hand, doubled up in a way to show nails anything but immaculate, flushed of face, pushing away the plates and glasses, and laying down the law as if it were the gospel and there could be no mistake in his assertions or appeal from his decisions; Sir Robert as cool as the ice that tinkled in his glass, genuinely, not affectedly, indifferent, presenting a politely impassive exterior, and offending far more by saying too little than if he had said too much, while he imperturbably ate and drank, exchanged parenthetic courtesies with his neighbors on the right and left, begged pardon for the momentary inattention, and displayed other advantages besides the physical one of handsome hands with nails as pink and polished as a girl's.

It was not until "that quarrelsome, unpleasant fellow," as Sir Robert mentally dubbed the vehement member, had poured out the last phial of his wrath that discussion or conversation became possible, and then the national colors fell into the hands of "the member of the Upper House," whose reserved and dignified bearing had already contrasted conspicuously with that of his colleague throughout. The Senator had been listening to the member with the intellectual impatience of a clever man who sees a good cause weakened in the defence, and was not sorry to have an opportunity of setting things right. A lawyer of distinction, an authority on international law, thoroughly familiar with English politics, diplomacy, history, with either no temper at all or one that he kept habitually on ice, and an intellect of a high order, highly trained and disciplined, he entered the lists with no fanfaronade whatever, and dropped rather than threw down the glove, as if by accident. There was no direct, intemperate assault now, no apparent partisanship, not so much as an insinuation that could anger. The Senator was not bitter or scornful, wearisome or dictatorial. He did not enter into long expositions or protracted arguments. When Sir Robert spoke, he listened to perfection, intelligently and quietly, interjecting now and then a calm assent to some statement, or a courteous objection, a brief palliative of some damaging fact or explanation of a particular point. And when his own turn came, he gave full and eloquent expression to his views, and handled the subject with the felicity of illustration and apt repartee of a wit, the breadth of a statesman, the ease of a man of the world. The keen, cool, rapier-like play of his mind, so skilful of thrust and parry, so adroit of fence, so swift to see and sure to pierce the weak or unguarded points, and the vigorous and able resistance offered by his opponent, made the conversation a delightful one, and the other men present felt all the interest and fascination of such a contest, and some justifiable pride in their brilliant champion. Did Sir Robert arraign the Indian policy of America before the bar of justice, the Senator had a Roland for his Oliver in the Indian policy of England. Did Sir Robert deprecate the possible annexation of Canada or Mexico by the United States as "unpardonable rapacity," and insist on the moral right of the feeblest State to the preservation of its autonomy and the management of its own affairs, the Senator was able to show that the invariable policy of England had always been to get all she could and keep all she got, and took it for granted that Sir Robert was a Home Ruler. Was it a question of bribery and corruption in American elections, the Senator was ready with extracts from Parliamentary reports and respectable English journals, showing that the "right little, tight little island" was not Arcadia, or Liberals and Conservatives on one side of the water much purer and nobler than Republicans and Democrats on the other. And so on with various issues and questions, until a break of some kind made the talk general again.

This had hardly been done when the member, who was as dull as he was dogmatic, and had not been over-pleased at having the part of principal in the late duel

20

taken out of his hands, brought up what he considered a Krupp, and, *à propos* of nothing, stated that the English had blown five regiments of Sepoys from their guns after the Mutiny. To this Sir Robert deigned no response whatever, but the Senator pared it down to its proper proportions, and the host whisked the company off on a siding by asking if Sir Robert had been to Mount Vernon. Sir Robert had enjoyed, he would not say that pleasure, but that *honor*, and had seen as well the "home of the great Virginian, Lee."

Some one now began speaking of the various Presidents and their administrations; and, Johnson being mentioned, the member expressed an ardent admiration of him, and stated, with the uncalled-for emphasis that characterized any expression of his opinions, that Johnson was the "finest" President the country had ever had, and was as "perfect a gentleman as ever stepped."

Why this particular speech should have annoyed Sir Robert rather than the others, there is no knowing, but it was certainly distasteful to him. "It takes nine tailors to make a man; I don't know how many would be required to make a gentleman," he said, his side-whiskers bristling a little and his mouth drawn down at the corners. "A man of integrity, a man of talent, if you like."

"*An elegant gentleman*, every inch of him," insisted the member, determined not to abate a jot or tittle of the ex-President's aristocratic claim.

"You *carn't* mean to call the fellow a *gentleman!*" said Sir Robert incredulously, laying down his knife and fork and looking at the member.

"As much of a gentleman as you are, or me, or anybody!" shouted the member, and added a past participle that need not be given here, and a most awful thump on the table.

Sir Robert had gone far enough, he thought,—a good deal farther than he had intended, he knew. But he hated to retreat. "Ah! yes, to be sure," he said. "Just as you please. As much of a gentleman as you are, as you say. I yield the point. Here is his very good health," (sipping his sherry). "Is he still alive, by the bye?" (To the Senator), "How completely out of office seems to mean out of sight and mind in the case of Presidents! At least we never hear of them at home afterward. It is oblivion not even tempered by revolution or assassination. You remember that squib in ' Punch' about ' Abdul Aziz and Abdul as was'? When I was in the East—" Sir Robert grew agreeably reminiscent for a while, and so got off the ground that sounded so hollow beneath his feet.

Later in the evening, however, he said to the Senator, "Talking of politicians, who is this Honorable Alfred Hodges, of the State of Oheeo, that I have been reading about in the papers? He seems to be very celebrated over here, though quite unknown to me. Let me see. I think I have got about me a cutting from the morning paper that tells of him." He looked in his pocket-book as he spoke, and produced a paragraph which he read aloud, and which stated that the Honorable Alfred Hodges was "the equal of Clay, Webster, Calhoun, or Crittenden," that he was "a man of matchless eloquence and acute mentality" as well as "adamantine principle," that he was sweeping everything before him in his own "section," and was to be the next candidate for

President, although he abhorred public life and would never have sought any office had he been left in the obscurity so congenial to him, instead of being carried forward struggling by his friends. The Senator listened with a smile. Most Americans have heard these limpid, artless versions of the eternal verities, and he was not startled.

When Sir Robert had restored it to its place, where a good many other choice items were waiting to be embodied in the diary, he dryly said, "The Honorable Alfred, in the first place, is not an Honorable; in the second, he is a local politician of no particular note; in the third, he is advocating with his 'adamantine principles' the repudiation of the State debt. That waiter yonder will be President as soon as he. And as for office, there is not one so mean that he would not cringe to his worst enemy and deceive his best friend to get it, if he could not get a better. His is the old definition— Politics, the art of getting a place; Patriot, a candidate for that place."

"Is that an American saying? If so, universal suffrage has—" began Sir Robert.

"That is Fielding, my dear Sir Robert," replied the Senator, with a bow.

The two men laughed.

"'I owe you one,' as Dr. Ollapod would say. But really, now, a gifted, powerful demagogue like that may do a lot of mischief. A dangerous fellow, I should think, —a great orator, and so unscrupulous," Sir Robert continued.

"He is not at all dangerous, I assure you. And I never heard a more ordinary speaker. A penny

trumpet, believe me, to which no one pays much attention.".

"You surprise me! The newspaper speaks as respectfully of him as though he were a Gladstone or
Beaconsfield," said Sir Robert.

"Ah! yes. Newspapers must be newspapers, you
know. And politics will be politics."

"Well, say what you please about politics, for real
freedom and individual liberty—mark you, I don't say
*license*—there is no place like England," concluded Sir
Robert, with conviction.

Late as it was when he got back to his hotel, he
found a gentleman waiting to see him, in the shape of
a reporter, who had been instructed to "interview" him
and find out whether the rumor that he owned seven
hundred thousand acres in Wyoming, and represented
an English syndicate bent upon buying five million
acres more, was true or not; also his opinion of the
Rugby Colony, its founder, and a dozen other subjects,
germane and foreign to it. "The representative of the
'Columbia Eagle,'" as introduced by himself, was a very
tired and sleepy young man, who had been sitting, pen
cil and book in hand, for more than an hour waiting for
Sir Robert to come in, and who was not unnaturally
anxious to dispatch the business in hand as soon as
possible and recoup himself by a little supper and such
slumber as might follow. Long experience of the crass
dulness and almost inconceivable vanity, garrulity, and
rudeness of the "interviewed" (of which little account
is taken in estimating the crime of the unhappy reporter who earns an honest living by the sweat of his
soul, often) may have had its effect upon the gentleman,

20*

who, with a brief explanation of his mission, said, with brisk, business-like directness, ' I tell you what you want to do. You need not talk at all. You just answer my questions, and I'll fix the rest."

It certainly would have saved a great deal of trouble if the baronet had acted on this suggestion in all simplicity and sincerity. But in all that related to his private affairs Sir Robert was almost as reserved as the Englishman whose servant told an inquiring friend that his master was dead, but did not wish it to be generally known. He abhorred such English papers as were said to have adopted " the American method" and dealt in personalities disguised as " fashionable intelligence."

" To think that a man cannot be the heir to the throne or the Premier of England without being like a beetle under a microscope and having a calcium light cast continually upon his home is bad enough; but when it comes to describing a private gentleman's bedroom and telling the world that he always uses Pears' soap and Turkish towels at his bath, I, for one, will do something more than complain of the insufferable impertinence. I will prosecute to the full extent of the law any one presuming to show me up in the public prints before I have done something to disgrace myself," he would say.

As the owner of a " show place," Sir Robert had his trials, and, in the spirit of the ancestor who had built the beautiful old house in which he lived and had then carved over the entrance, " Walk, knave! what lookst at ?" he had sternly forbidden his servants to admit any one connected with the press, had once discharged the whole staff for disobeying his orders, and had put up a board in his grounds on which was inscribed, instead of the usual warnings to trespassers, "No authors, editors, reporters, or scribblers of any kind admitted here." In the matter of notices he was apt to be a little eccentric, as was witnessed by another version of a prohibition grown so stale that it is seldom heeded :—"Idiot, keep off the grass!" It is hardly remarkable, then, that in a very few minutes after negotiations began the representative of the "Columbia Eagle" was racing down the street with a feverish energy born of much inward heat, and a temper ruffled almost beyond precedent, while Sir Robert was congratulating himself upon "sending that chap off with a flea in his ear."

Mrs. Sykes's exquisite delicacy received a severe shock when she heard of it. "Was there ever anything to equal the impudence of these Yankees?" she asked. "Fancy the clerk of this 'otel trying to introduce to me one of the women stopping here to-day! I sent for him to come up to me in the drawing-room, that I might explain to him about sending off my packets to England, and the other things to go to Canada by parcels express, and having my boxes mended, that have been more injured already than in going round the world. I shall have them thoroughly overhauled—they have needed it for some time—and relined, and all that, and send the bill to the railway company. Yes, a regular introduction: 'Mrs. Arundel Sykes, Mrs. Valentine—Mrs. Valentine, Mrs. Arundel Sykes;' they always give my name in full here. I took no notice of it, of course; but *fancy!*" It will be seen that Mrs. Sykes, with her usual acumen, had found ways of utilizing what might otherwise have been a wasted force,—Mr. Maffy's gallantry.

"I had an idea—I don't know where I got it—that society over here would be organized on a rigidly Puritanic basis of plain living and high thinking, and that I should be citizen Heathcote, as it were," said Sir Robert. "It seems, on the contrary, if not so long established, as well defined as our own, and fully as luxurious and artificial; more ostentatious, I should say. Americans may disclaim caste as much as they please, but what of their cliques shading by remarkably fine degrees from the class of which the duke was speaking at the De Witts', and the highest official class, through the wholesale grocer who will not visit the retail grocer, and the dress-maker who will not know the butcher's wife, down to my friend the 'lady' who has got the Patent-Office washing and objects to being confounded with 'dose low niggers dat warn't raised by de quality,' and that she 'don't have nuffin' to do wid, noway'? I don't say that I understand the system. On the contrary, it is quite a mystery to me; many of the distinctions made seem very arbitrary,—uncommonly fine we should think them; but I see that it exists. As to titles, if they deny them to their own people, they certainly do not to others. I have been more Sir-Roberted here in a few weeks than in the whole previous course of my life. It is tacked to every sentence, almost. I don't like it, especially in public places; but I see that they use it as the French do 'Monsieur,' and not in the least from a snobbish liking for the sound, as English people of a certain class would. Just so. And I can't agree with you in calling them impudent, except that newspaper fellow who wanted to 'interview' me. They evidently respect themselves too much not to respect others. I notice that very much. I keep my eyes as wide open as possible. I wish to form just ideas of the country for myself, instead of taking second-hand, ready-made opinions. Its material civilization has astonished me, and cannot but surprise any European; but its social order, moral progress, and political experiments interest me far more."

"What I most notice and admire in them," said Miss Noel, "is their politeness. It is most striking. I do not now speak of their attentions to us, although those have certainly been such as we could have had no right to expect, but of their treatment of each other. I observe that they ask of each other a thousand little services without any thought of being denied or rebuked, and accord them as a matter of course, not as a favor. It is a very unselfish and charming feature in the national character. I was looking about in the street one day in New York for the nearest pillar-post, and, not seeing one, asked the first passer-by, a workingman, who not only gave me the information civilly, but offered to post the letter himself, which is more than a Parisian *ouvrier* would have done, I am sure. In the tramway, too, I was not only invariably offered a seat, if it proved to be crowded, as a woman of the better class, well dressed, might expect, but I saw with pleasure that when a poor woman with a great basket or little children got in, or out, there was always some one to help her. The general good nature and willingness to oblige seem almost universal. It is not so with us, you must acknowledge. We apologize elaborately before making any demand upon a stranger, and he does not always stop to hear our excuses, much less the request.

'Would you mind?' doing so and so, is one of our formulas for the reason that people generally do mind, and don't relish being called upon to do anything or being put out in any way. I am sorry to say it, but it is quite true. And as for courtesies, you know, Robert, that if you were caught out in the rain at home and some one offered you an umbrella, you would say—what should you say?"

"'Confound the fellow! What does he mean by offering me his umbrella?' most likely," replied Sir Robert laughingly. "You are right, Augusta. We have got a ridiculous amount of buckram about us. But when it is all taken out of us, as it sometimes is by long residence abroad, there seems nothing left but a coarse sieve through which nearly everything has run that makes an English gentleman. And I agree with you about American politeness: it is the genuine thing, and not the French veneer. Have you noticed that in the shops one is treated with civility, but not servility? Many of our tradesmen cringe when they must, and bully when they can, in a way that is disgusting."

"I have found, so far, but one exception to this polite, self-respecting behavior, and that was the other day when I took my umbrella to a little shop in a back street: it was my dear father's, and this is its twenty-sixth new coat. After I had waited some time, a young person in flaunty attire, with her hair in curl-papers at noon, came in and quite shouted from the back of the shop, 'What do you want?' I beckoned to her, and she at last condescended to come forward and hear what I had to say; but she was very crusty and sullen, and would hardly give herself the trouble to look for the stuff I required, but just turned over a few things and said she was out of it. So I told her that she was not likely to succeed as a shopkeeper if she behaved in that way, and she got angry, and said that she wasn't a shopkeeper, she was a 'saleslady, and as good as anybody.' It did no good, of course, and Ethel laughed at me afterward for doing it, but I could not help reading her a little lecture and telling her that rudeness was not republicanism, and that if equality meant anything it meant equal regard for the rights and wishes of others on the part of individuals of every class."

"As you admire everything American," said Mrs. Sykes, "I suppose you noticed the dressing in the train and liked that. Every other woman in a twenty-guinea silk and diamonds. They evidently think of nothing but dress. Even the bishop's wife at the De Witts' was more interested in the fashions of this world, even if they do pass away, than in anything else. But then, to be sure, there are all those daughters of hers,—six of them,—and the bishop with no dean, chapter, curates, or so much as a private chaplain, as far as I can find out, to palm them off upon in return for good livings. Mr. Porter told me all about them, and I asked her after dinner if, as there was so many of them, and all plain, with no private fortune, I understood, their settlement in life did not weigh heavily upon her. But she seemed to have no Belgravian anxieties whatever. She said she never thought of it; that if the Lord intended them to marry he would provide them with husbands,—which even in a clergyman's wife does seem to be presumption. I told her that in England they would not have the ghost of a chance, but that men were more plentiful over here, I knew."

"Why *did* you say that to her?" said Miss Noel. "It is like your putting up your glass and looking at the De Witts' *épergne* as you did. You will give great offence, really."

"Oh, no, I shan't! And it doesn't matter very much if I do. I shall never see any of them again after I leave America," replied Mrs. Sykes calmly. "I have taken good care of *that*. I don't mean to be overrun by them when I go back, as you very likely will be. I have only met two people so far that I cared to keep up with, and to those I have given my proper address. To the others I always give my bankers', and if I am inquired for there I shall instruct them to say that I have gone abroad. They come over now in hordes every year, you know, and if one did not take some such precaution one would *never* be safe. They would be asking themselves down to stay indefinitely at the most inconvenient seasons, and all that." Mrs. Sykes laughed cheerfully over her little *ruse* as she spoke, but Miss Noel flushed with indignation.

"You are very much mistaken if you think that," she said warmly. "Indeed, you mistake them altogether. You do not in the least understand them."

"I don't pretend to understand them, or like them either," retorted Mrs. Sykes.

"And I, if I do not quite understand them yet, like them immensely," insisted Miss Noel. And so the little conversation between them, one of many, ended. Sir Robert had not stayed to hear its conclusion, having an appointment with a friend to listen to an argument in the Supreme Court, where Justice seemed to hold the scales more evenly for wearing a gown, although the connection between them is not always evident, as Mrs. Sykes was proving at that very time. That lady embroiled herself afresh that night at a party to which she went, where she met Sir Robert's friend the Senator. A quiet alcove and a comfortable sofa, or rather sofas, made a pleasant refuge for the non-dancing and flirtatious members of the assembly during the evening, the former being represented at one time by Mrs. Sykes and the Senator, the latter by the *beau* Ramsay and a *belle* Louisianaise. For a while Mrs. Sykes contented herself with affable generalities, to which her companion made courteous if not copious response; but, considering, probably, that there had been quite enough preluding done, she was soon introducing the theme of her heart, her American experiences, and was expressing great disappointment at not having found the magnificent primeval forest that she had expected. "I have seen no really fine, wide-spreading, ornamental timber," she said. "Nothing that can compare with our Warwickshire oaks and Gloucestershire elms, for instance. They tell me here in the North that the British destroyed it, and I dare say at the South they will declare that the Yankees burnt it all down; but my belief is that it never existed."

The Senator gave her one of his cool, quiet glances and took her measure, but only said that the early settlers in America, and their successors, had been very reckless about cutting down fine trees, and added, "We still have a sapling or two, though, that would compare favorably even with English trees, especially in California." The talk then drifted away to the timber **of** other countries for a few minutes; but Mrs. Sykes was soon ready with two questions, unusually fine examples of her powers of interrogation.

"Sir Robert tells me that you are a member of the Upper House; and I should like to ask you whether it is true, as I have heard, that American politicians are sadly lacking in political honesty, and have not very much education,—don't go to universities, and all that, you understand?" she said.

"Perfectly," said the Senator dryly. "Most of them read quite fluently,—English, of course,—and they can all cipher a little, say on the Alabama Claims and such problems. As for honest men, madam, I refer you to Diogenes's experience. If that philosopher were to turn his bull's-eye upon either Parliament or Congress, who shall say what he would find? You surely do not mean to force me personally to reveal the crimes that have disfigured my official career?"

Question second was not to be stayed by sarcasm or badinage. "There is another thing," said Mrs. Sykes. "Why is it that American men are so conspicuously and notoriously inferior to their wives, mothers, and sisters, who are often nice, really? Some of the prettiest and most accomplished women in American society are married to such oafs and clowns!" Mrs. Sykes felt that she had made the most liberal concessions to the Senator's nationality in what she had said, and awaited his response with what she meant for a smile and a look of flattering interest.

"Ah, my dear Mrs. Sykes, there is no explaining such things," said he very suavely. "I don't know why it

is, unless it is that our women can't be equalled. But
come, now, you surely can account for the fact that
Englishmen are notoriously better looking, better
dressed, and better bred than Englishwomen. The
reason must be the same, if we could only get at it.
It is evidently the same law operating differently in
the two countries." The Senator did not really think
all these ungallant things, but he had intuitively understood the Sykes and comprehended that this was a case
in which the bludgeon and not the rapier was required.
He preserved, too, such an air of abstract speculation
that Mrs. Sykes was quite checkmated for once, and
could only mutter gruffly something about "an extraordinary idea."

Five minutes later the Senator had bowed himself
out of the alcove; but Mr. Ramsay, who remained, had
overheard the latter part of the conversation, and repeated it to Mr. Heathcote that night. "Nasty one for
Mrs. Sykes, wasn't it?" he said. "But she deserved it
richly. Why doesn't she keep a civil tongue in her
head? She is always pitching into the Americans, and
I wonder they put up with it."

"She is a scrub," replied Mr. Heathcote. "I have
never liked her. Fetlock somewhere. Think I've
heard the grandfather was a corn-chandler, or something. Awfully good-natured, kind people, these; been
as nice to her as possible. That is the mistake they
have made. If they would 'everlastingly scrouge' her,
as they call it, she would behave herself, and not go
about with her nose in the air, giving two fingers to
people who are as superior to her as possible in real
refinement. We have got a lot of that kind of people

in England, and we understand how to deal with them
They require to be sat upon, *hard.* It isn't a pleasant
thing to do, but it has to be done; and how they do
thrive upon it!"

"I know. I hate 'em," said Mr. Ramsay. "I saw
Mrs. Sykes most beautifully served out, though, the
other day. Neatest thing I ever heard. It was at that
ladies' luncheon at the Rainsfords'. Gorgeous house,
gorgeously furnished, and nice people. I was the only
man asked, you know, and I was in an awful funk for
a while. The ladies of the President's family were
there: the thing was a swell affair given to them. And
when luncheon was ready Mrs. Sykes was standin' near
the door, and she pushed most rudely past everybody
and marched into the dining-room first, saying, 'You've
got no precedence in this country, and I'll just take my
place.' You should have seen Mrs. Rainsford. You
know her? Stunning woman. Looks your hat off, as
some fellow says. Well, she followed her, and said, so
that every one could hear, 'It is quite true. Will you
take a seat somewhere there, *near the foot of the table?*'
I was so disgusted to think she was an English woman
behavin' like that, that I could hardly face it out, and I
gave her a piece of my mind afterward. I told Mrs.
Rainsford, too, what I thought of it, and she said, 'It
*was* very rude, but pray don't feel annoyed about it.
None of us can afford to be responsible for what our
countrymen do. I should have enough to blush for, I
know, if I made a personal thing of all the ill-bred acts
committed by Americans abroad. And, to tell the
truth, I am rather ashamed of myself for taking any
notice of it.' Awfully nice of her, wasn't it?"

Mr. Heathcote agreed, and they had some further talk, in which he asked Mr. Ramsay if he was keeping a bright lookout for his future.

"Agreeable sort of place this, but I don't see anything to suit me," he replied. "You know I had a lot of letters to business-men in New York that I presented; but nothing came of it. They evidently took me for a counter-jumping Liverpool clerk of some sort; but I told them I hadn't come out here to slave away at that sort of thing,—that my intention was to make a lot of money out of hand and go home again. None of them seemed to know of any opening in mines and things; but they said they would bear me in mind. It don't matter. Something is sure to turn up, old fellow, and I'd like to have a little fling and a chance at some big game before settling down."

One thing he had done in New York which he considered to be a marvel of pioneer forethought, and that was to have a richly-chased gold whistle made from a design of his own at Tiffany's, on which was inscribed, "Look out for the locomotive when the whistle blows," —a sentence that, for some reason, had fascinated him at American stations and become a permanent mental possession. "I shall find it awfully useful, you know, out on the prairies," he explained. He had been in the habit of using a plain one when driving at home, to warn people that he was in the rear of them when he wished them to pull aside and let him pass, or wanted to attract the attention of some smock-frocked rustic and get a gate opened; but what application he meant to make of it to the conditions of life in Colorado deponent knoweth not. Probably there had been some delightful

21*

vision of driving a team of mustangs at a dashing pace across a vast plain, and whistling down buffaloes, wild cattle, Indians, or whatever might be in the way.

Novel as the life of the American capital was to the party, they had begun to feel at home in it, when an occurrence took place just before they left the city that revealed such unexpected social possibilities, such heights of Democratic aspirations and depths of Republican toleration, as utterly puzzled and confounded them, and reduced them to the position of strangers and aliens again for a time. It was this: Sir Robert came back to the hotel one afternoon when they had no thought of seeing him until dinner, and announced (*à l'Anglaise*), rather than suggested, that Miss Noel and Ethel should go to the President's reception, then already in progress.

"But, my dear Robert, how is it possible?" objected Miss Noel. "Parsons asked leave of me to go off on an expedition somewhere,—she did not say where, but she was to be with some friends she has made here; and you know how dreadfully dependent I am upon her. I don't see how I could get myself up for a state affair like that."

"Oh, pooh! make Ethel see to your buttons and strings," insisted Sir Robert. "Go you must. I have my reasons."

Go they did, *en grande tenue,* accompanied by Mrs. Sykes, and squeezed themselves somehow through the outlying crowd and got into line. Mrs. Sykes was their pilot, and so unscrupulously and vigorously did she push and elbow her way that she soon got them far ahead of the irresolute or indifferent majority. They had nearly reached the President, when they caught sight of a very familiar back, the back of a lady at that moment shaking hands with his Excellency,—in short, Parsons!—Parsons, looking quite as respectable as her neighbors, in her best black silk, her velvet bonnet, her handsome Paisley shawl, but still Parsons!

The shock to Miss Noel was so great that she fairly stood still for a moment and gaped. Then she felt herself pushed forward by the impatient procession, and followed exactly in her maid's wake, enjoying precisely the same honor, and hardly to be distinguished from her, as she indignantly felt. The wave which had carried her on now spent itself in ever-widening circles, and she could overtake the offending Abigail.

Parsons's expression when she heard herself called by name, and, turning, saw her usually gentle mistress all petrified dignity and offended majesty, was a sight for Hogarth or Gilroy. Her mistress, whom she supposed housed for the afternoon,—her mistress at the same entertainment with herself, and looking like the Duke of Wellington in petticoats!

" *You here!*" said Miss Noel, a fiery spark in her usually mild eyes. "You HERE, Parsons? You have presumed to come HERE? Go home at once!"

Home Mrs. Parsons went, and Miss Noel was too much upset to remain much longer. Instant dismissal was the very least penalty she could think of for such a flagrant liberty and impropriety. But she was a perfectly helpless old lady in a strange country, and Parsons was a model maid who had been with her for twelve years. And so, after much discussion with Sir Robert, her nephew, Ethel, and Mrs. Sykes, Miss Noel decided to "overlook it this time," and gave Parsons a long lecture instead, to which she listened respectfully as she went about her usual tasks. And then feminine curiosity came in. "I can't think how it is that you were allowed in. What did you think of it? So *very* wrong of you to go," she said to her a few days later.

"Yes, mem, I was allowed in,—there was no trouble about that; but it was no great sight, after all. I've seen far finer at 'ome, when I lived in Upper Grosvenor Street and used to see 'er Majesty going to the drawing-rooms, and again when we fought the Russians and beat them, and all London was illuminated,—you remember, mem. All London was up and about, and Primrose 'Ill one blaze, and me, and Mrs. Rich, the 'ousekeeper, and two of the men-servants was out till two o'clock. Not but that I'm glad I went, to be able to say that I've shook 'ands with the President of the United States, beggin' your pardon for sayin' so, mem."

"I suppose we shall be meeting Parsons wherever we go now," said Mrs. Sykes. "A beautiful state of affairs!"

"I don't know, I'm sure. I can't make it out, try as I will," replied Miss Noel.

They did not understand the situation any better when they were told that there was not one bit more probability of their meeting Parsons at any other house in Washington than in their own set in London.

"The Chief Magistrate's. I really can't understand it," repeated Miss Noel. "If she goes there, why not to other officials',—everywhere?"

"Of course you can't. You are hopelessly mixed, and no wonder. The woman Mr. Maffy introduced to me the other day, if you please, was a great swell. She is staying here. I met her at the French minister's last night, and she turned her back on me. The wife of a member of the Cabinet, and introduced to one by the clerk of the 'otel! Good heavens! what a country!"

## V.

"It is very odd: we have not seen any one in the least like 'Yankee' Robinson yet. I wonder what part it is that they live in?" said Mr. Ramsay to Sir Robert, alluding to a London actor who has been representing, or rather misrepresenting, an American for some years in a costume never seen on this continent and speaking a dialect never heard anywhere.

"I have no idea. One would have supposed that at the capital every type, almost, would be represented, and a national one clearly defined. But it seems to me that all the things I counted upon seeing either do not exist at all or have not come under my notice; and I was not prepared in the least for America as I find it, it is so different from America as I fancied it," replied Sir Robert. "I have not got enough mental elasticity to take it all in at once, but I see that the first step toward learning anything about it is to recognize that I know nothing, and that the language, unless I am careful, will only help to keep me in a fog. A most fruitful source of misunderstandings I find it. I really think sometimes that I should understand better if French or German were spoken instead,—it is so misleading to hear familiar words and terms with totally different meanings attached. But all the same why did that woman to whose house we went on Tuesday, —Pennypacker? Was that it? American names are many of them so queer that I can't keep them in my head,—why did she speak French to me and make her daughters do the same, I wonder? I have a fair knowledge of French, and answered a question or two; but, seeing they were .for keeping it up, I said to her, as politely as possible, 'My dear madam, you are an American and I am an Englishman. Why in heaven's name should we play the fool like this?' Yet she was offended. I saw that."

"She took you for a Frenchman, and so she began with her '*Parlez-vous, Oui monsieur, Bon soir, Au revoir.*'" (Mr. Ramsay made a rhyme of this, with his "*mushew*," and, like his companion, spoke with an aggravated "quatre ving-sang accent" that put him above suspicion, if, as has been said, no Englishman who speaks French without an accent is to be trusted. He laughed, too, and exhibited the finest teeth, if not wit, imaginable.)

"Take *me* for a Frenchman! Stuff! Impossible! If there is a thing that I thank my God for, it is that I am not a Frenchman; and no one in his senses could mistake me for one," said Sir Robert.

."Can it be that quite the highest class here speak that language habitually?" inquired Miss Noel. "I know they do in Russia. And I have noticed that in conversation a great number of phrases from it are used. In the case of that nice South-American girl from the State of New Orleans that I met so often everywhere it was very noticeable. You remember, Ethel dear, how she rolled her *r's* and used French idioms translated into English. She doubled all her vowels in a curious way, and drawled out her words; but there was something soft and pleasing about her. Not but that I liked Miss Marlowe better,—she is so superior; and so is her brother, though I am almost sure he doesn't like England. He always stays in Paris when he is abroad,—at least makes that his headquarters."

"Not like England! God bless my soul! What *does* he like, then? I should not have expected that of an American. It is inconceivable that there should be such narrow-minded prejudice against the mother-country," exclaimed Sir Robert in a disappointed tone, as unconscious as his neighbors of being at all inconsistent. "You should not say the State of New Orleans, Augusta, when you mean the city. Louisiana is the name of the State." Sir Robert had not studied the map for nothing.

"How very stupid of me!" said Miss Noel in mild lament. "I was always dull about geography, even as a child. It is down on my list" (taking a paper out of her satchel), "I see, as a State; but I suppose I must have mixed my pins. I took black ones for States, and white ones for the principal places. But you must acknowledge, my dear Robert, that it is no trifle to master the mere outlines. I shall never do more, I feel; for when it comes to detail, what with dozens of Washingtons, and villanous villes of all kinds, and Indian impossibilities as bad as Welsh ones, and then Sparta

and Corinth, Athens, Rome, Versailles, and a most marvellous jumble of places one knows already and is
amazed to find over here, and a great many that sound
like bad jokes,—such as Red Cow, and Lickskillet, and
Bad Axe,—I really *must* say that American geography
will always be more or less of a muddle to me. It has
given me three bad headaches in one week; and I can't
find the Amazon anywhere, try as I will, though I have
looked and looked, and I sure it was there when I
was in the school-room, for I remember going without my pudding and being kept in the house all one
afternoon to impress it on my mind, after missing it in
my lesson. I was asking that South American about
the natives along there being converted, and telling her
what an admiration I had of the missionaries sleeping
in the bamboo huts and living on a handful of rice for
years in order to Christianize and civilize them, cleverly
arousing their sympathies by making a black Madonna,
just like themselves. I forget where I read the account,
but I know I gave one pound ten to it and sent it as
a 'Protestant Christian.' And it can't have been true,
after all; for she said that she was a Roman, but that
she had never heard of anything of the kind in Louisi-
arner. She asked me if I meant the aborigines by the
natives; and I said, 'Of course.' And then she said
they were dying out very fast, or had been sent away,
and were wedded to a wild life for the most part, and
very miserable, wretched creatures. Poor things!
Speaking of color, have you noticed how extraordinarily
the blacks resemble each other? I can't tell one from
another. They all look alike. And I can't say I like
having them about me. It often gives me quite a turn

when I see a black hand offering me a dish at table, or when I glance up into their faces, which are really alarming and look capable of everything that is bad, somehow. I am not as foolish as Parsons there, though. She is afraid to stay in the same room with one of them alone. Eh, Parsons?"

"They people do look that dreadful, mem, as I should fear to be murdered if I crossed 'em," replied Parsons. "And this precious pet" (embracing Blanche, Miss Noel's cat) "won't go near 'em, coax as they will. It's somethink about the heye. Even the 'ead-waiter 'ad it at the 'otel, though in general respectable, free with the plum-cake, and willin' to bring what I harst for. I've seen the same in a Hitalian I kep' company with from Christmas till Michaelmas one year, w'ich he drew a knife on me, and us as good as called."

"Why, that was a low proceeding for a 'Hightalian,' Parsons, upon my word, and a narrow escape for you," commented Mr. Heathcote jocularly. "But don't despair yet: you may get another chance, you know, over here."

Miss Noel looked reprovingly at her nephew.

The decorous Parsons smiled significantly. "To tell the truth, I 'ave 'ad one already, sir," she said.

"An offer, Parsons? *Really!*" exclaimed Mrs. Sykes. "One of our acquaintances, very likely," she added behind her fan to Miss Noel. "Who was it, pray?"

"Tell us all about it. What did he say?" urged Mr. Heathcote.

"Yes, tell us at once," Mr. Ramsay laughingly insisted. "I'd like to know how they do the thing in this country."

"How is it that I have not heard of this before?" said Miss Noel.

"Go on, Parsons. What fun!" cried Ethel.

Parsons felt herself quite a heroine, and indeed had been not a little gratified by the episode.

"It was a young man,—a grocer in a small way of business on Heighteenth Street, mem," she said, address-ing herself to her mistress rather than to the company at large. "And he not more than 'arf my hage. Very foolish of 'im, as I told 'im; but he wanted a settled person to keep the shop, as could be trusted."

"Not half a bad thing for you, Parsons, if you like boys," said Sir Robert.

"Yes, sir; I suppose so. But it was all nonsense 'im thinkin' of me. And I couldn't bear to give up the old country and 'ome and friends besides. I told 'im I 'ad no wish to marry in America, not if I could 'ave the very President. You see, sir, I shouldn't know which end I stood on; I'd never know what my station was; and the 'abits different, and messy victuals, and English not rightly spoke, and 'im a Papist,—it was not to be thought of," explained the obdurate fair one.

"Quite right, Parsons. I'd not live here if the whole country were given me on that condition," said Mrs. Sykes sneeringly.

"Stuff! What nonsense you are talking! I'd not like to try you with an estate or two if I were an American," grumbled Sir Robert from his corner. "I know that."

"I wonder what they are all about in Washington now," said Mr. Heathcote irrelevantly. "I suppose that queer genius that bored me so with his wonderful gun that he had been trying to get the government to adopt for ten years, and that 'recoiled backward,' strange to say, is still hanging around button-holing strangers, like the Ancient Mariner."

"I remember that fellow," put in Mr. Ramsay. "I used to see him at the Capitol. They called him a 'crank.' Splendid word, 'crank.' My governor is one, and I'm glad to get a name for him. He'll never let my mother be ill in her own house. He sends her straight away out of the house until she recovers, and then she is allowed back. And it is just the same with the rest of us,—that is, it was when we were at home," replied Mr. Ramsay, with an air of *bonhommie.* "Sometimes we were packed off to hospitals with hired nurses, and sometimes put in lodgings and a 'sister' got down from town; but out we bundled the moment we got measles, or typhoid fever, or so much as a rash from indigestion. My father never takes any medicine himself or sees a doctor, and he says he is not going to have his house poisoned up by anybody and infested by a lot of quacks. Bill and I shammed several times when we got tired of being at home during the holidays, and got sent off to Eastbourne or Scarborough for a fortnight. Bill was a jolly old boy in those days, and we hit it off beau· tifully together. I can't think how it is he is so changed. He hasn't *done* anything. He is a respectable ass enough, but he has the nastiest temper I know, and is always lecturing me about getting on in the world, and altogether I know I was precious glad to see the last of him."

"I hate being sermonized myself. It's an awful bore," said Mr. Heathcote. "Some people have a talent for boring others. There was that dreadful woman that I took in to dinner the other day, who *would* talk about the royal family,—anecdotes, you know, about the queen, and the prince consort, and the Duchess of Kent, and what the Duke of Cambridge thought of the prince, and how the prince never dared to sit down in the queen's presence, and how Wales can't smoke because his mother objects, and all that stuff. I felt like asking her what the deuce it mattered to her what any or all of them did; but I only said that I knew nothing about them whatever,—which is true, except what the papers say. I never was at court but once in my life, and I had nothing to say about them. But I couldn't get her off the subject for the longest while, and when I did she went off upon another quite as bad,—a law lord that she had met abroad, and a mayor fellow, Sir Peter something, that got knighted somehow. Very great people she thought them. At last I thought I would give her aristocratic feelings a shock, so I told her that my grandfather was a Ramsgate tradesman, and that my associations had been principally with my mother's people,—chapel people, and the very salt of the earth, which I knew was more thought of in America than any mere worldly distinctions. And I also said that I had come over here to get a position as commercial traveller. It was such fun to see how she rose to it and swallowed the whole thing, hook, sinker, line, and pole, and gave herself airs of social superiority at once,—and she an avowed republican!"

Mr. Ramsay laughed gleefully over this little fiction of his friend: "Oh, she is nothing compared to that old maid from Vermont that kept chasin' me up into corners to talk about John Bright. She knew all about him already,—where he was born, and where he was educated, and all that,—lots more than I did. She quoted from two of his speeches as pat as possible about the franchise and all that, you know. I couldn't think what was up, when she suddenly clasped her hands and shook her curls at me, and said, 'I take the deepest interest in his noble career, with all its grand devotion to liberty. He has been a clear, strong reformer all the way through. And what a passionate love of the humanities he has! What is he doing now especially?' I told her that I didn't know at all what he was up to now in the way of stirrin' up a mob, and that, in fact, all I did know was that he was one of those radical fellows that are tryin' to ruin England, and that I'd like to transport the lot of them to Botany Bay if I could. And so I would, like a shot. I says to her, 'Why, some of those chaps object to the queen's birthday bein' celebrated!' And she rolls her eyes at me and says, 'If you want a royal birthday you should celebrate his instead,—the birthday of a royal nature, instead of that of a mere royal accident. I am surprised to hear a youth, an English youth, at the very period when all generous enthusiasm should glow most brightly—' "

"The old party was evidently punning," put in Mr. Heathcote. "Go on."

"I forget the rest. Talkin' like that, she meant. She talked like a book. Fancy me keepin' John Bright's birthday! I'd sooner keep Nebuchadnezzar's. That's my horse. The governor named him that, he said, because he went on all-fours and ate grass. There's something about it in the Bible. The governor's an awfully

r  22*

clever fellow, you know. He is down there now. I couldn't afford to keep him in town. And the governor is chargin' me quite enough for his keep, too. He is very near, is the governor; in fact, an awful screw."

"How did you get rid of your old woman?" asked Mr. Heathcote.

"Oh, she left me in high disgust. 'Have you n beautiful ideals, then? no large desires or earnest aspirations? What are your hopes and ambitions? Is there nothing you would like to do? Is there not *something* you would like to be?' she says to me. 'Yes : I should like to be the best cricketer in England, or to go about the world killin' big game as fast as I could load and fire. That would be glorious,' I says; 'and when I've made my fortune over here I'm goin' home to hunt six days in the week as long as I can sit in the saddle, or be tied in, like old Lord Mainwaring, who is over eighty and rides to cover strapped into place like an old mummy.' She got quite excited at that, and says she, 'You look as though you came off the façade of a Greek temple; and if life were an Olympic game, you and such as you would be well fitted for it. But there is the higher life. You should either go back to barbarism and work out on a higher plane, or make your electric light a coal from the altar of the gods.' Wasn't it a rum speech? 'I haven't the least idea what you are talking about, I give you my word,' I says. 'Whom the gods would destroy they first make deaf,' says she : 'I don't suppose you do.' 'I'm not deaf,' I says : 'I can hear a view-halloo across a dozen fields and the wind not in my favor.' 'Oh, you hopeless Philistine!' says she, and marches off. Awfully queer people, some

of these Americans. Why am I a Philistine? I am
nothing of the kind. I'd like to have been with Sam-
son, though, when he took the three hundred foxes and
tied them tail and tail with firebrands and turned them
into the corn-fields. That must have been jolly good
fun. Such sport! They read that in church the last
time I went, and I thought it uncommonly lively for
church, you know. Fact is, she was talkin' over my
head; I saw that; but it *was* deucedly queer, now,
wasn't it? I thought the Americans were not very
well educated, and all that, but hanged if they can't lay
me over! I met a girl of sixteen the other day that
set a lot of people laughin' at my expense. I'm not a
clever man, you see, and I always did hate readin'.
'Which of Thackeray's characters do you admire most?
I shall never forgive you if you don't adore my dear,
dear Colonel Newcome. I have been in love with him
for years,' says she. 'Have you? Really, I don't know
which I like best,' I says; for it was true. I didn't
know one from another, and the only Colonel Newcomb
that I know is that fellow that I see by 'Bell's Life' is
sellin' off his stud. Wouldn't I like to buy 'em! She
was down on me again in a minute. 'No wonder you
can't decide between them, they are all so interesting.
Ah! I see how it is: you prefer *Dickens.* Now, which
of *his* books do you like best? I've read them all, over
and over again,' she says. I was a 'possum up a gum-
bush, as they say over here, then, I can tell you. But
the governor is awful nuts on Dickens's books, and is
always talkin' about them, so I thought I was all right
and had remembered one when I said, 'Nicholas Cop-
perby.' You should have seen them tryin' not to laugh!

I saw I had put my foot into it, and I told 'em I had
been lyin' and hadn't read one of 'em, and that it was
no sort of use shammin'. The girl was nice about it.
She pinched her lips in a bit, and got very quiet, and
said that gentlemen didn't get much time to read, but
that she was sure I would enjoy both authors when I
got the leisure. She didn't keep the thing up at all."

"If gentlemen can't get time to read, I wonder who
can? You can put in a lot of that sort of thing out on
the prairies if you like," said Mr. Heathcote.

"That's it, you see. I don't like," replied Mr. Ramsay honestly. "It bores me tremendously. But I really
must do a little of it some time or other when there is
nothin' goin' on. Macaulay's History is about the only
stiff·piece of readin' I've ever done. My godmother
gave me five guineas for doin' that, and put me through
a toughish exam. afterward, and that impressed it on
my mind. I tried Plutarch's Lives the summer Haw-
kins, my cousin, and his coach spent with us, but it was
awfully dull work, all those dead men,—I couldn't tell
them apart,—and the weather was fine, and fellows
dropped in, and we'd take a b. and s. all round, and go
for a walk, or cricket, or somethin',—and I didn't manage more than fifty pages of the stuff. The governor
was in such a wax about it, I remember."

These conversations took place in the westward-
bound train in which our party were speeding away
from Washington, which they had left behind them
steeped in sunshine, the dome of the Capitol clear-cut
against a sky that Sir Robert unreservedly pronounced
as blue as any he had ever seen in Italy. Mrs. Sykes
had fixed her eyes on the ugly buildings in the vicinity

instead, and complained loudly of "the intolerable glare," finding that part of the city "a perfect eyesore," and its chief ornament "an absurdly pretentious, badly-proportioned pseudo-Grecian structure, thoroughly out of keeping with its surroundings."

"Have you noticed the guard?" Miss Noel said to her when they had been under way for a couple of hours.

"I never notice the guard," that lady very truthfully replied, "any more than I do the engine."

"I observe faces very closely, on the contrary. It is a habit I have formed, I rather think, from drawing heads so much. And the lines in his face are very strong. His expression, too, is so kindly and benevolent. It is not belied, either, by his conduct, as far as one can judge on the surface. You see what a comfortable bed he has made up for me, on hearing that I was not well, with Parsons's help. He brought a couple of boards and turned over a seat, and then with the wraps and dressing-bag he improvised a very tolerable substitute for a couch, for which I am grateful, as my head is really very bad. I see, too, that he is very thoughtful in other directions. I have amused myself watching him dose that poor woman at the back of the carriage. Just now he made a paper windmill for that poor baby of hers, that has got into such a fret."

"He is paid for all that, you may be sure. I don't see anything to gush over, I must say," replied Mrs. Sykes.

"I have no wish to 'gush,' as you call it, but it is very nice to see how obliging he is, helping people on and off the train, and carrying such quantities of bags and parcels. I can't think it is *all* done with an eye to the money he is going to get."

"I should think not. You had better be careful how you insult the American citizen who is acting as a guard by offering him a tip. I got into trouble that way myself the other day. He won't take it; and it's a toss-up whether he won't stop the train and put you off for your pains, aunt," put in Mr. Heathcote. "I really didn't believe there was such a *rara avis* in the world. I'd like to instil the sentiment into certain classes at home, I know. At a place where I was shooting last year I really thought of taking up a collection among the servants to pay my expenses back to town."

"I can't afford to go to any but the smallest establishments," said Mr. Ramsay. "If it wasn't that my brother-in-law takes pity on me and gives me some shootin' every year, I'd never get a chance at anything, unless it was a cat or two among the chimney-pots. It amounts to blackmail, that is what it does; and when I make my fortune and go back home I mean to discharge every servant that takes a shillin' from a guest of mine, much less five or ten pounds. Lots of poor devils like me haven't got it, don't you see, and can't rob a church once a week. I tell you what I do to save appearances at my brother-in-law's,—at least what I did, for I blurted it out right before the servants last time, and shan't be able to repeat it. Awfully stupid of me, wasn't it? But then I am a duffer, you know, and it was at luncheon, and I thought they had all been dismissed. It was this: I'd borrow it of the master and pay it out handsomely with a grand air to the ser-

vants. Capital idea, wasn't it? How I did haw-haw,
to be sure, when I looked round and saw Thomas behind my chair tryin' to look as though he hadn't heard!
And what a fury my sister was in! I'd never have paid
a penny to shoot there in the world. Higgs—that's my
brother-in-law—is a cotton-spinning fellow, anxious to
have the name of havin' good shootin', and he'd get his
birds down from town, and after they were killed they
were all sent back to Leadenhall Market. I was never
allowed to keep a bird, and it was only to keep my hand
in that I shot at all. Higgs can shoot. No doubt about
that. He put out his brother's eye, and has winged
three guests at different times. I always make him
keep his distance when we are out together; and it is
just as dangerous to have him in the front as behind."

They were laughing over this when the conductor
came round on an inspecting tour. When he got near
Miss Noel, she stopped him. "Would you tell me if
we are to stop anywhere soon? I have a severe headache, which will not be any better until I get a cup of
tea," she said.

"A headache? Why, that's too bad. I'm mighty
sorry for you. They are mean things to have, I know.
I'm subject to them myself. I've got some bay-rum back
yonder that I'll bring you presently to put on it. That's
about as good as anything, I reckon, for it: at least it
helps me. I'll fix you up some with some ice-water,"
responded the conductor, with friendly concern. "My
wife always makes me take some with me when I start
out on the road, and that's how I happen to have it.
She looks out for me, I can tell you. As for that tea, I
am afraid you'll have to go without that, ma'am."

He walked on.

Mrs. Sykes looked after him. "What an impudent fellow! To offer his bay-rum, and presume to say that *he* was subject to them. As if anybody cared about *his* head! Putting himself on an equality, as far as he could, like that!" she exclaimed.

"I really don't think he meant it," pleaded Miss Noel. "I think he meant to be kind. I do indeed. One can see that he is just a simple, homely creature."

"Meant it, indeed! Abominable familiarity, I call it. His wife made him put it up! A little more, and he'd have grown insufferable," Mrs. Sykes protested. "Give these Americans an inch and they will take a mile."

"I think it rather interesting to know that he is subject to them," said Mr. Heathcote. "And I think very well of his wife, thoughtful soul! It will be delightful, aunt, to see you anointing your poor head with the guard's hair-tonic, or whatever it is. You really must not be so giddy and receive such attentions from strange gentlemen, or I shall tell of you when we get back."

"What *am* I to do? One *can't* take his bay-rum; and one wouldn't for the world hurt the poor man's feelings," said Miss Noel, seriously concerned as to her future course.

"Couldn't you pretend to, aunt dear, and throw it out of the window when his back is turned?" suggested Ethel.

"I never heard such stuff,—never! Send the man about his business, and rebuke his impertinence properly," counselled Mrs. Sykes impatiently.

Miss Noel laid back her head: contention made it worse.

"Is your friend sick? Won't she have some of my cologne?" asked a lady opposite, holding out a bottle as she spoke.

Mrs. Sykes stiffly declined, making a distinction which conveyed no sense of difference. "She is not sick; she is ill. Her head aches," she said, with *hauteur.*

Miss Noel had not expected the conductor to reappear for some time, or that when he did he would come from another direction. He turned up, however, quite unexpectedly at her elbow a few minutes after this, a collapsion cup in his hand.

"Here you are, all right. This isn't the bay-rum: got this from a doctor in the next car. Here." And, without further ceremony, the worthy man took up the handkerchief lying in her lap, dipped it in the cup, and laid it, ice-cold and grateful, on her burning forehead.

"Oh! oh! Really!" exclaimed Miss Noel, startled and half struggling up; but he was off again, and she saw only the smiles of her friends.

"I wonder at you, really! How can you permit such a thing?" said Mrs. Sykes indignantly.

"I wasn't consulted. You must have seen that. And really it is very grateful,—very. I was very surprised, of course,—very. But I don't think he *meant* anything," Miss Noel plaintively replied.

In ten minutes more he was back again. "I dunno about that cup of tea. We are behind time now. But I'll see. I'll pull up if I can somewhere and hold the train till I can get it for you," he said, in his slow way and low voice.

"Not if we are behind time. Pray don't do that, I beg. *Pray don't,*" remonstrated Miss Noel, a remem-

M                                    23

brance of "American recklessness" and the risk of col·
lision flashing before her.

"Lor' bless your heart! I ain't a-going to run no
risks. No, indeed," he replied, and shook his head
wisely as he walked away again.

After a bit Miss Noel sat up, and presently, when the
train came to a full stop, she looked out of her window
and saw the conductor outside. He had hurriedly
seized a train-boy, and was saying, "Kite it up to Colonel Barlow's farm, and bring back a cup of tea, if
they've got it, and a slice of light bread. And hurry
all you know how, my son."

"Is that his son? What a very dirty little boy! But,
then, one does get such a sweep in travelling, and,
living on the train as he does, he can't keep himself
tidy," she thought.

It was not long before the conductor came beaming
down the aisle toward her, saying, "Here it is. Nice
green tea; hot and strong. I don't drink tea myself,
but I know the ladies like it. I hope it'll do you good."

"Thank you very much. How good of you!" exclaimed Miss Noel, who was glad indeed to get the
refreshment her exhausted system demanded, and
eagerly devoted herself to it at once.

"Not at all; not at all," said her smiling benefactor.
"I like to be accommodating when I can, especially to
a lady." He moved off again, with a last, "Don't mention it, ma'am."

"Well, I must say that the American guard is quite
the most remarkable thing I've seen in the country yet,"
commented Mr. Heathcote.

"Fancy holding a train over for a thing like that in

England!" said Sir Robert; but nobody could fancy it for one moment.

"He *is* a kind creature, you see," said Miss Noel, between her spoonfuls. "And respectful, too, in his way. He said ' ma'am;' though he neglected to touch his hat." ·

"I've not had a hat touched to me since I landed, except by the Hitchcocks' Irish coachman and English footmen," said Sir Robert. "I must really go and thank the fellow, if you are sure it wouldn't do to tip him and that thanks is all he will have."

Sir Robert rose, and was gone some time. "Quite a character," he said on his return, dropping back into his seat. "A warrior, and a bit of a philosopher, and a Christian, I should think, unless he is a humbug. When I thanked him, he said, 'That's nothing. You like to be accommodating when you can, don't you? I reckon we wuz put here to help each other along. Life is travelling all the way through for us all, and when we hand in our checks we'll feel bad if we ain't done nothing to help each other along. Now, won't we? It warn't no trouble for me to send up to Colonel Barlow's. He's a friend of mine,—an elegant gentleman. He often sends down things that way.' I told him that I shouldn't like to offer him money for a service of the kind; but I said it rather doubtfully, I suppose, for he said, as if shocked, '*Money for waiting on a lady?*' and I hastened to make the *amende honorable.* He told me he had been in the Southern army; and he's called 'Cap'n,' I notice, —a non-commissioned officer, perhaps; but I don't think there can be any doubt that he was in Stonewall Jackson's command, and that is title enough. 'Old Blue-

Lights' he called him. He boasts of having been ten years in the service of this company as though it were forty, and thinks it, he told me, 'the greatest road on the top of the earth,' which is certainly conclusive, though not proved. Altogether, I was amused by my talk with him; and he was a little too 'accommodating' about one thing,—introductions to two or three men sitting there."

"Fancy being introduced to people by the guard!" Mrs. Sykes exclaimed; but this also was an effort to which the English imagination was wholly unequal. "I wonder where it stops! Do bootblacks and sweeps introduce their patrons to each other? Is there no limit to this dreadful radicalism? What kind of men were they?" asked Mrs. Sykes.

"Two of them appeared to be gentlemen; the third looked to be a respectable grazier, or something of that sort," said Sir Robert.

As a matter of fact, the two "gentlemen" were a couple of clean-looking, well-dressed, side-whiskered Boston drummers, with handsome portmanteaus containing "samples," light overcoats, velvet caps, and an easy air of proprietorship of the train and lordly superiority to their fellow-passengers that had not been without its effect, while the "grazier" was a judge of the Supreme Court of the State through which he was passing, a man of property and influence, whose address was better than his dress, fortunately, and whose reputation could stand the clothes-test when it was applied to him, though it never occurred to him that such a test would be applied, much less that he might with advantage give a little more time and thought to the

adornment of the outer man. The caps aroused Sir
Robert's envy. "So stupid of me not to have provided
myself with something of the sort. This stiff hat of
mine is not the thing at all for these long journeys. I
wonder— Let me see," said he. And, opening his
Gladstone bag, he presently fished out a white cotton
night-cap with a red tassel, and, putting it on, settled
himself for a nap, saying, "Very comfortable substitute,
—very. I wonder I did not think of it before."

He did not see the ripple of amusement that ran
through the car over this incongruous addition to the
toilet of a highly-respectable elderly gentleman; but
it would have made no difference if he had. He had
not given a thought to its effect on his fellow-travellers,
but would have been quite indifferent to any such expression of public opinion, knowing the impossibility
of his ever being ridiculous.

He was still asleep when they reached Point of Rocks,
where they were to change cars for the West. As soon
as they could collect their various effects, they scrambled down the steps of their car, near which the conductor was standing with a lantern, the engine of the
next train puffing impatiently as it pulled in alongside.

Mrs. Sykes was first, and was met by a warning
caution, "Mind you don't step there. This way."

Then came Miss Noel. The conductor seized her
arm firmly. "Be careful, grandma. Mind that broken
rail sticking up there," he said. And then to Ethel,
"Come on, young miss;" and to Parsons, "Give me
them things, lady. This way. Follow me."

A general scramble ensued, after which they found
themselves transferred to the new train, and caught a

23*

glimpse of their "accommodating" ex-conductor climb-
ing up the steps of the car they had vacated, with a fat
baby in his arms, or rather left arm, and a carpet-bag
in the right hand, both the property of a lady he had
just assisted to enter.

"He called Parsons 'my lady,'" commented Mrs.
Sykes, when they had somewhat composed themselves,
"and *you* 'grandma.' I told you what would be the
result of encouraging him as you did, instead of putting
him down. It is a mercy your distinguished relative
didn't say, 'Walker,' with his fingers spread out from
his nose, by way of farewell. Another time you will
believe me, perhaps. The impertinence of it!"

The young men, who now heard of it for the first
time, were exquisitely tickled by the situation, and gave
way to regular guffaws, and half choked in their efforts
to control themselves. Ethel could not help joining in.
Miss Noel looked what she felt, completely bewildered,
but attempted a faint "Perhaps it was not 'grandma,'
but something else. Such a civil creature as he appeared."

Sir Robert growled out something about "an impudent Radical rascal."

Parsons looked altogether unconscious, which is the
well-bred English "domestic's" way of taking part in
such scenes. At least, she did until Miss Noel's eyes
wandered to her, and she said, "Did you hear the man?
*Was* it that?" when she appealed in her turn.

"It was, mem. I 'eard it as plain as plain. What sort
of a country 'ave we got to, mem?" she said, vague
alarm and vivid disgust painted on her prim countenance.

"1 don't know, I am sure," responded her mistress plaintively.

There was nothing that struck them as eccentric about the next guard, a severe official of few words, in whom they only missed that general *bouquet* of subservience to which they were accustomed in men of his class. Mr. Ramsay's one idea of travelling in America was getting to that vague region, misty, illimitable, fascinating, where there was a profusion of game of all kinds, and from time to time he would hazard a "I say, my man, we are getting out pretty fast, aren't we? Is it far from here to—to the wild part?" which he had gleaned in Washington must not be looked for immediately along the Atlantic seaboard, or a brisk "Is there good sport about here, do you know?" and felt himself snubbed by the answer:

"I don't know what you mean. Are you talkin' about Harper's Ferry? Some people call that wild: and there was shootin' enough about there during the war."

There was the usual small excitement at the Ferry to see the arsenal and the *exact* spot where John Brown was imprisoned. Sir Robert was concluding his nap, and Mrs. Sykes asked of a neighbor, "What's all this talk about the queen's gillie?" and was given a not very lucid account of the insurrection at that spot, which she afterward repeated to her companions, and from which they learned how "a Southern desperado stirred up the Northern whites against the blacks, and got hanged for his pains." On being told by the same neighbor that the scenery "'bout there" was "unsurpassed in the world," and implored to look out, she put

her head out of the window and regarded the Virginia
and Maryland heights, and the rivers rippling in the
moonlight, for a moment, and then settled back in her
seat, saying that she knew dozens of prettier places in
Derbyshire alone, and that it was all nonsense talking
like that,—a speech that greatly disconcerted the person
to whom it was addressed.  Miss Noel, on the other
side of the car, and Ethel, at the next window, pronounced it "Lovely!"  "So bold!"  "Beautiful!" and incidentally found the suspension bridge of interest.  The
young men found the bridge absorbing: all during their
brief stay they stared at it from the platform; and they
waked Sir Robert that he might not miss it.  As for
the view, it was "not half bad."  Parsons, like Mrs.
Sykes, took one glance at it, and fell to nibbling furtively
at a sandwich, public attention being safely diverted
for the time.

After this, they rolled and rattled on without incident,
until it became a question of disposing of themselves
for the night.  None of them had ever taken a sleeping-
car before, except Sir Robert, and they found it a proceeding as amusing as it was novel.  But a hitch arose
in it before many minutes, the same berth having been
sold by mistake to two persons, Mrs. Sykes and a nice
old lady from New York, going to Chicago to see a
daughter at the point of death.  A dispute arose, in
which Mrs. Sykes showed an angry and determined
spirit and the old lady a kind of feeble violence.  Each
insisted that she had bought and paid for that berth
and meant to have it, claim it who might.  The conductor, being summoned, could only say that there had
been a mistake, and he suggested that as the berth was

the lower one they could share it,—a compromise which could not have been more emphatically rejected if the nice old lady had been a recently-recovered smallpox patient. If it had rested with her, the poor old woman would certainly have been compelled to sit up all night; but happily, while Miss Noel was anxiously thinking of some plan for preventing this, a gentleman who had overheard the discussion cheerfully gave up his bed, saying that the idea of a woman of that age being made to undergo such discomfort was "shameful."

When at last they were all disposed of, Mrs. Sykes was not able to immediately reap the fruits of her selfish triumph, for there was in the company the perennial communicative traveller who, like the poor, is always with us in America. This time it was a man from Florida, who in a loud voice gave a full account of himself in the past and present, supplemented by his plans for the future, to a fellow-passenger with an apparent thirst for pure detail, who asked question upon question and filled any chance silence with commonplace comments that grew gradually shorter and sleepier. On and on went the Floridian, until his auditors were fairly desperate, telling of what he considered "good eating" and what he "never could touch," of his plantation, his "awrangos," the average yield of the trees, the causes of abnormal success or failure, and then of his wife, where he met her, how he had "courted her" in the teeth of opposing parents and married her "in spite of the whole crowd," of how she had made "a first-rate wife,—no discount on her," of how he was "perfectly devoted to her," and she "worshipped" him, with illustrations of this fact. And then came an account of her death, that somewhat roused his tired companion, who languidly asked if she was "a professin' Christian," upon which it appeared that there "never was on the green earth a piouser woman or one that kept her house better."

"What was her las' words? do you disremember 'em?" asked the companion again, with revived interest.

"They was, 'Ha! ha! ha! call in the friends!' She sorter laft, you understand," said the bereaved husband. "And when it come to choosin' a verse for her tombstone, Brown he couldn't think of no verse except R. I. P., which sounded to *me* disrespectful, like 'let her rip,' and *I* couldn't, and me and him bothered over it till he sez to me, 'Look here, Joe, what was her las' words?' And I told him, and he said that was the very thing, and put that, with a weepin' willow over it,—the handsomest tombstone that ever you saw in all your born days!"

He was going on with some further particulars of his domestic life, the appearance and peculiarities of "Jane," sole daughter of his house and heart, when Mrs. Sykes, who had been bouncing about in a fury behind her curtains, sat up in bed, and, in a voice whose raucous and excessively British accents contrasted most ludicrously with those of the preceding speakers, said, "*Would* you be good enough, whoever you are and wherever you are, to keep yourself and your affairs to yourself, and allow an English lady, who doesn't care a pin about you, or your wife, or your daughter, or any-thing connected with you, to go to sleep?" She thought of and spoke for herself alone, but so admirably expressed the general exasperation that a loud laugh followed.

"Well, I never!" said the Floridian in subdued tones. "Did you ever?" commented his companion.

"Haw! haw!" burst out Mr. Ramsay, and then shut off his laughter so suddenly that a snort would force its way out.

"Confound the woman!" thought Sir Robert, annoyed.

"Dear, dear! how can she make herself so dreadfully conspicuous? I wish she wouldn't," Miss Noel remarked under her breath to Ethel. Some little tittering and whispering followed this outburst, but in ten minutes Mrs. Sykes had gained the day, or rather night, and the car was as still as a car can be.

When Mr. Ketchum went down to the Kalsing Station to meet his friends, he made an early start, to be sure of welcoming them, and found his clerk, Tom Price, already on the ground, waiting to pick up such crumbs of information as might be lying about for the early bird. It was one of Mr. Price's crosses that he could not see all the trains come in.

"Mornin'. How are you?" asked Mr. Price, promptly joining him.

Mr. Ketchum nodded, and responded by a curt "All right."

"Pretty day, ain't it? Expecting anybody?" inquired Mr. Price, knowing as well as he did the errand upon which he had come.

Mr. Ketchum nodded again, and lit a cigar.

"Which way are they coming from?" said Mr. Price, pursuing the subject.

"Washington," replied Mr. Ketchum laconically.

"Washington!" repeated Mr. Price, fixing on him his

small red eyes. "Is that so? Pleasant place, Washington, I've heard. Ladies or gentlemen?"

"Both, I think; but you had better take my affidavit," said Mr. Ketchum, the twinkle coming in his eye.

"Known them long?" asked Mr. Price.

"Well, that depends," replied Mr. Ketchum. "Counting by the Pyramids, I met them yesterday; and by the dentist's chair, I have known them a thousand years."

"You are joking now, ain't you? I'm not curious about it myself, but they do say in Kalsing that you've got a lord coming to make you a visit,—an English lord. Is that so?" Mr. Price continued.

"The lord knows that to be a pure invention," replied Mr. Ketchum.

"What! You haven't got anybody coming, then? Fool who? Why did you bring the big carriage, and the little one, and a cart besides, and leave them over yonder by Stites's store?"

"I didn't say that," replied Mr. Ketchum.

"You have got somebody coming,—somebody particular. If he isn't a lord, what is he, eh?" said Mr. Price, in the tone of a man who has a duty to society to perform and doesn't mean to be put off.

"A baronet," said Mr. Ketchum.

"A baronet! You don't say so!" exclaimed Mr. Price, with the liveliest interest, though he had no idea what a baronet was, perhaps for that very reason. His eyes dilated, and the next question was still more eagerly put: "Where did you know him? A baronet! Well, well! You are not trying to deceive me now, are you? because it's no use. You are not joking?"

"No, I'm not. He is a real, genuine, simon-pure, blown-in-the-bottle, send-for-circulars, none-genuine-unless-stamped-with-the-lion-and-unicorn, British baronet, and no mistake," maintained Mr. Ketchum.

Mr. Price looked puzzled for a moment. His employer was often an enigma to him. "He's a sort of lord, I guess, now, ain't he? And a friend of yours, you say. Rich?" he said, pursuing his inquiries as seriously as before.

. "Well, I don't know about that. He hasn't nursed me through smallpox, and I never have tried to borrow any money from him, if that is what you mean by a friend. And I don't know what the wages of a baronet are when he is at home. You'll excuse me, Tom, if I step out of the witness-box for a moment now. There's the whistle." Mr. Ketchum walked away briskly toward the approaching train. When he got to the last car, containing his friends, Sir Robert was already out on the platform, peering through his eye-glasses, with a wall-of-Troy wrinkle of anxiety on his forehead, and the doubtful air of a man whose surroundings are unfamiliar.

"Has there been a Mr. Job Ketchum—" he began.

"That was my maiden-name!" exclaimed its owner, and, bounding up the steps, he seized both of Sir Robert's hands and shook them with the utmost heartiness, his face beaming forth a welcome that required no translation. "Well, here you are at last! Delighted to see you, all of you! Delighted! Where are the others?" said he; and the sight of so friendly a face and the warmth of his cordial greeting made Sir Robert unusually effusive in return. "Got you on my own ground

24

now ; can scalp you at my leisure," said Mr. Ketchum, describing as he spoke an imaginary circle around Sir Robert's head, and then, running an arm through his, he drew him into the car, saying, "I am as glad to see you as though you were my long-lost brother with the mark of a strawberry on the end of your nose."

Greetings followed, and introductions, Ethel and Miss Noel and Mr. Ramsay being strangers to him. More hospitable assurances followed as they left the car. Mr. Ketchum was neatly dressed, but wore a crumpled linen "duster;" his hat was pushed a little back in impatient protest against some question of Mr. Price's; the day being warm, his face was flushed, and he fanned himself vigorously with a large palm-leaf fan as he talked.

Altogether, Mrs. Sykes disapproved of him, and responded but coolly to his welcome. Her ideas of refinement being purely conventional ones, she privately at the time, and publicly later, pronounced him "vulgar," and—what she meant to be conclusively crushing —"*so* American." She asked tepidly after "Mrs. Ketchum" (meaning his wife), and fell to fondling her "precious angel Bobo," paying small attention to his reply, in which he explained that she had twisted her ankle the day before, and that she regretted very much not being able to meet them. The others were not so critical, and were much pleased by the friendliness he showed and the welcome he gave them.

"My shebang is around here just a step," explained Mr. Ketchum. "The horses are not used to the locomotive."

"You are sure you have got all the parcels, Parsons ?"

Miss Noel stopped to inquire, her anxiety being a chronic one.

"Here, give those to me. That bag is too heavy for a woman to carry," said Mr. Ketchum, his attention thus attracted to Parsons loaded down with various articles. He took the heaviest from her as he spoke, and marched a little in advance of the party, leading the way to where the carriages stood,—a handsome landau and a dog-cart drawn by two pairs of beautiful Kentucky horses. If there was a thing that Mr. Ketchum liked, it was fine horses, and his stable boasted no less than sixteen, while his coach-house sheltered a great variety of vehicles, it being his favorite amusement to ride and drive. The turn-outs were a surprise to Mrs. Sykes, who had argued, from the careless appearance of her host, poverty. And, as poverty was the only hopelessly vulgar thing in her eyes, some animation and satisfaction began to dawn in her manner. "What perfect beauties! Do you give them much oil-cake, that they shine so? And those dear ponies over there, with the white faces and stockings! Really, it is too bad that Mabel could not have come out. I hope it is nothing serious," she commented affably, as she was helped into the landau, followed by Miss Noel and Ethel, while Parsons was put up on the box next a coachman of ineffable blackness and terrible appearance from her point of view,—a most harmless creature, from whom she shrunk as from a gorilla. The three gentlemen were standing a little apart, discussing the points of the ponies, and Mr. Ramsay and Mr. Heathcote, who were always laying wagers about trifling matters, had disagreed as to their height and staked ten shillings apiece on the infallibility of their

judgments, when Mr. Ketchum joined them. On being
asked about it, he gave his verdict, with the usual result,—a distaste for abstract truth on the part of the
loser, who determined to make accurate measurements
later.

"I go where beauty waits me," said Mr. Ketchum,
waving his hand toward the landau. "Get in, Sir Robert. Get in, you fellows." Then, noticing Mr. Ramsay's
eyes still fixed admiringly on the ponies, he said to
him, "Would you like to drive? If so, go ahead; that
is, if you know what you are about, as I suppose you
do, being a Britisher," he said.

"I should like it," said Mr. Ramsay, preparing to
avail himself of the permission. He had a passion for
horse-flesh, was a capital whip, and was longing to get
the ribbons in his own hands. "I don't think I shall
come to grief. I don't pretend to be a swell at it, but
I've got Heathcote here to advise me, and it is not the
first time," he modestly added.

"All right," acquiesced Mr. Ketchum, and, calling
their coachman, an immense Irishman with what his
master called "a six-inch smile," he gave him instructions to get certain things in Kalsing and follow in the
wagon with the luggage; after which he took his seat
in the landau, and they rolled away through the streets
of a handsome city and out into the open country beyond. Mr. Ketchum was not one of those superla-
tively-cultured, globe-travelled persons who would never·
dream of committing such a solecism as admiring anything in an American town of modest pretensions. On
the contrary, he had a natural honest pride in Kalsing,
and a decided interest in everything that appertained

to it, though he was not in the habit of boring people
with its perfections. He found a great many things to
point out,—the wide, cleanly avenues, watered by a
newly-invented machine daily, and delightfully free
from dust, the broad asphalt pavements, bordering them
the fine shade-trees, the new market, the Roman Catholic cathedral, and a dozen other features of the prosperous, pleasant town, such as the gas, electric lights,
handsome private dwellings, the just-finished opera-
house that "cost a million," and so on; all of which
Sir Robert was noting for himself in the rear, further
wondering about the city's water-supply, sewerage, fire-
brigade, municipal management, thinking that his previous conceptions of the "Western wilds" would have
to be decidedly modified, not to say changed altogether,
and honestly confessing the amazing spread of civilization over a country so very lately, as he counted time,
in the possession of "a few instincts on logs, holding
tomahawks." The churches were not like the vener-
able buildings whose towers and spires stood so thickly
together in his own beautiful island, the stones of whose
gray walls seem to have a prayer in every pore; the
houses had not the historical, architectural, and æsthetic
charm of many that he could easily recall, nor the land-
scape upon which they were now entering the mellow
· perfection of that lovely garden, England; but he saw
here, as he had done everywhere in America, something
better than the bloom of a great civilization, its roots
already vigorous and far-spreading, and, having a strong
love of humanity, it rejoiced him more to see evidences
that there was bread, work, shelter for all, than if he
had come continually upon a Chatsworth or Alton
24*

Towers projected mentally against a background of hovels and squalid misery. His imagination was touched by the thought of the future stretching before a country of whose extent and resources he was getting a better idea every day, and that of its people, in whose conquests and triumphs he was growing to feel an interest, to whose fresh and joyous energies everything seemed possible, and from whom he hoped better things than merely material results, however splendid. He was deep in speculation about the America of a hundred years hence, when the landau drew up, and Mr. Ketchum's voice was heard calling his attention to the well-wooded, fertile valley into which they were descending. "Pretty rolling country, isn't it?" he said. ("I suppose he means undulating," thought Sir Robert.) "Best land in the State," Mr. Ketchum went on.

"What is the name of that beautiful stream? Some very important river, I'm sure, whose name I ought to know without being told, to judge from its appearance," said Miss Noel.

"Oh, that is a little river called the Miatomo," replied Mr. Ketchum, not meaning to boast, any more than he had meant to sneer when he first saw the Thames and asked, "what little river that was."

"Miatomo. How very soft and pretty! What does it mean?" asked Ethel.

"Oh, daughter of the Sun, or Sister of the Clouds, or something. I forget exactly," responded Mr. Ketchum.

Sir Robert was about to ask what the yield of wheat was to the acre, Mr. Ramsay was eager to know if there was good fishing in the river, and Ethel was about to reproach Mr. Ketchum with his indifference to the poetry of its nomenclature, when Mrs. Sykes broke in:

"Why do you build those hideous white wooden houses with green blinds, all exactly alike wherever we go, and so inexpressibly ugly, and set in such wretchedly unsightly grounds?"

"Ahem! Those are very curious but very picturesque fences," put in Miss Noel hastily. "What should I call them, now? Timber must be very plentiful in this part. And you *must* tell me the name of that charming little brook over there, overhung by pollard willows. Look! near that copse of arbor-vitæ, beyond the rick-yard."

"Where?" asked Mr. Ketchum, who had some difficulty in identifying these landmarks.

"Right away to the left of that bullfinch there, and running like a mill-race," said Mr. Ramsay, pointing with his whip.

Mr. Ketchum's eyes followed the direction. "Oh, *that!* That is Hog Creek; and the one running parallel with that deep gully on the right is Snickers' Creek. The fence you asked about is called a snake-fence, Miss Noel," he said.

("'Gully:' that is a Devonshire word. I wonder how it got over here? I must look into that," thought Sir Robert.)

"Is that because they afford refuges for serpents in the corners? Are there many reptiles about here? and are they very venomous?" asked Miss Noel, raising her voice purposely to drown Mrs. Sykes's murmur, "What shockingly vulgar names!"

"I remember to have read such alarming accounts of

the American serpents, the boa-constrictors, and coach-
whips, and anacondas, and rattlesnakes, and a lot more
that I can't recollect, in the swamps and savannas. But
these are the prairies: we haven't come to the savannas
yet: so I suppose there is not much to fear. I have
such a horror of the creatures." Miss Noel could not
divorce South America from North America, though
Sir Robert had read her quite a lecture on the subject
that very morning. She had so long mingled them in
a kind of mental phantasmagoria of Indians, prairies,
gigantic palms and tropical undergrowth, gorgeous
flowers and birds, terrible beasts and reptiles, that she
could not all at once reduce them to their true proportions and set them in the right latitude. "I really never
feel quite safe about insects even, out of England. I
dislike the whole tribe of flying and crawling nuisances,
gnats, midges, moths, flies, harvest-bugs, slow-worms,
that we have there, and of course they are much worse
here, and there must be others of which I know nothing. I remember to have read of your terrible white
ants. Have they any particular habitat? And the ta-
rantulas. Do you get many of those about here?"

"None larger than a soup-plate, and their bite is not
*instant* death. You have probably heard that it is: exaggerated reports are spread about them. The patient
frequently recovers, though paralysis sometimes sets in
afterward," Mr. Ketchum replied. And then, seeing
that he was being taken quite seriously and the concern
on Miss Noel's kind face, he hastened to explain that
they had nothing to fear, and that he had been joking,
—a welcome assurance to a nervous old lady devoted to
botanizing. "Our aunts are not very terrible in this

coury: it is the mothers-in-law that make us stand around and look out for squalls.—Mr. Ramsay! oh, Mr. Ramsay! suppose you pull ahead, now, and take the lead. The piebalds seem restless. Straight ahead for about a mile, and then turn to the left."

Mr. Ramsay dashed past the landau in fine Hyde-Park-Corner style, saying to Mr. Heathcote, "I wish I owned these little beasts and was tooling over Brighton Downs or through the Park with them. This fellow must have picked up a lot of money somehow. Wonder how he did it? Queer sort of chap, isn't he? Gentleman?"

"M-m. Hardly," replied Mr. Heathcote.

"He seems a jolly sort, anyway, and knows a decent horse,—unless he gets somebody else to choose them for him," said Mr. Ramsay.

The landau followed briskly. "How much nicer this is than being shut up in that stuffy carriage! I was so crowded, and it was so hot and dusty. I thought the journey would never end, and over quite the most monotonous, uninteresting country that I ever saw," said Mrs. Sykes.

The complaint of being crowded was a frequent one with her, made with much bitterness,—the fact being that it was her practice to get a couple of seats turned to face each other, and, with her boxes and bags, take up the place intended for four travellers; an arrangement in which they naturally did not acquiesce, and which gave room for sundry comments on her part upon the "rudeness and selfishness of the Americans. We were told at Washington that we should get in an hour earlier than we did; but it seems there is no reliance to be put upon any information that one gets here. A most unpleasant journey, with a disagreeable, dirty lot of people around me, too. And such a time about it! It took an hour to go twenty-five miles, in one place."

"I noticed nothing of the kind. I am sure that I should have found a journey of equal length at home far more fatiguing. One is so cramped there," hurriedly supplemented Miss Noel.

"The mistake you made was in not letting the president of the road know that you meant to travel over it. He would have put a special car at your service, and changed the schedule, and very likely have managed the engine himself. He always does that for distinguished foreigners," said Mr. Ketchum. And so entirely had Mrs. Sykes convinced herself that she was a pivotal centre about which all Americans would and should revolve in profound humility, that she absolutely swallowed in perfect good faith a statement that Mr. Ketchum had supposed would reach the dullest apprehension and convey the most unmistakable moral.

"Oh, really!" she said. "Another time I shall remember that. I didn't think of that."

"Yes, bear it in mind,—do. You ought not to neglect these little precautions in travelling," said Mr. Ketchum.

"What a fine red sun!" said Miss Noel, not blinded by her friend's colossal conceit, and wishing to introduce another topic. "If the weather will only be so obliging as to hold, I make no doubt we shall get all the sketching we covet; and it is very lovely about here. We have been so fortunate, thus far. For twenty-five days and eight hours after we landed there was no rain. Think of that!"

"It may not rain quite as often as it does at home, but I am sure when it does rain there is a regular downpour,—it fairly comes down in buckets," persisted the malcontent.

"Oh, we can easily arrange that for you," said Mr. Ketchum. "We—"

But what his meteorological scheme for regulating the American rain-fall was they never knew, for—an interruption came, the landau stopped, and Mr. Ketchum jumped out and ran down the road. The others craned their necks to look after him, and Parsons, who loved a sensation, reported from the box, "Oh, there has been a hupset! They have gone down a precipice, and are all killed!"

What had really happened was this. Mr. Ramsay had for some time been "chaffing" Mr. Heathcote about being "nothing of a whip," and the latter had criticised his way of handling the ribbons, until Mr. Ramsay said, "Come up here and show us how the thing ought to be done, can't you?"—when Mr. Heathcote, more for the fun of doing it than with any idea of the kind, took his place. All went as before for a while, for Mr. Heathcote was in the habit of driving his uncle's four-in-hand, and knew what he was about; but, unluckily, at a certain point in the road they saw a wagon approaching. There was a long heap of stones piled up just there, intended for the repair of the turnpike, on one side; on the other there was an embankment sloping down to a small pool of water. There was just room by the closest shave for Mr. Heathcote to get by.

"Lay you five to one that you can't pass," said Mr Ramsay.

"Done!" said his friend, and gave the ponies a flick.

He could have done it "easily," he always insisted afterward, but that the wagoner and himself "shilly-shallied,"—Mr. Heathcote obeying the English law of the road and keeping to the left, or trying to, and the other man the American, but not keeping to either. Result,—a fall down the not very steep embankment for piebalds, dog-cart, and all, the gentlemen being shot into the pool like so many champagne corks. The horses, after a flounder and scramble, would have bolted, but the cart was on its side, a dead weight, and Mr. Heathcote picked himself up with amazing promptness, and, running to their heads, swung on boldly,—an example followed by Mr. Ramsay. So that when Mr. Ketchum came up he found three dripping but not much injured guests, two trembling horses, a furious wagoner berating an equally furious gentleman, an enraged baronet abusing both roundly, a broken dog-cart, and the material for as pretty a quarrel as can be imagined.

Down he sprang and promptly cut the traces; then he began soothing the horses. "Anybody hurt?—Soh, Punch, soh! Soh, Judy!—How did it happen?"

Explanations poured in so contradictory and inflammatory that there is no saying what might not have followed had he not taken things into his own hand, pacified and dismissed the carter, wrung a gallon, more or less, of water from Sir Robert's coat, found his hat,—and such a hat!—and beckoned to his coachman to approach.

Ethel and Miss Noel had scrambled out, and were regarding the scene with dismay. Mrs. Sykes's anxiety had not been uncontrollable, and she had kept her seat.

While Sir Robert, who had now got up on the road again, was abusing "that confounded pig-headed idiot of a nephew, who is always trying to take the very spokes out of every wheel that passes him," Mr. Heathcote was explaining to Mr. Ketchum and apologizing for what he had done. "I have often done it before; and if that blockhead had kept to the left it would have been all right. But I had no right to run any risks with your trap, and I beg your pardon. Whatever expense—" he began.

"None of that. Say no more about it. Accidents will happen. Don't make yourself uncomfortable about it. There is no great harm done. None of you are hurt, fortunately. May I ask you to take the reins there and drive the ladies home, and let Washington take these horses?" said Mr. Ketchum. "Sir Robert can take my place, and Ramsay and I will walk. It is not more than half a mile."

"'And this is the man that I've been telling Ramsay wasn't a gentleman!" thought Mr. Heathcote remorsefully; and he blushed most furiously over his response, which was not an eloquent one and yet somehow brought the two men nearer than they had ever been before. Mr. Heathcote declined to do any more driving that day, knowing that his uncle was "too awfully riled" to accept such a substitute for the accomplished Washington; and it was finally settled that Mr. Ramsay should be his successor. Mr. Heathcote and he had exchanged a very sheepish sort of laugh when they were alone for a moment, for several reasons,—Sir Robert being at hand for one. At another time, under more favorable circumstances, they would have roared; for had not Mr. Ram-

say, in the very act of shooting over the embankment,
cried out, " Won !"

" Keep dark about that. If my uncle knew it, he
would cut me off with a shilling," Mr. Heathcote, had
said.

And so it came about that Mrs. Ketchum, waiting on
the gallery for the arrival of her guests in formal array,
with Mrs. Ketchum senior, Mrs. Vane, and Fräulein
Schmidt about her, also attired with unusual care, and
her son and heir befrocked and curled and ribboned at
the last moment, so as to strike everybody dumb by his
noble beauty, saw the landau roll up, and received Sir
Robert with Miss Noel's water-proof on, three excited
ladies, and a strange coachman of the handsomest and
most pleasing exterior. Even her phlegm was not
proof against such an astonishing state of affairs, and
she opened her pretty eyes very wide and rounded her
rosy mouth in wonder, and actually almost bustled
about for a few minutes, seeing that Sir Robert got
"something hot to keep the cold out," and dry things,
and that the others lacked for nothing.

" Would you like to lie down ?  Do you feel upset at
all ?" she asked of Miss Noel.

" No, dear, thanks ; but I'll just go up and make myself a little smarter for dinner," that lady said, and
Mabel accompanied her, and then, having shown Mrs.
Sykes to her quarters, went down to welcome Mr.
Heathcote and her husband. She found Mr. Ramsay
on all-fours, with the boy on his back, and he scrambled
up on seeing her.

" Jolly little fellow this. We are great friends already," he said, by way of apology for the situation,

when Mr. Heathcote, too, had gone off to his room. "What's his name?"

"Don't mention the subject. You are on delicate ground," said Mr. Ketchum, seizing the child and thrusting him up on his shoulder. "You see, my wife wanted to call him 'Reginald Egbert Ponsonby D'Arcy,' and I had a notion that I would like him to have my father's name, 'Jared Elijah,' and between us we almost got up a divorce-case."

"And no wonder," said his wife. "Could he expect me to give him such a name? It is not a pretty name; and, while I should be more than willing to pay husband's father any mark of respect if he were living, I did think that, as he was dead, Boy need not go through life with an ugly name."

"And so we compromised, and he was baptized Jared Ponsonby, and I call him 'son' for short, which answers every purpose, and his mother leaves off the Jared whenever my back is turned, and, I am sure, got a Montmorency in the church register somehow. Eh, Daisy?" said her husband.

"Pray do not think that I would deceive husband. He is jesting," explained Mabel, as though the fact were not patent. "Now we really must separate there goes the dressing-bell."

Mr. Ramsay at once took himself off, leaving the couple alone.

"Dear Job, where did you get that coat? You looked so nice when you left this morning. How could you spoil it all with that coat? And only look at your hair!" she said, in soft reproach.

"Nothing wrong with that coat. It is a little tumbled

from being rolled up under the seat, maybe, but it is first-rate for keeping off the dust. And I've played my last card, you know: I'm married. Sad, but true," he replied, pinching her round cheek.

"It is vexing, certainly. Dear Job is really handsome when he takes pains with his dress; and my cousin lays great stress on such things, but still, if she can't see what he is, I pity her, that is all, and I'll not tease him," she thought; and, though she had that morning parted his hair and tied his cravat and generally superintended his toilet herself, that he might make the best possible impression on his guests, she only called him "an incorrigible careless fellow," in a tone far more musical than ireful, and begged him to "rush up and make himself beautiful in just five minutes by the clock."

## VI.

The Ketchums' house was the largest of eight handsome villas built by various magnates of Kalsing a few miles out of the city, in a kind of natural park improved by the most careful culture, the whole being known as Fairfield. It was impossible to say what was the extent of the grounds attached to any particular house, for the reason that there were no visible boundaries of any kind, the owners of the different properties having agreed to share the park amicably without insisting upon individual rights to the extent of building high brick walls, or fences of any kind, sightly or unsightly.

except such light wire affairs as might be required immediately around the houses. At the same time there was individual care and taste everywhere,—not general neglect such as had been predicted when the experiment was first talked of. The rivalries were only friendly ones about the earliest strawberries and finest roses, and the effect was worthy of the clever landscape-gardener in whose hands Fairfield had been placed by common consent.

Instead of the aggravated jealousies and perpetual dissensions which some persons had confidently declared inseparable from such a scheme, there was a great amount of peace and good will in the little colony. Each proprietor not only improved his own place to the full, but cheerfully paid his quota toward certain paths, bridges, roads, and lamps intended to benefit all, and seemed to take scarcely less pride in the whole estate than in his share of it. A plan pronounced Utopian had become an accomplished fact.

The Ketchums' house struck Sir Robert as the sort of one that called for about a thousand acres at its back, and, not doubting that his host had felt that earth-fever that always seizes an Englishman when he has made a fortune, he supposed him to have bought a handsome estate and set up as a country gentleman,—the *ne plus ultra* of dignity, respectability, and everything that is desirable from an Englishman's stand-point. He knew nothing of the gregariousness, love of excitement, and indifference to country pursuits that make such posses sions seldom coveted, or, if coveted and possessed, soon tired of, by American millionaires, and he was surprised to see from his bedroom window the red mansard roof of Mr. Brown's elaborate mansion. He met Mr. Ketchum on the steps as he was going down to the drawing-room, and they walked out on the veranda, where they got into comfortable chairs and fell to talking of many things,—of their meeting in England and the interval that had elapsed, of mutual acquaintances, and a little of what the party had been doing.

"Well, and how do you like these United? You have seen worse countries, haven't you?" said Mr. Ketchum.

"Immensely, my dear fellow," replied Sir Robert, answering the first question. "I am even more interested than I expected to be, which is saying a great deal. I have not had the chance to think what I do think yet. We have been so constantly on the wing that it was not possible to digest the facts I have collected; but, if I can only boast an intimate ignorance of it so far, it is quite certain that I mean to know it as well as any foreigner can. Are you an American at large, or primarily a Westerner and only very incidentally an American?"

"Oh, I claim the whole pocket-handkerchief; but of course I hold up my corner," said Mr. Ketchum.

"Doesn't that rather dilute your patriotism?" asked Sir Robert,—"confining yourself to one State?"

"No American does that. We all sit on a couple of States at least, take another for a footstool, and lean back against the rest. We like to do our own house-keeping, that is all, and have a prejudice in favor of managing our own affairs."

"It is all an experiment yet, you know," said Sir Robert, and went on to attach a good deal of significance to several "dangerous tendencies," notably the

riots of the preceding year, from which he deduced
"agrarian outrages" and other evils.

"We are not afraid of 'agrarian outrages' or 'Molly
Maguires' or Communists or anything of the kind," asserted Mr. Ketchum, who had listened with an indulgent
smile. "It is just the story of the buffalo and the fly."

"What is that?" asked Sir Robert.

"Oh, nothing, except that the fly gets shaken off and
the buffalo goes ahead. It takes things easy, does that
animal, but it don't do to fool with it. Even the politicians have found that out. When it does get its dan
der up, somebody is bound to get hurt."

It was Sir Robert's turn to smile when, on asking
about his friend's health, Job said,—

"First-rate, as a rule, and mother-in-laws' stock below
par. But about two weeks ago I got a fine large cold
that has been giving me a rough time,—one of the sort
that makes you feel as though your head had been *boiled*
for a few weeks, and, when you have made a key-bugle
of your nose for a week, decides which is your weakest
point, and goes for it. It has been working on the
ulcerated root of a tooth of mine that retired from business some time ago as a tombstone, and I'll be hanged
if it wouldn't have waked the dead. It has pretty well
used me up, I know. I feel like a fiddle with the bridge
down to-day."

"I am sorry to hear that. I suppose you have consulted your medical man?" said Sir Robert.

"H-m! No. There is a medicine-man in the neighborhood; but I generally do my own doctoring when I
require any,—which isn't often," replied Job

"What is the extent of your place, if I may ask?

Who is that living near you?" inquired Sir **Robert.** "Or is it a dower-house?"

Mr. Ketchum explained the Fairfield system to Sir Robert, who understood it well enough, but to whom it was not so clear why men who could afford to live in any other way had agreed to it.

"But there is plenty of land around here, isn't there? Or, if you must have neighbors, why don't you fence them out?" he asked.

"Oh, I *could* build a wall fifty feet high, with a frill of broken glass; but why should I? I don't want to shut myself in or shut my neighbors out. I came out here to be near them," said Mr. Ketchum.

"But you have no privacy," objected Sir Robert. "It must be disagreeable to have them prying in here and using their opera-glasses on you and your friends from the upper windows." (This was a novel idea to Mr. Ketchum, who laughed at it.) "I don't think I should like it myself. I don't like to be part of a system. I like to be independent."

"There is the solar system, you know: you can't escape from that. No, I have got all the privacy I could want. If I wanted solitude, I'd buy Pitcairn's Island, three thousand miles from anywhere, and have the birds exterminated. And of course if I found it unpleasant I should go somewhere else. I have got a lot of stuff about me that my wife has accumulated, and it wouldn't be quite as easy to pull up sticks as it is in East Tennessee, where all you've got to do is to call the dogs and shut the doors; but, still, I think sometimes I should like it. Brown lives just there,—the Brown you met in New York."

"I remember. Do you like him?" asked Sir Robert. "Pleasant family?"

"I have always liked him; but he has got a brother living with him who is the meanest man in America," said Mr. Ketchum, with decision. "There are three brothers; but the third hasn't been in the family show-case for some time. He never was good for much. Brown got him situations over and over again; but he was like a second-hand postage-stamp,—he wouldn't stick; and at last he did something or other and had to go to Mexico to look after his estates there. Brown's married daughter lives with him, too; and you have met Miss Bijou. Very pleasant ladies. The eldest one married unfortunately, and has got a separation and come back to her father. They have got an Englishman staying with them now. I haven't seen much of him, but he has been grovelling at Mabel's feet for two weeks." This last was intended principally for his wife, who had joined them.

"How can you say such things? How can you wilfully exaggerate so?" she replied. "It isn't true, at all." And then, as he rose and preceded them into the drawing-room, she said to Sir Robert, "Husband was jesting. And do not suppose that I meant that he was untruthful. I am quite sure that he would not tell an untruth for the world. But husband rather distorts things sometimes for amusement,—you may have noticed it,—and I always fear it may be misunderstood." A speech that served the baronet as a kind of *mot de caractère* and interested him in his sweet, simple little hostess, whom he had known only casually in Cheltenham

The other guests had all assembled by this time, and some of them had clustered about a charming wood fire that Mabel had ordered, the evening having turned chilly.

"Ah. here we are. Not drowned, not hurt, and, like the politicians, 'in the hands of our friends,'" Mr. Ketchum said, as he caught sight of them, and, going forward, he held out a hand to Mr. Heathcote and one to Mr. Ramsay at the same time, saying, with the genial warmth that made him an irresistible fellow to some people, "I am right-down glad to have you here, I de-clare,—all of you; and what I want you to do is to make yourselves perfectly at home and as contented as you can.—Mabel, this fire might be improved, I think. Where is the Congressman?"

"It is burning beautifully, dear; and if you disturb it it will very likely spark about and burn holes in the rug," she said. But, as he continued to look about him restlessly, she got the blower obediently and gave it to him, and he, stooping down, held it up in front of the fire until it was all roar and crackle, and then put it away satisfied.

"A little too hot for you, isn't it?" he said to Miss Noel, who was pushing her chair back. "Getting a little personal, isn't it? Hold on. I'll fix that all right." He was about to drag forward a plate-glass screen to place in front of her, when the dining-room door was thrown open and "dinner" was announced by Sanford (the new butler, just imported from New York), napkin in hand and eyes down-dropped.

Mrs. Sykes's eyes almost bade farewell to their sockets when she saw Fräulein Schmidt's bugled head-dress and jimp-waisted black silk disappear through the door in front of her, a lank arm and wrinkled, tremulous old hand so adjusted as to make it certain that she was being escorted by Mr. Ketchum. There had been a discussion between Job and his wife beforehand about this very matter. She had wanted him to do the conventional thing, which he refused utterly. She had suggested that he should make some apology—or let her do it, if he disliked the idea—for conduct so unprecedented from Miss Noel's point of view, not to speak of the others. Mrs. Vane had interested herself deeply in it as a vital question, and, not daring to tackle her son-in-law on the subject, had talked it to tatters with her daughter, and had prophesied that the whole party would leave the house on the following morning in mortal offence. Mrs. Ketchum senior had felt it her duty to tell her son that his English guests would certainly think that he had no respect for his own mother if he persisted in putting upon her a public affront, and that his duty, as she had said before and would say again, was to take *her* in to dinner. The result was that Mr. Ketchum calmly closed his ears to these appeals, declined to do, leave undone, or explain anything, and told Mabel that she might say what she pleased to the guests. Mrs. Ketchum, therefore, all soft deprecation and pretty, troubled concern, had explained to Miss Noel that it was "Husband's invariable rule," had imploringly "hoped she wouldn't mind," and had incidentally painted her lord's portrait as a kind of domestic archangel. And Miss Noel had "quite understood," and not been vexed at all; but Mabel was timid, and Mrs. Sykes was very awful to her, and she had not been

able to make the dreadful declaration in that quarter.
The thought of the Sykes stare, which certainly was
Gorgonian and alarming to less shy persons, and the
remembrance of the Sykes tongue, paralyzed this gentle
young person at the very door of her cousin's room,
and sent her down-stairs with the revelation unmade,
leaving her amiable relative wholly unprepared for the
shock that awaited her. "What's that for?" said Mrs.
Sykes imperiously to Mrs. Vane, actually pointing in
the direction of the retreating figures. But there was
no time for explanation. Mabel in a few murmurs had
already paired the company, and they all followed in
their host's wake.

The dinner was a well-ordered one, as was everything
about the establishment; for to American abundance
and variety, as shown in the ample provision for his
household made by Job, Mabel added English management and thrift, and the result was a *ménage* which even
their guests, accustomed to the almost military punctu-
ality and mellow, stable comfort of the most perfect
domestic system in the world, found delightful. It may
be a pardonable digression to say here that Mabel had
suffered almost as much from overplentifulness in
America as she had ever done from undue scarcity in
England. She had a conscientious horror of waste that
made it a great moral question what she should do with
the enormous quantities of food alone provided by her
liberal-minded spouse, who had no practical experience
of catering and a horror of being or seeing others
stinted. It drove her quite wild at first to see the
boxes, barrels, crates, coops, that he was always sending
out from Kalsing, and her distress vented itself in an

occasional mild exclamation, "What a dreadful country for waste, mamma dear!" To consume in any one house all that her husband provided was impossible. She could not have done it with a double staff of London servants, with their five meals a day and unlimited perquisites. To throw anything away, according to her creed, was wicked, and, according to Mrs. Vane, would certainly bring its retribution in personal want. At last, happily for all parties, a solution was found of the problem. A poor man, with a numerous progeny, moved into a particularly hopeless-looking cottage about a mile away on the Kalsing road, and that happy conjunction between food and mouths was effected which cynics declare does not often occur, and which lightened more hearts than Mabel's.

Gastronomically considered, the dinner, to which we must get back, presented no very striking features from first to last, unless it be accounted one that Sir Robert pronounced "the ices" quite the most delicious stuff he had ever tasted, and made acquaintance with pecans, which he thought so well of that he may be said to have become intimate with them on the spot and never to have separated from them afterward, as the pockets of all his coats testify to this day. Mrs. Sykes, whose appetite was immense, not only ate with great relish of such things as she was accustomed to, but absolutely made the daring experiment of trying one American dish, and reported on it promptly. "It is not as nasty and messy as it looks," she said to Miss Noel. "You might try it, if you like, but I should say it was perfectly indigestible. Still, one always likes to be able to say that one has tasted the native dishes, and after

26

taking birds'-nest soup, as I did in Hong-Kong, I can stand a little of anything."

"A little of some—things goes a very long way," said Mr. Ketchum; and there was something in the way he said it that made Miss Noel rush into an account of her journey, which, containing as it did the episode of the conductor, completely restored his good humor. He laughed over it in a way that quite surprised his wife, and called out to her, "Only hear, Mabel, what dreadful liberties the great American citizen has been taking with the British aristocracy!"

At which Miss Noel said, "Oh, pray don't fancy that I was really annoyed! Do you know, I think it must have been a little way of his to give nicknames? Parsons tells me that he called two children that sat behind her 'Bub' and 'Sis.' I am quite sure that he meant nothing, and it didn't signify: it was only a little odd just at first."

This sent Mr. Ketchum off into a fresh explosion of merriment, but he caught Mrs. Sykes's next speech. "The impertinent man actually laid his hand on my arm, once, to attract my attention, and was most unpleasantly obtrusive," she was observing to Mabel.

"Good heavens! you don't mean it? I wonder that it was not paralyzed up to the shoulder! Such audacity—" he began, but catching Mabel's eye and seeing that she was shaking her pretty head, he stopped abruptly and offered Miss Noel a dish she had already declined. He and Mr. Ramsay then got into a conversation about hunting and shooting, in which they talked very much at cross-purposes until they found out where the trouble was and defined their terms, Mr. Ramsay's red deer turning out to be Mr. Ketchum's elk; the European elk, the American moose; English thrushes, American robins; English grouse, American partridges; and so on. The other gentlemen were naturally attracted by topics so congenial, and a brisk discussion of guns, powder, shot, camp-life, Comanche-stalking, and the like, ensued that made Mr. Ramsay's eyes sparkle with interest. "How I should like a shy at one of those red devils!" he exclaimed. "I am going out to the far West, you know. I have come over to settle here, for a while at least."

"I am glad to hear that," said Job, who thought Mr. Ramsay looked the sort of man that ought always to be coming down the steps of the Guards' Club, and not a subduer of nature, a miner, herdsman, ranchero, pioneer, but did not feel called upon to express uncalled-for opinions.

"Yes, Ramsay is tired of the dry-rot of an idle life in London, and is going to sit down out in the bush and wait for civilization where there is only a fortnightly post and he will be quite out of the reach of telegrams, six men sleeping in the same tent, and that kind of thing. Just so. It is a fascinating sort of life for a young man. I have tried it myself, but I like my comfortable arm-chair and my newspaper now. '*Tempora mutantur, et nos mutamur in illis.*' I envy the fellow tremendously, except when I am pitying him with all my heart," said Sir Robert, running one hand through his side-whiskers and gazing benevolently, with his head a little on one side, at Mr. Ramsay.

"I don't mind roughin' it. I like it," said Mr. Ramsay. "And I think I have brought everything that I shall need. I was afraid you'd think I was goin' to give you the pleasure of my company for the rest of my life when you saw what an awful lot of luggage I had brought; but it is only that I am goin' out into the backwoods, where I've heard fellows say there wasn't so much as a corkscrew to be had for love or money. I hoped you'd excuse me bringin' it."

"Certainly, certainly: the more you bring, and the longer you stay, the better I shall be pleased. But, if you will let me, I'd like to see your outfit. I have lived out there, and may be able to give you a hint or two," said Mr. Ketchum.

"*Have* you, now? I shall be delighted! I'll get into my Colorado rig after dinner and show you what I'm like. Splendid get-up! Not very nobby, you know, for the Park, but quite the thing," replied Mr. Ramsay beamingly.

Miss Noel meanwhile had a very full and agreeable chat with Mrs. Ketchum senior about gardening, and sewing, and other practical topics, and very much surprised that lady by her mastery of them, as well as by her pronunciation of a certain word which she rendered unmistakably as "cowcumber." Mrs. Ketchum also noticed, this time with the most decided disapproval, that her left-hand neighbor was taking what she considered a scandalous amount of stimulant. Beer, sherry, champagne, claret, maraschino, and chasse-café made up a total that she had never seen a woman dispose of before, and, although Mrs. Sykes tossed them off with entire nonchalance as she had her glass filled and refilled by the butler, and did not seem in the least affected by any or all of them, Mrs. Ketchum felt the

most decided uneasiness about her, and was relieved
when Mabel gave the signal and they all trooped back
*en masse* to the drawing-room. Here Mrs. Sykes and
Mrs. Vane got together on the sofa. Mrs. Vane was
complimented on her "cleverness" in securing a son-in-
law like Mr. Ketchum for a portionless daughter, and,
on truthfully disclaiming any share in the marriage,
was playfully accused of being "deep, awfully deep."
Some very searching inquiries were also made by Mrs.
Sykes as to the amount of Mr. Ketchum's fortune
and the position and means of every one in the household, and her astonishment on hearing of what he had
done for Mrs. Vane alone was unbounded. "It will not
last," she said. "I suppose it results from a temporary
infatuation for Mabel's pretty face; but such an extraordinary state of things can't last." Mrs. Vane found
just the audience she had long craved to appreciate her
views of Fräulein's position in the house. "A fire to
dress by, burning in her room *all day long!* Silk dresses
given her! Spending all her evenings with the family!
Allowed the use of the carriage when she chooses!—
upon my word, I never heard anything like it in all my
life!" said Mrs. Sykes. "Has she got any hold over
him? An ugly secret of some kind, eh?" Poor Fräulein, who had shrunk up into a corner and was doing
some of her interminable tatting, divined from Mrs.
Sykes's scornful glances and short laughs that she was
under discussion, and was shrivelling morally under the
process, when Mr. Ketchum called out cheerily, "Why,
Mother Schmidt, where have you got, off there in the
cold?" and, getting up, placed an arm-chair for her near
the fire.

*u* 26*

Sir Robert was wandering aimlessly about the room, taking in the details of an international interior, turning over the books on the tables, the "Peerage" and "Who's who," some bound volumes of the "Penny Magazine," Miss Edgeworth's "Parent's Assistant" and similar works, "Tennyson's Poems," along with "Longfellow's Works," "Poe's Poems," the "Innocents Abroad," and a copy of the "Red Rover," on the fly-leaf of which was written, "Job Ketchum, from his devoted friend $1.50," the "Morning Post" and the "Queen" jostling "Texas Siftings" and the New York dailies.

The pictures and photographs, too, were eloquent of the two countries,—Mabel's father in his Oxford cap and gown, and again "having tea on the lawn with dear mamma," as Mabel put it, "and the Rectory (gabled and ivy-festooned) in the background." "My cousin Guy Huddlestone, taken just after he was gazetted." "Beatrice's baby that she sent home, taken with her Ayah." "Canon Ponsonby and the Bishop of Curds and Whey, both great friends of dear papa." "Husband when he was a little boy." (A most wonderful little boy, in very long trousers and a jacket that ended in the middle of his back, hair long and shiny, suggestive of Rowland's Macassar Oil, parted a little above the left ear, chubby hands clasped as if in prayer, eyes rolled up to match,—considered "perfectly sweet," when taken.) "Husband at school, a half-grown lad." "Husband, taken the year he came of age." "Husband in the uniform of his military company." "Husband after typhoid fever,—a perfect libel upon him." "Husband, done last year in New York; not as handsome as

ho, but the best of all the likenesses." "Husband's
father." (Preternaturally solemn and mortally ugly in
the picture, but really a pleasant-faced, benign old gen
tleman.) "The ancestral home of Husband's people"
(a square stone house of a dear old fashion, homely and
human, with a devoted-couple-and-twelve-children expression about it, the living-house of a God-fearing,
hard-working, rosy-cheeked, spinning, sleighing, snow-
balling, apple-eating family, set in a grove of fine trees);
and, underneath, a silhouette of "Husband's grandmother," a stately old lady, with a great deal of cap
and a Roman nose. It is by no means certain that, if
left to herself, Mabel would not have spoken of this
planet, supposing her to have occasion to allude to it,
as "Husband's world," and of Paradise as "the world
to which Husband is going." Baby Ketchum was now
brought in to bid good-night, and the ladies congregated
about him admiringly.

"Such a dear boy!" said Miss Noel. "Mayn't I take
him for a bit?" She held out her arms as she spoke,
and was soon passing her hand gently over his curls
and cataloguing his charms. "Now let us see, childie,
who you are like."

"Oh, *Husband!*" said Mabel decisively.

"Really a nice child, Mabel," commented Mrs. Sykes
tepidly, regarding him from her seat on the sofa. "Good,
fresh color, nice mottled legs. He looks healthy and as
though he would not give trouble. What name have
you given him?"

"Jared Ponsonby," said Mabel bravely, the ready
color mounting to her cheeks.

Mrs. Sykes looked as though she had heard of an

Irish Jew or a Japanese Presbyterian, but, for a world's
wonder, she made no actual comment: she only arched
her brows eloquently and expressed silently Sir Pertinax
MacSycophant's "Such an admixture!"

Seeing that the child was getting restless, Miss Noel
said, "Where are you going, and to whom? Mammy,
daddy, or granny?" And the boy for answer slipped
off her lap, and, running across the rug, clambered up
on Fräulein's knee, where he was rapturously received
with cries of "*Das herzliebste!*" his curly head being
pressed against her heart, her broad German face beaming gratification at this little mark of preference.

Heartily was Job loved and honored by the Fräulein.
and she loved and obeyed Mabel without reservation.
But as for the child, she adored him, and was his abject
slave, over whom he ran like a small car of Jugger-
naut whenever he felt the need of motion. Unconscious
of any sacrifice, and fully conscious of his power, he
had a hook in her nose before he could walk, and ever
after led her where he chose, accepted her devotion as
his right, and repaid it with the careless regard which
seems the portion of the too fond worshipper the world
over. His grandmothers squabbled over him, corrected
him, and in their way loved him, but it was "Frou" (as
he called her) who might have been seen anxiously
going through her Silurian hair-trunk in search of some
fresh trifle to please his royal highness, he standing by,
overseeing the job, with her gold watch on and an ag-
gravation of his father's restless energy. One grandmother—the American one—had been shocked by this
talk of "Granny," and "Daddy," and "Mammy," titles
which had only a cob-pipe and patchwork-quilt associa-

tion for her, "vulgar terms that it amazed her to hear from the lips of an English lady," as she afterward told Mabel. There had been a family discussion about some other titles and what "Boy" should call his parents. Mabel disliked the American variations of an old theme as heard in "Mar," "Maw," "Mair" (short, with a bleat), "Marmer," "Mommer," and their correlatives "Par," "Paw," "Pair" (another bleat, if you please), "Parper," "Popper." She was in favor, "Husband" permitting, of Papá and Mamá, as being more or less in vogue in both countries. Mr. Ketchum objected to even this compromise. The grandmothers ranged themselves under one or other of these banners, did a good deal of sharpshooting, and would have liked nothing better than to keep the question on the hob for a year or two. Mr. Ketchum, however, decided that the original air should reappear for once, and "father" and "mother" became the earliest utterances of the boy, undergoing only the necessary—if temporary—modification of "farzy" and "mozzy."

But to return. Mr. Ketchum was prowling up and down the drawing-room, stopping occasionally to glance out at what remained of a beautiful sunset, when a ring came at the bell, and Sanford admitted a gentleman, who could be plainly seen through the open door divesting himself of his overcoat and hat. Mr. Ketchum recognized him and smiled. He had expected him to call, but not quite so promptly. Elsewhere he would probably have greeted him with a careless "How're you, Bates? How was the queen when you left Windsor Castle?" Or, "What did 'Wales' say in his last letter?" But, punctilious in his ideas of hospitality, he now advanced, shook hands heartily, and presented him to the others. Mr. Bates was a tall man, whose figure was constructed on a few bold lines, as though he had been a towel-horse. Mr. Ketchum once said of him that when the workmen had finished building him they forgot to take down the scaffolding. He was dressed in the exaggeratedly British style, had an air of feeble gentlemanliness, and for the rest was rather a pronounced specimen of a not uncommon sort of snob. Heaven had denied him the boon he most coveted,—the happiness of being an Englishman; but an Englishman he had determined to be, in spite of the accident of birth. He lacked a great many gifts that a lesser soul would have thought indispensable to the *rôle* he proposed to play. His physique was not up to the mark, his tastes and habits and speech were formed, his voice was nasal, he had really nothing except his money and himself to depend upon,—yet mark the result. In a few short years he was more English than any Englishman in England,—such is the power of a resolute will. He was taken for one over and over again by Americans, who keep a portrait of John Bull hung up in their mental picture-galleries, just as John Bull does of his neighbor Johnny Crapaud and Monsieur Crapaud in his turn of Hans Schneider,—remarkably good likenesses all of them, of course, perfectly faithful, if not entirely flattering. Count D'Orsay once painted the picture of a friend and submitted it when finished to that friend's wife for criticism. "It is a good picture," was her verdict, "but not a good likeness." "Ah, madame," said the artist, "you see de beast," (meaning the best). We all see the beast in these national portraits, and do not greatly care about the likeness being preserved.

The English craze was only the last expression of a constitutional thirst for distinction that had long tormented Mr. Bates and had led him in the earlier stages of his career to talk only of the most fashionable people, and of these as his most intimate friends,—of their yachts, carriages, jewels, opera-boxes, and enormous fortunes,—of the best hotels, where he invariably stayed, —of the best clubs, at which every one hastened to put him up,—of his tailor, Poole, and his boot-maker, Biffins, the best in Europe, though (with an uneasy laugh) "frightfully expensive,"—of his cigars, which Cubans thought superior to any they had ever smoked,—and his wines, which a well-known *bon vivant* of New York had pronounced the best he had ever found on this continent. There was so much sweetness and light in Mr. Bates's accounts of himself at this period that it was doubtless only from the most charitable motives that society supplied the shadows in the brilliant picture and mitigated his else intolerable radiance by whispering that he was a simpleton and a bore and the son of a successful grocer in Tecumseh, Michigan.

The sight of so many English people was naturally refreshing to an exile like Mr. Bates, and he bestowed upon them the seven bendings, if not the nine knockings, with which Chinese dignitaries are saluted. Mrs. Sykes made him a present of a stare and took no further notice of him. Sir Robert divined the ass in the lion's skin, but made himself agreeable as usual. Mr. Ketchum played with a paper-knife and contributed intermittently to the conversation, as did Ethel and Mr.

Ramsay. As for Mabel, she had gòne up to the nursery, and so missed hearing Mr. Bates tell the company that he had been "yahs and yahs abroad, and was perfectly devoted to England," compare the climate, customs, and what not of the two countries, always to the disadvantage of his own, and round off every other sentence with a "Don't *you* find it so?" to Sir Robert.

"I think this a most delightful, exhilarating climate. I wonder at your liking ours better: it is so notoriously bad that we spend half our time abusing it," Sir Robert said in reply to one appeal.

But the visitor continued to set forth only the more plainly the impossibility of America's ever proving a congenial home to a Bates. Everything about it offended his exquisite sensibilities. It was "raw," it was "cold," it was "bare," it was "frightfully new." The grass, the skies, the architecture, all distilled torture upon this delicately-organized poet-soul. But the people,—last, worst, most unendurable and unescapable pang of all,—the people!

Mr. Ketchum broke his paper-knife as he listened, and as he threw the pieces aside he heard Mr. Bates saying, "Give me solid old England, I say," and looked up, to see " *Que diable fait-il dans cette galère?*" written so legibly in Sir Robert's honest English face that his vexation was replaced by amusement.

"Ah!" said Sir Robert, and the exclamation expressed something of the contempt he felt; "I should have thought, now, that you would have preferred your own country to any other; most people do." Sir Robert would very probably have been bored by the American who is always insisting blatantly upon the absolute superiority of everything American; he would have understood the American who in speaking of his country shows the loving pride and enthusiasm that a son feels for his mother; but he utterly despised the creature who held in such light esteem that for which most men are ready to lay down their lives.

The conversation languished rather, except so far as Mr. Bates was concerned. Bent upon posing as a personage and a social authority, he rambled on inconsequently, chiefly about himself and his affairs, opinions, experiences, what he considered "good form" and knew to be "bad form," of something that was "not the correct thing," and something else that was "no longer fashionable," and, finally, of some people who had bought a house near his whom he characterized as "low people,"—"tradespeople," he believed, whom he should have nothing to do with, of course.

"Quite right, Bates," said Mr. Ketchum. "You can't afford to know everybody: it would be a 'boah,' as you say. But don't be too hard on them. We can't *all* be upper crust, you know; somebody has got to be bedrock. We aristocrats should remember that." And, having dived after Miss Noel's ball of wool, which had rolled toward him, he added, "Pretty sunset that for a new country, isn't it? I like that view that we get of the valley through the trees, there, better than any other in America. I say America because it sounds as though I had been all over the world and prevents my being identified with my own country, which is my great object in life."

At this Sir Robert and Mr. Ramsay laughed and exchanged glances, and Mrs. Ketchum, coming in, called

o                              27

for an *aide-de-camp*, as she meant to "turn out the tea
that instant, but was not going to trot about with it,"
—a summons which both Mr. Bates and Mr. Ramsay
obeyed with alacrity.

"You go in tremendously for china, don't you?" Mr.
Ramsay said, looking admiringly at the exquisite service before him and removing the crimson cosey that
smothered the teapot. "Prettiest I ever saw, I think.
Nice tone, and all-overish design."

"It *is* rather nice, isn't it?" said Mabel. "I often
wish that I could go to China and prowl about the shops
a bit, picking up things. You will take me some day,
won't you?" (to her husband.) "It would be quite
delightful."

"It would be; but the question that presents itself
to the intelligent and reflective mind is, 'Where the
mischief is the money to come from?' The inclemency
of the times makes no impression on you, Mrs. Ketchum,
whatever. China, indeed! Haven't you enough of that
sort of thing yet? I assure you, Mr. Ramsay, that my
wife's extravagance in this matter is only equalled by
her parsimony. She is always buying china; but when
we have no company I am made to eat my dinner off a
tin plate on the back steps, to save wear and accidents.
Ah, there is Brown; come just in time to save me from
joining the noble company of cashiers in the woods.—
Glad to see you, Brown."

"Husband does jest so! The idea of his saying—"
Mabel began, but had to go forward to receive Mr.
Brown, his brother Mr. Albert Brown, and their maiden
sister Miss Susan Brown. The last was a great friend
of Fräulein Schmidt's, and joined her very soon; the

brothers proceeded to make their compliments to the English ladies; Mr. Bates attached himself to Ethel; and Job and the baronet were left to their own devices for the moment.

"Is that the brother you dislike?" asked Sir Robert, nodding toward Mr. Albert Brown. "Not a pleasant face, certainly: receding forehead, protruding eyes, thin lips."

"Oh, it is not his personal pulchritude that I look at: it is his pellet of a soul. A dozen such would rattle in a mustard-seed," replied Mr. Ketchum, giving his chair an energetic hitch. "He is so mean that if you were to bait a trap with a postage-stamp you would catch Albert six nights out of seven every week in the year. He was very ill last winter,—said to be dying,—but the doctor held a nickel under his nose, I suppose, at the last moment, and brought him back again. Strange to say, Brown is no more like him than if he had never heard of him. His heart is as big as all out-doors. Streaky family,—like breakfast bacon. I have known them all my life, but I never could stand Albert; and I have never asked him to my house. He's no friend of mine, and I feel at liberty to express myself pretty freely about him. I wonder what brought him here to-night. Bug under that chip."

Sir Robert would willingly have stayed with his host for the remainder of the evening, but just as they had changed the topic of conversation and settled down into a comfortable talk about several things that interested him,—such as the wages of servants, agricultural laborers, and artisans in Michigan, the price of bread and cost of living, the advantage of the great lakes as a commercial highway, expense per bushel of transporting grain to England, and the merchant-marine of America, —Mabel joined them, and asked Sir Robert if he would not play a game of whist with her mother for a partner and Mr. Brown and Miss Noel as his adversaries. Agree ing to this, he walked over and took his seat at the card-table, and was soon horrifying Mr. Brown by pro posing to play for money,—only sixpenny points and "hardly an object," as he explained when he found himself, to his great surprise, indirectly accused of gambling. "There isn't a clergyman in England who wouldn't do it," he said; "but don't let me undermine your principles over here," and forthwith proceeded to give himself up to the game with immense gravity and such philosophy as he could command with a partner who revoked, trumped his aces, dropped her cards, talked across the board, announced what she had in her hand, never knew what the trump was, and had every other fault that a player possibly could have or that could infuriate a veteran member of a London whist-club.

As Mabel went back to her seat she heard Mrs. Sykes saying, "I can't say that I care for American scenery: it seems to consist chiefly of St. Jacob's Oil on rotting fences, and stony, badly-tilled fields, and weazly sheep or cows, with an occasional telegraph-pole thrown in. But still I am glad to have seen it. One *must* see America nowadays, or one is nobody. What do I think of this house? Oh, comfortable enough. The library is good, the pictures barely tolerable—"

What more fault she was about to find did not appear, for just then the door opened, and Mr. Ramsay came in, accoutred in the "rig" he had spoken of, and blushing furiously at the sight of the additions made to the party in his absence.

"The haughty Briton, as he appears in the famous *rôle* of ' The Border Ruffian,' " called out Mr. Ketchum, laughingly. "Come here, Ramsay, and let us have a look."

Redder still, but radiating satisfaction through the veil of modesty, Mr. Ramsay joined his host on the hearth-rug and bore with entire good humor the general inspection that followed. He was dressed in a flannel shirt, a pair of corduroy trousers, enormous jack-boots, and a cork helmet, was belted and spurred, carried a haversack, wore gauntlets that came nearly up to his elbow, had a kind of wire coop with a gauze net stretched over it attached to his helmet, and as to arms was a peripatetic arsenal. " Green of the Fusiliers got me up this,—he's been out in Mexico a lot,—all but this," touching the coop. " I got that up to get ahead of those brutes of mosquitoes," he said, and glanced at himself in fond approval.

The sight was too much for Mr. Ketchum. He looked from the bristling, buccaneering Mr. Ramsay to the side-whiskered and generally Britished Mr. Bates standing a few paces off, and incontinently fled. Mabel followed him into the dining-room, and found him convulsed with laughter and fairly doubled up on the sofa. " What *is* the matter, husband? what is it?" she asked, seeing nothing to put anybody into such a state.

" Oh! It's th-o—ha! ha! ha! ha! ha!—those two —ha! ha! ha! ha! ha! ha! ha! ha!—those two *imitations!"* Mr. Ketchum got out, with great difficulty, and convulsed afresh, laughing until the tears rolled down

27*

his cheeks, to the no small amazement of his wife, who looked on quite anxiously at the demonstration. It was some moments before he could compose himself sufficiently to go back; and even then his features worked ominously, and he had the greatest difficulty in controlling his risibles.

Mr. Ramsay was still contemplating himself delightedly and talking of what he meant to do "out in Colorado and those parts."

Gradually sobering down, Mr. Ketchum joined in the conversation, telling him that they would have a serious talk about the Colorado plan next day, and saying what he could for the "rig." "You have been handed around on a rose-leaf all your life, my dear fellow. You'll find it exchanged for a cactus out there,—the roughest sort of life, and human nature in its shirt-sleeves. If you were not an Englishman, I should advise you either to go home again or invest in a quarter's worth of arsenic. You can't mine in hard-bake with a pewter spoon, you know. But I reckon you are made of the right metal and will come out ahead on that fight."

"I can't go home, you know. It is no good talking of that. I haven't got the money to live there, unless I turned mud-lark," said Mr. Ramsay. "The governor won't do anything for me, and I can't get tick, and I am obliged to try the colonies or America."

"Well, anything is better than being an English gentleman who can't keep up with the procession," said Mr. Ketchum; "and perhaps you may be the pigeon that is to pick up a pea."

After this there was some music, and then Sanford brought in the tray, with the materials on it for brewing what Mr. Ketchum called "the muriate of susquate of iodized potassium."

Miss Brown refused to stay long enough to either see the deed done or partake of the contents of the flowing bowl, and the party broke up, Mr. Bates kindly assuring Sir Robert that he meant to see a great deal of him.

Good-nights were exchanged, and the front door closed.

"I hope Mr. Brown did not take my hat," said Sir Robert, and walked up to the rack to assure himself that such was the case. His eye fell upon a little pile of narrow pasteboard strips, on which was engraved, "Mr. Bates, 10 Chapel Street, Belgrave Square." Mr. Bates's cards always bore this strange device. "What an ass!" commented the baronet, with a frown of disgust on his face; and to this Mr. Ketchum added something emphatic that will not be set down here.

The "muriate" having been mixed on purely chemical and medicinal principles and imbibed from a strong sense of duty, they all took their bedroom candles, and were about to ascend the stairs, when Sir Robert suddenly stopped, and said to his host, "How am I to dress to-morrow? What shall I wear?" An embarrassing pause followed. "What are we going to do?" he added.

The English people present understood that, accustomed to the carefully-arranged programmes of visits at English country-places, Sir Robert expected that certain occupations and amusements, involving suitable preparations for the same, were to be his portion in America.

"Oh, dear, how shall we amuse him?" thought Mabel dolefully.

It was Job who came to the general rescue. "Wear what you please," he said. "America was invented for the express purpose of getting one place where people could wear out their old clothes and do as they pleased."

Sir Robert laughed, as did the others in chorus, they resumed their march, and in another moment had disappeared into their respective bedrooms.

"We will show Sir Robert our old castles and ruins to-morrow, and our cathedrals and abbeys the next day, and so on," said Mr. Ketchum to his wife. "Wasn't Ramsay a spectacle for gods and men? When I see a fellow like that come over here, Daisy,—and they are coming by the dozen,—fellows with the tastes and habits of millionaires and only such knowledge of life and people as is to be gained on the right side of English park-palings, trained to no profession or pursuit, as ignorant of business matters as our little child, and suddenly set down in one of our frontier communities, like the Babes in the Wood, I always feel like saying to them, 'May the Lord have mercy on your souls!' The homesickness, the strangeness of everything, the hardships, and the almost certain failure make up a row of stumps, I tell you; the stoniest sort of patch to plough with a crooked stick and a strange heifer."

"But why need they plough with a crooked stick, dear? It is very sad for the poor things," Mabel replied.

"What do you think of all this?" Mrs. Sykes was asking of Miss Noel, their rooms communicating and both ladies passing to and fro.

"I think it is all very nice,—very nice indeed. I am sure we have every comfort and luxury we could possibly desire; and the people are most obliging, civil, and agreeable," replied Miss Noel.

· "You are positively infatuated about the Americans," grumbled Mrs. Sykes from her room.

"Oh, no; nothing of the kind. But we are not likely to agree about them; and, as I am considerably tired with the fatigues of the day, I may as well close my door and take myself straight off to bed," said Miss Noel, shutting the door of argument as well as the one of oak.

The next day was Saturday, and by half-past six o'clock Miss Noel was up and out, getting three hours of walking and botanizing before breakfast, and coming in full of praises of the beautiful day, a basket of wild flowers on her arm.

Mrs. Sykes also rose early, and, having written a great number of letters, in which she gave very spicy accounts of "the way they do things in America," proceeded to make herself entirely at home, as Mr. Ketchum·had urged her to do. There was a spare-room adjoining hers, into which she had her writing- and sketching-materials carried, and which she said would do very well for her boudoir during her visit. She made Parsons unpack her boxes first, instead of Miss Noel's. She had all her stockings collected that needed darning, and took them affably to "Schmidt," as she called Fräulein, telling her to "repair them neatly, Swiss fashion." She went on a grand prowl about the house to see what it was like, in the course of which she got as far as the lumber-room in the garret, where a maid was packing away the surplus winter bedding; and, seeing the store-room door ajar, she marched in there, and was staring

with lively interest at its wealth of "goodies," when
Mabel entered, followed by the cook. Not disconcerted
in the least, she said to Mabel, "What a larder you have
got, to be sure! I suppose you are very contented living over here on the fat of the land."

"I am contented; but it is not because I am living on
the fat of the land, as you call it," said Mabel coldly,
and then went on to give directions to the servant,
which she purposely spun out until Mrs. Sykes took the
hint and left.

Having exhausted her resources, Mrs. Sykes went out
on the front veranda, where any amount of amusement
awaited her in the person of "Hannibal Hamlin," the
first little darky she had ever met. In a moment she
was all rapture. "Oh, how delightfully black he is!
How he shines! What comical bow-legs! Poke him
up and make him laugh, or cry, or amuse me in some
way, somebody. Pray put him down there in front of
me, where I can see his eyes roll. Where did you get
the comical creature? I never saw anything so delicious and intensely interesting."

"He is Washington's son," said Mr. Ketchum.

"Rummest pickanniny I ever saw," said Mr. Heathcote. "Friend of yours?" (to Mr. Ketchum.)

"Yes; a particular one. I took a fancy to him first
because he looked so fresh from the cocoanut-tree; and
he's as smart as they are made. Come here, Hannibal,"
said Mr. Ketchum. Fishing in his pocket, he pulled out
a quarter, whistled a lively air, and fell to executing the
motion known as "patting juber." Up sprang Hanni
bal, and, small as he was, danced a breakdown, as a
pouter-pigeon inflates his breast, by sheer instinct. His

grins, his bare brown legs, his tatters, the indescribable African swing that he put into the movement, delighted the spectators beyond measure. They laughed uproariously through the whole performance; and Ethel and Mr. Ramsay, having only got down in time to see the final shuffles and whirls, insisted on an encore. Miss Noel arrived in time for that, and it was received with as much enthusiasm as the first, even Sir Robert giving out a series of painfully obstructed snorts and chuckles that indicated his appreciation.

"Never saw such a little nigger; drollest specimen of a blackie possible," he said.

"Sh-sh! colored person, you mean. We are having our English history rewritten so as to bring out the figure of the Colored Prince properly," said Mr. Ketchum. "Would you like to see him cut a few more capers?"

A general cry of "Oh, do!" and "That we should!" went up, and Mr. Ketchum began to whistle again. But he had reckoned without his Hannibal, who had thrown himself down on his back and declined to stir.

"I'se tired. Ain't gwine to dance no mo'," he said.

Threats, temptations, cajolery, were tried in vain. The impudent and independent attitude of the child amused them almost as much as his dancing, but they could not understand how he dared refuse to obey Mr. Ketchum. They would have kept him spinning away for another hour, if he had not shown the caprice of the artist and strutted off with the funniest swaggering air while Mrs. Sykes was gone in search of her block and pencil, intending to sketch him. This she did later, in a great variety of attitudes; and during the remainder of their visit Hannibal was an unfailing source of interest.

Breakfast over, they nearly all returned to the veranda again,—the ladies bringing out their work, the gentlemen smoking and reading. Sir Robert and Job each had a pile of newspapers to look over, and effected an exchange from time to time of the English for the American, though of the latter Mrs. Sykes remarked, "I can't see what interest you can find in them. They are ill written and abusive, and the ridiculous vulgarity of the advertisements is very tiresome."

Sir Robert was a man who read every part of his paper; and, having mastered the contents of his copies of the "Times," "Standard," "Pall Mall Gazette," and "Guardian," he tackled some of the leading American dailies, and then some of the minor and more provincial sheets. It was a funny sight to see his expression as he wrestled with the allusions to the Chicago girl's foot, the Rig-Veda and baked beans paragraphs about Boston, and such jokes as, "Mrs. Wills Hackett lit her new fire with coal-oil on the morning of the 23d of February: her clothes fit the present Mrs. Hackett to a T;" or the refined pleasantry of such stories as, "'Yes, Adolphus, there is a terrible gap between us,' said Araminta, when her parlor young man gave a yawn at 1.30 A.M." Bewilderment gave place to a different emotion when he saw that a certain quack medicine was "reliable,—being what it was in the beginning, is now, and ever shall be;" that "Jim Phelps" (vide a police report) "had blasphemed his Maker five dollars' worth;" also a verse from the Sermon on the Mount used to advertise a "Professor" of chiropody; and a leading article in which

with much delicate editorial raillery the Queen of England and the Princess Louise were cruelly belittled by
being called "Vic" and "Lou."

Mr. Ketchum, meanwhile, was enjoying the "Court
Chronicle," in which "Her Majesty walked out on
Friday morning attended by the Duchess of Bam-
borough," and evidently returned quite safely to luncheon, as the next paragraph proved: "Her Majesty drove
in the afternoon, attended by the Duchess of Bam-
borough." He was revelling in the advertisements for
"a serious cook;" an "Evangelical footman," a housemaid to whom no "flounces or followers" would be permitted, "a young, musical, cheerful High-Church curate,
with decided views on the eastward position, who would
be expected to take two services on Sunday, train the
choir-boys, and teach Latin, Greek, French, and English
branches in a school; graduate of Oxford preferred:
£50," and of "Tomes & Dollop, wig-makers to all the
crowned heads of Europe." He had got to "sermons
for busy rectors, High, Low, or Broad, at 12/6 the dozen,"
when he heard an exclamation from Sir Robert, and,
looking up, saw him clutching fiercely the "Columbia
Eagle," his face brick-red with anger and excitement.
"Look at this!" he cried: "this infamous, lying article
about me!" He pushed the paper into Job's hands, who
saw a long article chopped into short paragraphs and
spiced with sensational head-lines: "*A Bloated Baronet!*" "*British Vampires and Land-Grabbers!*" "*Millions of Acres Wrested from the American People!*" "*Congressional Legislation Needed!*" "*Rascally Earls and
Bankrupt Dukes!*" The writer of the article was the
reporter who had "interviewed" Sir Robert in Wash-

28

ington. He purported to give a verbatim account of that interview, and was very particular to state the kind of chair Sir Robert sat in, where his arm rested, his changes of position and expression. He painted the baronet's portrait in India ink, ridiculed and abused him in the most grossly personal and shameless fashion, invented for him an entire conversation containing his "views," motives, thoughts, and plans, and then took him as a text for a violent attack upon the Englishmen of rank who have bought extensive properties in this country. Not that a word was said about the purchase-money. It was stated that "the blue blood of England had pro duced nothing but rascals, sots, and libertines for the last two hundred years." A magnificent image of "free America stalking athwart the stage of English politics like Banquo's ghost, terrifying tyrants and inspiring serfs," was drawn. In connection with the well-known tendency of rats to leave a sinking ship, it was pointed out that "a number of so-called noblemen had come over here and gone to the virgin West, where they had wrung from the horny-handed sons of toil the blood-bought domain which constituted the sole inheritance of their children." And why? "*That they might plant the Upas-tree of aristocratic institutions upon the free soil of Columbia!*" While Mr. Ketchum read this veracious, dispassionate production, so creditable in every respect to American civilization, Sir Robert walked rapidly backward and forward and roared and raged in a pretty fury.

"Oh, these Americans! these Americans!" exclaimed Mrs. Sykes, and smiled hatefully.

Mr. Ketchum shot an angry glance at her, but ad

dressed Sir Robert. "I shouldn't care a claco, if I were you," he said. "It is some fellow that would rather tell a lie on credit than the truth for cash, I guess. Nobody will attach any importance to it. Don't let it worry you." But Sir Robert was of a different opinion, and attached great importance to it. It was not only that it did not contain a word of truth, but that "the rights of others were involved, the public mind would be inflamed, it would lead to acts of spoliation." Mr. Ketchum would greatly oblige him by recommending "a respectable solicitor in Kalsing" whom he might consult and instruct to prosecute at once. Nothing would do but that he should have legal advice; and, after using every argument he could think of to dissuade him from this course, Mr. Ketchum agreed to drive him into town that afternoon.

The day was one of those warm lovely ones in early summer that are enough to draw the very nails out of a house, so that the ladies had lingered outside. There was nothing thunderous or electrical in the atmospheric conditions, but all the same it was destined to be a day of disturbances. His talk ended with Sir Robert, Mr. Ketchum walked back into the dining-room to give Sanford an order, and while there he was surprised to hear loud sounds coming from the hall. ".Can my old ladies have locked horns?" he thought, and walked quickly back to see what was the matter. The matter was this. Shortly before the arrival of the English guests Mrs. Ketchum had lost a model housemaid, and had hired as a stop-gap an Irish girl of the genus Biddy, a hopeless incapable, with what the French call a *flamberge au vent* in the way of a temper. Mrs. Sykes noticed her, and promptly asked Mabel where she got " that flauntily-dressed sloven, with no idea of her position or duties, and positively flounced up to the waist." Thanks to mistress rather than maid, all had gone smoothly for a few days; but this morning the degrading task of polishing two grates and hanging up the cascades of tissue-papers that Mabel had made for fire-screens had been assigned to her, and her Milesian soul had utterly revolted at the idea. So down she came to her mistress, and, with arms akimbo and face aflame, poured out a Niagara of impertinence and rebellion that utterly amazed the guests and made Mabel turn pale. Sir Robert, in the absence of Mr. Ketchum, was about to tell her that he would "give her in charge,"—a threat he would have found some difficulty in carrying out,—when Mr. Ketchum appeared on the scene and took such active measures that in fifteen minutes a scornfully erect female figure might have been seen sitting in a cart that was bowling out of the grounds *en route* to Kalsing.

Ten minutes later another interruption came that contrasted comically with the previous one. It was Parsons this time,—Parsons with her exaggerated deference and propriety of manner, saying, " If you please, mem, Master Bobo and Miss Blanche 'ave been fightin' that dreadful I could 'ardly separate 'em, and Master Bobo's h'ear is all tore and bleedin' frightful! What would you please to wish done about it? Will I bathe it with a little loo-warm water and h'arnica, if there's any hotted ?"

This dreadful news sent both Miss Noel and Mrs. Sykes in-doors with cries of " Oh, my poor cat !" and

"That beastly cat! To touch my dearest angel!" leaving a smiling company behind them, and one person—Mr. Ketchum—extravagantly merry.

"Parsons ought to be exhibited in all our towns and cities," he said. "'Miss Blanche! Master Bobo!' Moses in the bulrushes!" He was in full enjoyment of this, when some visitors were seen approaching. These . proved to be some ladies from the neighborhood, one of them being Miss Bijou Brown. Miss Noel and Mrs. Sykes were sent for, and, reappearing, gave an account of the late fracas, each proving that the pet of the other was alone to blame. Bijou stayed some time, was extremely effusive and cordial to Miss Noel and Ethel, and, when she left, cast a good many quick, bright glances about her, which, being translated,—though she would never have admitted as much even to herself,—meant that she had expected and hoped to see Mr. Ramsay, who chanced to be out of the way. A second batch of callers followed,—Dr. Rhodes, the Ketchums' family physician, and Governor Bunnell, from a neighboring State, a florid, fluent politician, who was staying with the doctor. Both gentlemen made an agreeable impression, and were urged by Mrs. Ketchum to stay to luncheon, but declined.

About two hours later the carriage came round, and Miss Noel, Mrs. Sykes, Sir Robert, and Mr. Ketchum started for Kalsing. Washington was instructed to take a certain route, that an especially fine view of the valley might be enjoyed; and they were about half-way when they saw quite a large crowd gathered at the cross-roads near a blacksmith's shop. As they approached, they saw the figure of a man uplifted above

28*

the rest, who seemed to be gesticulating wildly ; a little nearer, and they could see him plainly.

"Pull up, Washington," called out Mr. Ketchum, and the carriage stopped.

"Dear, dear! *Can that be the governor-general ?"* asked Miss Noel, hardly believing her own eyes. "What is 'he doing ?"

"Ranting like a street-preacher, evidently," said Mrs. Sykes, but nobody paid much attention.

The governor was beginning the summer campaign that was to culminate at the polls in the autumn. He was a ready-witted man and a capital speaker. He knew how to interest his audience and keep them interested. He perfectly understood the art of turning interruptions of every kind to account. He knew how to tell a joke or story, and did not tell too many. He was affable, grave, satirical, jocose, statistical, by turns. He got off two Latin quotations that were not the less effective for not being understood. He fused the mass before him with his fervent oratory, and swept them along by the force of an eloquence not of the highest order indeed, but extremely effective for his purpose. The crowd roared and cheered with a will. Cries of "Give it to 'em, Johnny!" "That's right! waltz into 'em, Jack!" "Hand 'em another!" rang out. Sir Robert listened with all his ears. Even the ladies caught the excitement, and for an hour the governor had the pleasure of printing his sentiments on the agricultural mind as plainly as if he had represented a mould and they so many pats of butter. Then he relapsed into private life, put on his coat, which had been laid aside, poured some water from a pitcher (standing on a keg in front of him) into a glass, drank it off, and scrambled down from the wagon in which he had been enthroned.

"Splendid, governor! splendid!" called out Mr. Ketchum. The governor bowed his acknowledgments, and Washington was told to drive on.

"A rattling good speech," said Sir Robert, and plunged into a discussion of the whole electoral system of America, that gave Mrs. Sykes no chance to express her views then. Demosthenes could not have excited her admiration or retained her respect in the governor's place; and her asides to Miss Noel were so contempt uous that it was a lucky thing that they were not overheard by her host.

"It was a clever speech," said Miss Noel,—"Robert says that; but I can't think why he took off his coat. So dreadfully improper! And the wagon and that. Why didn't he take up his quarters at an inn, and have committees and all that, and speak from a balcony, I wonder? He certainly is not supported by anybody. The principal gentlemen of Kalsing and county-people must be in favor of the opposite party. I fear he must be a sad Radical. They call him 'Jack,' as if one of themselves!"

Arrived at Kalsing, the ladies did a little shopping and Sir Robert secured a lawyer. He also saw while in that part of the town a notice affixed to a door that caused him to stare very hard for a moment and then laugh outright. It bore this legend every day at the same hour: "Gone to dinner. Be back in ten minutes." "Ten minutes for *dinner*, by George!" he mentally exclaimed, and drove back to a good dinner of his own, over which he spent so many hours that poor Mr. Ketchum, forbidden by his wife to leave the table, wriggled about on his chair as if impaled.

That evening no one came except Mr. Price and his sister, an extremely vivacious and soulful, not to say silly, young woman, who, considering how little there was in her to express, contrived to throw an astonishing amount of expression into a pair of large brown eyes. By an amusing chance, Mr. Price undertook to talk to Mrs. Sykes; and if ever Greek met Greek it was on that occasion. They mutually plied each other with questions until they were both exhausted, and then parted with a hearty mutual dislike. His *first*, to put it in charade form, was, "Pleasant journey out here? Scalper's ticket or regular one?" and the information she gleaned from him about railway-tickets alone ought to have made her more lenient in her judgment of him, especially as she made it the basis of a settlement with Sir Robert a few days later when they went over their accounts for travelling expenses, and she refused to pay for any but a scalper's ticket from New York to Kalsing, on the ground that Sir Robert ought to have managed better and not have put her to "unnecessary expense." She ungratefully spoke of Mr. Price as "an inquisitive little beast," however, and he said of her that she could ask more questions than anybody he had ever met since he was born, and was "eaten up with curiosity." "Asking me who Mr. Ketchum was, and what he is worth, and whether they knew many nice people, and a hundred things," he said. "I hate a curious woman. I've got no use for them." Nor had he.

Meanwhile, Miss Price rattled on and on, and rolled her entire eyeballs at Mr. Ramsay, who, having had a tiff with Ethel that afternoon, was obliged to fall back on Miss Price for amusement. This she afforded ; and after a long *tête-à-tête* she rose to make her adieux, clapping her hands breezily in his face by way of impressing on him that he had promised to come and see her, and assuring him that she would be "perfectly desperate" if he didn't come. She then said good-by to Miss Noel in her own peculiar fashion. She took her hand, shot a glance of almost tragic emotion not so much at as into Miss Noel, and murmured, "*So* glad to have met you! So glad! *Let* me kiss you, won't you? I pine to kiss the cousin of a duke." Without waiting for an answer, which Miss Noel was too much taken aback to give, she saluted that lady, and, still holding her hand, shot a glance expressive of a heart-rending pang of separation at Mrs. Sykes, and murmured, "So glad to have met you, too! Charmed. *You* will come and see me, too, will you not? *Say* that you will."

"I will, if I can manage it conveniently, and if I can't I won't," said Mrs. Sykes. "You had not best look for me : it is hardly probable that I shall have time to return visits."

"*So* sorry,—so ve'ry sorry!" said Miss Price, more deeply expressive of irreparable loss than ever, and taking her hand lingeringly. In this way she made her sentimental rounds, Mr. Ketchum looking on impatiently the while. When at last she was safely outside the front door, he came back, sank into a chair, rolled his eyes up to the ceiling, and exclaimed, "For this and all thy mercies, yours respectfully," in a way that brought down the house.

Even Mrs. Sykes condescended to laugh. "Really,

now, you have an odd, striking way of saying a thing sometimes. You have, really," she said and was surprised that he did not seem more gratified by her commendation. "I have been amused two or three times myself," she added, in a tone of good-humored patronage.

"No! Have you? Kyind heaven, thou art merciful and hast gratified my highest earthly ambition!" cried Job, striking a mock dramatic attitude.

"Husband, will you see that the gas is not left burning in the butler's pantry all night?" said Mabel. "It is such a waste."

---

## VII.

It has not been concealed that, with all his fine qualities, Mr. Ketchum was an obstinate man, and so, in spite of his wife's remonstrances, he came down-stairs next morning—Sunday morning—in a dress that she had assured him was "only fit for one's bedroom,"—namely, a very gorgeous Oriental dressing-gown (Mabel's gift the preceding Christmas), with a fez on his head, and on his feet a pair of slippers of amazing workmanship and soundlessness, the joy of his feet, if not of his heart. Thus accoutred, he prowled about on the lower floor, looking after various things, and, going into the pantry for something, he chanced to look through the small window used for the transmission of dishes from the next room, and saw Parsons holding a pile of letters one by one over a steaming kettle. Unconscious of his proximity, the respectable Parsons dexterously and neatly opened several envelopes with a practised hand, and then transferred the letters to her pocket, to be enjoyed at her leisure, after which she laid hold of the kettle and retired to the kitchen beyond.

"Well, upon my word, if that isn't the coolest thing I ever saw!" exclaimed Mr. Ketchum mentally, and, feeling that he had made a great discovery, was at first for sharing it immediately with Parsons's mistress; but on reflection he thought differently. "It is her funeral: I guess I had better not meddle: there would be a great scene," he thought. "At any rate, I'll wait until they are leaving before putting her on her guard." He went back to the dining-room to his newspaper, and sat there until the others came down.

Miss Noel was not long in the room before an idea struck her. "Did you not say that your post-bag containing the night's mail would be sent over this morning," she asked.

"I did. It came about an hour ago," said Mr. Ketchum.

"How very nice! I hope there may be something for me. It is so very trying to get no news from England," said Miss Noel.

"Why, Mabel had twenty-three letters laid aside for you until you should come. Didn't she give them to you?" asked Mr. Ketchum. "Were none of those from England?"

"Oh, yes. But that was three days since, and I've heard nothing for a fortnight. If Parsons has *quite* finished with the letters, I suppose I may as well have them. And she must be, by this. Would you kindly ring and send for them?" said Miss Noel.

"What! you know that she reads your letters?" exclaimed Mr. Ketchum, surprised.

"Oh, dear, yes. They all do. It is very tiresome, but they will do it. Parsons is generally good enough to let me have them quite promptly; but she reads them, of course,—all but my cousin Blanche Best's letters. Blanche has always been my most intimate friend, and can't bear the idea: so she blocked the game by a most ingenious device. She writes one sentence in French, the next in Italian, the third in English,—at least she did until a happier plan suggested itself: now she writes English in German text. It answers perfectly; but it is having a great effect on Parsons, quite undermining her constitution, I fear, especially when important things are happening at 'The Court,' where I often go. I sometimes wickedly slip one of Blanche's letters under the pin-cushion, as if with the intention of concealing it, and I have so enjoyed seeing Parsons whip it under her apron when she got the chance, knowing that she could not make out a single word. She really looked quite green afterward for a week: pure chagrin."

"I am sure I have done everything that I could think of to keep my letters from my man," said Sir Robert, "but quite without success. I think he finds my correspondence a little dull sometimes, as compared with that of a former place. He came to me from the greatest scamp in England; and I can fancy that the letters there were very various and diverting. My own must be altogether too ponderous and respectable for a taste formed on sensational models."

"Well, all I have got to say is that if I caught a servant of mine at that little game I'd make my letters uncommonly interesting reading to him; and if the style suited him, I'd see that he got a little leisure in the penitentiary to copy them and impress them on his mind. Do you mean to say that you don't even discharge them for it?" said Mr. Ketchum. "I never heard anything like it!" •

"One could discharge the culprit easily enough; the trouble is that his successor or successors would do exactly the same thing," replied Sir Robert. "When the Barons rose, they neglected to provide a remedy for an unforeseen nuisance, and I suppose this literary partnership of Master & Servant, Limited, will always exist. I wrote a note once to Beazely (my man), addressed to myself, and told him that if he disapproved of the Conservative tone of my correspondence, as was likely, seeing that he was a Radical, I would make an effort to get at Dilke or Bright, with a view to an *occasional* note at least. The envelope had been resealed, I saw when it reached me, but Beazely had no more expression in his face than the Sphinx. My letters, however, were not tampered with for about a week."

Mrs. Ketchum senior became fluent in her amazement: "How perfectly dreadful! Good gracious! What did you do about your husband's letters? The idea of sharing his letters with a servant!"

She was addressing Mrs. Sykes, who said very cheerfully in reply, "Oh, there was never anything in his letters, except warnings to put the servants at board-wages before I went away, and look to expenditures, and not ask him for any more money soon. I didn't mind much. I was rather ashamed of the spelling,—

that was all. Poor dear Guy never could spell, and I never read anything so dull as his letters,—the same thing over and over again, till it hardly seemed worth while to open them, only for knowing what he was up to, or when he was coming. How my poor sisters did laugh one Christmas when I got a letter from him in Italy, saying, 'The cole here is intense; but I have got a projick in my head, which is to get back to England as fast as ralo and steme can possibly carry me'! It wasn't often that bad; but there was always something wrong. I can't think how it is, for he had no end of tutors and masters, except that he certainly was a very thick-headed fellow." She laughed merrily over the epistolary deficiencies of her late lord as she spoke, and every one joined her except Mrs. Ketchum, who was too shocked to countenance her.

"I saw Parsons in the very act of opening your letters this morning as I was roaming around in my Jesuit creepers, and thought you would be horrified; but it seems to be all right," said Mr. Ketchum, glancing down at his slippers. "Suppose, now, we have some breakfast: it is late. We haven't nearly as much time as the patriarchs, anyway, and so much more use for it."

"I have been thinking it would never be ready," said Mrs. Sykes.

"And I am quite ready for it. Isn't that a nice new-laid egg for me?" asked Miss Noel, taking her place with the others.

"Mabel, eggs for Miss Noel every morning, if she likes them, and don't you forget it," said Mr. Ketchum. "'Trouble'? Not the least that ever was. I have them for myself always. An egg for me must be like Cæsar's wife,—above suspicion. I have provided myself with a conscientious High-Church hen that lays one every day of the year; though how she can think it worth her while, when they are selling for ten cents a dozen, I can't imagine.—What's the matter, Heathcote?"

The matter was the "Jesuit creepers" and the hen combined, which had sent all the party into a little fit of laughter, from which Mr. Heathcote could not recover.

"I don't see anything to double you up like a jack knife," said Mr. Ketchum, in allusion to his guest's way of stooping over and having the laughs, as it were, shaken out of him by a superior force, while he got out at intervals,—

"Jest—creep—High—such a fellow!" in staccato jerks that made every one else laugh from sympathy.

"I call 'em that because Mother Schmidt made them for me so that I could steal a march on my mother-in-law, and she's a Catholic and knew how to do it. Talking of Catholics and what Washington calls the ' 'Peskypalians,' who is going to church to-day?"

"I am going to walk over to Dale with Bijou Brown and her father," said Ethel.

"That isn't as nice a church as ours. We will take the others into Kalsing, eh, husband?" said Mabel; "that is, if they will come."

"I will go to the scaffold with Mrs. Ketchum," protested Sir Robert gallantly. "What do you youngsters say?"

"Ramsay and I thought we would walk over to that little village on the crest of a hill that one can see from my window," said Mr. Heathcote.

"You had much better go to church,—much better But of course your soul is your own," said Sir Robert.

"You won't have much body left when you get back: it is a good twenty miles," remarked Mr. Ketchum.

"Oh, that is nothing," replied Mr. Ramsay.

"Forty miles there and back! Are they crazy?" Mrs. Ketchum asked of Mabel *sotto voce;* to which a smile and shake of the head came in answer.—"The day is very damp, Job. I am almost afraid to go out; but it is my duty, and I will."

"That's right, ma. Do your duty. It is a good earthly as well as heavenly investment," replied Mr. Ketchum.

"But I wish, son, that you would live in Kalsing, next to the church, or in New York, which will would be better. I saw a beautiful house advertised in the neighborhood of Trinity Church the other day, and wrote to ask about it," said Mrs. Ketchum, who was always in spirit moving the family away from Fairfield.

"You are too speculative, ma, entirely," said he. "You are like my partner, Richardson, who would write to ask the Czar what he would take for the Winter Palace, if I'd let him, when if steamships were a dollar a dozen he couldn't put up enough to buy a gang-plank. I can't move next to a church, because all you womenites belong to different ones; but I can take a room for you in the steeple and have an elevator put in that will make close connection with the services, if you like."

"Don't be irreverent, my son," said Mrs. Ketchum, who, like some other Protestants, believed in an infallible steeple, if not an infallible Pope. "I don't expect *my* wishes to be considered in anything."

"Oh, come, now, ma; that isn't fair. Except that I

married to suit myself, which is about the only foolish thing that I have done, I have been tolerably obedient, I think," said Mr. Ketchum, aware that he was on dangerous ground.

"Do tell us about it. You wanted him to marry some one else,—some one with a fortune, didn't you?" said Mrs. Sykes. "Quite natural, I am sure."

"She wanted me to marry the ugliest woman east of the Rockies," said Mr. Ketchum. "But I couldn't stand that face behind my cups and saucers three hundred and sixty-five days in the year, and I bolted to England, where my wife picked me up."

"She wasn't so ugly at all, Job, except that her nose was a little aquiline," protested Mrs. Ketchum.

"Aquiline as a camel's back," asserted her son, in an aside.

"And her hair *was* rather auburn," Mrs. Ketchum went on, in reluctant concession.

"Call it pink, as the English do their hunting-coats," suggested he, smiling.

"But such a dear, *good* girl, you quite forgot that she wasn't exactly handsome" ("No, not precisely," interjected he) "when you came to know her."

"That I *never* did. It might as a speculation have done to get a cast of her face for andirons to keep the American child from falling into the fire; but *marry her!* Good Lord! When I eat anything now that disagrees with me, I dream of Emily's mouth," affirmed Mr. Ketchum, with the most laughing mirth in his eyes, his mobile features expressing volumes.

"Her mouth *was* large, and her teeth *a little* prominent. But you shall not abuse Emily any more. You

29*

would have been very happy with her, I can tell you,"
asserted Mrs. Ketchum. "You would have got over
her mouth."

"I might in time have got *around* it, and I could
easily have got *into* it, but I should never have got *over*
it in the world," affirmed Mr. Ketchum, with decision.
"I would rather be married to that Puseyite there, un
happy as I am."

This closed the little duel between the mother and
son, and another laugh drowned Mabel's remark to Miss
Noel, which was, "Husband is in one of his joking
moods, and does not mean that he is *really* unhappy at
all. He should not say such things, they are so very
misleading."

When quiet was restored, a discussion followed about
the parties in the English Church, and, the question
being raised as to who was the head of the Low Church
party, Mr. Ketchum had just said, "Why, *Lucifer*, of
course," when, amid general merriment, Miss Brown
walked in, saying, "I never heard of such an uproarious
Sunday party. Are you ready, Ethel? We ought to
be off,"—which practically ended the meal, for first Mr.
Ramsay and then the others left the table, he to talk to
Bijou, they to get ready for church. Job's eyes followed Mr. Ramsay, and he said to Sir Robert, "What a
charming girl Mrs. De Witt was in the old Cheltenham
days! Heathcote didn't make the landing there, and
I'm sorry."

"So am I. She is an immense favorite of mine," said
Sir Robert. "As charming as ever! It was a more
serious thing than I thought it would be. I doubt
whether he ever marries."

" She was a born enchantress, Jenny was," he replied. ". Some women are like poison oak,—once get them in your system, and they will break out on you every spring for fifty years, if you live that long, fresh and painful as ever. But as for his marrying, some one of our girls will enter for the Consolation stakes, very likely, and he will be married before he knows what has hurt him."

" A consummation devoutly to be wished," said Sir Robert. " He is my heir, you know."

In a few minutes Ethel joined Bijou, who looked at her rather hard, as she felt. Ethel wore a simple serge dress, heavy boots, a stout frieze jacket, and a hat of a shape unknown in America, that seemed to be all cocks' plumes. Her eyes being weak, she had put on her smoked glasses. The day being damp, and her chest delicate, she had added her respirator. " I am nicely protected, am I not?" she said contentedly. " I had a severe cold last winter, from which I am not quite re- covered, and auntie thinks I had best be prudent. Are you ready ?"

" Not quite," said Bijou. " I want to see Mrs. Ket chum a moment." She ran off, accordingly, into the library in search of the old lady, whom she found there looking out the lessons, it being her practice to verify every word the clergyman read, and no small satisfac- tion to catch him tripping. " Do, Mrs. Ketchum, speak to Ethel and get her to take off those machines and put on something stylish," said Bijou. " I am really ashamed to take her into our pew ; people will stare so. She is a perfect fright. The idea of a girl making her- self look like that !"

Mrs. Ketchum, however, declined to interfere, and when Bijou got back to the drawing-room Ethel was missing. Taking advantage of Bijou's absence, she had gone up-stairs, and, during the library interview, was saying to her aunt, "You never saw anything got up as she is,—silk, and satin, and lace, and bracelets, and feathers, and what not. And for church, too! I wonder she should turn out like that: she should have better taste. I really don't quite like going with her. she looks so conspicuous,—just as if she were going to a garden-party or flower show, for all the world." When they met again, both girls looked a little conscious, and Ethel said, "How very smart you are!"

"Why, this is an old dress that I put on for fear it might rain," said Bijou. "Don't you hate having to wear goggles and cages and things? It must be perfectly horrid."

"I don't mind. Of course one isn't looking one's best; but that is of no consequence. Health is the first consideration," said Ethel. "Ah! there comes your father."

Of the walk it need only be said that it was very pleasant going, and rained a little coming back; that Ethel produced her "goloshes," put up her umbrella, and walked home as serenely as her concern for Bijou would admit. That young lady had on paper-soled boots that got soaking wet, a fine summer parasol that she seemed to think fulfilled every office that was desirable in shielding her bonnet, a dress ill fitted to resist chill or dampness. She persisted that she was "all right," while her pretty teeth chattered; but she caught a violent cold, and was in bed a week, while

Ethel came down to dinner as rosy as Baby Ketchum, and ate as heartily as Mr. Ramsay and Mr. Heathcote, who certainly showed themselves good trenchermen. Mrs. Ketchum persisted in regarding the two young men very much as though they had been returned Arctic travellers, and amused them not a little by suggesting that they should lie down all the evening.

"Why, we haven't turned a hair. We are as fit as a fiddle," they exclaimed, and looked anything but unstrung.

Ethel had made one speech that morning that astonished Bijou considerably. "Do you know, I have been watching you ever since I have known you," she said, "to see if it was true? That is, that the American ladies *spat* on all occasions, as I have read. Don't think me rude to mention it."

"We don't quarrel any more than any one else," said Bijou, quite misunderstanding.

"I don't mean that, you know: *expectorate.* And I see it was not true at all. I have not seen it once," explained Ethel.

"I should think not! Well, I do think! How could you believe such ridiculous nonsense?" asked Bijou indignantly.

"Don't be vexed, Bijou dear. I did not mean to make unkind reflections. It was only that I had read a stupid book about America," said Ethel; and peace was restored.

As for the other members of the party, they had gone to a handsome church in Kalsing, which boasted the best stained glass in the country and was thoroughly churchly and attractive. Here they not only heard

good music, but one of the most eloquent preachers in
"the American branch of the English establishment,"
as Sir Robert called the Episcopalian communion.

It amused Mr. Ketchum not a little to see the way
in which the baronet conducted his devotions,—his pre-
liminary prayer in his silk hat, from which streamed a
halo of side-whiskers, the heartiness with which he
joined in the service, especially the way in which,
avoiding all the compromises the male American prac-
tises in prayer-time (such as bending forward a little,
or leaning back pensively with the hand shading the
face), he plumped squarely down on his knees, turned
up a pair of shoes half as long as his very respectable,
tightly-rolled umbrella, and made his responses in a clear,
audible voice, like an honest gentleman and a miserable
sinner.

It did not escape Mr. Ketchum's keen eyes, either,
that although Sir Robert contributed a five-dollar bill
to the offertory, he first rolled it up into a tiny, unrec-
ognizable wad before dropping it into the alms-basin.
The service over, Sir Robert and the eminent divine
were made acquainted. The latter said he would call
as soon as he could snatch a moment, and Sir Robert,
his hands folded behind his back, holding his hat and
gloves, made the rounds of the church, inspecting every
bit of carving, frescoing, glass, and brass, and making
the most intelligent criticisms upon what he saw to
Miss Noel in a whisper. Mrs. Sykes sat still in the
pew, fuming at being "let in for a charity sermon," for
some inexplicable reason, seeing she had given nothing
to the charity. Miss Noel was stopped at the door by
no less a person than Captain Kendall, who had suddenly

discovered that he had a great-aunt living in Kalsing, whom he must see, and now stood there saying, "Where is Miss Ethel? How is it that you are here without her? I hope she is quite well."

"My niece, Miss Heathcote, is quite well, thanks, and has gone to church elsewhere," said Miss Noel, with dignity, intending to mildly repress a young gentleman whom she thought a little too free with his "Miss Ethels."

"Then I will have the pleasure of calling upon you to-morrow," said Captain Kendall, unabashed and joyous, as he walked away.

So active an intelligence as Sir Robert's requires plenty of food, and when Mrs. Ketchum senior issued from her room about ten the next morning, whom should she meet in the hall but the baronet in a state of the most overflowing energy and brilliant good humor, dressed in a suit of striped red-and-white "pajamas," having on his head a paper cap, under his arm a roll of designs, and in his mind the delightful intention of painting the ceiling of Mabel's boudoir!

"Good-morning, madam. Here we are," he said, shaking his box of paints and stencils at her. "I have improvised a scaffolding, and am now going to work on my outlines. I planned the whole thing in bed last night, and, unless I am much mistaken, we are going to have the prettiest boudoir in this part of the country. I shall do a panel or two to get the effect, and any workman can finish it."

"But can you do it?" asked Mrs. Ketchum, amazed, but interested.

"You shall see. *I* frescoed the chapel on my place

at home, and I may say there have been worse pieces of work," replied Sir Robert, descending the stairs as he spoke, eager to get to work.

" Is he *raving crazy*, Mabel? What on earth has he got on? He isn't *respectable*. I declare to goodness, he has set my heart beating so I shan't get over it all day," said the startled lady to her daughter-in-law, who joined her just then.

" Oh, for shame, ma, to give yourself away like that! Fashionable men wear those costumes altogether now," said Mr. Ketchum, coming up. " You see, Daisy, that if I shocked him beyond expression yesterday morning, as you said I should, he has horrified me to death to-day: so I guess we are quits. Come along: let's go down to see the trapeze-performance."

Down they went, and, meeting Mr. Ramsay, who was coming up, Job stopped a moment to tell him to take out any of the horses that he fancied. " Take the piebalds," said he, " if you'd like to have a drive, and take some nice girl—Miss Ethel or Bijou Brown—for a two-forty shine."

" Thanks awfully," said Mr. Ramsay. " But I think I had better—that is, I had rather ask Heathcote."

" You are horribly welcome, but I don't think much of your taste," replied Mr. Ketchum, not understanding what a proposition he had made.

In the lower hall they found the eminent divine, irreproachably clerical and dignified, and Captain Kendall, just arrived. Sir Robert, hearing voices, came out, brush in hand, to welcome them, producing quite as great an impression on them as on Mrs. Ketchum. " I belong to the working-classes now. Just you come here

and see how the fine arts are prospering in the State of
Michigan," said he, and led them into the boudoir
where, after some conversation, he nimbly ran up a
step-ladder, laid himself out on the scaffolding, and,
with a bold, free touch, went on sketching a procession
of Cupids which was to go around the base of the small
dome, talking all the while with the utmost animation
to the guests below. "As soon as I get in this fellow
riding a dolphin, I shall be entirely at your service,"
said he. "No considerations of respect and attachment
to the Church or fear of the Army can influence me
just now."

The two gentlemen begged that he would go on; the
ladies came in, and together they passed an agreeable
morning, Sir Robert declaring that on the scaffold he
was entitled to benefit of clergy, and begging the eminent divine when he left to let him have his ghostly
counsel every day for at least a week. In spite of his
eminence, this gentleman had no very great breadth of
view. To sit about on boxes and window-seats, pic-
nicking in an empty room, while the stranger upon
whom he had come to call lay above him in red pajamas, painting Cupids on the ceiling, was to his mind
monstrously indecorous. It was amusing to see the
dignified way in which he took the pleasantries of the
party; and he made no response to Sir Robert's farewell overture except a bow. "Your guest is a very '
entertaining man," he said to Mr. Ketchum, who accompanied him to the hat-rack, "but is he quite—quite
—you understand?"

"Perfectly so," said Job, with a laugh. "Head and
heart both of the best, as you will find out when you

know him better. You are coming back to dinner,
ain't you, to help us out with the fatted calf?"

The dinner was a very elegant affair of twenty-five
covers, given to the guests, the first of a series of enter
tainments planned in their honor. All the notable
people of the neighborhood were represented at it.
The scandalized divine returned to partake of it, and,
seeing Sir Robert in a dress-suit, dignified, polished, of
preternatural respectability, not to say distinction, looking the pillar of Church and State that he was, and
talking with due gravity of the tariff, free trade, and
the like ponderous subjects, concluded to overlook the
mad behavior of the morning, and, joining him, gave
him a long account of the Indian missions of the
Church. Unconscious of having done anything that
might be regarded as eccentric, Sir Robert was all affa-
bility, soon grew interested, asked a number of questions as to the death-rate among the tribes, the preva-
lence of smallpox and cholera among them, the spread
of civilization, confirmed nomadism, traces of Jewish
rites, and so on, thanked him for a "very profitable
half-hour," and said he should send a little check to be
applied in any way he might see fit, obliterating thereby
the last trace of the previous prejudice. This, indeed,
was replaced by something very like enthusiasm when
there came next day a slip of paper representing five
hundred dollars, also a note from the donor, saying that
he should be glad to know that some portion of the
sum enclosed had gone to an industrial school, if any
such existed, where the young Indian women could
learn to boil a potato properly, and the use of brooms
and pails and scrubbing-brushes. "You must first clean

them and then convert them : get them into the bath-tub, and you can take them anywhere," said Sir Robert, with great truth and perspicacity.

"One doesn't get such a dinner, except at a few great houses, outside of London or Paris," Mrs. Sykes was pleased to say when it was over. "I have found out that almost everything was ordered from New York ; and a pretty penny it must have cost. Not that this man cares. I dare say he is only too glad to have the chance of entertaining me,—that is, us. I was sent in with a waspish little man that turned suddenly crusty on my hands and was an owl for the rest of the time ; but I was rather glad to be able to devote myself to my dinner for once."

Mrs. Sykes's escort had "turned crusty" because that lady, following her instinct of ingratiation, had said to him, "All the gentry of this country are in the South, aren't they ? They don't live about here, do they ?"— not from a prejudice in favor of Southerners at all, as was proved when she went to New Orleans later and promptly asked the first acquaintance she made whether all the education was not at the North.

The week that followed was a very gay one, the Ketchums' friends in the neighborhood and in Kalsing being most intent on hospitable thoughts and providing something agreeable in the shape of an entertainment for every night. Every moment of the day, too, of every day was filled up. It seemed to Mrs. Ketchum that "those English people," as she called them, were never idle, and had discovered the secret of perpetual motion.

Sir Robert had the boudoir, to which he devoted exactly two hours after breakfast. He had a geological chart of America, with what he felt to be melancholy blanks for the chalk and oolite beds of his own country, and appropriate fossils indicated by an index-finger in red ink. He had the Poor-Law and electoral systems to master, as well as the prison systems of the different States. He had to prove that the Mound-Builders and the race that built the buried cities of Central America were one and the same. He had innumerable questions, political, social, agricultural, pressing upon him, from the history of spiritualism, the purity of the ballot, and the McCormack reaper, down to certain expressions that immensely struck and pleased him, which had to be entered in the diary as "unconscious poetry of the Westerners,"—such phrases as "the fall" (of the leaf), "morning-glories," "dancing like a breeze," "Daphnes" (instead of laurels), and many more, which he hoped would be "permanently engrafted on the mother-tongue." There were other entries to be made,—"customs of the Westerners," their "descent," "taxation," "climate" (as affected by the Great Lakes), "population in 1900," and so on. There were books, books, books, to be read, referred to, ordered. There was even a little taxidermy to be done, and the "native birds" to be first sought, then bought, then prepared, and packed to be sent back to England. The others, if not quite so busy, were anything but idle. Miss Noel walked her five miles a day. She was out sketching for hours under her umbrella, no matter what the weather was, and only said, "Thank you for your kind concern, but I am quite equal to it," when Mrs. Ketchum, astonished to see a woman of her own age enduring such fatigue

and running such risks, undertook to remonstrate with
her. "One must get one's constitutional, you know,
and one must not mind a drop or two. There has been
no really bad weather yet,—nothing to keep one in-
doors, at least." If she stayed in-doors, she and Mrs.
Sykes (when the latter was not scouring the country on
foot or horseback) interested themselves in their plants,
minerals, seeds, drawings, the herbarium, the Ward
case, the diaries and letters and fancy-work, the beautiful collection of sea-weed sent by Miss Marlow from New
England, and a dozen things besides. Mr. Heathcote,
meanwhile, was walking, and riding, and visiting, and,
above all, photographing. He got a small covered cart,
into which he would put his photographic apparatus
and go the rounds of the country-side alone, getting his
luncheon as he could, and coming back late in the evening, flushed with heat and victory, bringing amusing
accounts of his experiences, a bouquet as of an apothe-
cary-shop, and "proofs" of "a lane,—quite an English-
looking lane," "a dog on the chain," "rear view of an
American public" (house), "Saint Lieuk's Church" (five
different aspects), "what the natives call an 'ash-hop-
per,'—came out beautifully," "children among the hay-
cocks,—very indistinct," "squatter's hut on the edge of
a common," "Western American farm-house," "negro
dust-man," "village beauty," and many others. He
was much complimented upon them all by Mr. Ketchum, who enjoyed the whole collection and made
comments and suggestions of the most delightful kind.
Mr. Heathcote looked infinitely pleased and flattered
when told by him that they had "a cold, professional
air," and asked for copies of some of them, after which

x 30*

he was eclipsed behind his black cloth and instrument for two days, had his room darkened to a Cimmerian pitch, worked very diligently, and presented the fruits of his labors to his host with the modest depreciation but secret delight of the artist, smiling indulgently at Mr. Ramsay, with his, " I say, old chappy, what an out-and-out swell you are at it, to be sure ! You must do the horses." Thus encouraged, Mr. Heathcote did the horses, the house, the family grouped inside and outside, Master Jared Ponsonby, Hannibal Hamlin, Master Bobo and Miss Blanche, the poultry, and (aided by mirrors) himself in almost every dress and attitude which it is possible for a man to assume. He must have spent a small fortune in chemicals alone, and all his talk was of light and shadow, background, draperies, foreground, plates, and proofs ; every table was strewn with photo-graphs, finished and not finished, mounted, or curled up like paper crumpets.

Mr. Ramsay, too, had his little diversions, not pre-cisely scientific, but amusing. He was in and out of the stables all day long, and was loved by every animal on the place. Such long-suffering and good nature Master Ketchum had never seen, except in Fräulein Schmidt ; and then the strength, the resources, the con-versation of his new friend enchanted the child, who followed him about, perched on his shoulder, played games with him, and had to be carried away from him struggling by his nurse. Mr. Ramsay had other occu-pations : he rode, he fished, he cleaned his guns, he got over leagues and leagues of ground, he killed several snakes and captured scores of insects. He caught dozens of tree-frogs, for one thing, and shut them all

up together in the drawing-room coal-scuttle, where he
peeped at them from time to time, well satisfied. He
played little tunes on his chin, asked conundrums,
showed Job a great many tricks at cards, and two
French puzzles (saying, "Those French beggars are
awfully sharp at that kind of thing, you know"); he
played "God Save the Queen" with one finger on the
piano, held skeins of wool for the ladies, shut doors, got
shawls, and really need have done none of these arduous duties, for in looking so handsome and so jolly from
Monday morning until Saturday night he contributed
his quota toward the carrying on of society, and all
beside were works of supererogation. When these
palled upon him a little, one morning, as was shown by
his picking up a book, he looked very unhappy for ten
minutes, and then, making a pass at his face with one
of his beautiful hands, he cried out, "No fellow can read
badgered like this. There's a regular brute of a fly
that has been lighting on my nose every half-second
since I sat down," closed the book, smiled, and said, "I
may as well call upon Mr. Brown while I have time,"
and took himself off. This happened on the ninth day
after his arrival, and with it began a new era in his existence. He not only went to Mr. Brown's that day,
but the next, and the day after that. In short, he had
found an amusement best expressed in the French
equivalent *distraction.* He rode with Bijou, and reported to Mr. Heathcote that she was "a clinker at her
fences, and went at them as straight as an English girl."
He taught her a good deal about the management of
her reins and animal, and admitted that she was "a
plucky one." If she had only consented to get an Eng-

lish saddle (which she declined to do, with one of her customary exaggerations, saying that she "didn't want a thousand pommels"), to rise in that saddle, and to have the tail of her horse cropped properly, he would have been quite happy. As it was, he acknowledged that in her own fashion she was a most graceful and fearless horsewoman, and approved of her accordingly. It soon struck him that she did other things well. Used to the reserved and rather constrained manner of most English girls, he found a great charm in her bright gayety, her frank cordiality, the good-humored comradeship and absence of stiffness, untainted by vulgarity. For, although Bijou was not high-bred, distinguished, or clever, she was a girl of real refinement, and he had the wit to see it. Her merry tongue and generous and affectionate heart, neither chilled nor hardened·yet by contact with the world, were very attractive, and it is just possible that he felt the influence of her piquantlypretty face. At any rate, he had found a great number of imperative reasons for going to Brown's, when one morning, as he was opening the little wicket-gate that admitted him to their croquet-field, he saw something that gave him an unpleasant shock. It was a buggy in front of the door, in which sat Bijou, charmingly arrayed, smiling upon a gentleman who had just helped her in and was only deterred from taking the seat waiting for him by her calling out, "Stop, till I fix my skirts and put up my parasol," the gentleman being his cousin, Mr. Edward Plummer, *alias* Drummond. The sight of Mr. Plummer enraged him. Bijou's cheerful air did not improve matters, and for the first time he felt irritated at her American speech and accent. "'Fix my skirts,'" he quoted discontentedly, as he watched them drive off, and then, after a moment's indecision, he stalked angrily up to the front door, pulled the bell fiercely, and asked to see Mr. Brown. He was almost immediately ushered into the library, where Mr. Brown was sitting.

"Good-morning, sir. I am glad to see you. I am sorry to say that Bijou is out. She has gone driving with our guest: an English guest, by the way,—Mr. Drummond. He came on with us from New York, and has been here ever since, except the last two weeks which he has spent in Chicago," said Mr. Brown.

"That's what I've come about," blurted out Mr. Ramsay, the moment there was a pause. "His name isn't Drummond at all: it is Plummer. And he isn't fit to be a guest in any decent house, and I've come to tell you so and have you give him the sack and put him to the door at once. Excuse me meddling, but you have been very kind to me and received me most hospitably, and I am not going to see you taken in by a rascal and a blackguard."

Mr. Brown was shocked, but did not show it. He prided himself on being very logical and dispassionate and judicial, and was privately convinced that he would have greatly adorned the legal profession if Fate had been kinder. Besides, Mr. Drummond was his guest and there by his invitation, which to his mind was strong presumptive proof that Mr. Ramsay's charges were without foundation. "Grave accusations these, Mr. Ramsay,—very grave accusations. I trust you are making them upon some better grounds than mere personal prejudice or idle rumor, if you expect me to believe them. Not that I mean any discourtesy to you.

sir, in saying this," he said, in his roundest, most impressive tones.

"What do you mean? The fellow was sent to Coventry by his regiment and forced to resign, his father has cut him off with a shillin', he can't show his face in London, and he has been kicked out of his club for keepin' too many aces up his sleeve. I should think that was grounds enough for an accusation. Do you suppose I go about inventin' lies to take away other people's characters?" said Mr. Ramsay excitedly.

"Do not exaggerate. Be calm; be reasonable," said Mr. Brown. "Observe, I do not accuse you of wilful misrepresentation, but of misapprehension, perhaps of prejudice. There is a difference. Note it, and do not take offence, my young friend, too readily."

"I am not offended, but what I say is true, and I hope you will act upon it, so that Miss Brown shall not go out ridin' round the country with that—" began Mr. Ramsay, only to be interrupted by—

"No violence; no excitement. Let us look at the thing rationally," from Mr. Brown. "Mr. Drummond is my guest,—my guest, remember; introduced to me by one of the first men in New York; received everywhere. You are both strangers to me. This is a matter of purely individual testimony," Mr. Brown went on, feeling that he was growing exquisitely subtile, and clothing himself in imaginary ermine as he spoke. "He may tell me that *you* are a rascal. In that event, how am I to know who is the honest man and who the villain? Shall I believe you, or shall I believe him, in the absence of documentary evidence and disinterested statement? As my guest, he has, if anything, the prior claim to consideration; though I am far from saying that whatever views you may advance will not have equal weight with me,—*as views*, mark you."

"You can believe who you please and what you please," said Mr. Ramsay; "but remember that I have given you warnin'. He may be your guest, but he is my cousin, and I should think that I ought to know what I am talkin' about. There is no necessity for mè stayin' any longer."

He rose to go, but Mr. Brown stopped him by a gesture. "A cousin!" he exclaimed. "Do not excite yourself; be calm. On the face of it, that would seem conclusive; but appearances are notoriously deceitful. Will you assure me on your honor that there is no motive, no family feud, at the bottom of this? Cousins do not go about the world denouncing each other—*as a rule.* Family pride, affection, a thousand things, prevent them from making such things public; but still it is not impossible. I do not say that it is *impossible;* only *improbable,*—very improbable. Give me your word, though, that there is *no motive,*—we must always look for a motive in these cases,—and I will promise to give the matter full and impartial investigation."

"I'll do nothin' of the sort. I will bid you good-morning," exclaimed Mr. Ramsay, reaching out impetuously for his hat.

"You have meant well, perhaps. I am obliged to you, if such be the case. I will bear what you have said in mind, and let you know my decision," said Mr. Brown, delivering a verdict from the bench.

"Just as you please," replied Mr. Ramsay haughtily · and so they parted.

Left to himself, however, Mr. Brown ceased to be judicial, and became practical. He recalled, as he sat there, a number of circumstances that had not impressed him favorably in connection with his guest. Mr. Drummond had borrowed a considerable sum of him, on the ground of delayed remittances. Mr. Drummond had filled his pockets with his host's Havanas in the most scandalous fashion, yet never had a cigar. Mr. Drummond had done a number of ill-bred things that he had not liked,—such as ordering the carriage to be got ready on his own responsibility, lending valuable books without so much as asking permission, and the like. The longer Mr. Brown thought of the late interview, the more uneasy he felt. The paper had dropped from his hand, and he was still deep in his uncomfortable meditations, when the door opened, and his daughter ran to him and threw herself into his arms, crying hysterically, "Oh, popper, popper! Oh! oh! oh!"

We will extricate the story of what had happened from the sobs and interruptions to which Mr. Brown had to submit, and preface it with some account of the relations between Bijou and Mr. Drummond-Plummer or Plummer-Drummond.

They had met in New York the previous winter, where Mr. Drummond had suddenly appeared, put up at a fashionable hotel, and, with no other credentials than his handsome person, good manners, and bold assertions that he was related to certain great people in England, had been accepted in society with that beautiful faith and charity that believeth all things an Englishman of supposed position may choose to say of himself, in spite of much disastrous experience of

foreign adventurers both painful and ludicrous. Attracted by Bijou, he promptly satisfied himself of the
stability and reality of her father's fortune, and began
to lay siege to her hand: about her heart he gave himself small concern. Now, Bijou was a Western belle,
and was in the habit of receiving any amount of
attention. At seventeen a famous racer and a steam-
boat had already been named for her. The local newspapers chronicled her toilets and triumphs. Her little
sitting-room was a sentimental hall of Eblis, full of
shapes with hearts that were one burning coal, bright
with the sacred flame. She had a large album which
she called her "him-book," because it contained nothing
but the photographs of her admirers. She had hats,
and bats, and caps, and whips, and cravats, and oars,
and canes disposed about it tastefully, souvenirs of
various persons, times, and places, and talked of the
original owners in a way that made Ethel's blue eyes
open their widest when she came to be admitted there,
that decorous young person not being used, as she
frankly said, to hearing "a person of the opposite sex"
called "a perfectly lovely fellow," and his nose pronounced "a dream," though not in the sense of its
being broken or disjointed.

"Why, you wouldn't have me call *you* a lovely
fellow, would you?" said Bijou laughingly, as she
tripped about doing the honors of her den;—showing
locks of hair (of which she had almost enough to stuff
a sofa-cushion), dry bouquets of vast dimensions, little
gifts she had received, verses and valentines that she
thought "perfectly splendid" or "too utterly killing
for anything," and bundle after bundle of letters,—the

adorers' letters, all of them, written from all parts of the country, in every style. She read Ethel choice passages from them with great glee, and gave spirited sketches of her correspondents; how she had met them at Saratoga, Mt. Desert, "and pretty much every place;" how she had danced, flirted, walked, driven, sailed, "crabbed," read, sung, talked with them, apparently without either fear or reproach; and of their appearance, dress, character, position, prospects,—a full, if not perfectly complete, history of her relations with them that almost made Ethel's lower jaw drop as she listened. There was no mention of mother, aunt, governess, or maid throughout. Bijou had gone away from home with friends who had let her amuse herself in her own fashion; and at home she was what De Tocqueville has pronounced "the freest thing in the world,—an American girl in her father's house." Yet it was a liberty that was worlds removed from license. Undisciplined she was, impulsive, indulged beyond all European conceptions, but, in spite of a good deal of innocent coquetry and vanity, effervescing in some foolish ways very pardonable in a motherless girl, and of which a great deal too much has been made in discussing American girls, there was never one of any nation more pure-hearted and womanly. Her worst deviations from rigidly conventional standards were better than the best behavior of some very nice people, as Swift defines them.—"Nice people: people who are always thinking of and looking out for nasty things." Different training would have improved her, just as a hot-house rose is more perfect than the wild one; but she, too, was pink-petalled, had a heart of gold, and was full of lovely, fragrant qualities, like the English variety near her.

"You correspond with twelve men! Good heavens!" exclaimed Ethel, when these open secrets had been revealed to her. "Don't tell auntie of it, I beg. She will —will misunderstand, I fear, and think it dreadful, and perhaps prevent me being here so much. It is not at all in accord with English ideas, you know, dear; and auntie is rather stricter than most, even there."

"Not tell! Why not?" asked Bijou. "What is there to shock her? She must be easily shocked. I have got nothing to be ashamed of; and I shall tell the old dear to-morrow."

"Does your father know it?" said Ethel.

"Why, *of course* he does," replied Bijou impatiently. "I generally read him the letters, and he laughs fit to kill himself over some of them. Popper don't care one bit. He says I am old enough to paddle my own canoe; and so I am. And he knows I don't care a pin about any of them. It's great fun until you get tired of it. I am tired of it now, rather. I used to write to twenty; but it has dwindled down to twelve, and I'm going to drop two of those, because they are in the army and are both stationed at the same post. You see, it is too much trouble to write different letters to each one, so I get up one bright, smart one that suits all around, and copy it for them all, with some changes."

This speech almost stunned Ethel for a while. "But doesn't it vex them very much to get such letters? What if they should find it out? And if you don't at all care for them, why do it at all?"

"Why, for the *fun* of the thing, goosie. Angry?

No. They do the same thing themselves. Will Piper sent Kate Price and me letters that were exactly the same, word for word; we compared them. That is where I got the idea. Splendid one, isn't it? I am just bent and determined on having stacks of fun before I am married, because after that, you know, I shall be laid on the shelf completely," said Bijou.

"But why should you be 'laid on the shelf'? I can't make it out. Your life will be just beginning," said Ethel.

"Well, because what is so is *so*," replied Bijou, showing her some patterns for slippers, watch-pockets, tobacco-pouches, and so on, that she meant to work up for birthdays, anniversaries, Christmas, "philopœnas," and other festive occasions, as presents for the adorers.

It is perhaps clearer now why Bijou laid no stress whatever on Mr. Drummond's attentions, while she seemed to him to be receiving them with marked favor. When, on their leaving New York, Mr. Brown had asked him to go home with them and spend a month, he looked upon the prize as won. Before going to Chicago he had shown this so plainly that Bijou had snubbed him roundly,—a course so foreign to her amiable nature and hospitable creed that on his return she had received him with a kindness that had revived all his hopes,—or rather designs. He utterly misunderstood it, and easily persuaded himself that he was practically irresistible. The drive of that afternoon had been planned by him that he might ask the fateful question. He had asked it, and, presumptuously taking her answer for granted, had slipped an arm about her waist, when, to his great surprise, he had found himself half ordered, half pushed out of the buggy immediately, after which Bijou, transported by fury, had laid the whip once smartly across his shoulders and driven away at a gallop, leaving him standing in the middle of the road, an angry man.

She went home, as we have seen, and told her father, who was distinctly excited on hearing it, ordered Mr. Drummond's effects to be packed and sent to the hotel in Kalsing at once, forbade her ever taking another drive with a stranger "the longest day she lived," and would certainly have caned the offender with unparliamentary fervor, instead of being "reasonable" and letting the affair drop, had he known where to find him.

What Mr. Drummond did was to walk into Kalsing and put up at a boarding-house there, where he spent the evening glowering into vacancy blackly enough, and showed his high breeding and respect for the other boarders by taking off his shoes in the parlor and sitting with his stockinged feet propped up on a chair in front of him while he gave himself up to his reflections,— bitter thoughts of the past in which he had been an English gentleman, desperate plans for his future as a *chevalier d'industrie,* fierce abuse of Americans in general and the Browns in particular, culminating in a fixed resolve to leave "this beastly hole" next day; which was happily carried out.

Mr. Ramsay, offended, held aloof for a little while; but, getting a note from Mr. Brown couched in few words, and those to the effect that his warning had been acted on and Mr. Drummond dismissed, he called next day at the house, assured Mr. Brown with earnestness that his cousin was "a precious rascal," gave some par-

ticulars of his shady career, and took up the threads of
his intimacy again, unvexed by any such ideas as that
he was at all responsible for or could be affected by his
kinsman's disreputable behavior.  Mr. Brown concealed
from him that he had lost some money by Mr. Drummond.  Bijou imagined that he must be "feeling dreadfully about it," and took great pains not to say anything
that could wound his imaginary susceptibilities as the
relative of a *mauvais sujet*.  But the simple truth was
that, once assured that respectable people were not
being deluded or cheated by his cousin, Mr. Ramsay
had no further sensitiveness on the subject.  The Browns
kept what he had told them even from the Ketchums,
only to hear him announce in all assemblies that a
cousin of his was "goin' about over here,—an awful
swindler and 'leg,'—and that the best thing people could
do would be to give him the widest sort of berth until he
got himself into the penitentiary, as he certainly would,
—at least it was quite on the cards," smiling in cheerful
enjoyment of the possibility.  Entertainments were
going on all the while in the neighborhood, and he had
ample opportunities of advertising the fact, all of which
he improved, while a puzzled audience knew not what
to make of so novel a situation, and were sorely put to
it for suitable replies as they stared at an Adonis in
Poole-cut clothes who sat and looked alternately at them
and his patent-leather court pumps and gay silk socks
while he affably denounced his father's nephew and
"hoped the blackguard was goin' to New Orleans and
would get the yellow fever there, which was beginnin'
to be had over from the Havana."

This last speech was made at a dinner-party which

Mr. Ketchum's partner Mr. Richardson had felt called upon to give in honor of the English guests, and was almost the only amusing feature of the evening to Job. The Richardsons' house was one of those in which everything is provided on such occasions except amusement. When their invitation came, Job said to his wife, "I wish we could get out of going; but we can't. I don't know what is the matter with that house. It is one of the handsomest in the city, elegantly furnished; they always have a crowd of people at their entertainments, some of them delightful people to meet anywhere else, but somehow there seems a kind of pall draped above the front door that drops down behind you when you enter and never lifts till you leave. Mrs. Richardson puts on all her war-paint and feathers and goes around all the evening anxiously trying to make the thing go off, and it gets worse and worse every moment, so dull and stupid that you can hardly keep awake and not quite quiet enough for a good nap. Richardson buys everything that is to be had, and then sits around and looks as though he had a note to meet in bank and no money to do it with. Altogether, it is about as lively as a water-tank on the Pacific Railroad after the train has gone. But it won't do to hurt their feelings: we have got to go."

So they did, and it was stiff and formal beyond even his expectation. The dinner was interminably long, over-elaborate, and slowly served. They were all sent in with the wrong people. The conversation all but died again and again. Sir Robert was afflicted by a deaf man, who shrieked, "Ha-ow?" and "What say?" at him with brief intervals all during the meal.

Mabel shrank into herself, and only ventured on a few trite remarks. Mr. Ketchum's liveliness utterly evaporated after the first ten minutes. It was quite ghastly, and the move back to the drawing-room was a most blessed relief. Mrs. Sykes had made no effort to lighten the tedium of the dinner, and no sooner found it at an end than she lolled back indifferently on the sofa, and, picking up a book, coolly read it for more than an hour, though twice interrupted by Mrs. Richardson, who vainly tried to substitute polite conversation the first time, and offered a cup of tea the second.

"English breakfast?" asked Mrs. Sykes loftily, raising her eyes for a moment. "No; I am afraid not. It is green tea, I think."

"But do take some," replied Mrs. Richardson. "It is very nice indeed."

"No, thank you," said Mrs. Sykes very shortly, her eyes on her book.

"Just one cup. Let me make it for you?" suggested Mrs. Richardson.

"Not for a five-pound note would I drink the poisonous stuff. Say no more about it," replied Mrs. Sykes, with delicate consideration, and turned over a page.

"Do take some coffee, then, or chocolate," insisted Mrs. Richardson.

"Nothing of any sort or kind whatever," snapped Mrs. Sykes, turning away decidedly, to get a better light on her book, apparently, but really to get rid of her hostess.

Mr. Ketchum, fearing to show indecent exultation when the carriages were announced, repressed the satisfaction that would have expressed itself in gay speeches

. of farewell. A decorous exit was made; and as they
rolled away he gave a great sigh of relief, and exclaimed,
"I haven't had as much fun since I had the measles.
Mussiful Powers! what an evening! I feel like the boy
whose mother gave him a good beating for his own
sake. But all the same I shall have a word to say to
Mrs. Sykes to-morrow; and of course I shall have to
apologize for her behavior to Richardson."

"Most insolent, unpardonable conduct, I call it," said
Sir Robert. "She's an innately vulgar woman."

"Puts on an awful lot of side. I can't stand her. She
gives me the jumps. And she can tell a buster, too,
when she likes: I have found that out," put in Mr.
Ramsay.

"Well, I don't exactly hanker to be cast away on a
desert island with her, even supposing I was one of the
royal dukes and had taken the precaution of being
introduced while we were tying on the life-preservers,
in case of accidents," said Mr. Ketchum.

What he said to Mrs. Sykes next morning no one ever
knew but the discreet Mabel. Not much, probably, but
that little was so much to the point that it had a decided
effect,—two of them, indeed, one interior, the other ex-
ternal. It increased her respect for him, and it made
her perfectly civil to all his friends, as far as constitution
and habit would allow.

"I cut her comb for her, and handled her without
gloves," was his report of the interview to his wife, who
was amazed at his nerve.

When Sir Robert got a note addressed to "Lord
Heathcote, Baronet," beginning "Dear Sir," and signed
" Very respectfully your obedient servant," and read it

*u*

aloud at the breakfast-table as "a most extraordinary production," Mrs. Sykes had absolutely no comments to make. And when Ethel opened her letters and found among them an invitation to take a buggy-drive, commencing "Dear Miss," Mrs. Sykes still held her peace, —a fact that was full of significance.

It was Miss Noel who said, "Really, Ettie dear, I can't have you driving about furiously in a gig without a groom. But pray thank Mr.—what is the name?—Price for being so kind as to propose it, meaning to give you pleasure. He has been so obliging, too, as to procure tickets for us to the play, and has kindly offered to escort us: I have a letter from him as well. A most lovely day, this. There seems no end, really, to the fine weather. Remind me to look at the thermometer after breakfast, before the sun catches it, love. It must have been *quite* two degrees hotter yesterday than the day before; but I neglected to make the entry in my journal, and so cannot be quite positive. Only fancy! Is it not annoying? I am getting sadly forgetful about everything. And I so dislike guess-work and conjecture in a record of the kind. I should like to see the rose-trees at home this morning: the garden must be gay with flowers by this,—though the last time I went pottering about it in my pattens there was nothing out but the blackthorn."

Other entertainments followed closely upon the dinner, of which Mrs. Sykes complained to Miss Noel, saying, "Why will they ask me out? Why can't they leave me alone? Really, I shall not let any one know that I am here, if anything ever brings me back to America,—which is most unlikely."

"There is nothing to prevent you staying at home if you do not wish to go out," replied Miss Noel. "But do you not like it? I enjoy going to the Browns'. Mr. Brown is a man of cultivated mind and Christian courtesy; I like him very much; and the people one meets there are generally of superior station and refined education. Why should you object to meeting them?"

"American society may be nice some day,—that is, if it ever grows up. There doesn't seem to be anybody in it now over twenty," grumbled Mrs. Sykes.

One result of the parties was that Mr. Ketchum, going over to Mr. Brown's one morning, found all the young people assembled there practising steps, the "two-and-a-half," the "polka-glide," and other cheerful evolutions. After watching Mr. Ramsay's efforts to do as Bijou did, for a moment, he called out to her to know what she was doing to a British subject under his protection, and, being shown by Bijou (skirts held up a little, the prettiest feet imaginable, daintily shod, and the gliding, swaying, pirouetting, galopading, graceful beyond expression), cried out, "Teaching him to dance, are you? I thought he was practising heading off a calf in a lane." This so exactly expressed the awkward desperate plunges to the right and left which Mr. Ramsay was executing at the moment, that Mr. Heathcote had another of his acute attacks of appreciation, and became almost a subject for sal volatile and burnt feathers, Mr. Ramsay saying good-naturedly, "What a fellow you are for chaffin', Ketchum! Just you hook it out of this, will you, and let us get on with this? One and two and a kick, you say, Miss Brown? I am such a duffer I can't get the kick."

"You do the one and two make one, and leave the kick to Miss Bijou," said Mr. Ketchum suggestively. "Why aren't you gambolling like the playful antelope, Heathcote?"

"I don't often gamble. I leave that to Ramsay, who is an all-fired jewhillikens scratch at it, as you say over here," replied Mr. Heathcote.

"You gamble a little differently, that is all. You have dropped a good deal on loo first and last, for all your wisdom," retorted Mr. Ramsay between his steps.

"Get out your 'Hand-Book of American slang,' my boy,—two dollars a volume,—and you will retrieve all your losses, I'll engage," said Mr. Ketchum laughingly, as he walked away.

The dancing had been interrupted, however, and Bijou and Mr. Ramsay retired to the bow-window to talk. "Odd that I can't get it, isn't it?" said he. "I never was much of a dancin' man; and I ought to be, you know. I am not a readin' man; and a man that is not a readin' man is nearly always a dancin' man. The governor is a readin' man, and took a double-first; but I am like my poor mother, who was dull." Thus launched, he gave her a full account of his relatives and home with all his own frankness, and she, listening with her heart as well as her ears, did not know whether to smile or sigh: the phraseology of the recital and its completeness amused her, but she also divined the loneliness of such a boyhood. To her great embarrassment, the tears rose in her eyes in quick sympathy when she came to hear of the way he was treated in his childish maladies.

"Poor little fellow!" she said softly, and, as she was

obliged to drop the white, thickly-fringed lids and fall to pleating her handkerchief industriously, she felt rather than saw that he was looking at her narrowly.

There was a moment's silence, and then Mr. Ramsay began talking again. "You are very happy here, aren't you. You wouldn't like to leave it and go away to India, or Egypt, or—or—England, or anywhere?" said this particularly deep young man, and, without waiting for any answer, except such as was afforded by her rosy silence, went on: "American girls do have lots of fun, I see that. I am afraid they are too fond of flirting, though. English girls don't get much of a chance at that, as girls. They don't amount to much until they are married and get their own way."

"Why, they don't flirt after they are *married*, do they?" said Bijou, in a horrified tone, her ideal of post-matrimonial conduct being the exact opposite of the ante-matrimonial.

"Oh, don't they, just!" said Mr. Ramsay cheerfully. "You see, as girls they are heavily handicapped. They can't do anything they like, or go anywhere; it's awfully slow for them, poor things. And so they naturally look forward to the time when they will get their liberty as well as a husband. But the competition must be something awful. A fellow that has got a fine property or money is regularly hunted down; and even a poor devil like me has to be monstrous careful. Cowrie, of the Carbineers, who has got sixty thousand a year, says that he can't go to certain houses, for fear they may have a clergyman secreted about the place and will get him spliced to the ugliest daughter before he can escape. Awfully clever chap, Cowrie,—a match for any mamma

32

in England, I can tell you. He is not going to marry
any woman but the one he wishes to marry. No more
am I. That's why I can't marry. I've got no money.
The governor picked out a young woman from Liverpool for me last year,—a brewer's daughter, with pots
of it,—and wanted me to make up to her."

"Oh, he did! What did you do about it?" asked
Bijou, in a low voice.

"Well, you see, just then I was most awfully hard
up, and couldn't afford to break with the governor; and
so—"

"I'd be ashamed to say any more about it. Addressing the girl just for her money!" interjected Bijou
warmly, disappointed that he had not scorned the
proposition utterly.

"It didn't go that far. I thought it might be a good
thing, you know. And so I tried it,—spoonin', you
know," said he placidly.

"Oh, indeed!" commented Bijou sarcastically. "Very
honorable of you, I am sure, and delightful for the girl
to have such a disinterested admirer. How did it end?"

"How you do pick a fellow up!" remonstrated Mr.
Ramsay amiably. "It sounds awfully conceited to say
so, of course, but I think I could have carried off the
cup if I had liked. At least every one said she was
hard hit. And she wasn't long in the tooth, or very
ugly, or vulgar, or anything; but somehow I couldn't
stand it. I got to hate her. She breathed so hard
when she danced, for one thing. Regular grampus.
Upon my word, she almost blew my gibus away from
under my arm sometimes. Regular snorts. And then
she was always smilin'. And she talked an awful lot

about Goethe and Schiller, and those chaps. Altogether, I cried off, and told the governor I would try the Colonies. And he told me that if I was such a consummate ass as to let a good thing like that slip, I could take my little pittance and go to the deuce as soon as ever I liked; and here I am. Some may think I acted foolishly, but one's relatives are not always the best judges of what is good for one, you know, though they may think they are actin' for one's good; and what one wants to do is to do one's best in whatever position one finds one's self in, you know, no matter what one— Hang it all! I know what I want to say, but I can't say it. You understand, I fancy, without me tryin' to explain."

Having tied himself up in this conversational bow-knot, Mr. Ramsay waited to be extricated. His idea had been to convey in the most delicate and roundabout way to Bijou that he was not the man to marry any woman for her money, and that if he had seemed to like a certain person a good deal it was not because she was the daughter of a rich man. To her, however, he seemed to be posing as a conqueror of heiresses, indifferent to the pain he might inflict upon any girl silly enough to be captivated by his good looks and good manners,—a breaker of tacit engagements, and a wicked worldling. So she rose very stiffly, and said that she neither knew nor cared to know what he meant, and was obliged to leave him, and so went away, and left him extremely puzzled and disconcerted by the behavior of his charmer.

After this, the summer of Mr. Ramsay's discontent set in. There was nothing that he could actually complain of in Bijou's treatment of him, but it was plain that she had changed. She was vastly more polite than before, but much less kind. Their intimacy seemed a thing of the past century. It was Mr. Heathcote now who, partly from idleness, partly from a desire to tease his friend, went constantly to the Browns', and showed Bijou various attentions, which she accepted with very pronounced satisfaction. It was with Miss Price now that Mr. Ramsay rode and walked and talked. Miss Price, whose free-and-easiness, vapid chatter, artificiality, and sentimentalism contrasted unpleasantly with Bijou's frankness and sincerity. By this course each confirmed the other in the impression of untrustworthiness and flirtatiousness both had received, and they ought to have been perfectly satisfied with this result. But, considering how perfectly happy she was in Mr. Heathcote's society, it was odd that Bijou grew paler and thinner every day. And if Miss Price was so perfectly delightful, why did she send Mr. Ramsay home always as gloomy and morose as any young man very well could be? With blundering honesty, Mr. Ramsay once taxed Bijou with a preference for Mr. Heathcote, not knowing that when a jealous lover accuses a girl of being fond of some other man she never fails to encourage the idea, unless it is really true, when she denies it with the utmost vehemence. Bijou, with much feminine circumlocution, insinuated that he was devotedly attached to Miss Price, to which he truthfully replied that he did not care "one rap" about her. Women are born incredulous in such affairs. When sure of themselves, they doubt the lover; when sure of the lover, they invariably doubt themselves. And so the misunderstanding grew, and continued in mutual mistake and suspicion, and no two people were ever more thoroughly and foolishly miserable. Mr. Ketchum, when enlightened by his wife, could see that his guest was in a bad way; and one day it chanced that they were left alone in the library, where Job was most unromantically engaged in looking up plans for a model pig-stye, while he incidentally refreshed himself with his favorite confection, molasses candy.

"Man alive!" said he, after directing a keen glance at Mr. Ramsay's face, "what is the matter? Take some of the Dentist's Friend, won't you?" (pushing a plate toward him.) "I like it better than all the French stuff that was ever made, and Mabel keeps me liberally supplied. You look awfully down in the mouth, Ramsay, as though you'd enjoy howling like the lone wolf on far Alaska's shore, if you were sure nobody was looking. Suppose you tell me what has impaled you. Is it love, money, or indigestion, old fellow?"

The words were light, but the tone hearty and kind; and, thus encouraged, Mr. Ramsay laid bare his woes, Mr. Ketchum listening attentively, and saying, when he had finished, "I know; I know. When I thought I had lost Mabel once, I carried the universe around on a sore back all day, and then my heart would get up on its hind legs and yelp half the night; and there have been other times when I got caught in the machinery, and I know how it hurts. I think of those times often. They grind a man down to the quick, and send the chaff flying; they teach him valuable lessons. I remember I started out in life with two violent prejudices,—one against Jews, and the other against Roman Catholics

32*

Well, in the greatest strait I have ever known, the
Christian that came to my relief was a Jew in a town
of seven thousand people; and when I had the smallpox a Sister of Charity took me to the hospital and
nursed me, when every one had deserted me and left
me to die or live without any meddling from them to
bias me in my decision.    After that I said to myself,
'Job Ketchum, if the Lord can make and stand as great
a fool as you have been, he can make plenty of good
Jews and Roman Catholics, and if they have got his
hall-mark they can do without your valuable endorsement; and when smelting-day comes I reckon you'll
find that the Protestants' or even the Christian quartz
won't pan out *all* the silver that has been put in the
earth's veins.    You needn't go around blushing for
David and Thomas à Kempis any longer, my son.    Take
a holiday.'    My advice to you, Ramsay, is to keep a
stiff upper lip.    Perhaps the buzz-saw has only got your
clothes, and you will be all right when you cut loose;
but if it has got *you*, all you can do is to stand and take
it, and if you can remember who set it going it will be
better for you."

The last phrase Mr. Ketchum got out in a shamefaced
way, as if very much ashamed of it, as indeed he was;
but Mr. Ramsay was the better for the talk, and, though
not "a readin' man," had easily understood the illuminated characters in this page of human experience.    He
brightened perceptibly from this date, and was able to
take a healthy interest in certain match-games of base-
ball and la-crosse in neighboring cities, which he attended with Mr. Ketchum and Sir Robert, who, besides
these diversions, had to visit the prisons and all the

public schools, and to gather a mass of information in regard to these two subjects, with criminal and educational statistics, systems, theories, that had to be examined, sifted, recorded in the diary with the pains, study, and reverence for facts that characterized every entry made in it. Meanwhile, quite an intimacy had sprung up between the ladies of the Ketchum and Brown households, or rather the existing one soon embraced the Englishwomen. Mrs. Sykes and Miss Noel were struck by a number of things in the latter establishment.

"Do you suppose that *all* American households are organized in this extraordinary, miscellaneous way, so as to include, besides the head of the house, his wife and children, all sorts of relatives, outsiders, and strangers?" said Mrs. Sykes to Miss Noel. "Mrs. De Witt told me, quite as a matter of course, that the sister of her husband's first wife lived with them, though she was away when we were there. And look at the Ketchums and Browns. It is most remarkable. Why do they do it, I wonder? I must really ask about it, how it ever came about. And on such an extraordinary basis, too! Only fancy, that poor, thread-paper creature, Mr. Brown's daughter, has married badly and come back to her father with a troop of children; and she married in opposition to his wishes, and she hasn't a farthing of her own; and yet she seems to have no proper sense of her position whatever. She does nothing to make herself useful and get her living, but sits up in her bedroom, rocking and sewing, all the day long. She bids her father buy this and that for the children, just as though they were not actually beggars, dependent upon him for shelter and every mouthful. She meddles in household matters to any extent, giving the servants orders, having fires made, and even the dinner-hour changed to suit her convenience; and one would think she was mistress there. I wonder she dares do it. Yet, so far from being sat upon or put in her place, I heard Mr. Brown tell Bijou the other day, when some little disagreement took place between them, that she must let her 'poor sister' have everything to suit herself, and do her best to make her happy and contented and help her to forget all the trouble she had known, as far as possible. Just as if spoiling her like that, and giving her false ideas of her importance, could be a good plan. Not that it will last. She is a pauper, and will be made to see that she is one, sooner or later. She has nothing but what he gives her, I know, for I have asked her; but she would not tell me why she separated from her husband. Americans are so absurdly secretive and sensitive! Do you know, she was vexed by the inquiry? A great mistake, as I told her, to get rid of him, unless he was a dangerous brute: men are so useful, and 'grass-widows,' as they say here, are always looked down upon. Did you ever know anything so idle as those Brown women? The men here are very active and 'go-ahead,' as they call it, but the women seem to do one of two things,—either they hold their hands altogether and are a thousand times more idle than any queen or duchess, or they work themselves to death, and are cooks, sempstresses, maids, housemaids, nurses, governesses, ladies, and a dozen other things rolled into one,—poor things! Thank heaven I am not an American lady."

"1 see what you mean," said Miss Noel. "That dear, sweet girl Bijou has had no practical training whatever. She was amazed that I should make Ethel dye her white kid slippers (when they were soiled) for morning use; and when she saw me getting up some dainty bits of old point that I do not trust to Parsons, she asked me why I bothered with the old stuff and didn't buy new. She has absolutely no idea of the value of money or of household management. On the other hand, that little Mrs. Grey, their friend, told me that she did all the sewing for her twelve children; and Mr. Grey has not taken a holiday of even a few weeks for twenty years. I can't think how it is they don't break down altogether."

But it was the children of the Brown household that awakened the liveliest surprise in the minds of these ladies,—an astonishment wholly free from admiration or approval, for they were children of a type with which Americans are sadly familiar, but which had never come under their notice before. The little Graysons were utterly undisciplined, and got their own way in everything. Their grandfather, aunt, mother, and nurses combined were powerless to control them, and would give them anything but what they most needed. They pervaded the whole house, and were the hub of it; they ate at all hours, and of whatever they fancied. They had no regular hour for going to bed, but fell asleep everywhere, and were removed with the utmost precaution. Mrs. Sykes, going there, would find them jumping up and down with muddy feet on the drawing-room sofas or playing on the new grand piano with the poker. Miss Noel one day found Mr. Brown in a great

state of perturbation, calling out, "Helen! Jane! Bijou!
Come here, quick! The baby is bumping his head on
the floor!" (The baby being three years old.) "Don't
get angry, darling. If you won't bump your head,
grandpa will bring you a wax doll from Kalsing to-
morrow." Another day, baby's sister in banging on the
window-pane struck through the glass and cut her fist.
"Poor little dear! Poor childie! Let me bind it up
quickly. Harry, love, bid nurse fetch the arnica at
once," exclaimed Miss Noel; but the patient stamped
and shrieked, and would not have her hand examined
or doctored by anybody, whereupon her admiring
mother said, "Jenny has always been that way. She
has a great deal of character, Miss Noel."

"A very undisciplined one, I fear," replied that lady
emphatically. She could scarcely believe that she
heard aright when, on asking this model parent what
her plans were for the summer, she said,—

"I am going to try Saratoga again. We were there
last year, and I went prepared to stay until the 1st of
October. I liked it very much; it was very gay and
pleasant; but Harry got tired of it, and wouldn't stay
after the second week, so I packed up and went to
Long Branch, which he has always liked."

"Your brother, or uncle?" inquired Miss Noel, in
perfect good faith.

"No; my little Harry," replied the placid mother.

The very appearance of the children, fragile, delicate-
looking, nervous, was in striking contrast to the solid,
rosy, somewhat stolid English children to whom she
was accustomed. They were pretty, quite abnormally
intelligent she thought, and as attractive as such rear-

ing would permit them to become; but their habits
and manners positively afflicted her. She pined to put
them to bed at seven o'clock, keep them four or five
hours of every day in the open air, give them simple,
nourishing food,—in short, inaugurate the wholesome
nursery system of her own country. To see them
sitting down to table without saying their grace or
putting on their pinafores, and order of the servant
soups full of condiments, veal, any or all of eight vege-
tables, pickles, tarts, pudding, jelly, custard, fruit-cake,
bon-bons, strong coffee, cheese, almonds, raisins, figs,
more custard, raisins again, and more fruit-cake, all
despatched in great haste, with no attention to the
proper use of napkin, knife, fork, or spoon, was acutely
disagreeable to her; and it was amusing to see her
efforts to insinuate, as it were, better things into their
daily life. "They are nice, clever children," she would
say,—"so delicate-featured, and so refined in appearance, but, heavens! what a monstrous system of education!"

There were other things in that household that Miss
Noel was not blind to. She saw, for instance, what
quite escaped Mr. Brown and Mrs. Grayson, namely,
that Bijou was not herself, and shrewdly guessed that
she was suffering from a malady that had once made
a certain part of her own life very happy and very
miserable. She had taken a fancy to Bijou from the
first, and she soon noticed in her a great many little
evidences of weariness, discontent, unhappiness; also
that she was alternately very pale and depressed or
flushed and animated. She took the girl therefore
under her motherly wing, lectured her a little in her

gentle way about some things, praised her in others, and was very kind to her.

"My dear," she would say, "do you not eat entirely too many sweets, bon-bons, and what not, and then go without proper food at the regular meals?" Or it would be, "How do you occupy yourself, as a rule, dear child? Do you district-visit, botanize, sketch, learn a language? What do you do? You would enjoy a course. of belles-lettres, and should take that. And that head in crayons that you did at school was pleasantly executed: why not study from life constantly?" Bijou had to confess that she did nothing, and not even that industriously: "But, my dear, you are not an Asiatic. You surely don't wish to be a doll, a plaything, self-indulgent, helpless, leading a life of mere luxurious indulgence and artificiality?"

. No, Bijou had no such wish; but what was the use of learning or doing anything now as a girl? If she married, it would be different; but then she would never, never marry. But Miss Noel insisted that an idle woman was a miserable woman, married or single, and was brisk and cheerful and kind, and devised a number of small employments for Bijou, whom she kept with her a great deal, and so befriended her as effectually as Mr. Ketchum had done Mr. Ramsay. Mrs. Sykes found fault with her once or twice, but did not find her all meekness.·

"Why do you talk of 'an elegant breeze'?" she said to her one day.·

"For the same reason that you spoke of 'a beautiful roast' yesterday," retorted the young lady, who might be broken-hearted, but was certainly not broken-spirited.

"I know better, and I suppose you do, but we are both careless."

Matters drifted along in this way until a certain morning spent by Mr. Ramsay at the Browns',—eventful because a little thing happened which convinced him that Bijou cared for him. He came home with a new pang substituted for those he had been enduring for a lover's age. After dinner he tramped off for a long walk alone, in the course of which it may fairly be presumed that he decided what course to take, for early on the following day he called especially, for the second time, upon Mr. Brown.

"I have come to tell you that I can't come here any more," he said, holding his hat with his accustomed grace, and going in his straightforward fashion immediately to the subject in his mind. "And I wish to thank you for bein' so kind to me and receivin' me as you have done, and to tell you why I am actin' in this way."

"Why, what's the matter? Going away? Isn't this rather sudden?" asked Brown *père*, all unsuspicious of what was to come.

"Oh, it isn't *that!* Though of course I shall be goin'. It is that I can't marry. That is what it is. You should have been told of it before, by rights, only I kept puttin' it off. You have a perfect right to blame me for not sayin' so long ago, when you were good enough to admit me here on an intimate footin'. It was a shabby, dishonorable thing of me, and I hope you'll forgive it, rememberin' that it was not my intention to deceive you," said Mr. Ramsay. "It wasn't, now, really."

" But, my dear fellow, of what are you accusing your-self? There must be some mistake. What has that got to do with your visits here?" asked Mr. Brown.

" Why, don't you see?—don't you object to me bein' thrown so much with Miss Brown, under the circum-stances?" stammered out Mr. Ramsay.

"Not the least in the world,—not the least in the world, I assure you. Delighted to· see you, I am sure, whenever you like to come," said Mr. Brown, with hospitable warmth. "Why should I? There is no necessity for your marrying anybody, that I can see. What put such a foolish idea in your head?"

" But I thought you would think—she would think I thought—that is—as you might say—"

A hearty laugh from Mr. Brown interrupted him: "Why, you seem to have thought a good deal on the subject. The most extraordinary idea! Excuse my saying so. This house is always full of young men dancing attendance on Bijou, who is as popular a girl as there is; but I don't trouble *my* head about them, I can assure you. No, indeed. Half of them don't want to marry Bijou, and she don't want to marry any of them that I know of. And I guess I shall be told when the affair comes off, so that I can order the wedding-cake. Why, they are just all young people together. It don't mean anything. They just naturally like each other's society. They are amusing themselves,—that's all; and quite right, too."

Mr. Ramsay had never conceived of such a philo-sophical parent or agreeable state of affairs. He was very much embarrassed, and caught at a familiar idea in his confusion. "That's what I thought you would think,—that I was amusin' myself. And I wanted to tell you that I am not, you know. I have far too much respect for Miss Brown to dream of doin' such a thing," he said very eagerly.

"Oh, you mean at her expense? I understand now. Well, now, let me make your mind perfectly easy on that score. Bijou can take care of herself as well as any girl in America, and I never thought of such a thing. If you are thinking of *her*, that's all right. If you are thinking of yourself, of course that is another thing. She isn't thinking of marrying *you*. She doesn't care anything about you in that way, I am certain. I should have noticed it if she had been," said Mr. Brown, who labored under the usual parental delusion as to his daughter's heart having a glass window through which he could see all that went on there.

"I am tryin' to do what is best for both of us," said Mr. Ramsay honestly, blushing profusely. "And I came to say good-by. And here is a little note I have written Miss Brown. I have left it open, in case you wished to see it."

"Not at all,—not at all. Bijou would blow me up sky-high if she caught me reading it, I can tell you. I'll give it to her, certainly. I think you are giving yourself unnecessary concern; but your scruples, though novel, do you honor. If you think it best to give us up, you are, as far as you are personally concerned, the best judge. Good-by. Send us a line to say how you like the West. Good-by," said Mr. Brown, and smilingly accompanied him to the front door.

Papa Brown gave his daughter the note, which ran as follows:

" My dear Miss Brown,—I am going away, and you have been so awfully kind to me that I know you will excuse me writing to say how awfully grateful I am to your family for receiving a stranger as they have done."

Here " I shall often think of you" was carefully scratched out, and " I shall always remember it and the pleasant hours I have spent with them" substituted.

"And now I have got to say a disagreeable word, which is good-by. I hope you will have a fine hot summer and will think of me sometimes. when you are spooning tremendously at croquet,—as you know you do, though it isn't fair. With best regards to all the members of your household, I am

" Faithfully yours,

" Arthur Ramsay.

" P.S.—If I should drop into a good thing you will hear of it."

Mr. Ramsay had taken four hours to compose something that should not be actionable or compromising, and yet that should convey some idea of the state of his mind and feelings, and had turned out this masterpiece, which Bijou read in bitterness of soul over and over again.

" Excuse me writing," " fine hot summer," " croquet," she quoted mentally. "After all that has passed between us ! If he had really cared for me, and anything had separated us, he would have had the common honesty and manliness to say so. No ; he thinks me another Liverpool girl, 'hard hit.' He is running away from *me*." At this cruel idea, so abhorrent to her vanity, pride, affection, and general womanhood, the poor girl sank down on her bed overwhelmed, and did not leave her room for three days,—or rather eternities,—at the end of which time she met Mr. Ramsay by accident on the high-road and cut him dead.

"I must pull myself together and get away out of this," said Mr. Ramsay to Mr. Ketchum that evening. "I have bought of Albert Brown his ranch in Colorado, near Taylorsville, and I leave in the morning."

"WHAT!" cried Mr. Ketchum. "Has he sold you that tumble-down claim on a burnt prairie, miles from any wood or water? I know the place."

"I haven't examined the property; but he assured me it is a fine one. And, anyway, it is settled. I am going. A thousand thanks for all your kindness, Ketchum. An Englishman that I met in New York wants me to go huntin' with him, and I shall join him at St. Louis and go on out from there."

"Why, I thought you had all promised to go to Niagara as my guests in a few days. Do change your mind and stay, won't you?" urged Mr. Ketchum.

But Mr. Ramsay was obdurate, and took himself and a car-load of property off in the direction of the setting sun by the mid-day train next morning.

"Ramsay, I want you to promise me one thing. If, owing to that skunk Brown, you are disappointed out there, or don't get on, write or telegraph me, and I'll stand by you to the tune of ten thousand or so. Good-by, old fellow. Remember, I'm your *friend*," said generous Job, at the station. And as he went home he stopped and presented Mr. Albert Brown with a piece of his mind that any other man would only have taken in exchange for a flogging, delivered.

33*

" How very nice and kind of the dear duke to give Mr. Ramsay an invite to join him !" said Mrs. Sykes, with emotion, at dinner that day.

---

## VIII.

Not the least delightful of Sir Robert's qualities was his capacity for enjoying most things that came in his way, and finding some interest in all. When Mr. Ketchum joined him in the library, where he was jotting down " the *sobriquets* of the American States and cities," and told him of the Niagara plan, his ruddy visage beamed with pleasure.

" A delightful idea. Capital," he said. " I suppose I can read up a bit about it before we start, and not go there with my eyes shut. Ni-a-ga-rah,—monstrously soft and pretty name. Isn't there something on your shelves that would give me the information I want ? But we can come to that presently. Just now I want to find out, if I can, how these nicknames came to be given. They must have originated in some great pop ular movement, eh ? I thought I saw my way, as, for example, the ' Empire State' and the ' Crescent City' and some others, but this ' Sucker State,' now, and ' Buckeye' business,—what may that mean in plain English ?"

Mr. Ketchum shed what light he could on these interesting questions, and Sir Robert thoughtfully ran his hands through his side-whiskers, while, with an apologetic "One moment, I beg," or "Very odd, very; that must go down verbatim," he entered the gist of Mr. Ketchum's queer remarks in his note-book.

On the following morning he rose with Niagara in his soul. He had more questions to ask at the breakfast-table than anybody could answer, and was eager to be off. Mr. Ketchum, who had that week made no less than fifty thousand dollars by a lucky investment, was in high spirits. Captain Kendall, who had been allowed to join the party, was vastly pleased by the prospect of another week in Ethel's society. Mrs. Sykes was tired of Fairfield, and longed to be "on the move" again, as she frankly said. So that, altogether, it was a merry company that finally set off.

The very first view of "the ocean unbound" increased their pleasure to enthusiasm. Mrs. Sykes, without reservation, admitted that it was "a grand spot," and felt as though she were giving the place a certificate when she added, "*Quite* up to the mark." She was out on the Suspension Bridge, making a sketch, as soon as she could get there; she took one from every other spot about the place; and when tired of her pencil, she stalked about with her hammer, chipping off bits of rock that promised geological interest. But she found her greatest amusement in the brides that "infested the place" (to quote from her letter to her sister Caroline), indulged in much satirical comment on them, and, choosing one foolish young rustic who was there as her text, wrote in her diary, "American brides like to go from the altar to some large hotel, where they can display their finery, wear their wedding-dresses every evening, and attract as much attention as possible. The national passion for display makes them delight in anything that renders them conspicuous, no matter how vulgar that display may be. If one must have a fool's paradise, generally known as a honeymoon, this is about as pleasant a place as any other for it; and, as there are several runaway couples stopping here, and the place is just on the border, this is doubtless the American Gretna Green, where silly women and temporarily-infatuated men can marry in haste, to repent at leisure."

Mr. Heathcote gave his camera enough to do, as may be imagined. He and Sir Robert traced the Niagara River from Lake Erie to Lake Ontario, and photographed it at every turn, made careful estimates of its length, breadth, depth, the flow of currents, scale of descent to the mile, wear of precipice, and time necessary for the river to retire from the falls business altogether and meander tranquilly along on a level like other rivers. They arrayed themselves in oil-skin suits and spent an unconscionable time at the back of the Horseshoe Fall, roaring out observations about it that were rarely heard, owing to the deafening din, and had more than one narrow escape from tumbling into the water in these expeditions. They carefully bottled some of it, which they afterward sealed with red wax and duly labelled, intending to add it to a collection of similar phials which Sir Robert had made of famous waters in many countries. They went over the mills and factories in the neighborhood, and Sir Robert had long confabs with the managers, of whom he asked permission to "jot down" the interesting facts developed in the course of their conversations, surprising them by his knowledge of mechanics and the subjects in hand.

"Man alive! what do you want with *those?*" said he to one of them, a keen-faced young fellow, who was showing him the boiler-fires. He pointed with his stick as he spoke, and rattled it briskly about the brick-work by way of accompaniment as he went on: "Such a waste of force, of money! downright stupidity! You don't want it. You don't need it, any more than you need an hydraulic machine tacked to the back of your trains. You have got water enough running past your very door to—"

"I've told that old fool Glass that a thousand times," broke in the young man; "but if he wants to try and warm and light the world with a gas-stove when the sun is up I guess it's no business of mine, though it does rile me to see the power thrown away and good coal wasted. If I had the capital, here's what I'd do. Here."

Seizing Sir Robert's stick, the enthusiast drew a fondly-loved ideal mill in the coal-dust at his feet, while Sir Robert looked and listened, differed, suggested, with keen interest, and Mr. Heathcote gave but haughty and ignorant attention to the talk that followed.

"Yes, that's the way of it; but Glass has lived all his life with his head in a bag, and he can't see it. I am surprised to see you take an interest in it. Ever worked at it?" said the man in conclusion.

"A little," said Sir Robert affably, who could truthfully have said as much of anything. "Who is this Glass?"

"Oh, he's the man that owns all this; the stupidest owl that ever lived. I wish he could catch on like you. I'd like very well to work with you," was the reply.

"A bumptious fellow, that," commented Mr. Heathcote when they left. "He'd 'like to work with you,' indeed!"

"A fellow with ideas. I'd like to work with him," replied his uncle; "though he isn't burdened with respect for his employers."

Miss Noel meanwhile tied on her large straw hat, took her cane, basket, trowel, tin box, and, followed by Parsons with her sketching-apparatus, went off to hunt plants or wash in sketches, a most blissfully occupied and preoccupied old lady.

To Mr. Ketchum's great amusement, Miss Noel, Mrs Sykes, and Mr. Heathcote all arrived at a particular spot within a few moments of each other one morning, all alike prepared and determined to get the view it commanded.

Miss Noel had said to Job *en route*, "Do you think that I shall be able to get a fly and drive about the country a bit? I should so like it. Are they to be had there?"

And he had replied, "You will have some difficulty in *not* taking 'a fly' there, I guess. The hackmen would rather drive your dead body around town for nothing than let you enjoy the luxury of walking about unmolested. But I will see to all that."

Accordingly, a carriage had been placed at their disposal, and they had taken some charming drives, in the course of which Parsons, occupying the box on one occasion, was seen to be peering very curiously about her

"A great pity, is it not, Parsons, that we can't see all this in the autumn, when the thickets of scarlet and gold are said to be so very beautiful?" said Miss Noel, addressing her affably.

"Yes, mem," agreed Parsons. "And if you please, mem, where are the estates of the gentry, as I 'ave been lookin' for ever since we came hover?"

"Not in this part," replied Miss Noel. "The red Indians were here not very long since. You should really get a pincushion of their descendants, those mild, dirty creatures that work in bark and beads. Buy of one that has been baptized: one shouldn't encourage them to remain heathens, you know. Your friends in England will like to see something made by them; and they were once very powerful and spread all over the country as far as—as—I really forget where; but I know they were very wild and dreadful, and lived in wigwams, and wore moccasins."

"Oh, indeed, mem!" responded Parsons, impressed by the extent of her mistress's information.

"A wigwam is three upright poles, such as the gypsies use for their kettles, thatched with the leaves of the palm and the plantain," Miss Noel went on. "Dear me! It is very odd! I certainly remember to have read that; but perhaps I am getting back to the Southern Americans again, which does so vex Robert. I wonder if one couldn't see a wigwam for one's self? It can't be plantain, after all: there is none growing about here."

She asked Mabel about this that evening, and the latter told her husband how Miss Noel was always mixing up the two continents.

"I don't despair, Mabel. They will find this potato-patch of ours after a while," he said good-humoredly.

But he was less amiable when Mrs. Sykes said at dinner next day, "I should like to try your maize. Quite simply boiled, and eaten with butter and salt, I am told it is quite good, really. I have heard that the Duke of Slumborough thought it excellent."

"You don't say so! I am so glad to hear it! I shall make it generally known as far as I can. Such things encourage us to go on trying to make a nation of ourselves. It would have paralyzed all growth and development in this country for twenty years if he had thought it 'nasty,'" said Job. "Foreigners can't be too particular how they express their opinions about us. Over and over again we have come within an ace of putting up the shutters and confessing that it was no use pretending that we could go on independently having a country of our own, with distinct institutions, peculiarities, customs, manners, and even productions. It would be so much better and easier to turn ourselves over to a syndicate of distinguished foreigners who would govern us properly,—stamp out ice-water and hot rolls from the first, as unlawful and not agreeing with the Constitution, give us cool summers, prevent children from teething hard, make it a penal offence to talk through the nose, and put a bunch of Bourbons in the White House, with a divine right to all the canvas-back ducks in the country. There are so many kings out of business now that they could easily give us a bankrupt one to put on our trade dollar, or something really *sweet* in emperors who have seen better days. And a standing army of a hundred thousand men, all drum-majors, in gorgeous uniforms, helmets, feathers, gold lace, would certainly scare the Mexicans into caniptious and unconditional surrender. The more I think of it, the more delightful it seems. It is mere stupid obstinacy our people keeping up this farce of self-government, when anybody can see that it is a perfect failure, and that the country has no future whatever."

"Oh, you talk in that way; but I don't think you would really like it," said Mrs. Sykes. "Americans seem to think that they know everything: they are above taking any hints from the Old World, and get as angry as possible with me when I point out a few of the more glaring defects that strike me."

"I am surprised at that. Our great complaint is that we can't get any advice from Europeans. If we only had a little, even, we might in time loom up as a fifth-rate power. But no: they leave us over here in this wilderness without one word of counsel or criticism, or so much as a suggestion, and they ought not to be surprised that we are going to the dogs. What else can they expect?" said Mr. Ketchum.

"Husband, dear, you were very sharp with my cousin to-day, and it was not like you to show temper,—at least, not temper exactly, but vexation," said Mabel to him afterward in mild rebuke. "She has told me that you quite detest the English, so that she wonders you should have married me. And I said that you were far too intelligent and just to cherish wrong feelings toward any people, much less my people."

"Well, if *she* represented England I should drop England quietly over the rapids some day when I could no longer stand her infernal patronizing, impertinent airs, and rid the world of a nuisance," said Mr. Ketchum, with energy. "Excuse my warmth, but that woman would poison a prairie for me. Fortunately, I happen to know that she only represents a class which neither Church nor State there has the authority to shoot, *yet*,

34

and I am not going to cry down white wool because
there are black sheep. Look at Sir Robert, and Miss
Noel, and all the rest of them, how different they are."

Captain Kendall certainly found Niagara delightful,
for, owing to the absorption of the party in their different pursuits, he was able to see more of Ethel than he
had ever done. He was so different from the men
she had known that he was a continual study to her.
Instead of the studied indifference, shy avoidance, shy
advances, culminating in a blunt and straightforward
declaration of "intentions," which she would have
thought natural in an admirer, followed by transparent,
honest delight in the event of acceptance, or manly sub-
mission to the inevitable in the event of rejection, Captain Kendall had surprised her by liking her immediately, or at least by showing that he did, and seeking
her persistently, without any pretence of concealment.
He talked to her of politics, of social questions in the
broadest sense, of books, scientific discoveries, his travels,
and the travels of others. He read whole volumes of
poetry to her. He discoursed by the hour on the manly
character, its faults, merits, peculiarities, and possibilities, and then contrasted it with the womanly one, trait
for trait, and it seemed to her that women had never
been praised so eloquently, enthusiastically, copiously.
At no time was he in the least choked by his feelings or
at a loss for a fresh word or sentiment. Such romance,
such ideality, such universality, as it were, she had
never met. When his admiration was most unbridled
it seemed to be offered to her as the representative of a
sex entirely perfect and lovely. Everything in heaven
and earth, apparently, ministered to his passion and

made him talk all around the beloved subject with a
wealth of simile and suggestion that she had never
dreamed of. But, if he gave full expression to his agitated feelings in these ways, he was extremely delicate,
respectful, reserved, in others. He wrapped up his
heart in so many napkins, indeed, that, being a practical woman not extraordinarily gifted in the matter of
imagination, she frequently lost sight of it altogether,
and she sometimes failed to follow him in a broad road
of sentiment that (like the Western ones which Longfellow has described) narrowed and narrowed until it
disappeared, a mere thread, up a tree. If he looked
long, after one of these flights, at her sweet English
face to see what impression he had made, he was often
forced to see that it was not the one he had meant to
make at all.

"Is anything amiss?" she asked once, in her cool,
level tone, fixing upon him her sincerely honest eyes.
"Are there blacks on my nose?" Although she had
distinctly refused him at Kalsing, as became a girl destitute of vanity and coquetry and attached to some one
else, she had not found him the less fluent, omnipresent,
persuasive, at Niagara. It was diverting to see them
seated side by side on Goat Island, he waving his hand
toward the blue sky, apostrophizing the water, the
foliage, the clouds, and what not, in prose and verse,
quite content if he but got a quiet glance and assenting
word now and then, she listening demurely in a state
of protestant satisfaction, her fair hair very dazzling in
the sunshine, an unvarying apple-blossom tint in her
calm face, her fingers tatting industriously not to waste
the time outright. It was very agreeable in a way, she

told herself, but something must really be done to get
rid of the man. And so, one morning when they
chanced to be alone, and he was being unusually ethereal and beautiful in his remarks, telling her that, as
Byron had said, she would be "the morning star of memory" for him, she broke in squarely, "That is all very
nice; very pretty, I am sure. But I do hope you quite
understand that I have not the least idea of marrying
you. There is no use in going on like this, you know,
and you would have a right to reproach me if I kept
silent and led you to think that I was being won over
by your fine speeches. You see, you don't really want
a star at all. You want a wife; though military men,
as a rule, are better off single. I do thank you heartily
for liking me for myself, and all that, and I shall always
remember the kind things you have done, and our acquaintance, but you must put me quite out of your
head as a wife. I should not suit you at all. You
would have to leave the American service, and I should
hate feeling I had tied you down, and I couldn't contribute a penny toward the household expenses, and,
altogether, we are much better apart. It would not
answer at all. So, thank you again for the honor you
have conferred upon me, and be—be rather more—like
other people, won't you, for the future? Auntie fancies
that I am encouraging you, and is getting very vexed
about it. Perhaps you had better go away? Yes, that
would be best, I think."

Thus solicited, Captain Kendall went away, taking
a mournfully-eloquent farewell of Ethel, which she
thought final; but in this she was mistaken.

Our party did not linger long after this. Sir Robert

met a titled acquaintance, who inflamed his mind so much about Manitoba that he decided to go to Canada at once, taking Miss Noel, Ethel, and Mr. Heathcote; Mrs. Sykes had taken up on her first arrival with some New York people, who asked her to visit them in the central part of the State,—which disposed of her; Mabel was secretly longing to get back to her "American child," as Mrs. Sykes called little Jared Ponsonby; and they separated, with the understanding that they should meet again before the English guests left the country, and with a warm liking for each other, the Sykes not being represented in the pleasant covenants of friendship formed.

"I am glad that we have not to bid Ketchum good-by here," said Sir Robert. "Such a hearty, genial fellow! And how kind he has been to us! His hospitality is the true one; not merely so much food and drink and moneyed outlay for some social or selfish end, but the entertainment of friends because they *are* friends, with every possible care for their pleasure and comfort, and the most unselfish willingness to do anything that can contribute to either. I am afraid he would not find many such hosts as himself with us. We entertain more than the Americans, but I do not think we have as much of the real spirit of hospitality as a nation. The relation between host and guest is less personal, there is little sense of obligation, or rather sacredness, on either side, and the convenience, interest, or amusement of the Amphitryon is more apt to be considered, as a general thing, than the pleasure of the guest: at least this has been growing more and more the case in the last twenty years, as our society has broken away

*aa* 34*

from old traditions and levelled all its barriers, to the detriment of our social graces, not to speak of our morals and manners. As for that charmingly gentle, sweet woman Mrs. Ketchum, it is my opinion that we are not likely to improve on that type of Englishwoman. A modest, simple, religious creature, a thorough gentlewoman, and a devoted wife and mother. My cousin Guy Rathbone is engaged to a specimen of a new variety,—one of the 'emancipated,' forsooth ; a woman who has a betting-book instead of a Bible and plays cards all day Sunday. He tells me that she is wonderfully clever, and that it is all he can do to keep her from run ning about the kingdom delivering lectures on Agnosticism ; as if one wanted one's wife to be a trapesing, atheistical Punch-and-Judy ! And the fellow seemed actually pleased and flattered. He told me that she had 'an astonishing grasp of such subjects' and was 'attracting a great deal of attention.' And I told him that if I had a wife who attracted attention in such ways I would lock her up until she came to her senses and the public had forgotten her want of modesty and discretion. This ought to be called the Age of Fireworks. The craze for notoriety is penetrating our very almshouses, and every toothless old mumbler of ninety wants to get himself palmed off as a centenarian in the papers and have a lot of stuff printed about him."

"I see what you mean, Robert," said Miss Noel, "and it certainly cannot be wholesome for women to thirst for excitement, and one would think a lady would shrink from being conspicuous in any way ; but things are very much changed, as you say. And I agree with you in your estimate of the Ketchums. · She is a sweet young thing, and I heartily like him. Only think! his last act was to send a great basket of fine fruits up to my room, and quite an armful of railway-novels for the journey. Such beautiful thought for our comfort as they have shown!"

"He is rather a good sort in some ways, but a very ignorant man. I showed him some of my specimens the other day, and he thought them granitic, when they were really Silurian mica schist of some kind," put in Mrs. Sykes, who never could bear unqualified praise. "Still, on the whole, the Americans are less ignorant than might have been expected."

"*I* consider Mr. Ketchum a most kind, gentlemanly, sociable, clever man," said Miss Noel, with an emphatic nod of her head to each adjective, "geology or no geology. And I must say that it is very ungrateful of you to speak of him so sneeringly always."

Sir Robert only waited to write the usual batch of letters, including a last appeal to the editor of the " Columbia Eagle" to know whether he intended to apologize for and publicly retract a certain article, and asking " whether it was possible that any considerable or respectable portion of the Americans could be so arbitrary, illiberal, and exclusive as to wish to exclude the English from America." This done, he left for Canada with his relatives. With his stay there we have nothing to do. It consumed six weeks of exhaustive travel and study of Canadian conditions and resources, resulting ultimately in the conclusion that Manitoba was not the place he was looking for. The ladies, who had been left in Montreal, were then taken for a short tour through the country, which they all enjoyed, after

which Sir Robert asked Miss Noel whether she would
be willing to take Ethel back to Niagara and wait there
a fortnight, or perhaps a little longer, while he and Mr.
Heathcote came back by way of New England and
from there went down into Maryland and Virginia,
where, according to "a member of the Canadian Parliament," lands were to be had for a song.

"A fortnight? I could spend a twelvemonth there,"
exclaimed she. "Had it not been that I was ashamed
to insist upon being let off this journey, I should have
stopped there as it was."

To Niagara the aunt and niece and Parsons went, as
agreed, and there they found Mr. Bates wandering languidly about the place in chronic discontent with everything for not being something else. He had burned a
good deal of incense on Ethel's shrine when she was at
Kalsing, and now hailed their advent with some approach to enthusiasm, and attached himself to their
suite, *vice* Captain Kendall, retired. He liked to be
seen with them, thought the views from the Canadian
side were "deucedly fine," was cruelly affected by the
advertisements in the neighborhood, which he denounced as "dreadfully American," trickled out much
feeble criticism of and acid comment on his surroundings, gave utterance to fervent wishes that he was
"abrard," and in his own unpleasant way gave Ethel
to understand that she might make a fellow-countryman
happy by becoming Mrs. Samuel Bates if she liked to
avail herself of a golden opportunity. "I would live
in England, you know. I am really far more at home
there than here," said the expatriated suitor. "I have
been taken for an Englishman as often as three times

in one week, do you know. Curious, isn't it? I ought
to be down in Kent now, visiting Lady Simpson, a great
friend of mine, who has asked me there again and again.
You would like her if you knew her. She is quite the
great lady down there."

"A foolish little man, and evidently a great snob, or
else rather daft upon some points," Ethel reported to
her aunt. "And such a dull, discontented creature, with
all his money!" Ethel had some trials of her own just
then, and it was no great felicity to listen to Mr. Bates's
endless complaints, nor could she spare much sympathy
for the sufferings of the exile of Tecumseh, with his
rose-leaf sensibilities, inanities, absurdities.

Meanwhile, the young gentleman who was indirectly
responsible for many a sad thought of two charming
girls that we know of—and who shall say how many
more?—was enjoying as much happiness as ever fell to
any man in the capacity of ardent sportsman. He had
joined the duke and his party at St. Louis, and from
there they had gone "well away from anywhere," as
he said in describing his adventures to Mr. Heathcote.
He had at last reached the ideal spot of all his wildest
imaginations and most cherished hopes,—"the wild
part,"—really the great prairies, about two hundred
miles west of the Mississippi and east of the Rockies.
The dream of his life was being fulfilled. He related,
'n a style not conspicuous for literary merit, but very
well suited to the simple annals of the rich, how, having
first procured guides, tents, ambulances, camp-equipage,
they had pushed on briskly to a military fort, where,
having made friends with "a pleasant, gentlemanly set
of fellows," the commanding officer, "a friendly old

buffer," had courteously given them an escort to protect
them from "those dirty treacherous brutes, the Indians."
Not a joy was wanting in this crowning bliss. The
guide was "a wonderful chap named Big-foot Williams,
so called by the Indians, good all around from knocking
over a rabbit to tackling a grizzly," with an amazing
knowledge of woodcraft, "a nose like a bloodhound,
an eye as cool as a toad's." No special mention was
made of his ear; but the first time he got off his horse
and applied it to the earth, listening for the tramp of
distant hoofs in a hushed silence, one bosom could
hardly hold all the rapture that filled Mr. Ramsay's
figurative cup up to the brim. And the tales he told
of savageness long drawn out were as dew to the
parched herb, greedily absorbed at every pore. A portrait of "Black Eagle," a noted chief, was given when
they got among the Indians,—"a great hulking slugger
of a savage, awfully interesting, long, reaching step,
magnificent muscles, snake eye, could thrash us all in
turn if he liked. The best of the lot."

Even the noble red man was not insensible to the
charms of this graceful, handsome young athlete who
smiled at them perpetually and said "*Amigo! amigo!*"
at short intervals,—a phrase suggested by the redoubt-
able Williams and varied occasionally by a prefix of his
own, "*Muchee amigo!*" The way in which he tested
the elasticity of their bows, inspected their guns, the
game they had killed, the other natural objects about
them, aroused a certain sympathy, perhaps. At any
rate, they were soon teaching him their mode of using
the most picturesquely murderous of all weapons, and
Black Eagle offered, through the interpreter, to give

him a mustang and a fine wolf-skin. The pony was declined, the skin accepted, a *quid pro quo* being bestowed on the chief in the shape of one of Mr. Ram say's breech-loaders, a gift that made the snake eyes glitter. But what earthly return can be made for some friendly offices? Could a thousand guns be considered as an adequate payment for the delirious thrill that Mr. Ramsay felt when he shot an arrow straight through the neck of a big buffalo, and, wheeling, galloped madly away, like the hero of one of his favorite stories? Was not the duke, who "knew a thing or two about shooting" and had hunted the noble bison in Lithuania, almost as much delighted as though he had done it himself? Is it any wonder that these intoxicating pleasures were all-sufficient for the time to Mr. Ramsay? Perhaps Thekla would have been forgotten by her Max, and Romeo would never have sighed and died for love of Juliet, if those interesting lovers had ceased from wooing and gone a-hunting of the buffalo instead. Not the most deadly and cruel pangs of the most unfortunate attachment could have taken away all the zest from such an occupation, provided they had had what the Mexican journals call the *"corazon de los sportsmans."* Youth, strength, courage, skill, exercised in a vagabondage that has all the nomadic charm without any of its drawbacks, are apt to sponge the old figures off the slate of life, leaving a teary smear, perhaps, to show where they have been, and room for fresh problems. At night over the camp-fire Mr. Ramsay gave a few pensive thoughts to the girl who regularly put two handkerchiefs under her pillow to receive the tears that welled out copiously when she was at last alone and unob-

served after a day of virtuous hypocrisy. Poor child!
The pain was very real, and the tears were bitter and
salty enough, though they were to be dried in due time.
If he had known of them, perhaps he might have kept
awake a little longer; but when he wasn't sleepy he
was hungry, and when he wasn't hungry he was tired,
and when he wasn't tired he was too actively employed
to think of anything but the business in hand. Happily, at five-and-twenty it is perfectly possible to post-
pone being miserable until a more convenient season;
and, though he would have denied it emphatically afterward, he certainly thought only occasionally of Bijou
at this period, and of Ethel not at all.

Miss Noel heard very regularly from Mrs. Sykes all
this while; and that energetic traveller had not been
idle. She had made her new friends "take her about
tremendously," she said. She had seen all the large
towns in that part of the country, and thought them
"very ugly and monotonously commonplace, but pros-
perous-looking,—like the inhabitants." The scenery
she had found "far too uninteresting to repay the bother
of sketching it." But she had made a few pictures of
"the views most cracked up in the White Mountains,"
—where she had been,—"a sort of second-hand Switzerland of a place; really nothing after the Himalayas,
but made a great fuss over by the Americans." She
described with withering scorn a drive she took there.

"We came suddenly one day upon a party in a kind
of Cheap-Jack van," she wrote,—"gayly-dressed people,
tricked off in smart finery, and larking like a lot of Ramsgate tradesmen on the public road. One of the impudent creatures made a trumpet of his great ugly fist and

spelt out the name of the hotel at which they were
stopping, and then put his hand to his ear, as if to listen
for the response. Expecting *me* to tell *them* anything
about myself! But I flatter myself that I was a match
for them. I just got out my umbrella and shot it up in
their very faces as we passed, in a way not to be mistaken. And—would you believe it?—the rude wretches
called out, 'The shower is over now!' and 'What's the
price of starch?' and roared with laughing." A highly-
colored description of "a visit to a great Dissenting
stronghold, Marbury Park," followed: "I was immensely curious to see one of these characteristic national exhibitions of hysteria, ignorance, superstition,
and immorality, called a 'camp-meeting,' to which the
Americans of all classes flock annually by the thousands, so I quite insisted upon being taken to one, though
my friends would have got out of it if they could. I
fancy they were very ashamed of it; and they had
need to be. I will not attempt to describe it in detail
here,—you will hear what I have said of it in my
diary,—but a more glaringly vulgar, intensely American performance you can't fancy. I have made a number of sketches of the grounds, the tents and tent-life,
with the people bathing and dressing and all that in
the most exposed manner; of the pavilion, where the
roaring and ranting is done; and of the great revivalist
who was holding forth when I got there, and who had
got such a red face and seemed so excited that it is my
belief he was *regularly screwed*, though my friends denied it, of course. With such a preacher, you can
'realize,' as they say, what the people were like. A
regular Derby-day crowd having a religious saturnalia,

—that is what it is. It would not be allowed at home,
I am sure. Disgusting! One can't wonder at the
state of society in America when one sees what their
religion is. An unpleasant incident occurred to me
while sketching in the pavilion, that shows what I have
often pointed out to you,—the radicalism and odious
impertinence of this people. I was just putting the
finishing-touches to my picture of the Rev. (?) 'Galusha
Wickers' (the revivalist: such names as these Americans have!), when I heard a voice behind me saying,
'Lor! Why, that's splendid!—perfectly splendid! Well,
I declare, you've got him to a t. Lemmy see.' And, if
you please, a hand was thrust over my shoulder and the
sketch seized, without so much as a 'By your leave.'
Can you fancy a more unwarrantable, insufferable liberty? But they are all alike over here. I turned
about, and saw a woman who was examining the rev-
erend revivalist with much satisfaction. 'Well, you
*have* got him, to be sure,' she said, returning my angry
glance with one of admiration, and quite unabashed.
'What'll you take for it? I've sat under him for five
years; and for taking texteses from one end of the
Bible to the other, and leading in prayer, and filling the
mourners' bench in five minutes, I will say he hasn't
got his equal in the universe. He's got a towering
intellect, I tell you. I'll give you fifty cents for this, if
you'll color it up nice for me and throw in a frame.'
Of course I took the picture away from the brazen
creature and told her what I thought of her conduct.
'Well, you air techy," she said, and walked off leisurely."
Before closing her letter, Mrs. Sykes remarked of her
hostess, "Quite good for nothing physically, and ab-

surdly romantic. She has been abroad a good deal, and
bores me dreadfully with her European reminiscences.
She is always talking in a foolish, rapturous sort of way
about 'dear Melrose,' or 'noble Tintern Abbey,' or 'en-
chanting Warwick Castle;' and she has read simply
libraries of books about England, and puts me through
a sort of examination about dozens of places and
events, as though I could carry all England about in
my head. I really know less of it than of most other
countries : there is nothing to be got by running about
it. If one knew every foot of it, everybody would
think it a matter of course ; but to be able to talk of
Siam and the Fiji Islands, Cambodia and Alaska, and
the like, is really an advantage in society. One gets
the name of being a great traveller, and all that, and is
asked about tremendously and taken up to a wonderful
extent. I know a man that didn't wish to go to the
trouble and expense of rambling all over the world,
and wanted the reputation of having done it, so he
went into lodgings at intervals near the British Museum
and got all the books that were to be had about a particular country, and, having read them, would come
back to the West End and give out that he had been
there. It answered beautifully for a while, and he was
by way of being asked to become a Fellow of the
Royal Geographical, and was thought quite an authority and wonderfully clever ; but somehow he got
found out, which must have been a nuisance and spoiled
everything. I can see that these people consider it
quite an honor to have me visit them, all because of my
having been around the world, I dare say. And of
course I have let them see that I know who is who and

what is what. They are imploring me to stay on; but I told them yesterday that it wouldn't suit my book at all to stay over two weeks longer, when I had seen all there was to see. That young Ramsay seems to be enjoying himself out there among those nasty savages; and, as hunting is about the only thing he is fit for, he had best stay out there altogether."

The unwritten history of Mrs. Sykes's visit to Marbury Park would have been more interesting than the account she gave. She took with her a camp-chair, which she placed in any and every spot that suited her or commanded the pictorial situations which she wished to make her own permanently. To the horror and surprise of her friends, she plumped it down immediately in front of Mr. Wickers (after marching past an immense congregation), and, wholly unembarrassed by her conspicuous position, settled herself comfortably, took out her block and pencil, and proceeded to jot down that worthy's features line upon line, as though he had been a newly-imported animal at the "Zoo" on exhibition, paying no attention to the precept upon precept he was trying to impress upon his audience.

She walked all over the place repeatedly, went poking and prying into such tents as she chanced to find empty, nor considered this an essential requisite to the conferring of this honor. When less sociably inclined, she established herself outside, close at hand, and in this way made those valuable observations and spirited drawings which subsequently enriched her diary and delighted a discerning British public. But this is anticipating. When she tired of New York, she wrote to Sir Robert that she wished to give as much time as possible to the Mormons, and would leave at once for Salt Lake City, where she would busy herself in laying bare the domestic system as it really existed, and hold herself in readiness to join the party again when they should arrive there *en route* to the Yosemite.

Sir Robert, being an heroic creature, felt that he could bear this temporary separation with fortitude, and, being about to start for Boston when he got the news, forthwith threw himself upon the New England States in a frenzied search for all the information to be had about them,—their exact geographical position, by whom discovered, when settled, climate, productions, population, principal towns and rivers. He studied three maps of the region as he rattled along in the south-bound train, and devoted the rest of the time to getting an outline of its history: so that his nephew found him but an indifferent companion.

"I suppose there are authorized maps and charts, geographical, hydrographical, and topographical, issued by the government, and to be seen at the libraries. I must get a look at them at once. These are amateur productions, the work of irresponsible men, contradicting each other in important particulars as to the relative position of places, and inaccurate in many respects, as I find by comparison," he said, emerging from a prolonged study of his authorities. "You don't seem to take much interest in all this. You should be at the pains to inform yourself upon every possible point in connection with this country, or any other in which you may find yourself; else why travel at all?"

Mr. Heathcote, not having his uncle's thirst for information, was reading a French novel at the time, and did

25*

not attempt to defend his position, knowing it probably
to be indefensible.

Before getting to Boston the air turned very chill,
and a fine, penetrating rain set in that for a while disturbed the student of American history with visions of
rheumatism. "God bless my soul! I shall be laid by
the heels here for weeks. Damp is the one thing that
I can't stand up against. And I have not left my coat
out!" he exclaimed, tugging anxiously at his side-whiskers and annoyed to find how dependent he had grown
on his valet. "What shall I do? Ah! I have an idea.
Damp. What resists it and is practically water-proof?
*Newspapers!*" With this he stood up, seized the "Times"
supplement, made a hole in the middle of the central
fold, and put it over his head. "Now I have improvised
a South American *serapa*," he observed, in a tone that
betrayed the pleasure it gave him to exercise his ingenuity. He then took two other sheets and succes-
sively wrapped them around his legs, after the fashion
in vogue among gardeners intent upon protecting valuable plants from the rigors of winter. This done, he
smoothed down the *serapa*, which showed a volatile
tendency to blow up a good deal, and, with a brief comment to the effect that "oil-skin or india-rubber could
not be better," and no staring about him to observe the
effect of his action on the passengers, replaced his hat,
sat down, picked up his book again, readjusted his eye-
glasses, and went on with the episode he had been
reading aloud to his nephew, who, mildly bored by
King Philip's war, was mildly amused by the spectacle
the baronet presented, and surprised to see that their
fellow-travellers thought it an excellent joke. A loud

"Haw! haw!" and many convulsive titters testified their appreciation of the absurd contrast between Sir Robert's highly-respectable head, his grave, absorbed air, and the remarkable way in which he was finished off below the ears ; but he read on and on, in his round, agreeable voice, unconscious of the effect he was producing, until the train came to a final stop, when Mr Porter and a very dignified, rigid style of friend came into the car to look for him.

"My dear Porter, I am delighted to see you, and I shall be with you in one moment. I shall then have ceased to be a grub and have become a most beautiful butterfly, ready to fly away home with you as soon as ever you like," Sir Robert called out in greeting, and in a twinkling had torn off his wrappers, and stood there a revealed acquaintance, carefully collecting his "traps," and beaming cheerfully even upon the friend of his friend, who had not come to a pantomime and showed that he disapproved of harlequins in private life.

Mr. Porter, however, was all cordiality, and very speedily transferred his guests to his own house in the vicinity of Boston.

The season was not the one for gaining a fair idea of the society of the city and neighborhood ; but if all the people who were away at the seaside and the mountains were half as charming as those left behind and invited by Mr. Porter to meet his friends, it is certain that Sir Robert lost a great deal. On the other hand, it is equally certain that if they had been at home Sir Robert would most likely be there now, and this chronicle of his travels would end here. As it was, he found something novel and agreeable at every step, a fresh

interest every hour of his stay. He began at the beginning, and promptly found out what kind of soil the
city was built on, went on to consider such questions
as drainage, elevation, water-supply, wharves, quays,
bridges, and worked up to libraries, museums, public
and private collections of pictures, and what not. He
ordered three pictures of Boston artists,—two autumnal
scenes, and an interior, a negro cabin, with an hilarious
sable group variously employed, called " Christmas in
the Quarters." Then the questions of fisheries, maritime
traffic, coast and harbor defences, light-houses, the ship-
building interests, life-saving associations, and railway
systems, pressed for investigation, to say nothing of the
mills and manufactories, wages of operatives, trades-
unions, trade problems, and all the pros and cons of free
trade *versus* protective tariff. Over these he pondered
and pored until all hours every night; and the diary
had now to be girt about with two stout rubber bands
to keep it from scattering instructive leaflets about promiscuously and prematurely. And by day there were
sites literary, historical, or generally interesting to be
visited, engagements with many friends to keep, endless
occupations apparently.

There was so much to see and do that the place was
delightful to him, and he certainly made himself vastly
agreeable in return to such of its inhabitants as came
in his way.

"I have added to my circle some very valuable acquaintances, whom I shall hope to retain as friends," he
wrote back to England, "notably a medical man who
confirms my germ-propagation theory of the ' vomito,'
which is now raging in the Southern part of the States

(I had it, you remember, on the west coast of Africa, and studied it in the Barbadoes),—an exceptionally clever man, and, like all such men, inclined to be eccentric. I think I was never more surprised than to come upon him the other day in a side-street, where he was positively having his boots polished *in public* by a ragged gamin who offered to 'shine' me for a 'dime' He behaved sensibly about it,—betrayed no embarrass· ment, though he must have. felt excessively annoyed, made no apologies, and only remarked that he had been out in the country, and did not wish to be taken for a miller in the town.

" I was led to believe before coming here that I should not be able to tell that Boston was not an English town. It did not so impress me on a surface-view, but it was not long before I recognized that the warp and woof of the social fabric is that of our looms, though the pat tern is a little different,—a good sort of stuff, I think, warranted *to wash* and wear. The variation, such as it is, tried by what I call my differential nationometer, gives to the place its own peculiar, delightful quality."

The rigid gentleman was a great deal at the Porters', and proved, when thawed out, to be pleasanter than he looked,—rather square in manner, and upright and downright to the point of dogmatism sometimes, but digestible, on the whole, to a man of catholic constitu- tion and kindly temper like Sir Robert. The process of melting into good-fellowship was usually one of from fifteen to twenty years' duration with the Bostonian, but somehow he was no' sooner exposed to the genial and delightful rays that radiated from the baronet—the combined effluence of a rubicund visage, a bright mind,

*hh*

and a cheerful spirit—than he began to warm up in a
wonderful way. He not only freely contributed his
idcas in the talks the three gentlemen enjoyed daily
over their cigars, but his notions, some of which were
not without originality. For one thing he held that
the English tongue in the American mouth was heard to
better advantage than anywhere else. It was the Tus-
can Romanized. The tongue of Shakespeare would owe
its preservation to the Colonies he was sure. Macaulay's New Zealander would find only the remains of
the ancient tongue among other ruins. The descendants of Maori chiefs, American Indians, Dutch Boers,
and Hindoo princes were to become the conservators of
it. In this connection he showed what the United
States had done to preserve her share of the common
heritage, and, by way of illustration, what one citizen
of the great republic was doing, with the same end in
view. He was, indeed, rather inclined to insist upon
the great purity and beauty of his own English, to
which he repeatedly invited attention, and, as Mr. Ramsay would have said, "went in for" certain philological
refinements which Sir Robert had never heard before,
and thoroughly disliked. But as there are more Scotch-
men in London than in Edinburgh, and better oranges
can be bought for less money in New York than in New
Orleans, so it may be that if you want to find really superior English you must leave England altogether,—
abandon it to its defective but firmly-rooted *patois*, and
seek in more classic shades for the well-spring of Saxon
undefiled. But Sir Robert was not inclined to do this.
There were limits to his liberality and spirit of investigation. When the rigid gentleman instanced certain

words to which he gave a pronunciation that made
them bear small resemblance to the same words as
spoken by any class of people laboring under the disadvantage of having been born and bred in England,
Sir Robert got impatient, and testily dismissed the subject with, "Oh, come now! I can stand a good deal,
but I can't stand being told that we don't know how to
speak English in England." Something, however, must
be pardoned to a foreigner. If Sir Robert would not
consent to set Emerson a little higher than the angels,
as some other Bostonians could have wished, and had
never so much as heard of Thoreau and other American
celebrities not wholly insignificant, he had an immense
admiration for Longfellow, and could spout "Hiawatha"
or "Evangeline" with the best, associated Hawthorne
with something besides his own hedges in the month
of May, and was eager to be taken out to Beverly
Farms, that he might "do himself the honor to call
upon" the wisest, wittiest, least-dreaded, and best-loved
of Autocrats. When the day fixed for his departure
came, he was still revelling in what the Historical Society of Massachusetts had to show him, and actually
stayed over a day that he might see the finest collection
of cacti in the country, and at last tore himself away
with much difficulty and lively regrets, carrying with
him a collection of Indian curiosities given him by Mr.
Porter, whom he considered to have behaved "most
handsomely" in making him such a present. "I can't
rob you outright, my dear fellow. I feel a cut-purse,
almost, when I think of taking all these valuable and
deeply-interesting objects illustrative of the life and
civilization of the aborigines," he said to his host on the

morning of his departure. "Give me duplicates, if you will be so generous, but nothing unique, I insist." He finally accepted one gem in the collection,—a towering structure of feathers that formed "a most delightful head-dress, quite irresistibly fascinating," tried it on before a mirror that gave back faithfully the comical reflection, and incidentally delivered a lecture on the head-ornaments of many savage and civilized nations of every age, though not at all in the style of the famous Mr. Barlow.

Mr. Heathcote at least was not sorry to find that they were, as he said, "booked for Baltimore." The image of the beautiful Miss Bascombe had not been effaced. Perhaps he had photographed it by some private process on his heart with the lover's camera, which takes rather idealized but very charming pictures, some of which never fade. At all events, there it was, very distinct and very lovely, and always hung on the line in his mental picture-gallery. It was positively with trepidation that he presented himself before her very soon after his arrival; and an undeniable blush "mantled" his cheek—if a blush can be said with any propriety to mantle the male cheek—when he marched into the drawing-room, where she was doing a dainty bit of embroidery, and with much simplicity and directness said, "You said I might come, you know, and I have come; and I begged of Ethel to come too, but she could not leave my aunt," before he had so much as shaken hands. Of course no well-regulated and well-bred young woman—and Miss Bascombe was both—ever permits herself to remember any man until she is engaged to him; but she need not forget one that has

impressed her agreeably. Miss Bascombe had not forgotten the handsome Englishman she had met at Jenny
De Witt's, nor the little lecture she had given him on
the duties of brothers to sisters, and it did not strike
her that his inaugural address was at all eccentric or
mysterious. He had been told what he ought to do,
he had tried to do it, as was quite right and proper. · He
deserved some reward. And he got it,—though only as
an encouragement to abstract virtue, of course. The
young lady was pleased to be friendly, gracious, charming. Her mother came in presently, was equally
friendly and gracious, and almost as charming. Her
father came home to dinner, and was friendly too, and
hearty, and very hospitable. Her brothers were friendliest of all. He knew quite well that he had no claim
on them, that he had not saved the life of any member
of the family or laid them under any sort of obligation,
individually or collectively, and no reception could have
seemed more special and dangerously cordial, yet no
anxieties oppressed, no fears distracted him. The
weight of excessive eligibility suddenly slipped off him,
like the albatross from the neck of the Ancient Mariner,
leaving him a thankful and a happy man. In a week he
had established himself firmly at the Bascombes', declined
to accompany his uncle to Virginia, and definitely settled in his own mind that he would take the step matrimonial,—the step from the sublime to—well, not always
the ridiculous. · With this resolution he naturally
thought that the greatest obstacle to success had been
removed; but he was soon disillusionized. He had already come to see that American girls were very much
in the habit of being gracious to everybody, and saying

pretty and pleasant things, with no thought of an here-
after; also that they did not live with St. George's, Han-
over Square, or its American equivalent, Trinity Church,
New York, stamped on the mental retina. Miss Bascombe was "very nice" to him, he told himself, but she
was quite as nice to a dozen other men. She was uni-
formly kind, courteous, agreeable, to every one who
came to the house. Her cordiality to him meant nothing whatever. Yes, he was quite free,—free as air; he
saw that plainly, and perversely longed to assume the
fetters he had so long and so skilfully avoided. What
was the use of having serious intentions when not the
slightest notice was taken of the most compromising
behavior? It was true that he was perfectly at liberty
to see more of Edith than an Englishman ever does of
any woman not related to him, and to say and do a
thousand things any one of which at home would have
necessitated a proposal or instant flight. But no importance whatever seemed to be attached to them here, and
he was utterly at a loss how to make his seriousness felt.
Yet it was quite clear that if there was to be any wooing done, he would have to do it,—go every step of the
way himself, with no assistance from Miss Bascombe.
"How on earth am I to show her that I care for her?"
he thought. "Other men send her dozens of bouquets,
and box after box of expensive sweets, and loads of
books, and music without end, and they come to see her
continually, and take her about everywhere, and are
entirely devoted to her. I wonder what fellows over
here do when they are serious? How do they make
themselves understood when they go on in this way
habitually? It is a most extraordinary state of affairs!

And neither party seems to feel in the least compromised by it. There is that fellow Clinch, who fairly lives at the Bascombes', and when I asked her if she was engaged to him she said, 'Engaged to George Clinch? What an idea! *No.* What put that in your head? He is a nice fellow, and I like him immensely, but there's nothing of that sort between us. What made you think there was?' And when I explained, she said, 'Oh, *that's* nothing! He is just as nice to lots of other girls.' And when I suggested to him that he was attached to her, he said, 'Edith Bascombe? Oh, no! She is a great friend of mine, and a charming girl, but I have never thought of that, nor has she. I go there a good deal, but I have never paid her any marked attention.' No marked attention, indeed! Nothing seems to mean anything here: it is worse than being in England, where everything means something. No, it isn't, either. I vow that when I am at the Clintons' in Surrey I scarcely dare offer the girls so much as a muffin, and if I ask the carroty one, Beatrice, the simplest question, she blushes and stammers as if I were proposing out of hand. But what am I to do? I can't sing and take to serenading Edith on moonlit nights with a guitar and a blue ribbon around my neck. I can't push her into the river that I may pull her out again. I dare say there is nothing for it but to adopt the American method,—enter with about fifty others for a sort of sentimental steeple-chase, elbow or knock every other fellow out of the way in the running, work awfully hard to please the girl, and get in by half a length, if one wins at all. There is no feeling sure of her until one is coming back from the altar, evidently."

Some of his conversations with Edith were certainly anything but encouraging. At other times he felt morally sure that she shared that derangement of the bivalvular organ technically defined as "a muscular viscus which is the primary instrument of the blood's motion," whose worst pains are said to be worth more than the greatest pleasures. He was very much in earnest, and entirely straightforward. There were no balancing in decisions now, but the most downright affirmation of preference. His little speeches were not veiled in rosy clouds of metaphor and poetry and distant allusions, like Captain Kendall's, nor did they flow out in an unfailing stream of romantic eloquence, like that gifted warrior's. They were so honest and so clumsy, indeed, that Edith could not help laughing at them merrily sometimes, to his great discomfiture, consisting as they did chiefly of such statements as, " You know that I am most awfully fond of you. I was tremendously hard hit from the first. If you don't believe me, you can ask Ramsay. I told him all about it. You aren't in the least like any other girl that I have ever known, except Mrs. De Witt a little. I suppose you know that I would have married her at the dropping of a hat if I could have done so. But that is all over now. I care an awful lot for you now, and shall be quite frightfully cut up if you won't have anything to say to me,—I shall, really. I have got quite wrapped up in you, upon my word. And I shall be intensely glad and proud if you will consent to be my wife."

When Edith failed to take such speeches as these seriously, poor Mr. Heathcote was quite beside himself, and. in reply to her bantering accusations as to his being "a great flirt" and not "really meaning one word that he said," opposed either burly negation or a deeply-vexed silence. They looked at so many things differently that they found a piquant interest in discussing every subject that came up.

"There go May Dunbar and Fred Beach," she said to him one Sunday as they were coming home from church. "Isn't he handsome? They have been engaged *three years.* Did you ever hear of such constancy?"

"Do you call that constancy? Why, if a fellow can't wait three years for a lovely girl like that, he must be a poor stick. Why, my uncle Montgomery was engaged to his wife seventeen years, while he went out to India and shook the pagoda-tree, after which he came back, paid all his father's debts, and they married and went into the house they had picked out before he sailed," said Mr. Heathcote.

"Good gracious! what a time! I hope the poor things were happy at last. Were they?" asked Edith.

"H-m—pretty well. He is a rather fiery, tyrannical old party. She doesn't get her own way to hurt," he replied.

"I have heard that Englishwomen give way to the men in everything and are always, voluntarily or involuntarily, sacrificed to them. It must be so bad for both," said Edith sweetly.

"Oh, you go in for woman's rights and that sort of thing, I suppose," he said, in a tone of annoyance.

"Indeed I don't do anything of the kind," replied she, with warmth. "If I did, I should be aping the men when I wasn't sneering at them. But I respect your sex most when they most deserve to be respected, and

I don't see anything to admire in a selfish, tyrannical man that is always imposing his will, opinions, and wishes upon the ladies of his household and expects to be the first consideration from the cradle to the grave because he happens to be a man."

"But he is the head of his house. He ought to get his own way, if anybody does, and, if he is not a coward, he will, too," said Mr. Heathcote rather hotly. "Would you have a man a molly-coddle, tied to his wife's apron-string, and not daring to call his soul his own?"

"Not at all," replied Edith. "It is the cowards that are the tyrants. 'The bravest are the tenderest, the loving are the daring,' as our American poet says. And women have souls of their own, except in the East. Why shouldn't *they* be the first consideration and do as they please, pray? They are the weaker, the more delicate and daintily bred. If there is any pampering and spoiling to be done, they should be the objects of it. And as to rights, there is no divine right of way given to man, that I know of. I don't believe in that sort of thing at all. Of course no reasonable woman wants or expects everybody to kootoo before her and everything to give way to her."

"And no gentleman fails to show a proper respect for his wife's wishes and comfort, not to mention her happiness," said Mr. Heathcote. "But of course that sort of thing is only to be found in America. Englishmen are all selfish, and tyrants, and domestic monsters, I know."

"I didn't say anything of the kind," replied Edith quickly, her cheeks pink with excitement. "I don't know anything about Englishmen or the domestic system of England, and 1 never expect to. But, if what I have heard is true, it is a system that tends to make men mortally selfish ; and selfish people, whether they are men or women, and whether they know it or not, are *all* monsters. But I apologize for my remarks, and, as I am not interested in the subject *in the least,* we will talk of something else, if you please."

This very feminine conclusion, delivered loftily and with sudden reserve, left Mr. Heathcote in anything but an agreeable frame of mind, and for an hour or two made him doubt the wisdom of international marriages; but this mood passed away, and he remained a fixture at the *maison* Bascombe, where the very postman came to know him and generously sympathized with the malady from which he was suffering. Nor was this the only house in which he was made very welcome. Baltimore is one of many American cities that suffer from the vague but painful accusation of being "provincial;" but, admitting this dreadful charge, it has social, gastronomic, and other charms of its own that ought to compensate for the absence of that doubtful good, cosmopolitanism. Mr. Heathcote certainly found no fault with it, and did not miss the population, pauperism, or other institutions of Paris, London, or Vienna. On the contrary, he took very kindly to the pretty place, and heartily liked the people. There was nothing oppressive or ostentatious in the attentions he received, but just the cordiality, grace, and charm of an old-established society of most refined traditions, perfect *savoir-vivre*, and chronic hospitality.

"You are making a Baltimorean of me, you are so

awfully kind to me," he would say, pronouncing the *a*
in Bal as he would have done in sal; but the truth was
that he had become primarily a Bascomite and only
very incidentally a Baltimorean. The city counts hun-
dreds of such converts every year. He was so happy
and entirely content that he would have quite forgotten
what it was to be bored just at this period but for certain individuals,—a boastful, disagreeable Irishman, who
fastened upon him apparently for no other reason than
that he might abuse England at great length and talk
of his own valor, accomplishments, and "paddygree"
(as he very properly called the record that established
his connection with Brian Boroo and Irish kings generally), and a lady who seemed to take the most astounding, unquenchable interest in the English nobility, as
more than one lady had seemed to him to do, to his
great annoyance.

"I don't know a bit about them, I assure you," he
said to her; "but I have the 'Peerage.' If you would
like to see that, I will send it you with pleasure."

This only diverted her conversation into a different
but equally distasteful channel,—the great distinction
and antiquity of her own family. It really seemed as
though she had a dread of Mr. Heathcote's leaving the
country with some wrong impression on this important
subject and was determined that he should be put in
possession of all the information she had or imagined
herself to have about it. She talked to him about it so
much that the poor man was at incredible pains to keep
out of her way.

"I don't care a brass copper about her," he complained
to Edith; "and if the family has been producing women

liko her as long as sho says, and is going on at it, all I
can say is that it is a pity thoy havo lasted this long,
and tho sooncr they die out tho better. What do I
caro about hor family, pray? I never hoard as much
about family in all my lifo, I givo you my word, as I
have dono sinco I came to America. Tho stories told
mo aro somothing wonderful,—all about tho two brothoors
that left England, and all that, you know. Thoy soom
all to have come away in pairs, liko tho animals in tho
ark. I said to ono follow that was beginning with thoso
two brothors, ' *Couldn't you make it three*, don't you
think?' And you'll not believe me, but I spoak quito
without exaggoration, when I say that one woman out
in Kalsing assured mo gravoly that she was doscondod
from tho houses of York and Lancastor!"

" *She didn't!*" exclaimed Edith: " That is, if sho did,
sho must havo boon *crazy;* and I won't havo you going
back to England and giving falso imprcssions of us by
repoating such stories. Promiso mo that you will nevor
repeat it thoro."

" Oh, that's all right," ho replied soothingly. " It's
an oxtremo caso, I grant, and I'll say no moro about
it if it voxcs you, but it is a truo talo all tho samo.
Ilowo was her namo, I remember; and I folt liko saying, ' I'll cat my hand if I understand Howo this can
possibly be,'—that's in tho Bab Ballads,—but I didn't."

Sir Robort had small opportunity of making acquaintanco with Baltimoro. Ho was very eagor to get down
into Virginia, and stayod thoro but two days. On tho
sccond of these ho attended a gontleman's dinnor-party,
tho annual milc-stono of a military socioty composod
of men who had worn tho gray and markod tho well-

known tendency of tempus to fugit in this agreeable fashion. Their ex-enemies of the blue were also there, but not in the original overwhelming numbers, and the battle was now to one party, now to the other, the race to the best *raconteur*, rivers of champagne flowed instead of brave blood, and the smoke of cannon was exchanged for that of Havanas. Sir Robert's face beamed more and more brightly as the evening wore on, and reminiscences, anecdotes, stories, jests, songs, were fluently and cleverly poured out in rapid succession by the hilarious company. The fun was at its height, when he suddenly leaned forward with his body at an insinuating angle and smilingly addressed an officer opposite: "You must really let me say that I have been delighted by all that I have heard here to-night, and appreciate the compliment you have paid me in permitting me to join you. And now I am going to ask a great favor. Could you, would you, give me some idea of 'the rebel yell,' as it was called? We heard so much about that. I am most curious to hear it. It is always spoken of as perfectly terrifying, almost unearthly "

The gentleman whom he addressed looked down the table and rapped to call attention to what he had to say : "Boys, this English gentleman is asking whether we can't give him some idea of what the rebel yell is like. What do you say? If our Federal friends are afraid, they can get under the table, where they will be perfectly safe, and a good deal more comfortable than they used to be behind trees or in baggage-wagons," he called out.

A hearty laugh followed, and their blood having got bubbles in it by this time, a general assenting murmur was heard.

The next instant a shriek, sky-rending, blood-curdling savage beyond description, went up,—a truly terrific yell in peace, and enough to create a panic, one would think, in the Old Guard in time of war.

"Thank you, thank you. *I am entirely satisfied,"* said Sir Robert, in a comically rueful tone, as soon as he could say anything for the uproar. "I never imagined anything like it, never. Where did you get it? Who invented it? Is it an adaptation of some war-cry of the North American Indians? It sounds like what one would fancy their cries might be, doesn't it? It has got all the beasts of the forest in it; and I confess that I, for one, would have fled before it and stayed in the wagons as long as there was the slightest danger of hearing it. By Jove! it must have been heard in Boston when given in Virginia. It is curious how very ancient the practice of—"

But the company heard no more of curious practices, for their yell had been heard, if not in Boston, in a far more remarkable quarter,—namely, by the police, who now rushed in, prepared to club, arrest, and carry off any and all disorderly and dreadful disturbers of the peace.

If Sir Robert had been in any danger of being murdered, all experience goes to show that no policeman could have been found before the following morning, and then only in the remotest part of the city. As he was merely being wined, dined, and amused, quite a formidable body of these devoted but easily-misled guardians of respectability and innocence poured into the room, where at first they could see nothing for the smoke. Matters were explained, they were invited to "take something" before they went, and took it, and, quite placated, filed out into the passage again and from thence into the street.

Sir Robert sat up late that night, or rather began early on the following day, to copy the stories he had most relished into the diary, and do what justice he could to "the rebel yell," and, having added an admirably discriminating chapter on "the present political situation in the States," concluded with, "How striking is the good sense, the good feeling, that both the conquerors and the conquered have shown, on the whole! In other countries, how often has a war far less bloody and protracted left in its wake evils far greater than the original one, in guerilla warfare, murders, ceaseless revolt, and smoldering hatred lasting for centuries on one side, and centuries of tyranny, oppression, executions, confiscations, on the other! A brave and fine race this, not made of the stuff that goes to keep up vendettas, shoot landlords, blow up rulers, assassinate enemies. They can fight as well as any, and they have shown that they can forgive better than most,—taken together, true manliness. It may be that they are influenced by a consideration which is said to be always present to an American,—'Will it pay?' and of course so practical a people as this see that anarchy doesn't pay; but I would rather attribute their conduct to nobler, more generous motives, and in doing this seem to myself to be doing them no more than justice."

# IX.

AMONG the inhabitants of the United States there are
none that stand so firmly on the national legs as the Virginians,—though it would be more correct to contract
this statement somewhat, substituting "State" for "national," since it has never been the habit of Virginians
to make themselves more than very incidentally responsible for thirty-eight States and ten Territories occupied
by persons of mixed race, numerous religions, objectionable politics, and no safe views about so much as the
proper way to make mint-juleps. When Sir Robert
presented himself one day at the door of a fine old
house belonging to the golden age of ante-bellum prosperity in Caroline County, he was received by two of
the most English Englishmen to be found on this planet,
in the persons of Mr. Edmund and Mr. Gregory Aglonby,
brothers, bachelors, and joint-heirs of the property he
had come to look at. These gentlemen received him
with a dignity and antique courtesy irresistibly suggestive of bagwigs, short swords, and aristocratic institutions generally, a courtesy largely mingled with
restrained severity and unspoken suspicion until his
identity had been fully established by the letters of
introduction he had brought, his position defined, and
his mission in Caroline clearly set forth. An Englishman out of England was a fact to be accounted for, not
imprudently accepted without due inquiry; but, this
done, the law and traditions of hospitality began to

alleviate the situation and temper justice with mercy
The lady of the house was sent for, and proved to be a
wonderfully pretty old lady, who might have just got
out of a sedan-chair, whose manner was even finer and
statelier than that of her brothers (diminutive as she
was in point of mere inches), and who executed a
tremendous courtesy when Sir Robert was presented.
"An English gentleman travelling in this country for
pleasure, and desirous of seeing 'Heart's Content,'
Anne Buller," explained the elder brother. Miss Aglonby's face, which had worn a look of mild interest
during the first part of this speech, clouded perceptibly
at its close. She murmured some mechanical speech of
welcome in an almost inaudible voice, and sat down in
a rigid and uncompromising fashion, while her heart
contracted painfully. A gentleman to look at the place:
there had been several such in the last year, who had
come, and seen, and objected to the price, and ridden
away again; but perhaps this one might not ride away,
and the uneasy thought tormented her throughout the
conversation that followed. The brothers, meanwhile,
had quite accepted Sir Robert, and had insisted, with a
calm, authoritative air, on sending for his "travelling
impedimenta," which had been deposited at the hotel
in a neighboring town, and had expressed a lofty hope
that he would do them the honor to consider himself
their guest.

"The *res angusta domi* will not permit us to entertain
you in a manner befitting your rank and in consonance
with our wishes," said Mr. Edmund Aglonby, in his
representative capacity as head of the family, "but,
that consideration waived, I need not say that we shall

esteem it an honor and a pleasure to have you domesti-
cated beneath this roof as long as you find any satisfaction in remaining."

"It was not my idea, certainly, to intrude upon you
here, but rather to treat with your solicitor in this matter ; but if you find it more agreeable to set him aside,
which between gentlemen is usually altogether more
satisfactory, and will, in addition, allow me to become
your guest for a few days, I can only say that I shall
be delighted to accept your kind hospitality," replied
Sir Robert.

"Brother Gregory, will you see that our guest's effects
are at once transferred to his room here ?" said Mr.
Aglonby, half turning in his chair and giving a graceful
wave with one of his long, shapely hands toward the
door, after which he bowed with dignified grace to Sir
Robert, and said, "Your decision gives us great satisfaction, sir." Mr. Gregory Aglonby confirmed this
statement in Johnsonian periods before he left, and tiny
Miss Aglonby expressed herself as became a lady who
had been receiving guests in that very room for fifty
years with stiff but genuine courtesy. The atmosphere
was so familiar to Sir Robert that he could scarcely believe himself to be in an American household. Could
this be the American type of his dreams ? Was there
ever a country in which the scenes shifted so completely
with a few hours or days of travel ? "If this goes on,
America will mean everything, anything, to me," he
thought. "When I hear of a Frenchman, or German,
or Italian, I have some idea of what I shall find; but
it is not so here at all. This Mr. Aglonby is quite evidently a gentleman, and a high-bred one; but so was

Porter in Boston, and Colonel De Witt, and those Baltimore fellows; yet how different they all are! These
men remind me more of my grandfather and my great-
uncles than any Englishman of the present day. Perhaps they are English. I'll ask. Who would ever suppose them to be countrymen of Ketchum's?"

After dinner,—and you may be sure the dinner was
a good one, for Miss Aglonby was one of a generation
of women whose knowledge of housewifely arts was
such that, shut up in a light-house or wrecked on a
desert island, they would have made shift to get a nice
meal somehow, even if they could not have served it,
as she did, off old china and graced it with old silver,—
after dinner, then, a long and pleasant evening set in,
with no thought or talk of business-matters. Sir Robert
was charmed with his new acquaintances, and not less
by the matter than by the manner of their conversation.
Did they talk of travels, Mr. Aglonby "liked to read
books of adventure," but had never been out of the
State of Virginia, and had no wish to go anywhere.
He deplored his fate in being compelled at his age to
leave it permanently and take up his residence in Florida,
where his physician was sending him. He talked of
"Mr. Pope" and "Mr. Addison," quoted Milton and the
Latin classics, and had chanced upon "a modern work
lately, by a writer named Thackeray," "Henry Esmond,"
which had pleased him extremely. On hearing this, Sir
Robert took occasion to ask him whether he liked any
of the writings of this and that New-England author
of the day, about whom he had been hearing a great
deal since his arrival in the country, and Mr. Aglonby
replied, with perfect truth, that he had "never heard

of them," though he added that Irving and Cooper, the latest additions to his library, were, in his opinion, " writers of merit." In politics Mr. Aglonby declared himself the champion of a defunct party,—the " old-line Whigs,"—and explained " the levelling, agrarian tendencies of Tom Jefferson" and the result of his policy, which had been " to eliminate the gentleman from politics." Mr. Gregory Aglonby spoke with regretful emotion of that period of the history of Virginia in which her local magistrates had managed county affairs in such a way as to secure her " safety, honor, and welfare," when universal suffrage had not " cursed the country with ignorance and incompetence, legally established at present, indeed, but sure to be supplemented by a property or educational test eventually." In religion they were what " the Aglonbys had always been, —attached adherents of the Episcopal Church in this country, as of the Establishment in England." Quite early in the evening Sir Robert had propounded his question as to their nationality. " Are you an American ?" he had asked the elder of the two gentlemen, and both had replied, " We are Virginians," in accents that were eloquent of love and pride.

" Upon my word, if I were asked what your nationality was, I should say that you were English," remarked Sir Robert, feeling that he was making what they must see was a handsome concession. But he was not talking to a Sam Bates now. Mr. Edmund Aglonby regarded him with a reserved air, as if he had said something rather flippant.

Mr. Gregory said gravely, " You doubtless mean it kindly, but we would prefer to be thought what we are,

—Virginians. Not that we are ashamed of our parent stock, but Anne Buller here is the seventh of the name born in this country, and it is only natural that we should be completely identified with it. Unworthy as we are to represent it, we are Virginians." That anybody could be *more* than a Virginian had never crossed Mr. Aglonby's mind; but it should be said, in defence of what many regard as an exaggerated State pride, that to such men to be *less* than a Virginian (that is, an embodiment of the virtues represented to them by the title) is equally impossible.

Whist was now proposed, and played by the light of two candles in old-fashioned candlesticks, that towered high enough to allow mild yellow rays to illuminate a vast expanse of bald head belonging to Mr. Gregory, and made the dark sheen of the polished mahogany table dimly visible beneath. An oil-lamp on the high mantel-shelf enabled Sir Robert to get a ghostly impression of the large, bare room in which they were sitting, —the high ceilings, the black-looking floors fading away into grewsome corners, the spindle-legged furniture that had no idea of accommodating itself to a lolling, mannerless generation, and loomed up in some occasional piece in a threatening sort of way,—solid, massive, dignified furniture, conscious of its obligations to society and ready to fulfil them to the very end, however little a frivolous and degenerate world might be worthy of such accessories. More than once in the pauses of the game Sir Robert's eyes wandered to the pictures, of which there were a number, all portraits, two being half discernible,—a young matron in ruby velvet and pearls, with hair dressed in a pyramid, a coach-and-six

in court-plaster stuck on a snowy forehead, and eyes
that would have laughed anybody into a good humor;
and, opposite, a gentleman of the pursiest, puffiest,
most prosperous description, the husband of the young
matron, and so evidently high-tempered, dull, and obstinate, that he must have brought many a tear into
the laughing eyes.

" A handsome woman, that," he said, after one of
those moments of inattention, "and a good picture."

" It is an ancestress of ours on the distaff side,—Lady
Philippa Vane,—and is accounted a Lely.—Brother
Gregory, if you will have the kindness to cut the cards
we can proceed with our game.—The other is her husband and cousin, a man of rank and large property but
incurably vicious propensities, to whom we are rather
fond of attributing certain follies and weaknesses in his
descendants, and who we could wish had laid to heart
the maxim, ' *Nobilitatis virtus non stemma character.*'
They were of the Vanes of Huddlesford," said Mr.
Aglonby.

" Ah," said Sir Robert, " you suppose yourself to have
some connection with the Huddlesford Vanes ?"

Mr. Aglonby's white tufted brows arched themselves
in surprise above his dark eyes at the question, and
there was a little more dignified reserve than before in
his voice and manner as he said, " Descent and alliance
are not matters of *supposition* in Virginia, but of record.
—Anne Buller, I beg your forgiveness for having inad-
vertently revoked. My memory is really growing too
treacherous to permit of my long enjoying this diver-
sion, however great the horrors of an old age without
cards may be."

The deferential courtesy paid to Miss Aglonby by her brothers was the most remarkable feature of the game to Sir Robert, and, when it was over, the first thought of both was to place a chair for her in the corner she generally occupied. They were not in haste,—it was impossible to associate the idea of hurry or flurry with either of them,—but somehow there was a little collision between them in doing this, followed by formal bows and elaborate mutual apologies, which were broken in upon by Miss Aglonby's low voice, saying, "Brother Edmund, I feared that you had slipped again.—He sustained a grave injury in that way last winter" (this to Sir Robert), "and I am always afraid that the disastrous experience may be repeated.—Brother Gregory, I thank you. I am entirely comfortable, and I beg that you will be seated now. Perhaps our guest will do us the favor to resume the very instructive and entertaining discourse with which he was beguiling us earlier in the evening."

Thus adjured, Sir Robert proceeded to instruct and entertain, with such success that all three of his companions were charmed, though they gave no frivolous evidences of it, such as laughing heartily, interrupting him to interject phrases or opinions into the "discourse," or replying in an animated strain. They listened with intelligent seriousness to what he had to say, weighed it apparently, replied to it with gravity, responded to some jest with a smile; but, although they were not people to approve of crackling thorns under a pot, or any form of folly, they were, in their way, appreciative of the culture, humor, and insight he showed. Mr. Aglonby begged to be favored with his "observations" on America, and added that "the dispassionate reflec-tions of an intelligent foreigner should be esteemed of the utmost value by all judicious patriots and enlight-ened political economists, calling attention, as they often did, to evils and dangers whose existence had not been previously suspected." Mr. Gregory Aglonby wished to hear more of his travels among "that God-forsaken people the French." Miss Aglonby was eager to know more of the England of "Bracebridge Hall."

When bedtime came at last ("the proper season for repose," dear old Anne Buller called it, when she rose to "retire"), another courtesy was executed in front of Sir Robert by the châtelaine of "Heart's Content," who said, "How truly it has been remarked that we owe some of our keenest pleasures in life to strangers! You must permit me to thank you again for your improving and pleasing conversation, which I shall often recall, and always with lively satisfaction. May your slumbers be refreshing and your awakening devoid of all pain! I wish you a very good night, sir." With this Miss Aglonby took up one of the top-heavy candlesticks, and glided, like the shade she was and ghost of a past period, up the stairs.

While Mr. Gregory was looking to bolts and bars, Sir Robert strayed about the room with his hands behind him, looking at the pictures, followed by Mr. Aglonby, who made no extensive comment on them, but gave a word of explanation occasionally when his guest halted longer than usual before a canvas, such as, "The First Edmund, who came here in 1654;" "Edmund the Second;" "Edmund the Third, in his Oxford cap and gown;" "Gregory Aglonby, a colonel in the Revolution-ary forces;" "Red-haired Edmund, as we call him, because the others are all dark;" "Colonel Everard Buller Aglonby, who represented this county in the House of Burgesses for thirty years, and his wife, who was a Calvert,—a great-aunt, a woman of extraordinary piety, who reduced herself from a condition of affluence to comparative poverty by the manumission of her three hundred slaves."

When he had shaken hands with his host at the door of his bedroom (which was emphatically the room of a bed, a huge, be-stepped, pillared, testered contrivance that waited at one end of the large apartment to murder sleep), Sir Robert fell to winding his watch with what looked like interest, but all his thoughts were with the Aglonbys.

"English gentlefolks of the eighteenth century preserved in Virginian amber. What a curious survival! 'Gentlemen of a period of manners, morals.' Remarkably interesting! Delightful types of a society as extinct as the dodo," he was saying to himself. "There is but one mould for the gentleman; but nature changes its shape with every century, I suppose,—though I sometimes think she has gone out of the business altogether in utter disgust. We have got a lot of plutocrats that are tailors' blocks, and nobles that talk like stable-boys and act like blackguards, and both fancy themselves gentlemen; but when I contrast them with the men of my father's day even— And this dainty, charming old bit of Chelsea-ware, Anne Buller! Her brothers treat her as though she were a reigning princess. I wonder what she would say if she could see, as I did the other day, a group of Nuneham girls calling each other by

their last names and smoking cigarettes with a half-
dozen Cambridge men, who chaffed them and treated .
them exactly as though they were so many boys in
petticoats.  Well, well, the world moves, I know, and I
am an old fogy; but I shall not make myself hoarse
shouting 'Huzza' until I find out whether we are going
to the devil or not.  I hope I am not getting as cynical
as old Caradoc, who declares that he can always tell a
countess from an actress nowadays by the superior
modesty and refinement of—the actress."

In the next few days Sir Robert carefully inspected
the rambling, substantial old house, which, to Miss Aglonby's chagrin, he pronounced "quite modern ;" though
he smiled when she informed him that "Heart's Content"
had been "refurnished quite recently,—in '48."  He also
went over the land, only about four hundred acres. put
the most searching questions as to its practical value
and uses, filled a tin box with the earth, meaning to
have it analyzed by "a respectable chemist," and went
into details generally with much energy.  Nor had he
anything to complain of in the way of unfair dealing
in Mr. Gregory Aglonby, who accompanied him and
gave him the fullest and frankest particulars about the
property, which he pointed out was going to rack and
ruin, or rather had gone there.  Every broken gate
and stony field was dear to his heart, and it was a melancholy pilgrimage to him ; but had not Mr. Aglonby
said to him that morning, " Brother Gregory, the place
must go,—there is no help for it,—and this gentleman
seems likely to become a purchaser.  Will you see that
the disadvantages of the property are set before him
clearly, especially such as a stranger would certainly

overlook? I cannot entertain a proposition of any kind looking to its ultimate purchase until I know that this has been done, anxious as I am to have this matter definitely concluded. I had thought to die here. But it has been otherwise ordered by an overruling and all-wise Providence."

It did not escape Sir Robert that he was not likely to be overreached in his bargain, however much he might repent of it; and when Mr. Gregory pointed across the road and said, "The 'Little England' farm lies over there, but produces less and less every year. The land is exhausted," Sir Robert thought, "The fellow is either quixotic or doesn't wish to sell. I rather think the first: there has certainly been no shuffling and pretending." Aloud he said, "The soil can't be exhausted. It is virgin still compared to that of England, and all that it needs is careful cultivation. It seems to me that what Virginia needs is immigration."

Mr. Gregory looked displeased. It was as though Sir Robert had criticised Anne Buller's dress. "On the contrary, we wish to keep Virginia for Virginians," he said slowly. "We have no desire to see it overrun by a horde of Irish and Dutch, and heaven knows what besides. The proper place for that kind of people is the West and Northwest. If we could get the *right class* of English emigrants, that would be another matter. But it is scarcely likely that they will come here in any considerable number, now that the poor old commonwealth offers so little remunerative return to the most honorable enterprise."

When Sir Robert had quite made up his mind that he would like to possess the place, he telegraphed im

peratively for Mr. Heathcote, who joined him most reluctantly. Together they walked all over the county,
saw a great many people, and having bought two hundred acres that marched with, and, indeed, had formerly
been a part of, the Aglonby estate, Sir Robert made a
liberal offer for "Heart's Content," expressed his thanks
for the kind and honorable treatment he had received
there, and, his terms being accepted, paid the purchase-
money, and begged that the family would suit their
own convenience entirely in giving it up. This settled,
he went his way to the Natural Bridge, which he considered should rank second only to Niagara in this
country in point of interest, and then went on to Lex-
ington, to visit General Lee's tomb, and from there to
see Stonewall Jackson's grave, which, to his intense
astonishment and indignation, he found half covered
with visiting-cards,—the exquisite tribute of the sentimental tourist to the stern soldier. He could do nothing
until he had cleared the last bit of pasteboard (with
"Miss Mollie Bangs, Jonesville," printed on it) away
from the mound. This he did energetically with his
umbrella, after which he sat down quietly to think of
his favorite hero, who seemed to be "resting under the
shade of the trees over the river" rather than there,
and fell to repeating "Stonewall Jackson's Way,"—a
very favorite lyric, which he knew by heart. "'Appealing from his native sod In *forma pauperis* to God,' ought
to be his epitaph. I think he would like that," he said.
"I am glad England can claim such a son, however
indirectly. Fancy 'Miss Mollie Bangs' leaving a card
—and such a card—on old Blue-Light! A decent one
might do for Beau Brummel's grave, but Jackson's—!"

Mr. Heathcote was with him, and, after one careless glance, had strolled up and down, absorbed in his own thoughts, which were not of war or death. He only half listened to his uncle's praise of the great soldier, and presently said, *à propos* of nothing that had happened that day, " Uncle, what would you say if I should ask you to let me live at 'Heart's Content'?"

" Eh ? What's that?" asked Sir Robert, forgetting in his surprise to blow out the lighted match he had just applied to the offending cards. " You live in America? What idea have you got in your head, my boy ?"

Mr. Heathcote could not tell his uncle that Edith had said that she would never marry an Englishman, never! but that if she ever did, she should insist upon his living in America, for to go away from mamma and papa and the boys and everybody she cared for was a thing she could not and would not do, not if she adored the man that demanded such a sacrifice of her. What he did say was that he was tired of his aimless life in London, and liked his uncle too well to look forward with any pleasure to succeeding him, and that he should like to have a small property to manage without aid of bailiff, steward, agent, or factotum of any kind. " I could go over whenever I liked, or you needed me, and you could come to me to see that I wasn't making ducks and drakes of the property," he said. " And it is an experiment, I grant; but you have always been awfully gen- erous and kind to me, and I have something laid by that would cover the possible losses my inexperience might cause, for the first year at least. I am sure I can learn the trade, and am willing to pay for my appren-

ticeship, if you will only let me try my hand at farm-
ing."

"The boy is thinking of marrying," was Sir Robert's
mental comment; but he only said that he had bought
the place with a very different idea, but that he would
think the matter over.

"You must remember that it will not be child's play,"
he said. "And if you should grow attached to it and
wish to stay, you will be practically giving up your own
country, you know. But America is hardly a foreign
country. It is the representative institutions, moral
ideas, social atmosphere, and mental habits that make a
people, not the mere physical features of the country,
and in character the Americans are, as Mr. Aglonby
would say, 'Englishmen once removed'—across the Atlantic. You might be quite happy and content among
them. Just so."

"Oh, yes, I am sure I shall. You are quite in the
right in what you say of them," Mr. Heathcote eagerly
replied.

And Sir Robert, who had purposely laid this trap for
him, thought to himself, "The boy is certainly in love.
I must find out all about it, unless he has the grace to
tell me himself."

Much as she liked Niagara, Miss Noel was not sorry,
after long delay, to get a letter from Sir Robert, asking
her to join him in Chicago, and telling her of a delightful visit he had made to Richmond, where he had been
received "with particular kindness" and had met a
great number of agreeable people, most of them Virginians of the modern type and scarcely so interesting,
in a way, as the Aglonby family, who, as he saw from

other individuals, were survivals of a generation rapidly disappearing, to be found only occasionally here and there now,—"a class of aristocrats long a curious anomaly in a republican state, hardly to be matched in Europe to-day outside of Austria, and never to be reproduced."

It did not take Parsons long to do the necessary packing; but Miss Noel consumed a whole day in putting up her carefully-labelled "specimens of the flora of New York;" and Ethel had to settle with Mr. Bates, who would doubtless rather have been rejected by an Englishwoman than accepted by any American, and was not denied that luxury.

From Chicago the reunited forces went off almost immediately to Salt Lake City, having only three days to give to a little hurried sight-seeing in the "marvellous Sphinx city," as they called it in their letters home.

At Salt Lake Mrs. Sykes was awaiting their arrival, and betrayed a radiant satisfaction at the first glance.

"You can't think how busy I have been and what a lot I have accomplished," she related exultantly. "I have found a whole village of Thompsons with a *p*, and went and boarded there, and have got up a book that Bentley will give me a hundred pounds for. And I have done a lot of sketches to illustrate it, and, so far from being out of pocket, shall have made by my American tour. It has been the greatest fun imaginable, poking about in their houses and dishing them up afterward. And, only fancy, I've got a lock of Brigham Young's hair, *well authenticated.* I palmed myself off on a person that I met as being a very great admirer of

his, and she gave me it. When I get home I'm going
to have a ring made of it, like the one Lady Bottsford
has got made of King John of Abyssinia's wool, which
has been so talked of. People have taken to noticing
my rings very much ever since I had that tooth of darling Bobo's polished and mounted in brilliants; and this
will be unique,—there will not be another like it in all
England. I told the person of whom I got it what I
meant to do with it, and she said that I must revere
him deeply; and, do you know, I quite forgot my part
that I was playing, and said that I didn't care a fig for
the old sinner, but that it was a great curiosity. And
she was so angry, quite fiawrious, and wanted it back;
but of course she didn't get it. When do we leave
this?"

They left as soon as Sir Robert had satisfied himself
on certain points, and Miss Noel had been sufficiently
shocked by a service in the Tabernacle, and Mr. Heathcote had indulged in a bath in the lake, which he persisted in taking, and in the course of which he went
through any number of antics in addition to his usual
feats, in themselves remarkable, for he was a vigorous
and powerful swimmer. The ex-Devonshire Elder
(whom Mrs. Sykes had seen more than once slinking
about the streets, she said, but who had not come near
her) was pleased to be very polite to Sir Robert, or
would have been if he had been allowed; but, not wishing to conduct a Salt Lake campaign *à la* Sykes, Sir
Robert was content to see the place in his own way, got
a phial of water from the lake, which Miss Noel said
reminded her of Sodom and Gomorrah and was "very
suited to the odious place," looked at and into such
*dd*        38*

things as could be seen in a short stay, and made temperate, careful records of the same in his note-book.

The next point of interest to the party was "'Frisco and the Yosemite," toward which they pushed as fast as steam could take them, Sir Robert and Miss Noel being vividly interested in many things *en route*, Ethel and Mr. Heathcote pleased by a few, Mrs. Sykes grumbling ceaselessly about the length, monotony, bareness, aridity, stupidity, and general hideousness of the journey. The only thing that really amused her was a quarrel that she got up with a lady who sat near her. The acquaintance promised to be friendly enough for a while, for the lady was an amiable soul,—the wife of "a dry goods merchant in Topeka," she told Mrs. Sykes. The latter was pleased to ask her a great many questions and to patronize her quite extensively in default of other amusement, so that all went well at first. But the second stage of Mrs. Sykes's friendship was not apt to be so pleasant as the first, and accordingly she much astonished her neighbor one morning by saying to her curtly, "Why don't you speak English?"

"Why, I do. I talk it all the time, don't I?" replied the lady.

"No, you don't. Just look here. I have made a list of the things you say. They are not English at all. I don't know what you mean, often."

"Do you mean to say that you never heard anybody talk like me?" asked the lady indignantly, as she fumbled in her bag for her glasses.

"Oh, I didn't say that. I've heard *some* of the words among our lodging-house-keepers; but you have invented others, and your pronunciation is abominable.

You should really mend it, if you can," replied Mrs. Sykes, with decision.

The list which had been so civilly put in the Topekan lady's hands was a long one, and ran as follows: "Chawcolate, pawk, hawrid, cawd, squrl, stoopid, winder, lemmy, gimmy, years (for ears), 'cute, edgercation, conchienchous," etc., etc.

The fingers that held it trembled with rage long before it was finished, for the Topekan lady had wealth and social aspiration, if not "edgercation;" and when Mrs. Sykes broke in with, "Well, what do you say to that?" she had a good deal to say, and said it very forcibly, in such English as she could command, after which she swelled in speechless anger opposite for the remainder of their journey.

"There it is again. If I say the least thing to these Americans they fly out like that," complained Mrs. Sykes to Miss Noel.

But for sheer ill humor nothing could have surpassed her own conduct when they had "done" San Francisco, which she declared to be "a dull, dirty, windy place, with a harbor of which entirely too much is made,—ridiculously overpraised, in fact," and got under way for the Yosemite. The roads, the rough vehicle, the country, could not be sufficiently abused. However, when the spot was reached, she relented, as she had done at Niagara, and, looking up at the giant trees, graciously conceded that they also were "quite up to the mark."

It was a pleasant spectacle to see Sir Robert's enthusiasm. Such gazing and neck-craning and measuring and speculating! Such critical inspection of bark, leaves, soil, lichens! Such questioning of the guides!

Such keen delight, wonder, remeasuring, recraning, theories, calculations, endless contemplation! The enjoyment of the others was as nothing, compared to his, —for if there was a thing that he loved it was a fine tree, and had he not some of the best timber in England, which he knew as some generals have known their soldiers and some shepherds their sheep? "Stupendous! Prodigious! Wonderful!" burst from his lips as he walked slowly around them and rode between them as in a dream, perfectly entranced. He could scarcely be dragged away, and at last was only moved by the thought that there was so much that he "must positively see" in the surrounding country which was waiting to be considered volcanically, botanically, geologically, and otherwise. It was one of his vexations that nature, art, science, history, commerce, were so long, and time and a voraciously intelligent but mortal and limited baronet so fleeting. He would have liked to spend several months on the Pacific coast, looking into a thousand things with unflagging zeal and interest. It was really afflicting to turn his back upon the early Spanish settlers, the Jesuit missions, the grape and olive production, mining interests, earthquake statistics, the Chinese problem, annual rainfall on the great plateau, study of the Sierra Nevada range, and last, most alluring of all, that of the Santa Barbara Islands, described by a companion of Drake as densely populated by a white race with light hair and ruddy cheeks. When Sir Robert thought of that people and of all the bliss of investigation, he almost decided to make a winter of it in California and solve that mystery or perish. But he had still much to accomplish, and he had fixed the day for sailing before leaving England. So back the party came to St. Louis, where they found a mountain of mail-matter from the four quarters of the globe. There were five voluminous epistles from Mrs. Vane to Miss Noel, and others from that household; a simple domestic chronicle from Mabel, describing her daily round and stating her fears and anxieties about "Boy," who was getting "sadly wilful and unruly," and, like a youthful Ajax, had lately "defied husband;" and one of Mr. Ketchum's characteristic epistles:

"I send you a letter of introduction to my friend Fry in New Orleans (to whom my double-and-twisted), since you will go there. He will put you through all right. But I warn you that you will be nobody and won't be able to hold up your head there at all. No one can after an epidemic, unless he has lost half of his relations and had the other half given up by the doctors and prepared for burial. This reminds me that Brown's scapegrace of a brother has turned up here with a handsome Mexican wife and a million, and has deodorized his reputation by giving large sums to the yellow-fever sufferers, while I am thinking of colonizing all the mothers-in-law of these United there before another season opens, unless business improves. Fairfield has a Benedicts' Club now, and I chose the motto for it, 'Here the women cease from troubling and the wicked are at rest:' so when you want a little peace and comfort you will know where to come. My wife will have nothing less than her love sent you; but I am all the same your friend,                                J. K."

Having seen a certificate that New Orleans was entirely free from fever, "signed by all the medical men
of eminence in the city," Sir Robert was determined
not to be frightened out of his visit there altogether.
But it was only November, and he did not wish to run
any foolish risks, and the ladies were very nervous on
this score. He was still undecided what course to take,
when he one day picked up a paper and read an account
of the Indian Territory that interested him beyond
measure. In an hour he had got out his maps and
time-tables and arranged to "put in a week" at Tahle
quah, the Falls of St. Anthony, and the Mammoth Cave.
As none of the party cared for the first except himself,
he went there alone, and felt fully repaid for the effort.
Great was his joy at finding "a purely Indian legislative body" and assisting at their deliberations, his lorgnon glued now to one chief and now to another. And
then he talked to them, to get their "views," to sketch
them, to have a copy of their constitution and laws and
a newspaper in their own tongue and characters in
which an affinity to the Egyptian, Arabic, Chinese, or
any other might perhaps be traced! And then how
full his letters to his friends in England were of his
"visit to a Choctaw gentleman's plantation,—a most
deeply-interesting, well-educated man ;" " the first fruits
of the new civilization ;" "the opinion of a Seminole
person on the Indian policy of the American government ;" "the beauty of a young Chickasaw female"
whom he had seen at one of the schools, and "the extraordinary progress made by some of the other scholars,
showing that there is absolutely no limit to the intellect
ual development of the once-despised savage ;" " the ·

crystal clearness of the beautiful rivers, the lovely, fertile plains, framed by the Mozark Mountains, the balmy, delightful climate, and the brutality and wicked greed of an American of the lower class," who had told him that "the country was a million times too good for red-skins, who ought all to be exterminated, as ' Indians was p'ison wherever found.' " And then, while the glow of this interest still flushed his mind, he took up the Mis-sissippi River, which was a career in itself and beckoned him on to fresh conquests. He went up to the Falls of St. Anthony, which, after Niagara and the Yosemite, was accounted " tame and overrated" by Mrs. Sykes, bu' over which he pondered deeply. Before he left there the river had got a strong hold on his imagination that grew ever greater and greater. He spent all his time on the boat studying it. He talked to the pilot about it,—or rather made the pilot talk, and listened with all his ears; he took up the methods now practised for pre-venting the banks from caving in and forcing the Great Father to lie in the bed he has made, instead of driving honest folk out of theirs by scurvy turns and bends that break up thousands of homes. He drew diagrams of the pile-driving and wattling and willow mattrasses in the diary, with the improvements he thought advis-able, and some very scientific suggestions by which the river could be made to checkmate itself, like an automa-ton chess-player. He hung over the guards continually, observing all that was to be observed, and recorded the same under separate headings, such as " currents," " ve-locity," " flood-rises," with statistics without end show-ing that the carrying-trade of the great water highway would amount in 1950 to something so colossal that

there is no room for it here, while a future for the cities
that stud its banks was predicted that would satisfy
their most ambitious citizens.

.His heart was not in Louisville nor in the Mammoth
Cave, though he went over the first religiously and examined the latter carefully, collected specimens, and
even thrilled faintly over an eyeless fish, which aroused
considerable enthusiasm in Mr. Heathcote. He was not
really himself until he was again on the river, doing a
little dredging and sounding on his own account. At
Cairo he expanded almost as much as his subject, and
for a long while afterward was never weary of tracing
the blue and yellow currents that fuse so reluctantly
and imperfectly that out in the Gulf of Mexico, it is
said, one comes upon patches of the Missouri of the
most jaundiced, angry hue.

The sombre majesty of the stream was quite lost
upon Mrs. Sykes, who saw in it only "an ugly, wicked-
looking river, with a lot of dirty-white villages along
its mud banks." Her attention was given to the passengers and the clerk,—especially the latter. "A clerk
that talks to the ladies in the cabin about literature and
the dramar! Only fency!" she said to Miss Noel.
"And such comical blackies, that the ladies call 'aunty,'
and that call me 'honey' and 'child.' As like as not
you'll see a snag coming up through the bottom of the
boat presently, and you had better try one of the life-
preservers on and see how it works; though, after all,
we may be blown up instead. Of course we are racing.
I am sure of it."

"Dear, dear! How *very* dreadful! How did you
discover that? It should really be made known. I

shall speak to the captain. I really can't consent to
being *raced* with," replied Miss Noel, who did not make
sufficient allowance for Mrs. Sykes's love of the sensational. "Robert must call a meeting and protest, or
something."

She went to look for Sir Robert, whom she found
walking about on deck. He had been reading all the
afternoon, and his mind was full of La Salle, and De
Soto, and poor Evangeline, so cruelly near to Gabriel
and happiness once, only to drift away from both forever. So large was his grasp of any subject that the
imaginative phases of a situation appealed to him as
powerfully as the practical, and he was not the man to
take the Mississippi without its associations, any more
than he would have done the Hudson or the Sierras
without Irving and Bret Harte. So now he was pacing
backward and forward under the stars, thinking of these
things, and in no mood for bearding the captain in his
cabin; and, having calmed Miss Noel's fears, he stayed
on deck until very late, enjoying his cigar and surroundings.

When they got low enough down to come upon levees
and see that the river was actually higher than the
land, the questions of inundation, protection, blue-clay
banks, dikes, sluices, crevasses, water-gates, sediment,
currents, swept in upon Sir Robert, and he was still
working at them when they reached New Orleans.
Fresh interests and employments now awaited him, in
which he was soon absorbed, head over ears. Like
olives, New Orleans has a flavor of its own, so decided
that it is impossible to be indifferent to it: one must
either be very fond of it or dislike it heartily. It was

soon evident that Sir Robert belonged to the first class
and Mrs. Sykes to the second. Its brilliant blue skies,
and sunshine, and warmth, the lovely flowers, the good
opera and better restaurants, the infectious gayety of
the people, as light about the heart as the heels, with
enough Gallic quicksilver in their veins to give them a
genius for being and looking happy, and, lastly, the
warmth of his reception, and a hospitality as refined as
limitless, delighted this most amiable of baronets. He
had brought good letters, and was admitted to that
inner Creole circle which few strangers see, and in
which he found among the elders, as he said to Miss
Noel, " the atmosphere of the Faubourg Saint-Germain,
—a dignity like that of the period to which the Aglonbys belonged, with more grace and *savoir-faire.* And
such wonderfully pretty girls, my dear Augusta, with
eyes like sloes and skins like the petals of their own
magnolia-blossoms. And I observe a sort of patriarchal
tribal state of affairs among them,—grandparents, children, grandchildren, all living together in great numbers and perfect amity, apparently." Among the
Americans of the city Sir Robert found much to interest
him, and he went to visit their " sugar-estates," took
down in black and white the astounding number of
oranges that one tree is capable of producing, held conversations with many gentlemen about the emancipated
slaves, and with many emancipated slaves about their
late masters and present condition. And then was there
not cotton, the machinery employed on rice-, sugar-, and
cotton-plantations to " go into"? to say nothing of the
swamp-flora, the possible introduction of olives into
Louisiana, and Voodooism to trace back to the Vaudois

sorcerers of the fourteenth century and connect with
the serpent-worship of some parts of Italy, where he
had himself seen the peasants make their yearly procession with snakes wrapped about their necks, waists,
and wrists? And was there not, too, serious business
to be done? How could he secure and forward to England a few things that he must have, such as a gar alli-
gator, a pair of mocking-birds, a Floridian flamingo, a
ruby humming-bird, "a Texan horned frog, with a dis-
tinctly-developed tail, crustaceous, probably antedilu-
vian, and credibly reported to live upon air," not to
mention other treasures, and collections previously
made, which must be shipped before he left? All this
he finally accomplished, and was so pleased by his success
that not even a letter from his Kalsing "solicitor," saying that his suit against the "Eagle" had been brought
to trial and he had been awarded fifty cents damages,
could greatly cloud the content he felt.

Mrs. Sykes, meanwhile, was looking at everything
through her own bit of yellow glass or London fog, and
seeing only what her prepossessions would let her see
through a medium that distorted and magnified every
object. As the spittoons at the Capitol had seemed to
her far bigger and more striking than the dome, so now
the gutters of New Orleans made an immense impression upon her and affected her most painfully, although
the Mississippi failed to impress her at all. The climate
she found odious, the people spoke neither pure French
nor good English, and many a fault besides she found,
chiefly with what she politely termed "the Creowls,"
whom she was never tired of ridiculing as lazy, ignorant, effeminate, and morbidly conceited. She was not

an ideal companion when they made an expedition into
the lovely pastoral Tèche country, the Acadia of exiled
Acadians and Eden of Louisiana, but her lack of enthusiasm did not damp the ardor of Sir Robert. Miss Noel
thought it a beautiful country, but added that it looked
"sadly damp, and as if it might be malarious," and insisted on "dear Ethel's" taking ten grains of quinine
daily during their stay and wearing a potato in her
pocket,—precautionary measures adopted by herself,
and known to have nipped jungle-fever in the bud repeatedly in India, so she said. It seemed to Sir Robert's
heated fancy that even Ethel praised this ideal spot but
tepidly, and when she had started out of a revery three
times with an "I beg pardon" while he was reading
"Evangeline" to her under the shade of one of those
noble oaks "from whose branches garlands of Spanish
moss floated," fit monuments of the sorrowful maiden
of ever-green memory, he put down the book impatiently, saying, "It is only the old that are young nowadays; I am boring you,"—a speech that made her blush
guiltily, since she did not care to explain where her
thoughts had wandered. He was not bored. The
bayous were a fascinating novelty to him, the trees and
fields and glades were eloquent to him, the simple French
peasants who belong to the seventeenth century and by
some miracle lead its idyllic life in the nineteenth interested him, and he could see Basil, Gabriel, and Father
Félicien at every step.

The next week found them on a steamer bound for
Havana and New York, followed by friendly faces and
good claret to the last, leaving three baskets of champagne and about a ton of flowers out of account. For

an account of Havana, Matanzas, Spanish atrocities,
Cuban exports, coolie slavery, and the like topics, the
reader is respectfully referred to the book since published by Sir Robert,—"Eight Months in the United
States, Cuba, and Canada,"—a work pronounced in critical quarters "the best book of travels in America ever
published in England" (high praise, surely), though it
attracted less general attention than a very spicy, entertaining volume by Mrs. Arundel Sykes, called "A
Britisher among the Yankees," (to quote from another
English journal) said to contain "a not very flattering
picture of the life, society, and institutions of the Great
Republic, which must be a true one, since it is so uni
versally resented by the American press. People will
cry out when they are hit, as every one knows."

On arriving in New York our party went at once to
Mr. Brown's, that gentleman being established there
for the winter and having urged them to stay with him.
Their idea was to sail for home almost immediately, as
soon as Sir Robert had seen his friend General Bludyer,
with whom he had some business and who was bringing
out his two sons to establish them in America. But an
unexpected delay occurred. On the day after their
arrival, Mr. Heathcote ran up to his aunt's room to bid
her good-by before taking himself off to Baltimore,—-
he had made a full confession to Sir Robert, and received
much advice and counsel, together with a qualified approval of his plans and hopes,—and he found Miss Noel
still in bed, although it was mid-day and she not the
least punctual and energetic of her sex. In reply to his
playful reproaches she replied that she was "feeling
very, very queer," and he cheerfully assured her that

she " had best stop in bed a day or two and all would
be well," after which he told her that he was not going
back to England with the party, and, with a further
remark to the effect that she "was looking awfully
seedy," discovered that he was late for his train, was
again pleasantly sure that she would "be all right soon,"
and hurried off to the station, well pleased to think that
he should see Edith in a few hours.  It is not always
possible, however, for a woman to fulfil the optimistic
predictions of her careless male relatives, and in a few
hours Miss Noel was feeling really ill.  " Who is your
doctor, my dear?" she asked of Bijou, who had herself
arranged and carried up a little tray of delicacies with
which to tempt her.  " How very sweet of you to trouble!
Why did you not let Parsons do that?  Do you know
I am making myself quite wretched lest I should be
sickening with something,—something serious?  I must
have a doctor at once.  Would you kindly send for one,
or, rather, tell Parsons where to go?  I can't rest until
I get the opinion of a medical man."

" Now, don't you worry about *that*," said Bijou, be-
stowing an embrace upon her and then perching herself
on the foot of the bed.  " You are not going to be ill;
and if you are, why, you are with friends who will take
the best sort of care of you, that's all.  I'll nurse you;
and popper says I am just a natural-born nurse, if there
ever was one.  You can see the doctor if you want to,
but most likely you will be a great deal better to-morrow."

. " But, my dear, suppose I should be worse?  It would
be too dreadful!  I can't be ill in your house, you know,"
said Miss Noel disconsolately.

" Why, why not?" queried Bijou, in surprise.

"Why not? Can you ask why? Think of all the trouble I should be putting you to, the house upset, and the servants giving warning very likely, and all that. Oh, no! I hope and trust it is nothing; but if it should be serious I could not dream of putting you out like that," replied Miss Noel, with emphasis.

" Why, do you mean to say that anybody would care for *that*, or think of the *trouble*, with a friend lying sick in their house? I never heard of such a thing," exclaimed Bijou, expressing the liveliest emotions of astonishment and contempt in face and voice. " Of course we don't want you to get sick, for your own sake; but if you do we'll do everything in this world to make you comfortable and cure you. And the house won't be upset at all; and we don't care a snap what the servants think. You must put that perfectly ridiculous idea right out of your head, and turn over and try to go to sleep."

When the doctor came he looked grave even for a doctor, and felt it his duty to tell Miss Noel that she might have yellow fever. It was always to be had for the catching in Cuba, and her symptoms were suspicious, though he could not, of course, be positive. Here was a sensation. It was curious to see the effect this declaration had on the different members of the household. Sir Robert, after turning pale and saying " God bless my soul! you don't mean it," to the doctor, rallied from the shock as soon as he had left the house, and refused to believe anything of the kind, talked about " the art conjectural," and did all he could to impress this view on Miss Noel, who promptly gave herself up

as lost, told him that she had made her will "before
leaving town for the North" the year before, asked that
her body might be "taken back to dear old England,"
if this could be done without risk to others, and begged
that she might be "sent straight away to the hospital"
and no one allowed to come in contact with her meanwhile. Bijou, Ethel, and Parsons stoutly refused to be
hustled out of her room, declaring that they had already
been exposed to the danger, if danger there was, and
protested that they were ready to nurse her through
anything. Mr. Brown, coming home to dinner, was
horrified as by some impiety to hear it proposed that
Miss Noel should go to a hospital. "Admitting, for the
sake of argument," said this ever-judicial host, "that
the doctor is right, what follows? Why, that Miss Noel
will require great care, and, humanly speaking, will in-
cur additional risk in leaving my house. I cannot dream
of allowing it. My married daughter has taken her
children to see their grandmother; there are only Bijou
and myself to be considered, and neither of us has any
fear of the disease, or, indeed, any great belief in the
reality of the danger. I cannot think of letting a guest,
and that guest a stranger here, go to a public place of
the kind and commit herself to hired nurses. Oh, no!
That is out of the question."

"I never heard of such a thing,—never. It would be
perfectly shameful!" protested Bijou afresh. And so
Sir Robert was overruled, and, much touched by this
view of the matter, tried to express thanks on behalf
of Miss Noel, bungled out a few short phrases, very
different from his usually fluent utterances, shook Mr.
Brown's hand heartily, sat down with a very red face,

and then started up and dismissed the carriage, which pending this decision, had been waiting at the door.

It chanced that Mrs. Sykes had been out for some hours that day, and had then come back and gone into the library, where she spent some time in writing to the friends who had entertained her in Central New York. She had just finished putting up the morning paper for them containing a full and carefully-marked account of the defalcation and disappearance of a bank-president in Delaware in whom she recognized the brother of her former hostess, when Ethel looked in at the door and said, " Oh, you are here," and, coming forward, gave her the dreadful news. It was well that this final mark of her gratitude and graceful interest was complete down to the very postage-stamp, for after this Mrs. Sykes had no time for delicate attentions.

" Stand off! good heavens! Don't come near me. Get away !" she shrieked, and for once every particle of color left her face. The next moment she rushed up-stairs to her room, put on her bonnet and cloak in a flash, and, without farewells of any kind, or thought of so much as her darling Bobo, left the house immediately. She went first, and that as fast as her feet could carry her, to the nearest druggist's, where she invested lavishly in disinfectants and hung innumerable camphor-bags about her person. From there she went to the nearest hotel, from which she wrote to the Browns, giving instructions about her luggage, which she said must be packed by Parsons and sent over to England, to be unpacked at Liverpool, for fear of infection, by " a person" whom she would engage. She then took the first steamer leaving New York, and when she got

*ee*

on board gave vent to a perfectly sincere and devout exclamation, "Thank heaven, I have done with America!" From Liverpool she wrote back a lively account of the passage, and expressed the deepest interest in "dear Miss Noel," about whom she had been "quite wretched," but who she "hoped was doing nicely by this time and would make a good recovery." She also hoped, and even more earnestly, that "dearest Bobo was not being neglected in the general hubbub, and given his biscuits without their being properly soaked first, and his chicken in great pieces, not carefully minced," and begged that every care should be taken of him, imploring that everybody would remember that "*hot* milk invariably made the poor dear ill." She also sent Bijou a small and particularly hideous pin-cushion, which she said had been made for the Ashantee Bazaar by the Grand Duchess of Aufstadt.

The defection of Mrs. Sykes was not greatly deplored by anybody, but it was deeply resented by Parsons, who it is to be feared was not as devoted to Bobo as his mistress expected.

"I'm not one to run away,—not if it was lions and tigers,—like *some*," she remarked; "but if hever I get back to the hold country I'll go down on my bended knees, if it's in the very cab at Liverpool, and thank 'eaven I'm at 'ome again; which I 'ope I may live to see it."

Happily, Miss Noel did not have yellow fever. Unhappily, she had *a* fever, if not the dreaded one, and was ill for several weeks,—so ill that it seemed at one time as though she had done with travelling-days. Anxious weeks these for Ethel and Sir Robert and Mr.

Heathcote, trying ones for Bijou, who had at last found
"a rational occupation." For it was she who, with
Parsons's help, nursed Miss Noel faithfully, tenderly,
efficiently, Ethel being a most willing coadjutress, but
sadly out of place in a sick-room. The skill, the self-
reliance, and the unselfishness that Bijou showed surprised even those who knew her best, and quite endeared
her to Sir Robert.

"That girl is one in a thousand," he said to Ethel
more than once; "and I was such a wiseacre that I
thought her a useless, spoiled creature who would never
be anything but a domestic fetich. I shall ask her pardon, when I get the chance, for having so shamefully
underrated and misjudged her. Could there be a kinder
family? If Augusta had been a near and dear relative
they could scarcely have shown more solicitude. Every
luxury, every kindness that the most thoughtful affection could have suggested has been lavished on her.
Everything has been subordinated to the one object,—
her recovery,—and all their ordinary pursuits, amusements, occupations, cheerfully laid aside, apparently as
a mere matter of course. At least, they disclaim the
idea of sacrifice; and in all that they have done there
has been nothing perfunctory. If they have merely
been performing what they consider a duty, I must say
that they have had the grace and innate good breeding
to make it appear that it was a pleasure. Just so."

Miss Noel had been down-stairs on the sofa for three
days, having been officially pronounced convalescent,
when who should walk in upon her but the Ketchums,
—Mabel serene and smiling, and Job in a state of evident satisfaction and radiant good humor.

"Well, now, this is something like. Up and dressed, and looking first-rate for an invalid," he called out from the door, and then, advancing, took one of her thin hands with much gentleness, and said, "Getting well, ain't you? That's right. I am so glad. Creepin. through mercy, eh? as Father Root used to say."

Mabel slipped into a seat near Miss Noel, and, after some inquiries about Sir Robert, Ethel, and the Browns, told her what concern they had felt about her illness. "Husband telegraphed constantly to know how you were going on; but the replies were often most unsatisfactory; and it is so very nice to see you up again. You will soon be about, and the sea-voyage will set you up wonderfully. That puts me in mind of—Tell her, husband; show her."

Thus stimulated, Mr. Ketchum drew out an enormous pocket-book, stuffed full of papers, and attacked it rather than looked through it, drew out a handful of letters, bills, memorandums, tore up several, crushed others back into his case, walked swiftly into the hall, and came back triumphantly with his overcoat on his arm and a sheet of foolscap in his hand.

"Dear, dear, husband, you should not mess about like this," said Mabel, "littering up the carpet."

She would have picked up the bits of paper, but he interfered. "Here! I'll do that, Daisy; sit down. Daisy's occupation in the next world, Miss Noel, is going to be sweeping all the dirty clouds out of the sky, and polishing up the harps and crowns, and telling the small angels not to leave the ivory gates ajar, for fear of draughts, and to be sure and put their buckets and spades away tidily when they have done digging in the golden sands, and not to get overheated and fall ill, because they can't die and have got nowhere to go. Now, look at this" (getting up from his knees and holding up the foolscap, which was covered with drawings of some mechanical contrivance) : "I got thinking about you one day and your illness, and that you ought to stay on deck all you could, and to have the right kind of chair, and suddenly this idea hit me right on the head, and I got out my pencil and started in on it. And here it is. This is only the rough draught, you understand."

With growing enthusiasm he explained all the details, while Mabel looked intently and respectfully at the paper he held, and interjected admiring comments: "Isn't it a most wonderful thing?" and wasn't it clever of husband to think of it?—but, then, he is always thinking of things. Husband has got such a surprising talent for invention, and grasps an idea at once."

"Oh, no, I haven't. I think I could have found out the way to my mouth as soon as any other baby, that's all," deprecated Mr. Ketchum. "But this is a lucky hit. I am going to have it patented. It's a first-rate thing. This is the way you lash it to the mast when you want to ; and when you want to move about you let down the rollers and fasten them with this hook, and go where you please. Twenty-seven changes of position. Why, you can read, eat, sleep, ride, get married, run for Congress, die, and be buried in that chair, if you want to!" he said, by way of final recommendation.

"Thank you, but I don't wish to die. I would rather live," said Miss Noel, laughing cheerfully for the first time since her illness. "And did you really design it for me?. How very kind! I must really try to get it

40

worked out, if you think it will answer, as of course you do."

"Oh, don't you bother your head about that," he replied. "I worked it all out one night, and set a smart carpenter at it the next morning before breakfast. And it's a perfect success. And I've got it down at the hotel, ready for you. I'm coming up here to put you in it and take you down to the steamer myself like a first baby or a setting of ostrich-eggs."

Sir Robert and Mr. Heathcote now came in (the latter having returned from Baltimore an affianced man), and Ethel and Bijou followed, and everybody was delighted to see everybody else; and they had so much to talk about that Sir Robert almost forgot that he was engaged to preside over a children's dinner-party at the house of an intimate friend of the De Witts. He hurried off, though; and never had he "looked into" ten more charming little faces than brightened on his arrival. The way in which he radiated good humor, intelligence, benevolence, told stories and jokes that kept the little company shouting with laughter, and finally rose and got off an impromptu piece of doggerel with exactly ten verses, and each child's name and some peculiarity brought out in a way to convulse even mammas and the maids, was as indescribable as delightful. I am not sure that he did not enjoy it more than any of the grand entertainments that he had been asked to; and as for the children, they remember it to this day, although they are on the verge of young-ladyhood and at college now and have very serious demands made on their memories.

After a pleasant little interval of reunion and various

diversions, the day came at last for our English people to leave the country. What they felt about this necessity was well expressed for them by Sir Robert in the last letter that he wrote before going on the steamer.

"I am glad to turn my face toward the old land, which must always seem to me the best of all lands," he said; "but I take with me the pleasantest memories of the new. It has been a constant surprise and pleasure to me to find how like they are to each other in all essentials, greatly as they often seem to differ on the surface. I have had a most interesting and delightful tour. Such opportunities of observation as have come in my way, and such authentic information as I have been able to lay hold of, I have tried to make the most of; but in so short a time I could not do more than glean in a field that offers a rich harvest to more fortunate travellers. From the moment of landing until now I have been made the recipient of a hospitality too generous and too flattering to be appropriated to myself in my individual capacity. I must either set it down to the good-will which Americans feel toward England when not irritated and repelled by the insolent and overbearing among us,—who have done more to make a breach between the two peoples than you would fancy, and inflicted wounds that all the ambassadors and public-dinner fine speeches cannot heal,—or to that true politeness which Americans observe in the most casual relations, and the immense, apparently inexhaustible kindness which it is their habit to show to strangers. I find in them a certain spontaneity and affectionateness that has quite won my heart."

To the credit of Mr. Ketchum be it said that if **Miss**

Noel had been made of cobwebs she could have been
safely transported in his invention to the steamer.
This feat was comfortably achieved, at all events, and
Mr. Ketchum, having superintended it, left Miss Noel
in the chair on deck; and there were kisses and em-
braces between the ladies, a hurried rush to the wharf,
and the steamer moved out, with Miss Noel crying softly,
and saying, "Dear, dear Bijou!  Dear America!  How
good they have been to me!" and Ethel and Sir Robert
hanging over the side; and ashore the Browns, the
doctor, Mr. Heathcote, the De Witts, and Mr. Ketchum
and Mabel looking earnestly at them and waving their
adieux.

"You'll find a couple of barrels of pecans at your
place.  I forgot to tell you.  Good-by!  good-by!  Call
again!" shouted Mr. Ketchum.  And then, turning to
his wife, he said, " Don't you wish you were going home,
too ?"

Mabel stopped to straighten little Jared Ponsonby's
hat and settle his curls, somewhat disordered by the
wind from the river.  Then she turned a face full of
sweet content toward her husband; her simple and
serious look met his twinkling, bantering one for a
moment.  "No, dearest," she said, as she took his arm
and walked away.  "You know that I don't.  You are
my home."

The Ketchums went back to Fairfield, and spent the
two years that followed very happily and quite unevent-
fully in that simple round of duties and pleasures which
the foolish find so dull and the wise would not exchange
for any other.  And not the least agreeable feature of

this life was what was known as "the English letters," although this really included books, music, photographs, sketches, and a great variety of things, from the J. pens that came for Mrs. Vane and the larding-needles that housewifely Mabel had coveted that she might "set a proper fowl before husband," up to packages of a disgraceful size and bulk addressed to Mr. Ketchum in Sir Robert's hand. Sir Robert was a regular and delightful correspondent; Miss Noel and Ethel were equally kind about writing; Mrs. Sykes sent a very characteristic epistle or two to the family after her return, and then let "silence like a poultice" come to heal the blows she had inflicted.

"What do you hear from that idiotic young Ramsay?" "How is Ramsay opening the American oyster?" "What of poor Mr. Ramsay?" "Is Mr. Ramsay coming back to England?" were questions often asked by these correspondents; and Mr. Ketchum was able to give some account of that fascinating fortune-seeker.

Mr. Ramsay wrote to him occasionally, which was the more flattering because he repeatedly said in these productions that he "hated doing a letter most tremendously," and very truly remarked that "the worst of it is that you've got to be thinking what to say, which is an awful bore, and ten to one the pen is bad, and spelling takes a lot out of you if you are not used to looking up the words." Whether, "not being a literary chap," he would have written to Mr. Ketchum at all had not the Ketchum and Brown properties marched and the two families been good friends is one of those nice questions which it is hard to decide. His letters were headed "Out in the Bush" at first, and were full of the

40*

adventures and amusements that his novel surroundings afforded him. Then came more sober epistles from "The Ranch," with a good deal in them about "these dirty brutes of Mexicans and ignorant cowboys," the long, dull days, the doubts that had begun to agitate him as to the possibility of getting out of "old Brown's farm" the millions that had seemed almost within his grasp in London. Finally, after a long silence, Job got a letter one day, written in pencil, that betrayed the deepest depression and most utter disgust. He had "come an awful cropper from a mustang," and been laid up for three months; his money was all gone; he could get nothing to do. "I tried to get a clerkship in a 'country store' before I got my fall," he explained, "though if I have got to that I had better go back to England, where those fellows get a half-holiday on Saturdays and lots of bank holidays, and are in civilization at least. Perhaps if the governor saw me with a quill behind my ear, or riding down to the city on the knifeboard of a 'bus smoking a pipe, he'd do something for me for the honor of the family. But he's in a beastly humor now, and wouldn't send me a fiver to save my life. He says that I'm not worth my salt anywhere, and that he washes his hands of me. And Bill has taken to patronizing me so tremendously that I'd starve rather than ask his help. So I must just stick it out here, I suppose, unless you meant what you said when we parted, and will help me to get back home, where I have friends, a brother-in-law especially, an awfully good sort of fellow, that would stick to a fellow through thick and thin, no matter what other fellows said of him. There's a lot of 'fellows' in this last sentence.

but I never was a clever fellow— I had better stop.
I am getting worse mixed up than ever."

Mr. Ketchum's reply to this was a short, cordial,
hearty note, enclosing a check for five hundred dollars,
telling Mr. Ramsay to draw upon him for more if he
needed it, bidding him keep "a stiff upper lip," and
advising him to stop at Fairfield *en route* to England
and see if there wasn't some better way out of his diffi
culties. About two weeks after this Mr. Ramsay walked
into Mr. Ketchum's office and almost wrung his hand
off. "Awfully kind of you," "awfully glad to see you,"
"awfully good news to tell you," was poured out as in
one breath by the bronzed, thin, but still beautiful
Englishman, whose illness had given a last and quite
irresistible charm of spirituality to his handsome face.

"Sit down, man, and tell us all about it," said Mr.
Ketchum, when he had given him an embrace half real,
half theatrical. "Delighted to see *you*, if it comes to
that."

"Here's that check you sent me," said Mr. Ramsay,
going straight to his point, as usual. "I never got
it cashed, because I got by the very same post good
news from England. My great-aunt Maxwell is dead
at Bath and has left me all her money, twenty thousand
pounds. Isn't it the luckiest fluke that ever was? But
all the same it is a kindness that I shan't forget. You
are an awfully good sort to have done it. Most fellows
would have seen me in Halifax first, you know. And
if ever you want a friend you'll know where to find
him, that's all. Only fancy all this money fallin' in
when I hadn't a penny and was in perfect despair!
Such luck! And such a fluke, as I have said. You see,

·it was all to have been Bill's. He has always been my· aunt's favorite, though at first it was to have been divided between us; only when I was a little chap I blew off the tail of her parrot with a bunch of fire-crackers. Haw! haw! haw! I was never allowed there afterward, and she hated the very name of me. She and Bill have hit it off together so well that he never had the least fear of me steppin' in. But on last Val-entine's Day it seems that she got an awfully cocky, cheeky valentine of an old maid puttin' on a wig and paintin' her face, and it had the Stoke-Pogis post-mark. and she took it into her head that Bill had sent it, flew into a most awful rage, and sent for her solicitor and changed her will. And then, most fortunate thing, she died that night, and couldn't make another."

"Well, you are a doting nephew, upon my word," said Job.

"It is no use of me bein' a hypocrite and goin' about lookin' cut up and pretendin' that I am sorry when I am not," replied Mr. Ramsay. "I haven't seen her for years, and she was nasty to me even when I was a child, and she was a regular old cat, and no good to herself or anybody else. I don't see why I should pull a long face and turn crocodile because she made me her heir to spite Bill, though it comes in most beautifully for me. I don't mean to keep it all, though I could swell it considerably if I did. It would be a dirty thing to do, for Bill has been brought up to expect it and didn't send the valentine at all. I shall go halves with him; that seems fair all round." Mr. Ketchum agreed with him, and Mr. Ramsay went on to make further confi-dences, in which it appeared that he still cared for Miss

Brown, and had "thought an awful lot about her," and
now rejoiced to find himself in a position to address her
if she was still free. Tom Price, coming in, could
scarcely announce that the buggy was at the door for
goggling at Mr. Ramsay. The two men drove rapidly
out to Fairfield, talking all the way, and Mr. Ramsay
stared very hard at the Brown mansion and grounds,
and got a pretty welcome from Mabel that warmed his
heart not a little. What he said to Bijou in an interview that evening of four hours is no business of
ours.

It began after quite formal greetings with, "Do you
know that you are lookin' most awfully well, Miss
Brown?" on his part.

"You didn't dream that I cared for you, did you?"
said Bijou toward its close, anxious to reassure herself
upon a point that had made the last two years a bitterness to her.

"Oh, yes, I did. I twigged that long ago," replied
he. "That is why I cut my stick so suddenly. I couldn't
support a wife then, and I wasn't goin' to be thought a
fortune-hunter, you know." It must have been that he
was forgiven the sentimental blunder that is worse than
a crime,—a want of frankness,—or how else could they
have been married in six weeks and sailed for England?
Mr. Alfred Brown, being in California, did not witness
this ceremony, but Mr. Ketchum did, and "a large and
fashionable company of the *elite* of Kalsing" (*vide* the
local paper). And did not Mr. Ketchum give the groom
a pair of trotting-horses that afterward attracted much
attention in Hyde Park? and did not Mr. Brown
present the bride with a considerable fortune on her

wedding-day, which her husband insisted should be set apart for her exclusive use and control?

"Haven't you got any other name than Bijou?" he said to her. "That is—excuse me sayin' so—a most absurd name. Bijou Ramsay. What will my people say?"

"I was baptized Ellen," said she, "but I have never been called that."

"Ellen?— A nice, sensible name. I shall call you that," he replied, and kept his word.

And so the immigrant, who thought he had left England forever, went home in a little while and is living there now in inglorious ease and somewhat enervating luxury, while Mr. Heathcote, who thought that he was coming out for a short visit and couldn't possibly live out of England, is already more than half an American, a successful, practical farmer, and, it may be added, a happy man. "Heart's Content" has been renaissanced, papered, tiled, *portièred*, utterly transformed, and is thought quite a show-place now and much admired; but there are some persons who liked it better when it was only an old-fashioned Virginian home, before their mahogany majesties the old furniture, and those courtly commoners Anne Buller and her brothers, had been swept away with all the other cumbering antiquities.

Sir Robert is now looking into the military, monastic, and baronial architecture of the mediæval period on the Continent, and goes next year to Japan to begin the exhaustive researches which are to culminate in his next book, the "Lives of the Mikados."

THE END.

www.ingramcontent.com/pod-product-compliance
Lightning Source LLC
Chambersburg PA
CBHW052337110726
47901CB00005B/1256